No Need To Mention It

Mohsin Ahmed

ISBN: 978-1-916596-04-7
Hardcover edition

PublishNation
www.publishnation.co.uk

Chapter 1

Shopping with Sarah was a nightmare but what choice did he have? If his girlfriend wanted to go shopping, he had to go.

'I should have listened to what my friends used to say to me. I wouldn't be in this situation otherwise,' sighed Raheem.

The security guard, who had been listening to his monologue, frowned. 'What did they used to say?'

'I didn't listen, so how can I tell you what they said!?'

The security guard's phone started to ring, but he was laughing so hard that he didn't seem to realise. They shook hands as Raheem made his way to the fitting rooms carrying the horrible maroon jumper Sarah had chosen for him. She was examining still more jumpers in the corner, as if the one she had chosen for him wasn't bad enough.

Raheem joined the queue for the fitting rooms. Broadway Shopping Centre was always busy on a Saturday. It was the biggest shopping centre in Stalford, and one of the biggest in England. He had spent half his life in here since he had started dating Sarah.

He whiled away the time by reading an article on his phone about how, according to the Mayan calendar, the world was meant to end on 21st December 2012. Just over three months to go, so maybe there wouldn't be many shopping trips to endure after all. He was about to put on one of his favourite Punjabi Asian tracks on his phone but was told by the staff member that it was his turn to go in.

He entered the fitting room and slammed the door shut. He wasn't in the best of moods today. He had withdrawn fifty pounds from the cash machine earlier, which had printed off his receipt. It was only when he'd driven to pick up Sarah that he realised he had thrown the money in the bin instead of the receipt, which was in his back pocket. That fifty pound would have helped towards paying his speeding fine, which he had received last week. He had only been going 6 miles per hour over the limit. Then again, he was on the way back from a speed awareness course when the speed camera flashed, so he should have known better. He would have to sit through that stupid course all over again.

He stood in front of the mirror. His black hair, combed to the side and sticking up at the back, was a slight adjustment to the full spiked style he'd had during his second year at university. His stubble looked neat as he had gone to the barber's yesterday. But once he wore this jumper, he would look a mess. That was for sure.

Reluctantly, he started to change. It was a while before he noticed that he'd taken off his jeans instead of his top and was trying to fit the jumper onto his legs. Shaking his head, he removed his top and put on the jumper before walking out of the fitting rooms without checking his reflection. There was no point.

He walked up to Sarah and tapped her on the shoulder. As she turned her jaw dropped, which was a good sign; she must have also seen how horrible it looked.

'It's bad, isn't it?' Raheem said, looking around as the eyes of the other shoppers turned in his direction. Some of them started to giggle. Sarah was still gaping at him. 'What?' he asked.

'Where are your jeans?'

Oh no; he had forgotten to put his jeans back on and he was standing in the middle of the store in his boxers with thirty people laughing at him. He sprinted back into the fitting room and slammed the door shut. The laughter was still ringing out on the shop floor. Muttering angrily, he put on his jeans. He really hated shopping.

***

'Alright, it wasn't that funny.' Raheem reversed his car into a parking bay at McDonald's. Sarah had been laughing for the last ten minutes.

She finally calmed down and turned sideways in her seat. 'Can I ask you a question?'

'Whenever I've been asked anything in my life it has tended to be a question, so feel free,' he replied.

Sarah grinned. 'Alright, clever clogs. I've actually forgotten what I was going to ask you.' She turned the air condition on. 'Is it just me or are you hot?'

'It's not just you babe, lots of women think I'm hot.'

'Is that what they have been telling you? You must be so happy. Anyway, I'm glad I'm going to get Mondays off from work.'

'Did Julie approve it, then?' Raheem tried his best to look pleased.

'Not yet. She said she'd let me know sometime today. Bless her. She is working on the weekend but is still trying to get it sorted out for me.'

'The kid is not even born yet and you're already celebrating its birthday party,' Raheem said dully. 'At least wait for official confirmation that she has given you Monday's off before getting all excited. You love to pre-empt things all the time.'

Sarah's smile turned into a snarl. 'I thought you'd be happy with me having Mondays off. You could at least offer some encouragement while I wait for the decision.'

'I say we get a decision right now.' He slapped his thigh. 'Let's go to your office, bang on Julie's door and ask her. Julie will then say you *can't* have Mondays off.'

'Then?'

'Then you've got your decision, haven't you?'

He raised his hands to protect himself as Sarah began punching him. 'You're so annoying sometimes, Raheem!'

'What did I say wrong?' Raheem sniggered as he grabbed her wrist.

Sarah's phone began to ring. 'Hello?' she said, giving him a final punch as she answered it. Her face split into a wide smile. 'That's great! Thanks so much, Julie,' she said happily before disconnecting the call and turning back to Raheem. 'She's approved it! I'm going to do longer hours for the rest of the weekdays and have Mondays free!'

'So, I guess you're going to be at uni with me on Mondays to keep a— I mean, to keep me company?' Raheem forced a smile. Sarah nodded gleefully. 'Yes!' He raised his arms in mock celebration. Monday was the only day that members of the public could use the university library; just because the university was publicly funded didn't mean that the public should be able to use it.

This bad day was getting even worse. Sarah would not leave him for a second at university.

'Shall I go get the food, seeing as the drive through is closed?' Sarah asked.

'It's fine, I'll go get it.'

'No, I'll get it. So fish you can have from anywhere, but chicken has to be halal?'

'That sounds about right. When you order, ask them to fry it in vegetable oil though.'

'My Muslim friend at high school had once told me all about the rules. I'll go get the food.'

'Okay.' Raheem took out a cigarette. It wasn't one of his better habits and he didn't need Sarah to remind him, which she often did.

'How many times have I told you to stop smoking?' she demanded angrily as she got out of the car.

Raheem avoided the question as he got out too. He lit his cigarette. Sarah would never be satisfied with him. He could perform a miracle by walking on water in front of her and she'd say he was only walking because he didn't know how to swim.

'Do you want a milkshake as well, or just the Filet-O-Fish?' she asked, tossing back her silky brown hair. 'I'm only having a milkshake, doubt I will be able to have all of it.'

No matter what her mood, Sarah always looked stunning with that tanned skin, green eyes and perfect figure. The moment he'd seen her at Stalford University in his first year, he'd been attracted to her.

'I'm on a diet, so only the fish fillet, milkshake and fries. I'll have the rest of your milkshake if you can't finish it,' Raheem said.

'It's called "Filet-O-Fish", not "fish fillet". And remember, go online and report that pothole that we saw on the way here on Strentham road. I drive that way when I go to work, don't want it damaging my tyres.'

'Avoid driving on it then, simple.'

4

'Just do it.' She walked off to McDonald's.

Raheem gave her a salute before going on his phone and reporting it on the council website. Probably the only reason Sarah had gone in to get the food was because Cheryl, a student at the university, worked there. He had been friends with Cheryl during first year, but had kept his distance after he started dating Sarah. The fact that Cheryl had hinted that she wanted to date him meant that unsurprisingly, Sarah had never taken to her. He couldn't blame Sarah for that, but then again he couldn't blame Cheryl for wanting to date him either.

Sarah had graduated from Stalford University in the summer. She'd been a year ahead of Raheem and got a degree in accounting and finance. She had chosen to get a job in Stalford rather than go back to Birmingham, where she was from originally. Raheem supposed he should be glad she hadn't chosen to get a job in Manchester; he could imagine her opening her own accountancy firm at the end of his street just to keep an eye on him.

The sun had disappeared behind the clouds as a black Golf pulled up next to Raheem. 'Yes, Ryan,' he said as the driver wound down the window.

Ryan wasn't alone in the car. A woman in the passenger seat with a haughty face and black hair looked up from her phone. 'Who is he?' she asked Ryan.

'He is a human.'

'Looks like a devil to me,' said the woman, and returned to her phone.

Ryan turned back to Raheem with an apologetic look on his face. 'This is Melissa, by the way.'

'Hi, Melissa-by-the-way' said Raheem kindly. Melissa put in her earphones.

'We started going out together last week,' Ryan informed him.

'Don't know who to feel sorrier for,' Raheem muttered.

Ryan raised his middle finger. 'You still want those tickets for the United match?' he asked

'Make sure you save them for me. I'll give you the hundred quid next week at uni,' said Raheem.

'I'm sure you said one-twenty last time?'

5

Raheem finished his cigarette and dropped it in the bin next to him. 'I was going to give you £1.20 but I felt I was ripping you off, so a hundred it is, yeah?'

'Ha-ha. Prick. Just for you, I'll accept a hundred.'

After making plans to go to the gym together the next morning, Ryan drove off. Moody Melissa had taken out her earphones.

Sarah returned carrying two milkshakes and a bag containing the fish fillet and fries. Or the Filet-O-Fish. She tried to open the passenger door. Raheem unlocked the car and, after giving him an irritated look, she got in.

He waited thirty seconds before getting in himself. 'Hello, how are— What the—?' he muttered, getting out of his seat. There was a squashed box on the driver's seat; he'd sat on the fish fillet. 'Could you not have told me it was there?' he asked irritably as he picked it up. Why put it on his car seat in the first place?

'You sat on it before I could say anything,' Sarah replied coldly.

'So do I always have to ask you when I sit down?'

'Don't start please.'

He opened the box. The fillet was a bit squashed but there was no point in complaining.

They sat in silence for a few minutes, then Sarah asked unexpectedly, 'How's Samir?'

Raheem took his time sipping his milkshake before saying, 'He's fine. Do you want to have some of these fries?'

'Is he still with that Rachel? The blonde one?' *That* Rachel, as if she didn't know who she was.

'Can't you two sort it out?' Raheem asked as he took out his phone. He messaged Ashleigh back to say that he could swap work shifts with her the following week.

Sarah looked affronted. 'Me and Samir? Or me and Rachel?'

'One of them will do, both is asking too much.'

'No, we can't, so don't even ask! I've told you before Samir is a bad influence on you. When are you going to stop hanging around with him?'

Truth be told, Samir wasn't a big fan of Sarah's either.

'Look, I've known him all my life' Raheem said wearily. 'He's my dad's son's brother – I mean my dad's brother's son … my cousin! We are family. I can't just leave him like that. Anyway, ask me a good question.'

Sarah huffed before glancing down at his phone. 'Who's Ashleigh?'

He shouldn't have texted her while he was with Sarah. 'Just a work colleague,' he said defensively.

'Male or female?'

This was getting too much. It was like *Who Wants To Be a Millionaire*? except there was no money at the end of the questions. 'Tell you what, I'll ring the number,' said Raheem. 'If *he* answers then it's a male, and if *she* answers then it's a female, okay?'

He had nearly made her laugh with that, but then she turned her head to the side to hide her smile. It was time to be a bit more romantic. 'Do you want a bite?' asked Raheem politely.

Sarah looked at the half-eaten fish fillet in his hand. 'Go on, then,' she said sweetly.

Raheem moved his face towards her and bit her gently on the shoulder. 'What you doing?' she laughed as she moved his face away.

'I asked if you wanted a bite and you said yes!'

Sarah grinned mischievously. 'Well, let's go back to mine. I'll eat you over there.'

That had done the trick. Maybe the shopping trip would be worth it after all. Then he remembered that the horrible maroon jumper was in the car boot. Maybe not.

***

Samir was at the flat when Raheem returned from Sarah's. 'How many times have I told you to turn off the shower after you use it?' he asked the moment Raheem stepped into the hallway.

'You're the one who left it on yesterday,' retorted Raheem. 'And you didn't clean the kitchen this morning – I had to do it.'

'You said two days ago you'd clean the kitchen when I was about to do it.'

'That was two days ago. Doesn't mean I'm cleaning it all the time, you stupid idiot.'

The kitchen door opened and Rachel walked out wearing an apron. 'Hi, Raheem. I heard you met my cousins in Broadway earlier today.'

'They look so similar to each other,' said Raheem.

'It's amazing, isn't it? Even though they are sisters,' she said seriously.

There was a pause.

'Lasagne will be on the table in ten minutes,' Rachel continued. 'Feel free to have some. If you've just seen Sarah, I'm sure you'll be hungry.'

Talk about a sly dig. 'I'm okay, thanks, Rachel. But please put the lasagne on a plate and not *on* the table. I cleaned the kitchen this morning,' Raheem said politely before going into the living room.

Samir said something to Rachel and followed him inside.
'You better watch out, I've taught Rachel some good Asian swear words' he said as he closed the door and sat on the window ledge.

'Why have you brought her here? I told you I was bringing Sarah today,' Raheem demanded grumpily.

'I pay half the rent for this flat.'

'Does your dad pay the other half? Next Saturday is our turn here. It's not like Rachel sleeps outside on the street. She has a flat, go there sometime.'

Sarah had been complaining about not being able to visit his flat much during the previous year as Rachel was always there. Unsurprisingly, Rachel had been complaining to Samir about Sarah always being there. It really was hard when your girlfriend didn't like your cousin's girlfriend, and your cousin's girlfriend didn't like your girlfriend, and neither did you like your cousin's girlfriend and your cousin didn't like your girlfriend.

'Have you decided on your dissertation topic yet?' Samir asked.

'Women and crime,' said Raheem darkly. 'Are you still doing your dissertation on police powers?'

'Yeah, I think it's a good subject.'

8

'If I was you, which thank God I'm not, but if I was, I'd do the dissertation on the prison system,' said Raheem. 'It's where you're going to end up one way or the other in real life. It will be good preparation.'

'You'll go there before I do. Watch my dissertation get published and discussed in the Houses of Parliament.'

Raheem snorted. The chances of that happening were about as likely as Samir being loyal to Rachel. Samir had always been casual about his relationships with women. There was a period he was dating three women at the same time, until he got caught.

The good thing for Samir was that Rachel was studying architecture and her campus was a fifteen-minute drive from the city campus that they attended. That allowed Samir to chat to any other girl he wanted to. Raheem felt a bit sorry for Rachel, despite not getting on with her, but Samir had assured him that they were both just passing time and knew that nothing serious would come out of their relationship. Not that Raheem believed him. He had also told Raheem that Rachel had been going to the church a lot more recently, which made it all the less likely that the relationship was just casual. For Rachel at least.

A lot of people thought Raheem and Samir looked alike. Samir also had black hair, which was either flat or spiked depending on his mood. They were both nearly six feet tall, lean and muscular. They had been in the same classes from primary school until university. Add the fact that they were neighbours in Manchester, Raheem had spent more time with his cousin than he had with anyone else in his life. They were closer to each other than they were with their own brothers.

'Remember Natasha, Sarah's friend?' Samir asked.

He remembered her alright; she was the one who'd told Sarah that Cheryl was trying to be a bit too friendly with Raheem. Thankfully, Natasha had graduated last summer. 'Yeah, I do. Why?'

Samir looked towards the door to make sure it was closed. 'She was checking me out last night in Sensations. I was with Rachel. I might have to pick another nightclub going forward.'

'You wish. The only time you've ever been checked out is when you've left a hotel,' said Raheem. 'You stick to your ding dong ding's with Rachel and Katie.'

They both laughed. 'We need to make sure we're on time for our seminar on Monday,' Samir said. 'Ten o'clock start. If you want to get a job as a private investigator, you need to start being punctual.'

For once he was right. They needed to make sure they focussed more than ever in their final year. No more turning up late to lectures and seminars.

'Don't worry, we'll be on time. Trust me.'

**

Raheem hurried along the corridor with Samir right behind him. It was ten past ten, and they were ten minutes late for the first seminar of their third and final year.

Two girls were waiting outside the lift, which was on the way down. 'After you, ladies,' said Raheem politely, holding out an arm to stop Samir as he tried to enter the lift when the doors opened.

'Thanks.' They both smiled at him.

'He's very kind, isn't he?' said Samir as he pressed the button for the fifth floor.

'He sure is,' said the taller of the two girls, surveying Raheem with interest.

'It's not that I'm kind, it's just that if I let you in the lift first, I can get out first,' said Raheem, winking.

The girls giggled as the lift opened and Raheem and Samir walked out. The giggles had turned to shrieks by the time the lift doors had shut.

'That's a good one. I'm going to use it next time.' Samir looked impressed.

'You would never let anyone go before you anyway,' Raheem sniggered as their classroom came into view.

Samir peered through the glass pane in the door. 'He's already started – everyone's making notes. What shall we say this time?'

'Leave it to me, I know what to do.' Raheem pulled the door open. Aliyah gave him a death stare the moment he entered. Next to her, Hannah waved at them.

Before Raheem could do any more than give Aliyah an apologetic look, Martin, their seminar tutor, spoke. 'New year, but some things don't change,' he said in his deep voice. He was probably referring to his clothes; Martin was wearing the same white shirt, same black shoes, same round glasses that he always wore.

'Sorry sir. We would have been on time but we had a bit of a problem on the way,' said Raheem.

Martin raised his eyebrows. 'Did the lift break down like last time and the time before that and the time before that?'

'Oh no, sir, the *lift* didn't break down. This time my *car* broke down. Tyre punctured on the way here.'

'Are you sure about that?' Martin asked.

'I have never been more sure of anything in my life,' said Raheem confidently, knowing Martin couldn't prove he was lying.

'Then there is no issue from me boys. We can't do anything if a tyre suddenly punctures. It's not your fault.'

That was what you called an unprovable lie. 'You're right,' said Raheem.

Aliyah rolled her eyes and shook her head.

'Take a seat then,' said Martin. 'Actually, before you do I have a small task for both of you.'

'It's a bit early for a test I think,' said Samir.

'It's not the type of test you're thinking of.' Martin took a sheet of paper and ripped it in half. 'I want both of you to take a piece of paper.' He handed them both a pen. 'I want you to write down which tyre was punctured without showing each other,' he said pleasantly.

The class started to laugh and even Martin smiled. They had little chance of picking the same tyre. Knowing Samir, he'd probably pick the bonnet or something.

'Sorry, we'll be on time in future,' said Raheem resignedly.

'In that case, please take a seat,' said Martin.

With their heads bowed, Raheem and Samir trudged off towards their seats.

Chapter 2

'Listen, Aliyah, it won't happen again,' Raheem said as he caught up with her. He put his hand on her shoulder but she shrugged it off. She had not spoken to him at all during the seminar. 'Anyway, want to get something to eat?' he asked, knowing what the answer would be.

'No, thanks,' Aliyah said angrily. 'We were supposed to work on our dissertation plan this morning. I came in early just for you!'

'It doesn't matter. It's only the first day back – we got plenty of time to do it,' Raheem moaned. Why did women become so sensitive about little things? It wasn't like they'd have done much an hour before the seminar.

'That's not the point! You could have at least *rung* me to say you weren't going to make it! And you had your phone switched off when I was trying to ring *you*!'

'Help me,' said Raheem, looking for Samir, but he was walking thirty feet behind them, talking to Hannah.

Aliyah sped further ahead. Raheem jogged up to her again, nearly knocking over a library staff member who was carrying some books. 'Sorry,' he called as the books fell to the floor. He continued jogging until he reached Aliyah. 'Okay, well, I'm going to have to tell you the truth then, aren't I?' he said as they turned the corner towards the university main entrance.

'Go on, then. And don't even bother with the punctured tyre. That was proved to be a load of crap,' Aliyah snapped. She finally stopped next to the vending machine near the entrance to the library and leaned against the wall, her arms folded. She had an innocent face, but if looks could kill then her expression would have decimated half the university.

'It's not the tyre,' said Raheem slowly, with no clue what he was going to say next. He hadn't expected her to stop, but now she had he had to think of something.

'Well?' she said.

It was time to make up another story. 'Erm … actually it was … it was Ryan!' he said dramatically. 'He wasn't feeling well. He rang me this morning and asked if I could take him to the hospital. I couldn't take any risks, so I got up early and dropped him at the hospital. By the time I came back to pick up Samir, I was running late and my phone battery had died. We had to leave for the seminar so I didn't have the time to message you. I didn't want to say all that about Ryan in front of everyone in the class – data protection and all that.' It was worth a go. He would ring Ryan and ask him to confirm the story if Aliyah asked.

'That's so thoughtful of you,' she said unexpectedly.

Raheem grinned. 'I know, thank you.'

'Only problem is, I've seen Ryan this morning. He was going to a seminar.'

'Oh.'

Usually, Ryan didn't wake up until midday. He had to pick today of all days to wake up early.

'Did someone mention Ryan?' asked Samir as he joined them.

Aliyah jabbed a finger in Raheem's direction. 'Did I?' he said casually.

'Yes, you did,' she said shortly.

It was time for Plan B. 'I did indeed. You're right… But *this* Ryan ... is not *that* Ryan. The one I dropped off at the hospital, that's a different Ryan.'

There was a pause. Samir was looking confused; Raheem still had that cheesy grin on his face and Aliyah's eyebrows were raised. Unfortunately, it was Samir who broke the silence. 'So, who is *this* Ryan?'

Raheem looked at Samir and shook his head slightly. Samir nodded to show he understood. 'I meant, who is *that* Ryan?' he said, achieving nothing and making matters worse.

'Do you know all my fucking friends?' snapped Raheem, glaring at Samir, who seemed to have finally realised it was best to keep his mouth shut.

Raheem turned to Aliyah and laughed hysterically. 'I've got four friends called Ryan. He only knows the one on our course, the one you saw this morning! Let's get something to eat.'

13

'You wish,' snapped Aliyah and she stalked off towards the library.

He didn't want to start the year in Aliyah's bad books. He should have messaged her that he couldn't make it, but it wasn't that big a deal. 'I'll catch you outside,' he said to Samir.

'Hurry up, though. Hannah's coming with us, and the real Ryan has texted me to say he will meet us in town.'

'If I'm not back in two minutes, call the ambulance.' Raheem hurried after Aliyah and caught up with her at the library entrance. She had dyed her hair dark brown since the last time he'd seen her during the summer holidays and had put on a bit more makeup than usual.

They crossed the ground floor of the library. The IT team seemed to have relocated their office to the left-hand side of the building. It had always been a pain in the backside to walk to the other side of university to sort out IT issues on laptops. The bookshelves in the centre of the ground floor had been replaced with tables. The main floors of the library were usually very busy and, after many complaints by students, it looked as if the university had decided to take steps to accommodate extra study space.

Aliyah headed for the double doors opposite and began climbing the stairs. He followed her but stumbled on his untied laces. By the time he reached the first-floor landing, she was nowhere to be seen. He smacked his hand against the wall.

'Someone's having a bad day,' said an unpleasant voice from behind him.

Raheem turned around. Liam was leaning against the wall opposite the toilets. 'At least I haven't had a bad life, unlike you,' Raheem replied. A couple of students walked past them, seemingly oblivious to the tension in the air.

Liam chuckled. That long pointy nose on the thin face still looked the same; if anything, it looked slightly longer. His short back and sides haircut was the same as the one he'd had for the previous two years. 'You make me laugh,' he said.

'I can make you cry as well, like I did in first year.'

Liam had still not got over the fact Raheem and Samir had beaten him up in Sensations during first year. It was his own fault as he'd tried to touch Cheryl on the dance floor. Add to

14

that the fact that Samir had thrown his drink over Liam in the corridor last year for bumping into him, and there was no love lost between them. Not that it mattered to Samir that Liam had bumped into him by accident.

Liam tried to look as if Raheem's words weren't important, but his expression hardened slightly and a muscle twitched at the corner of his mouth.

The door behind Raheem opened and Samir walked in. 'There you are. You said you'd be—' He stopped as he saw Liam. 'Look who it is, our American friend.'

'Well, we are the superpower, aren't we? Not like your shitty island.' So why did he leave his superpower to study here?

'Don't be starting with me or I'll throw you down these stairs.' Samir gestured to the door behind him that led to the stairs.

'I'll just get the lift back up.'

'Lift's out of order, retard.' Raheem pointed at the out of order sign as Liam walked past them onto the first floor.

'No luck with Aliyah?' asked Samir as they headed back down the stairs.

'Nope,' said Raheem. 'I'll sort it out with her, though.'

'You take her for granted.'

'Me?'

'No you don't say? I was talking about your dad.'

'Shut up man, you're always chatting shit. Like we really would have done any work at nine in the morning. That is way too early.'

'Should have told her, that way she wouldn't have had to wait for you.'

'Sorry, big mistake!'

They reached the university entrance, where Hannah was waiting for them. 'Hiya,' she said, hugging Raheem. He hadn't had a chance to speak to her in the seminar as Martin had put them into groups.

'Hey! Missed you over the summer,' he said.

'I missed you guys, too. Have you found me Mr Tall, Smart and Handsome yet?' she asked.

'Are you not with Josh?' asked Raheem.

'You're so forgetful. I told you we broke up just before the summer holidays. That's why I asked if you'd found me someone.'

As if he didn't have enough issues in his own relationship to be finding people for others. 'That's our mission this year. Not many down your end?' he asked. It was close to mission impossible, as Hannah was six feet tall and wanted an even taller boyfriend. She should have stuck with Josh.

'Not many in Chelmsford,' she said grimly.

'Racist area,' muttered Raheem. He dodged out of the way as Hannah aimed a kick at him.

'It's not racist, it's just it's … erm…'

'Posh?' said Samir.

'Correct. Anyway, guys, come on. I need to eat. That seminar was so draining and I didn't manage to have any breakfast.'

They headed towards the car park together. Samir and Hannah were talking but Raheem's mind was on Aliyah. He hated seeing her upset, but they would make up. They always did.

Stalford University was at the top of the city centre, near some student accommodation. Raheem and Samir had decided to stay in the same flat for the third year running. Samir had wanted to move to the city centre, but Raheem had talked him out of it. They needed a break from the city centre because it was where they studied, worked and went on nights out.

They got in Raheem's BMW and he turned on the engine. The car lurched forward and his forehead skimmed the steering wheel; he'd forgotten to put the gear in neutral. Samir came off worse. He had been about to take a sip from his water bottle and now had a wet patch on his jeans. Talk about a perfect start to the university year.

***

The annual fun fair at Burydale Park wasn't one of Raheem's ideal hangouts. He had gone last year with Sarah and hadn't enjoyed it much, so he didn't see what would be different this time around.

He returned from the stall and handed Sarah her cappuccino.

'I don't know how you can drink black coffee,' she said, looking at his cup.

'It's not difficult – you drink it the same way you drink everything else.'

'I can barely breathe from laughing. Try my cappuccino. They make it really nice over here.'

Raheem took her cappuccino and tried it. 'Is this a cappuccino or a crapaccino?' he said, handing the cup back to Sarah.

'Excuse me, it's better than that boring coffee you're having! Anyway, Natasha says she'll meet us in Control later. She's coming with Darren.'

'Me and you will go to Sensations instead. Forget them two.'

'No, Sensations is always rammed. You always take me there. You need to be more open minded and try somewhere new.'

'*You've* opened your mind so much, your brain has fallen out' Raheem muttered.

'What's that?'

'Nothing.'

Sarah tossed back her hair. 'Darren and Natasha have got us VIP tickets.'

'Wow, how amazing…' He linked his arm with Sarah's and they walked past the dodgems they'd gone on earlier. Sarah had told him off for banging into her. Apparently they were supposed to be a team, hitting everyone else.

Raheem was just about to suggest they went for a drive in the warmth of his car when Sarah said she was going to ring her dad. She headed away from the blaring music towards a quieter corner of the fair.

As he was about to take out his phone, there was a tug on his jacket. A boy who looked no older than five was holding out a KitKat. He was standing next to a lady whom Raheem assumed was his mother. She had one finger in her ear as she spoke on her phone.

'Thank you,' said Raheem as took the chocolate. This kid was definitely going to be a noble human when he grew up. He

17

opened the wrapper and took a bite. For some reason, the child suddenly started to cry.

'Hey, what's up?' asked Raheem, just as Sarah returned.

'Aww, why is he crying? Is he lost?' She knelt down next to the boy and took his hand.

'I think that's his mum.' Raheem nodded towards the woman who was still on her phone.

'He's looking at your chocolate. I think he wants it,' said Sarah.

'It's not mine, he gave it to me.'

Sarah looked at him in bewilderment. 'And you ate it?'

'What? It's not poisoned, is it?' Raheem exclaimed.

Sarah clapped a hand to her forehead. 'He gave it to you to open the wrapper, Raheem! How could you be so dumb?'

Five minutes later, Raheem edged through the crowd with difficulty as he returned carrying candy floss. Sarah had made him get it for that not-so-noble kid, Oliver. His mother had laughed it off, but Sarah had insisted. He had asked Sarah if he could finish his coffee first. She had told him he could finish it on the walk to the candy floss stall.

'Where are you, Sarah?' muttered Raheem as he squinted through the crowd. A bark behind him made him jump and the candy floss fell to the ground.

'Sorry, love, he didn't mean to scare you,' said a woman walking past with her dog. It was sniffing the candy floss enthusiastically.

Fuck's sake. Now he would have to go get another one.

***

He would miss university when he finished his third and final year. The past two years had been the best of his life. He would even miss the Tesco Express store where he worked part time. As it was in the city centre, there were some interesting customers. There had been an occasion when a young lad who had stolen some beer from the store came back the next week and handed in his CV. Raheem had given it to Andrew, the store manager, who'd ripped it in half and thrown it into the bin.

18

It was after a shift at work that Raheem returned home to find Samir lying in his bed with Katie, his second girlfriend.

'What are you doing in my room?' asked Raheem as Katie lifted the duvet to cover herself.

'Hi Raheem.' She waved at him.

He waved back unenthusiastically and gestured to Samir to meet him outside on the landing. These two had been on and off since high school. 'Why are you in my room?' he hissed as Samir came out of the bedroom zipping his jeans.

'My bedroom radiator's not working,' Samir replied.

Raheem didn't have time to argue; it was already quarter to six and Sarah hated it when he was late. 'I'm going to Sarah's. I want my bed sheets changed and both of you out of my room by the time I come back.'

'Alright, but Katie is staying over, so we've got the living room for tonight.'

'Just make sure you're out of my room. There's a heater in my wardrobe, take that to your room if your radiator is not working. Catch you later. I'm going.' Raheem went downstairs and out of the front door. He tried to open his car door but it was locked. He trudged back inside to get the keys.

Twenty minutes later, he arrived at Sarah's apartment.

'Are you finally here?' she said as she let him in.

'No, it's my twin that's come' replied Raheem as he entered and gave her a hug.

'You look tired.'

'I was dancing all day at work, that's why.'

Sarah grinned and went in the bathroom. Raheem walked to the window and opened it as wide as he could before lighting a cigarette. The apartment was on the sixth floor and had a perfect view of the city. The lights of his university were visible in the distance. There was always someone in the library as it was open twenty-four hours.

'Don't smoke in here, Raheem. I'm making our tea once I have my shower,' called Sarah. She could smell smoke from anywhere; even if he was on the phone to her, she would probably smell it.

'Why do you call it tea? Just call it dinner,' Raheem called back.

'Because dinner is what I have around one o'clock, as I have told you enough times.'

'That's lunch, that's why it is called *lunchtime.*'

'You're still smoking, aren't you?'

Raheem threw his cigarette out of the window and walked grumpily back to the sofa. Sometimes he wished he could take the Samir route and not be in a serious relationship. Samir had always told him that he couldn't see a future for Raheem and Sarah; apparently they were two opposites that didn't attract.

Raheem had flirted with women a few times, mainly on nights out, but he had remained loyal to Sarah. She was just too controlling, that was the problem.

His phone buzzed with a text message from Aliyah.

Sorry about last time ☹

He smiled and texted back, telling her it was fine. Almost instantly, he got her reply. *Would be nice if you ever messaged first.*

Really sorry just busy atm I will message you later.

Ok.

Raheem waited a couple of minutes and then texted her. *Hi, Aliyah, how u doing? I hope this counts as me messaging u first btw* ☺

Lol, that was actually funny. I'll meet u at 10 tmrw at the uni café, have a coffee before our lecture?

Raheem replied that he would meet her at the café and stretched out on the sofa. Aliyah lived with her family in Stalford. She had some relatives in Manchester, a few streets down from Raheem's house. Whenever Raheem had come back to Stalford to work at Tesco Express during the summer, he'd always met up with her afterwards. Aliyah was different to the other girls he knew, but he could never understand why he thought that.

The bathroom door opened and Sarah walked out wrapped in a towel. 'I haven't made stew in a while, so don't complain if it's not perfect,' she said, with her back to him.

Raheem walked up behind her and turned her around. He put his arms around her waist. 'You look perfect, though,' he said. He tried to kiss her but she put her hand on his mouth.

'We're just eating tonight, nothing else. Behave.'

Raheem let go of her and collapsed back on the sofa as she went into her bedroom to get changed. Casual relationships might well be better than serious ones.

***

No matter how hard he tried, Raheem struggled to get to places on time. It was an old habit of his and, as the saying goes, old habits die hard. It was five past ten when he hurried through the university café entrance. Aliyah was already sitting at a table near the window.

'Hi, Aliyah' he said, hitching a smile on his face and sitting opposite her.

She looked up from her phone. 'Tyre punctured again? Or did you have to take a friend called Samir – who only you know – to the hospital?'

'Tyre punctured on the way to the hospital this time,' said Raheem innocently.

Aliyah shook her head, but at least she managed a smile. 'I think we have to go and queue for the coffees. They don't do table service here, even for you.'

They went and got their coffees. Raheem insisted on paying for Aliyah. The university café, or Parkview Café as it was known, was next to the university in a building that had five floors. It was the main building for lectures, and also had seminar rooms and staff offices. Businesses could book rooms for conferences, meetings and lunches. The café on the lower ground floor was where most students went for coffee and hot food. Raheem had spent a lot of time over the past couple of years with Aliyah in the café, having their chats.

'How's your family?' Raheem asked as they sat back down.

'Good, thanks. What about yours?'

'They are alright. My sister is stressing about her GCSEs, though.'

Aliyah nodded. 'I was so scared about them when I started Year Eleven, but I ended up doing okay. Tell her not to worry, she'll be fine. So, did you forget about me over the summer?'

'I could never forget you,' he replied simply.

'I'm sure you won't forget me, seeing as it's our final year and we have our dissertations to do,' she said sternly. There was a moment's silence before they both started laughing.

'So, you're accusing me of just using you for my work?' Raheem pretended to look hurt.

Aliyah grinned. 'Maybe.'

He knew Aliyah was aware how much he appreciated her. It had always been that way. 'So still besties?' he asked, holding out his fist.

'Yep, still besties' said Aliyah, fist bumping him.

They spent the next half hour discussing plans for their dissertations. Aliyah was doing hers on capital punishment. 'Everyone deserves a second chance,' she said when Raheem asked her why she was against the death penalty. He didn't pursue the subject; it was something she was passionate about it and he didn't want to be insensitive. If it was down to him, anyone who loved shopping would get hanged.

'So, what's the plan after graduating?' he asked.

Aliyah glanced around the café before saying, 'Job and marriage, I guess.'

That was the thing with the South Asian mentality: get married quickly. Even his parents were on his case about getting married within a couple of years of graduating. It was way too early for that; he was only twenty-one.

'Love or arranged?' he asked.

Aliyah shrugged. 'Either. I need to find someone good, though.'

'Cheers to that,' Raheem raised his cup.

'Cheers. I watched *The Lion King* last night with my niece.'

The Lion King was the most overrated Disney movie of all time, but Aliyah would not hear a word against it. 'I still don't get that circle of life thing in the movie,' Raheem said grumpily. Aliyah had mentioned it many times. It was her favourite quote.

'Circle of life is how things end the way they started,' she explained patiently. 'Remember we met outside this café two years ago on our first day at uni?'

He remembered it as though it were yesterday. Time really had flown. 'So when I was born, I was like one foot tall,' he said. 'Does that mean when I die I'm going to shrink to one foot again?'

There was a pause. 'Never mind, you won't understand.' Aliyah sounded prickly.

They sat in silence for a few moments before Raheem said, 'We should have done a degree in law. We'd have got a job straight away at my brother's law firm in Leicester.'

'It's who you know, not what you know, I guess. He specialises in property law, doesn't he?'

They continued to chat about their career options. 'How's Sarah?' Aliyah asked, once Raheem had finished telling her about his dream job of being a private investigator.

'She's fine,' he said a little too bluntly.

Aliyah frowned. 'Why so sappy? It was just a normal question.'

'You asked how she was and I said fine. What's sappy about that?'

'It's not *what* you said, it's *how* you said it.' Before Raheem could say anything else, she stood and picked up her bag.

'Are you angry with me again?' he asked.

Aliyah huffed, 'In case you hadn't noticed, we have a lecture at eleven.' She moved towards the exit. Women got upset over such small things. What had he done wrong?

He was just about to follow her when a soft voice behind him asked, 'Excuse me, is anyone sitting here?'

Raheem turned around. Wow. He'd seen many gorgeous women at the university, but the one in front of him right now had to be up there with the best. She was standing next to the chair Aliyah had been sitting on. She had long black hair and startling green eyes. She was wearing dark blue jeans and a denim top and carrying a Zara's handbag. She had that Latino look about her.

Raheem stood up and looked carefully at the seat Aliyah had vacated. 'Nope, don't think there is,' he said. She chuckled and sat down.

'Not seen you before. First year?' he asked as he sat back down. If he'd seen her before, he would have noticed her.

'I'm in my third year, just come to complete my final year here. I'm from Leicester originally,' she said pleasantly.

No one who knew him seemed to be in the café. He held out his hand. 'I'm Raheem, by the way. Raheem Khan.'

She shook his hand. 'Nice to meet you, "Raheem by the way". I'm Veronica.' She had a sense of humour as bad as his!

He laughed. 'Don't know why I said it like that.' He made sure he kept his eyes on her face, despite the temptation to look a bit further down. He could tell Veronica was used to attention.

She smiled, showing perfect white teeth. 'Aw, sorry if I'm making you feel nervous.'

His insides exploded with excitement at her words. He had to get her number. What more of a hint could he have asked for that she was interested in talking to him? 'I'm not nervous. I know your boyfriend, after all,' he said, crossing his fingers under the table.

Veronica looked confused. 'My boyfriend? I don't have a boyfriend.'

Talk about his luck being in today. Raheem sat back in his chair and winked. 'I'm joking. I just wanted to know if you had a boyfriend or not.'

Veronica stared at him before shrieking with laughter. It was now eleven o'clock, meaning his lecture had started. Oh well. Missing one lecture wasn't the end of the world.

Chapter 3

Raheem just wanted to be friends with Veronica. It was a bit of flirting and, as far as he knew, that wasn't against the law. Whether it was right or not was a different matter. He'd told her that he was single – but he was only having a laugh with her.

Aliyah messaged him to ask why he hadn't attended the lecture. He messaged back that the coffee had made him feel sick. The fact that she didn't ask him if he was feeling better confirmed to Raheem that she didn't believe him because Aliyah was the most caring and sensitive person he knew.

He wasted no time in telling Samir about Veronica.

'Could you shut up, please?' called the lecturer, Michelle, from the front of the room.

Raheem faked a look of surprise and turned his head around. There was no point, as he was sitting on the back row and there was no one behind him.

'I was speaking to you, Raheem,' said Michelle.

Raheem turned back to her, but this time he had two hundred students staring back at him. Giving him an irritated look, Michelle continued her lecture.

***

'I bet she's not even all that. She can't be, if she's into a guy who looks like you,' said Samir an hour later in the library. 'Shit. I'm going to have to start my dissertation plan all over again. I don't think I saved it,' he added as he plugged his charger into the socket.

'You only did two lines,' said Ryan, who had his head down on the table. He'd been out drinking again last night and had fallen asleep in the lecture. His blond hair was sticking up from the back, and his eyes looked rather red.

Raheem leaned back in his chair. 'Don't you worry Samir. Wait till you see her yourself.' Veronica had messaged him to say she would be in at one. It had just turned twelve.

Ryan raised his head from his hands. 'Are you not starting your literature review?'

'No chance. I got it all planned out. Unlike this joker,' said Raheem, nodding at Samir.

'Aliyah told me she wasn't helping you with it, now what you going to do?' said Samir.

Raheem tapped his nose. He always had a backup plan; in fact, he had told his backup plan to be here at twelve. He sent a text to Daniel asking him where he was, before looking around the library.

As usual, the first floor was almost full. It was a rectangular room with rows of computers. A large space in the middle had tables with sockets for those students who brought their own laptops, and another section had computers next to the printers. Being the busiest and noisiest floor, it had no books. Floors one, two and three were all designed in the same way. There was a smaller fourth floor, but usually only the construction students used it as it had special computers designed for their course. Raheem would usually bring his own laptop to work on.

It was common knowledge that the best-looking girls sat here. Raheem had spent most of last year with Sarah on the second or third floors. Unsurprisingly, she had always hated the first floor.

'Your best friend's here,' Samir nodded towards the computers. His best friend? More like Sarah's best friend.

Jason had put his coat on the chair and logged onto his computer. To Raheem's annoyance, he spotted them and came over. 'Hi, guys,' he said.

Samir and Ryan returned the greeting and, after a second's hesitation, Raheem did too. 'You working at the city campus today?' he asked politely. 'I'm sure the West Park Campus is nearer to where you live.'

Jason didn't look surprised by this less than warm welcome. 'Most of my classes take place here and I'm going into town with a mate after.'

26

'Sarah's working today, isn't she?' Samir winked cheekily at Raheem.

'Yeah, she will be. I'm going with someone else.'

Sarah and Jason had been friends since high school and, as luck would have it, had chosen to come to the same university.

'How do you know she's working today?' asked Raheem.

Jason frowned at him. 'Samir just mentioned it.'

'Oh. That's alright then.'

Jason stood there, as though hoping someone would continue the conversation. When no one did, he said, 'Well, I best get back to my desk. Good seeing you.' He returned to his computer, putting on his cap as he went.

The less Raheem saw of Jason, the better. Not that Jason would say anything wrong, but he was just so irritating. A tap on the shoulder made him look around. Jermaine was grinning at him; he was accompanied by Fiona.

'The best couple in uni have arrived,' said Raheem, shaking hands with Jermaine.

'Have we been promoted from second to first now?' Jermaine chuckled as he shook hands with Samir and Ryan before taking a seat.

'Seeing as Sarah has left, technically you two are the best couple in the uni now,' said Raheem as he greeted Fiona. She was one of those classy women who you could tell would go far in her career. She had an intelligent, sophisticated look about her. The glasses she wore certainly helped.

'You been working out over the summer?' asked Ryan, looking at Jermaine's arms.

'I've got him into the gym, so credit goes to me,' Fiona said as she sat down next to him.

Raheem had never met anyone who smiled as often as Jermaine. Even if he was waiting in a queue for a shop he would be smiling. He had met Jermaine and Fiona through Sarah in his first year, even though they were both on his course.

'How's Sarah, Raheem? How is she finding her job?' asked Fiona.

'Good, thanks,' Raheem replied.

'I always tell Jermaine that we need to be more like you and Sarah,' said Fiona.

'Really?' Raheem ignored Samir, who pretended to vomit.

She nodded. 'I think having a bit of difference is healthy in a relationship.'

'I agree,' said Jermaine, taking out his afro comb.

'Too much difference fucks it up, though,' said Samir. 'I know a guy, bit of prick, but he and his girlfriend always argue. I have tried telling him he needs to step away from the relationship but he never listens.'

A change of subject was needed. 'What are you guys doing for your dissertations?' Raheem asked. As Jermaine launched into an explanation about his dissertation (stress-management techniques), Raheem checked his phone again. Daniel had texted to say he'd be in the library in fifteen minutes. Daniel was a top lad, one of those students who you wouldn't think was intelligent but always came out with high marks.

After ten minutes, Jermaine and Fiona bade them goodbye and left hand in hand to attend their lecture.

'I should have done my dissertation on stress-management techniques.' Raheem yawned and stretched his arms.

'It would have been better if you did. Your stress is about to increase this year,' said Samir darkly as he returned to his laptop.

'Shut the fuck up,' Raheem snapped. 'Didn't you hear what Fiona said? Difference is a good thing. Even you and Rachel are very different.'

'How are we different?'

'You're a dog and she is a human, so quite a bit of difference if you ask me.'

Samir raised his middle finger before going back to his laptop, though Raheem doubted he had finished writing his first sentence yet. The door to the first floor opened and Daniel entered. He had lost quite a bit of weight during the summer; his clothes were loose and his skin looked rather pale.

'Danny boy!' exclaimed Raheem when Daniel reached their table. 'What you saying?'

'I'm … not bad mate. How have you guys been? Had a good summer?' Daniel asked in his Scouse accent. Thankfully, he supported Everton and not Liverpool in football.

'It was good. Me and Raheem went to Old Trafford to watch Pakistan play England in the cricket,' said Samir.

'You went to a football stadium to watch a cricket match?' Ryan asked. Only Ryan could come out with that one. Samir explained that there was also a cricket ground called Old Trafford.

'But you should be supporting England, Samir. Why you supporting Pakistan?' said Raheem pointedly.

Ryan said, 'It's up to him who he supports. I know an idiot who supports Pakistan in cricket, even though he was born here.'

'Who?' asked Daniel.

Ryan pointed at Raheem.

'Well, on the one hand you've got an underdeveloped, poor country, and on the other hand you got Pakistan, so I guess it's not difficult to decide,' Raheem sniggered. Samir and Ryan roared with laughter. 'I didn't see you in our lecture. Then again, I guess you don't need to attend; you always smash it when it comes to the exams' Raheem continued. He took out his water bottle and took a long swig.

'I'm still in second year, mate. I failed my exams last year.' Daniel looked at the floor.

Raheem choked.

'How the fuck did you fail? You were the cleverest out of all of us,' said Samir, staring at Daniel.

'That's not too hard,' muttered Ryan. For some reason, he looked at Raheem and Samir.

Daniel was obviously uncomfortable. 'I don't know what happened. But I'm going to have to make sure I pass this year,' he mumbled.

Raheem wiped his mouth with a tissue. That was the end of his back-up plan then. 'No worries, Dan, we can send you our notes from last year for the exams.'

'Don't worry, mate. Just let me know when you need them and I'll email them over,' said Samir reassuringly.

Daniel looked a little happier. 'Thanks, guys. I'll see you around. I have a seminar to go to.' He raised his hand in farewell and trudged off.

'Looks like you'll have to do your work yourself,' Ryan said as they watched him go.

Raheem had to agree. It wouldn't be fair to ask Daniel to help them if he hadn't passed himself. That was the thing with university: you could only fail a year once and resit, but fail a second time and that was it. 'We should have asked him what he failed on. He might have done different modules to us.'

'I'll ask him later, but I'm sure he was in all my seminars and lectures in second semester last year,' said Ryan, stifling a yawn.

Disappointed, Raheem stood up to go for a cigarette. 'You coming?' he asked Samir.

Samir shook his head. 'I need to start this dissertation plan, bro. Keep getting distracted.'

They only had a couple of weeks left to submit it. Raheem had managed to do his first paragraph yesterday.

'Can you get me a Red Bull from the campus shop?' Ryan asked. 'Got to go back to Sheffield this afternoon to help my dad in the takeaway, and I'm shattered.' He definitely looked shattered, but it was his own fault that he spent half his life in clubs and bars.

'Get me a chocolate as well,' said Samir, still searching his documents folder for the two lines he had typed in the hope that he'd saved them.

'Bloody hell,' said Raheem as he took his cigarette packet from his bag.

'Cheer up, Raheem. Now you get to be like everyone else and do your own literature review,' Ryan sniggered.

'Fuck off. Ask your dad that I'm coming to his takeaway tonight.'

Raheem had taken two steps when Samir shouted, 'That's not even a question! He said *ask* your dad I'm *coming* to his takeaway!'

Ryan cottoned on, and they both howled with laughter so loud that heads turned in their direction. Raheem grinned

30

sheepishly as he left. He pressed the button for the lift despite only being one floor up. Stairs weren't his thing.

When the lift doors opened, Hannah was inside texting on her phone. 'Hello,' said Raheem as he got in.

'Hey, how you been?'

'Not too good, not too bad,' he replied as they reached the ground floor.

Liam walked past them, shooting glances at Hannah. 'Why was he staring at me?' she asked, looking back.

'I get stares from women all the time. Nothing to worry about,' Raheem said casually.

'Ha-ha. Though now you mention it, I think my mate Lauren has a thing for you. Would you be interested?'

'I would if I could – but I can't.'

'You're seeing someone, aren't you?'

'Do you still work at that Morrison's in town?'

Hannah had never met Sarah because Raheem and Samir had only properly started talking to her near the end of their second year and by that time Sarah had left. Once they were outside, they said goodbye. Hannah headed back to her flat while Raheem lit his cigarette and chatted to Adam and Zack, a couple of mates from his course. Ten minutes later, he was back on the first floor handing Ryan his sandwich and a Mars bar to Samir.

'I said tuna, not tuna and sweetcorn,' said Ryan grumpily.

'What a dead chocolate,' Samir complained, looking at it as if it were something Raheem had picked up from the bin. 'Was this the only one you could find?'

'Ungrateful bastards,' Raheem muttered. Veronica had just sent him a message to say she would arrive soon. Quite a few people who knew him were sitting on the first floor; it might be better if he met her somewhere quieter. 'Listen, I'm going upstairs to sit down for a bit. Need to crack on with this literature review,' he told Samir and Ryan.

'No worries, we'll be down here,' said Samir.

Raheem glanced at Samir's laptop screen as he walked past. He *had* made a start: two words at the top of the page, *Dissertation Plan.*

Raheem checked his reflection in the mirror in the toilets before going upstairs to the second floor. Aliyah was sitting on a table directly ahead of him with Kiran and Catherine, two of her friends from their course. Instinctively, Raheem turned and walked back out of the door as it was sliding shut. His forehead smacked against the wood and he staggered back, clutching it.

Trying to act as if nothing had happened, despite the fact that his head was throbbing, he took the lift to the third floor and texted Veronica to meet him there instead. He found an empty table in the middle and sat down.

He had waited a few minutes before she walked in, her hair tied back in a ponytail and her handbag swaying in her arms, looking just as stunning as she'd done when he first saw her.

'You're looking nice,' said Raheem as they hugged.

Her lips briefly touched the side of his face as they broke apart. 'Thanks,' she said sweetly as she sat opposite him.

Raheem sat down again. Emma, one of Rachel's flatmates, was on the computers in the corner, but she didn't know Sarah.

'Got so much work to do already,' Veronica moaned, taking out her business management books.

A hand on Raheem's shoulder made him jump. For one mad moment, he thought it was Sarah, but it turned out to be Samir.

'I was looking for you,' he said. It was clear Samir had followed him all the way to the third floor to see what he was up to. They knew each other too well. When Raheem did not respond, he turned to Veronica. 'Hi, I'm Samir, but you can call me whatever you want.' They shook hands.

'Listen, this is Veronica,' Raheem said before Veronica introduced herself. 'We're just doing some work. We'll meet you on the first floor in a bit.'

Samir widened his eyes. 'How can I leave without you? We always do our work together,' he said innocently, though Raheem could hear the laughter in his voice. He felt like bursting out laughing himself, coupled with the desire to punch him.

'That's so cute.' Veronica looked at them admiringly. Raheem shook his head, cursing under his breath. 'Sit down Samir.' She indicated the chair next to her.

Raheem stood up and looked over Samir's shoulder. He raised his hand. 'Oi! Hi!'

Samir fell for it and turned around, allowing Raheem to sit on the chair next to Veronica.

'So you guys are on the same course?' Veronica asked as Samir finally took his seat.

'Same course, same flat—'

'But not the same bedroom,' Raheem interjected.

Samir reached across the table and clapped him on the shoulder. 'He's very funny, isn't he?' he said. 'We are actually cousins, but more like brothers.'

'Really? You're cousins?' asked Veronica keenly, as if having a cousin was something unheard of.

Raheem tried to kick Samir under the table but missed and hit his foot on the table leg. Now he had a throbbing foot to go with his throbbing head.

'Yeah, we are, but thankfully, God was very kind to me and I didn't end up looking like Raheem,' said Samir. What a cheeky git.

'Aw, that's mean! I stay with my cousin as well. It's good to have some family around,' said Veronica.

This wasn't going the way Raheem had planned. 'Ryan's probably waiting for you,' he said pointedly to Samir.

'Ryan's gone. Remember, he had to go to his dad's takeaway, the one that you were *asking* to come to?'

Raheem couldn't think of any reply to that.

'So how do you find your course, Samir?' Veronica asked.

Samir began chatting his usual gibberish, allowing Raheem time to convince himself that there was nothing wrong with innocent flirting. No doubt Sarah wouldn't approve, but he was just having a bit of harmless fun. Not like it was going to lead to anything.

He was just about to join in the conversation when he saw Aliyah walking towards them. 'Shit,' he said as she came closer. She had texted him earlier to ask where he was, and he had told her he was in a seminar.

'What's shit?' asked Veronica as Aliyah reached them.

'What?' asked Raheem, smiling at Aliyah. She didn't smile back.

'You said shit.' Veronica looked at Aliyah, who was standing with her arms folded.

'I said ... sit,' replied Raheem.

Aliyah said nothing and sat next to Samir. There was an awkward silence. It seemed the girls were waiting for someone to introduce them. It looked like he would have to do it. 'Erm... Sarah ... I mean Aliyah, this is Sarah – I mean Veronica. Veronica, this is Aliyah,' Raheem stuttered.

Samir shook his head in disbelief. Veronica smiled and said hello to Aliyah, who returned the greeting.

'Who's Sarah?' asked Veronica.

Raheem glanced at Samir, willing him to help, but just as Samir was about to speak Aliyah stood up. 'I need to go into town for some shopping. Come with me, please, Raheem.'

Samir looked as though his birthday had come early. 'Go on, Raheem. I remember you saying you needed to buy a few things.'

'Actually, I have some work to do,' Raheem began, but after looking at the expression on Aliyah's face he added, 'but it's not urgent. I can do it later.'

Aliyah would never let him forget about it if he didn't go with her, especially today of all days. He'd been planning to meet her later, after Veronica, but it looked as if he would have to go now.

'See you later, then,' said Samir.

'See you. I'd come with you but I need to crack on with my work,' said Veronica.

Raheem walked out with Aliyah, taking care to nudge his elbow into the back of Samir's head on the way. They walked in silence down the steps, past Liam who was going in the opposite direction. Raheem tried to bump into him as he walked past but missed. Things weren't going to plan today.

'Veronica is really pretty, don't you think?' asked Aliyah as they headed for the city centre.

Raheem could think of nothing to say except, 'She is okay.'

They walked for a couple of minutes.

'So how did you meet Veronica?' Aliyah asked as they entered Debenhams.

'We just started talking in the library.'

Aliyah, who had been examining a handbag, turned to look at him, her eyebrows raised. 'Oh, okay. I thought you got to know her that day you *forgot* to come to the lecture. When we were sitting in the café.'

If he really wanted to be a private investigator, he would need to lie better than this. Aliyah must have seen him talking to Veronica when she was going to the lecture. 'Oh, yeah, I think that was the first time. Must have slipped my mind,' he said unconvincingly.

Aliyah didn't respond. They didn't spend long in Debenhams; Aliyah had a brief look at some cardigans but didn't try any on. They went back out and sat on a bench. 'You seem to be forgetting a lot nowadays,' she said quietly as she took out her phone. She probably thought he hadn't remembered but, forgetful as he was, this was the one date he would never forget.

Raheem sighed. 'I know. But there are some things I don't forget.'

Aliyah looked up from on her phone. 'Like what?'

Raheem stared determinedly back at her, trying to keep a straight face. 'Like the fact that it's three o'clock and I know you got work tonight at five so I'll drop you off home.'

'Oh.' Aliyah looked taken aback. 'It's okay, I'll get the bus. I've booked a day off from work today but thanks anyway.'

He couldn't take the disappointment on her face any longer. 'Well, in that case all that's left to say is happy birthday, Aliyah.' He took a Chanel perfume gift set from his bag and held it out for her.

She stared at it for before her face split into a wide smile. 'Raheem, you're too much!' She hugged him. After a few seconds they broke apart.

'I can't believe you actually thought that I'd forget your birthday! I'm your bestie, aren't I?' said Raheem indignantly as they stood up.

Aliyah punched him on the arm and they started walking.

'Deep down I knew you remembered, but I told Samir not to remind you.' Aliyah seemed to have a new spring in her step.

'The twat will be chatting up Veronica,' muttered Raheem.

'What?'

'Nothing.' As Aliyah's bus stop came into view, Raheem said, 'I was actually going to take you to Grill and Pepperz tonight, but I know your family is waiting for you at home, so my turn is tomorrow evening, okay?'

Aliyah gave him a glowing look. Grill and Pepperz was her favourite place. 'You spent a lot on this present for me. We'll go tomorrow, but the bill is on me.'

'Fine, you pay my bill then. I'll go by myself,' he said moodily.

Aliyah pinched his cheek. 'Alright, the bill's all on you. You're being way too kind, but I prefer you this way.'

When they reached the bus stop Raheem stopped but Aliyah kept walking and grabbed his arm. 'And you're dropping me home as well. You really are so nice,' she said innocently.

Raheem turned to face her and started walking backwards, stretching his arms out wide. 'I know. After all, I'm a real gentleman.'

Chapter 4

The time was 6.30pm; still another thirty minutes to go before his shift finished. Raheem had just finished date checking the bread when Andrew, the store manager, walked up to him. 'Raheem, could you just jump onto the till for me?' he asked.

'I guess it would be a bit awkward if I said no.'

Andrew chuckled. 'It would be indeed, but it wouldn't take me long to go get your P45.'

'I'll go now, but if I jump on the till and it breaks I'm not paying any damages.'

Andrew clapped Raheem on the shoulder before walking off. One of the good things about Andrew was that he was always up for a joke. Some managers were strict and humourless, but Raheem was glad Andrew was different. For one thing, it made coming to work a lot easier. Secondly, it helped him get away with certain things. Last year Raheem had only been given a polite telling off from Andrew for throwing bread packets over the shelves at one of his colleagues. Under someone else he might have got the sack.

The Tesco Express where he worked was in the heart of the city centre and was usually very busy, despite only being a small store. Raheem served customers, constantly checking the time on the corner of the screen on the till. Ashleigh was taking ages stocking the drinks. Sooner or later, she'd be given a warning about bringing her phone to the shop floor and texting while on shift.

With two minutes left until 7pm, a lady with a child who looked like her son came up to his till. Why did they always come just as he was about to finish? 'Hi, you okay?' he asked as he began scanning her items.

'I'm good, thanks. How are you?' she said kindly.

'Very good seeing as I'm nearly finished for the day.'

'You're very lucky that you have a job.' The woman smiled at him. She'd only bought a sandwich, chocolate and a bottle of water, a nice little £3 meal deal.

'That's £3 please,' said Raheem as he placed the items in a bag.

The lady fumbled in her pockets and started placing coins in his outstretched hand. Her phone dropped from her pocket and she picked it up as she finished giving him the money.

'Do you have any cheaper water bottles? I'm twenty pence short.' She took out her wallet, which only held a bank card and what looked like a bus pass.

'No, sorry, it comes with the meal deal,' said Raheem apologetically.

The child was staring at the chocolate.

'We'll get the chocolate next time, Jamie,' she said. Jamie nodded. She turned to Raheem. 'I'll leave the chocolate, just the water and sandwich. Sorry about that,' she said, mustering a smile.

Something didn't seem right. He checked the time on his till screen. It was 7.01pm. Rebecca and Tyrone had just come onto the shop floor. Rebecca came towards him to take him off the till.

'Are you okay to wait a couple of minutes? I'll be back in a bit,' he asked the woman.

'Sure,' she said. Raheem told Rebecca not to serve the lady as he was sorting something out, then went downstairs to grab his belongings. He hurried back upstairs and went to the till. 'Don't worry about it, I'll get these for you,' he said quietly to the woman.

Ten minutes later, Raheem waved goodbye to Tracy and her son, Jamie, who was now opening a crisp packet having already finished his chocolate. He waved at Raheem from the top deck of the bus and Raheem smiled back at them.

As the bus started to move, Raheem walked to the car park near the market. Tracy would find another job soon. He was sure of it.

***

Ryan had already started his workout by the time Raheem arrived at the gym. Adrian, Ryan's flatmate, was lying on the bench clearly struggling to lift the weight. Ryan, who was on the treadmill hadn't noticed. Raheem hurried forward to grab the weight – it looked as if it would fall onto Adrian's nose at any second.

'I've got it, relax.' Raheem lifted it gently. All of a sudden there was extra pressure on his arms and the weight slipped from his grasp, landing on the bench where Adrian's face had been a second earlier.

'Fucking hell, man!' Raheem exclaimed as he jumped away. The weight tilted on the bench before landing with a thud on the ground.

'I thought you had it,' said Adrian breathlessly, rubbing his shoulder.

'You clown! You were supposed to keep hold of it as well,' said Raheem angrily.

'Sorry, pal. Thanks, though,' Adrian apologised, still pink in the face. Raheem had warned him before about lifting weights that were too heavy. Adrian was very thin with arms like matchsticks; his mop of hair probably weighed more than the rest of his body.

'What are you two doing?' asked Ryan as he joined them.

'Having a picnic. Do you want to join us?' Raheem replied.

'Eh?'

'Tell him not to try lifting shit that's too heavy for him,' said Raheem as he went to the treadmill section. He always did a quick run to warm up before starting the weights.

An hour and a half later, he stepped outside in the cool evening air. The freshness was a soothing antidote to his skin. He headed towards his car.

What the hell? Someone had parked their car very close to his. The gym's parking bays weren't exactly huge, but what made it worse was that the white Audi next to his BMW had not reversed into the bay, meaning that the driver would likely have scratched Raheem's car when opening their door.

'For God's sake,' Raheem muttered angrily as he squeezed through the gap. If he opened his door carefully he might be able to get in, otherwise he'd have to enter through the passenger seat.

'Sorry, I'll move my car.' A woman who'd been about to enter the gym jogged back to the Audi and slowly opened her passenger door.

'Can you try and park a bit further away next time? That way you won't scratch another person's car,' Raheem said irritably as he let her past.

The woman, who had just turned the engine on, switched it off and got out. 'Don't fucking accuse me, I never touched your car!' She had a long, arrogant face with a rather pointy nose. She resembled someone he knew, but he couldn't think who.

'Try using your common sense in future. Reverse park it so that two driver doors aren't facing each other,' Raheem snapped. It was common sense, but nowadays sense didn't seem to be common in people.

The woman looked at him for a split second before walking towards him. Thinking she was going to attack him, he raised his hands to cover his face, but she walked past him. 'I'm not moving it now,' she said stubbornly.

'Do I give a shit?' Raheem lowered his hands.

She turned around. 'My car is in the bay. I was just being polite, but to hell with you. Now I'm not moving it.'

'If it's parked correctly, why did you offer to move it?' asked Raheem loudly as he opened his driver-side door slowly. There weren't any scratches, so at least she hadn't hit his car, but it was still silly of her to park so close.

'Bye!' she called sarcastically.

'You're just stupid,' called Raheem, waving at her as he drove off.

'And you're just a stupid idiot!' she shouted back.

Raheem stuck his middle finger out of the window as he turned the corner.

***

Sarah. Whenever her name appeared on his phone screen, Raheem got a little nervous. He put his wallet back on the bed and took his phone off the charger to answer her call. 'Hello, dear, never fear, Raheem is here,' he said.

'Can't you *ever* just say a normal hello?' came Sarah's exasperated voice. Sense of humour was definitely not one of her better qualities. Either that, or he wasn't as funny as he thought. 'Are you going to say something?' she continued. She sounded annoyed and tired, which was never a good combination.

'Sorry babe.'

'I'm staying in Birmingham tonight. Just thought I would let you know.'

Yes! That meant he could enjoy tonight without looking over his shoulder every five minutes. Not that he was doing anything wrong. It was perfectly fine to go to a restaurant with a friend. Raheem cleared his throat. 'How come?'

'Dad has asked me to stay. Couldn't say no.'

Obviously: 'no' was reserved for Raheem. 'Is everything okay?'

'Yes. Can't my dad ask me to stay?'

'We live in a free country. He can ask you what he wants.'

'Stop it.'

'Okay.'

'I need to go. I'll come to yours tomorrow evening. I'll be back in Stalford by six. I took the train instead of driving so you can pick me up at six tomorrow from the train station. Don't be late.'

Raheem said bye and disconnected the call. He could cancel on Veronica. But she was just a friend…

***

An hour later, Raheem was standing outside Akbar's restaurant on Heybridge Road waiting for Veronica to arrive. For some reason, she had declined his offer to pick her up and said she'd make her own way there. Oh well, less driving for him.

A taxi pulled up and Veronica came out wearing a light-yellow skirt with matching high heels and a silver necklace. Raheem raised his hand and walked towards her, but he'd only gone three steps when Samir appeared from the restaurant

41

entrance. 'What the hell are you doing here?' said Raheem in surprise

'What the hell are *you* doing here?' asked Samir, who looked equally surprised to see Raheem.

Veronica joined them. 'Hey guys, you both called me here at the same time so I thought why not eat together?'

Raheem looked from Veronica to Samir. That idiot had messed up his date tonight. But he couldn't say anything to him in front of Veronica.

'Good idea' said Samir.

Veronica gave them a twirl. 'How do I look?'

'Great' said Raheem. 'Your booty... I mean beauty is out of this world.' Raheem linked his arm with hers. 'Let's go.'

Not to be outdone, Samir did the same with her left arm and they frogmarched her to the entrance. 'Both of you stop it!' She wrenched herself from their grasp and adjusted her dress. 'I'm going to the washroom. I'll meet you at the table.'

Raheem turned to Samir as Veronica went inside. 'You already have two girlfriends!' he said furiously, slapping his cousin across the head.

Samir slapped him back. 'Show me where it is illegal to have three? Trust me I'm doing you a favour. She is way out of your league.'

'Out of *my* league? Have you ever looked in the mirror you ugly bastard?'

'Didn't get a chance, all the ones in the flat are broken after you looked at them.'

An elderly couple were watching from their car. Raheem smiled at them before walking inside with Samir, jostling each other to get in first just like they used to do at the school canteen at lunchtime.

'Table for two?' asked the waitress.

'Table for three. My girlfriend's just gone to the washroom,' said Raheem. Samir snorted behind him as they followed the waitress to a table in the far corner.

'What happens if Sarah turns up?' Samir asked as he sat opposite Raheem.

Raheem took his time looking at himself in his phone camera before saying, 'She is staying in Birmingham tonight. Has Rachel gone back to Newcastle for the weekend?'

'Yeah. Katie wasn't feeling well, so she didn't come up.' Samir took out his phone. 'I needed something to do. All the lads were busy in Manchester.'

'Don't take any Snapchats!'

'Shit, you're right.' Samir put his phone on the table. He was so dumb sometimes. Putting it on his Snapchat story so that both Sarah and Rachel could see what they were doing.

'Why did you call Veronica here? You know I'm chatting to her,' whispered Raheem.

'I want three girlfriends. Are you scared of competition?'

'You wish I'm scared.'

Veronica arrived, which put an end to their conversation. 'What were you two talking about?' she asked as she sat down.

'Football,' said Raheem.

'Who do you support?'

'Man United.'

'I actually thought you were alright, Raheem.'

'Samir also supports them.'

Veronica picked up the menu and hit Samir on the head with it. 'Nobody is perfect, I guess,' she said moodily.

Twenty minutes later, their table was laden with starters. 'There you go, Veronica, try these lamb chops. I ordered them especially for you,' said Raheem. The lamb chops at Akbar's were the main reason he came here.

'I like your necklace,' said Samir, not realising that Veronica had taken it off when she went to the bathroom. Raheem sniggered as Veronica explained that she'd taken it off because she felt it didn't suit her.

They ate their way through the starters and mains before finishing off with the disgusting cheesecake Samir ordered, which he always had whenever they came here. Aliyah was the only other person who liked it.

'Thank you, the food was really nice. It's been a great evening,' said Veronica kindly as they got ready to leave.

'No need to say thanks. Anytime for you,' replied Raheem before Samir could get a word in. He was about to go and pay

43

when Samir took out his wallet. 'What you doing? Bill is on me today.' He grabbed Samir's arm.

'No, don't worry. It's on me today, bro,' replied Samir, trying to tug his arm out of Raheem's grasp. They struggled against each other.

'What are you both doing?' hissed Veronica as people turned to stare.

'This is a restaurant not a takeaway,' Raheem said as he finally let go. 'You just stick to giving the tip, I'll get the bill.'

Samir was about to argue when Veronica said, 'Come on, guys, don't fight. Samir, you can pay next time.'

Samir looked sulkily at her. 'Okay, then. Because *you* said, I'll let him pay today.'

'You remind me of my brother, he always pulls that sad face!' Veronica ruffled Samir's hair.

If Samir's face was sad before, it was nothing to how it looked now. Raheem winked at him and went to the till, grinning broadly.

'How was the food, sir?' asked the waiter.

'Good, thanks,' Raheem replied.

The waiter nodded approvingly before handing him the receipt. The bill had come to £63. Raheem searched his pockets but couldn't find his wallet. With a pang, he remembered that he had forgotten to take it off his bed after Sarah had called him. 'Erm, I think I've left my wallet in my car. Give me two minutes. I'll come back.'

The waiter nodded. 'No problem.'

'What's the table number?'

'It's table seven.'

'Back in a moment.' Raheem hurried out of the entrance. Good job Samir had come – it would have been embarrassing if Veronica had to pay. 'Samir, you were right,' he said cheerily as he joined them.

'What was I right about now?' Samir replied.

'This is your favourite place, so I think it's best if you pay the bill. It's table seven.'

'Aw,' said Veronica, beaming at him.

'Finally, you have spoken sense,' said Samir as he went back into the restaurant. He was only gone for a minute before coming back.

They both offered to drop Veronica home, but she said her cousin was waiting for her in the car park. 'Guys, this is Jasmine. She used to go to our uni, finished a couple of years ago,' she said as a white Audi pulled up in front of them. It looked horribly familiar.

'Hi,' said Samir as Jasmine got out of the car.

Fuck's sake. Of all the cousins Veronica could have had, it had to be her? No wonder Raheem had thought the woman in the gym car park had looked familiar.

'Is the parking okay?' Jasmine asked haughtily as she recognised him.

There was no way he could snipe back at her in front of Veronica. 'Very good,' he said, smiling. She didn't smile back.

'Do you know each other?' asked Veronica.

'Just had a friendly chat once outside the gym,' Raheem said cheerfully.

Jasmine raised her eyebrows before turning to Samir. 'Have you got a lighter?' she demanded. Samir handed her one his yellow Clipper lighters; they were the only ones he ever used. 'I need a cigarette as well,' she added.

Samir silently handed over his cigarette packet. Jasmine took out two cigarettes, pocketed one of them and lit the other.

It was time to break the ice. 'I'm Raheem – I need no introduction. This is Samir. He needs an introduction but he doesn't deserve one,' he laughed.

Jasmine glanced at Veronica before getting back into her car. Talk about awkward.

'Right, thank you so much for today. I'll see you both at uni.' Veronica hugged them both.

'Your cousin doesn't seem to like us,' said Raheem.

'Don't mind her, Raheem, she's just having a tough time since she moved up to work in Stalford. She's lovely once you get to know her,' Veronica said, squeezing his hand.

'I look forward to it,' Raheem muttered.

Jasmine drove off before Veronica had even closed the passenger door. She accelerated to beat the red light before zooming up the main road.

'She's got some attitude!' exclaimed Samir indignantly

'Tell me about it,' said Raheem as he lit a cigarette. 'She was the one who parked so close to me at the gym!'

'No way! I was wondering why she looked pissed off when she saw you. Nicked two cigarettes off me as well!'

'You should have seen the look on your face!'

'You should have seen the look on your face when she blanked you!'

'Should have seen yours when Veronica said you reminded her of her brother!'

'I was so gutted! You can have her. Two girlfriends are enough for me at the moment.'

Still laughing, they stayed outside the restaurant whilst they smoked. 'Listen, I got a question for you,' said Samir as he extinguished his cigarette on top of the bin next to the entrance.

'Go on,' replied Raheem.

'Why did you let me pay the bill? I know it's nothing to do with you feeling bad.'

'I left my wallet in my room.' They both howled with laughter again.

'They look fit,' said Samir suddenly as a group of girls walked out of the restaurant.

Raheem had to hold on to the door to keep himself steady as Samir started whistling. Samir would never change. Nor did Raheem ever want him too.

Chapter 5

Despite the fact that studying psychology was half his course, no amount of study would help Raheem understand how the female mind worked. Sarah had come back from Birmingham in good spirits but later that evening she had been very quiet. No matter how many times he asked if she was okay, he never got an answer other than, 'I'm fine Raheem, just tired.'

Veronica was now calling him daily. Even after they'd said goodbye to each other, she would call him again within an hour to ask him what he was up to. He did his best to convince himself there was nothing serious to it, but the more he thought that, the less likely it seemed.

It wasn't just the ladies who were acting oddly. Samir was spending a lot more time than usual on his phone. Raheem had walked past his bedroom a couple of times late at night on the way to the bathroom and heard him talking quietly. Rachel and Katie were certainly keeping him busy.

Raheem wanted to ask Aliyah for advice about Sarah and Veronica, but had resisted so far. After all, he was only friends with Veronica.

***

Third-year criminology and psychology students received an email to inform them if their dissertation plan had been approved. To Raheem's relief Steven, his dissertation supervisor, said that he was happy with the plan and asked him to come to his office for a quick chat about it.

It was a rainy afternoon when Raheem was sitting in his interdisciplinary psychology seminar. Aliyah was next to him as usual. He had not been paying much attention to Mathew, their seminar tutor; he'd spent most of the time looking out of the window, thinking about Veronica. He had taken her to a Shisha lounge the other evening along with some friends from

47

Manchester. He could sense that Veronica was waiting for him to make a move. He had resisted the temptation so far, but how long would that last?

Aliyah nudged him for the third time in half an hour, which relieved him of his thoughts.

'What is it?' hissed Raheem.

'Pay attention, otherwise I know you're going to be begging me for help with the essay. I'm not giving you my notes this time,' Aliyah whispered angrily. Her notes about the essay question *(Describe and evaluate the cognitive approach to psychology)* were almost five pages long.

'I'm listening with my eyes- I mean ears' said Raheem.

'No you're not. Good luck with the essay.'

Despite her words, Raheem knew Aliyah would eventually relent and give him her notes. He was more interested in his meeting with Steven, which would be taking place in twenty minutes. He went back to daydreaming until the sound of chairs scraping against the floor told him that the class had been dismissed.

Aliyah was already at the door. Hastily picking up his bag, Raheem followed her. She was halfway up the corridor when he jogged up to her, something he seemed to be doing a lot this year. 'You left me sitting there on my own!' he said, pretending to look horrified.

Aliyah narrowed her eyes. 'You don't listen in seminars and then you'll be stuck when it comes to your essay. If you fail, you'll deserve it.'

As he usually did whenever she was annoyed with him, he put his arm around her shoulder. 'I will listen next time, promise.'

Aliyah didn't reply. With his arm still around her shoulder, Raheem was not paying attention to where he was going. Only when he spotted himself in the mirror did he realise that he had just walked into the ladies' toilet with her. He quickly let go of her shoulder and ran outside, Aliyah's laughter ringing in his ears. Thankfully, the corridor was empty.

Aliyah re-emerged a few minutes later, still laughing. He tried to hit her with his bag, but all he ended up doing was stumbling because his laptop was inside it and the bag was heavier than Raheem had realised.

Laughing together, they made their way towards the library when he remembered that he had his meeting with Steven in five minutes. Aliyah said she'd wait for him on the second floor, so he returned to the rear of the university building where the members of staff had their offices. Hannah and a couple of her friends, including Lauren who was the one who apparently had a thing for him, were in the campus shop. Liam was also there and kept glancing at Hannah.

Raheem waited a full minute before the lift eventually arrived. He got in and pressed the button for the eighth floor. After many stops, he reached his destination, turned left and hurried towards the social sciences offices.

He knocked on the door before entering. Steven was waiting for him, Raheem's dissertation plan on the table. 'Hi, Raheem, come in and take a seat,' he smiled.

Steven was middle-aged, with a friendly looking face. Most of the students liked him because he often made lectures more interesting by cracking jokes when you least expected it. Raheem had Steven for one of his modules the previous year and found him to be a good lecturer who could make even the most complicated things sound simple.

Steven handed over Raheem's dissertation plan. 'Well, I think you've chosen a good topic, Raheem. There's a lot of source material available on women and crime. If you could just look at the notes I've made and tell me what you think.'

Raheem picked up his dissertation plan and read Steven's notes. There were a few corrections to his grammar, but mainly it was feedback on some of the areas he could expand on.

'Thanks. The only thing I'm a bit concerned about is my introduction. I don't really know how to start it.' He felt a bit stupid admitting it, but it was in these meetings that he had to ask about what he didn't know.

'A lot of students have asked me about that and I am going to give you the same advice I gave them,' said Steven. 'The last thing you write in your dissertation is the introduction. That way, you know what you've written about and it's a lot easier.'

That made sense; it would be easier to summarise the content for the introduction if he knew what was already in the dissertation.

Steven went on to explain the importance of making the dissertation flow and gave advice on both qualitative and quantitative research sources that he could use. Raheem made notes and, after arranging their next appointment near the end of November, left the office.

Steven had said that students were allowed to be either ten percent over or under the 10,000-word count for their dissertation. That was a lot of writing to do. Raheem would need to manage his time well and aim to do slightly over the word count to be on the safe side.

The lift doors were sliding shut. He hurried forward and managed to get in before they closed but banged his leg. Wincing, he pressed the button for the ground floor but the lift stopped on the fourth. Why did everyone have to use this flipping lift?

The doors opened and in walked Jason, accompanied by Chris, one of his friends. Raheem should have taken the stairs.

'Hey, Raheem, you okay?' Jason smiled at him.

'Hi, Jason. I'm good, thanks,' said Raheem automatically.

'This is Chris, he's—'

'One of your mates. I met him last year. Hi, Chris.'

Chris nodded but didn't speak, which suited Raheem perfectly. He kept his eyes fixed to the floor and walked out the moment the lift door opened.

'See you, mate,' Jason called.

'See you,' Raheem called back without turning around.

No matter how hard Jason tried, he was just one of those people that Raheem could not get on with. What did Sarah see in him that he was her best friend?

He headed up the corridor. Adam and Zack, who had ordered chicken wings and chips, were eating on the tables near the vending machine. 'When we next linking up for football?' asked Zack as Raheem joined them.

'I haven't been for a while, to be fair,' said Raheem.

'I'll sort something out soon. Want to try these wings?'

Raheem was tempted, but he was going to the gym later. 'I'm alright, bro.'

'Guess who I was chatting to in Sensations last night?' said Adam, showing him a WhatsApp contact on his phone. The picture in the contact was Cheryl.

'Check you out!' Raheem clapped Adam on the shoulder; he had pulled a good one that was for sure.

'Who is that chick you're always with?'

People loved asking him questions. Stupid, dangerous questions. 'Can you be more specific please?' asked Raheem, though he knew who Adam was referring to.

'The Latino one.'

Raheem explained that she was just a friend. Zack asked if he could set him up with her.

'She's got a boyfriend,' said Raheem sternly. 'Anyway, I thought you and Ashleigh were dating? She takes the piss at work – you need to tell her to get her act together. Took her half an hour to stock the drinks!'

Zack shook his head, looking glum. 'We aren't together anymore. We kept arguing all the time. That's why I asked if you could set me up with the Latino one.'

They had been together for one month and split up already? 'Can you still tell her to not take so long?' asked Raheem.

'You tell her! She's not my problem now. Just try some of these wings. Everyone can have a cheat day.'

'Oi, what you trying to say have a cheat day? Do I look like someone who cheats?'

'I meant in terms of food, everyone can have a cheat day. What did you think I meant?'

'Oh that's what you meant. I thought... anyway what's new with you?'

Raheem chatted to them for another five minutes before going to the library. Daniel was sitting on one of the sofas at the side of the ground floor, looking miserable. Raheem went over to him. 'What's up, Dan? You look like you've just been rejected by a lady,' he said.

Daniel looked up; it seemed to take him a few seconds to recognise Raheem. 'Hi, mate. I'm just tired. Not been sleeping

51

well recently,' he mumbled. His hair was all over the place and his eyes had dark shadows beneath them.

'Did Samir email you the notes?' asked Raheem.

'He did. Appreciate your help. I got a taxi waiting for me outside. I need to get some sleep.' He certainly looked as though he needed it.

'No worries, pal, you go home and rest. I'll see you later,' said Raheem, before making his way towards the stairs. He didn't need Daniel to say thanks to him all the time. It was their job to help him in any way they could now that he was having a hard time. It was still a big shock how Daniel had managed to fail.

Raheem continued up the stairs before turning right onto the second floor. Aliyah was sitting at a table near the back of the room but she was not alone. Catherine was with her, as well as Fiona.

Raheem went over to them, banging his knee on the computer desk as he went – the same knee he had banged on the lift. 'Hi, ladies,' he said as he sat down next to Aliyah and rubbed his knee.

'Hiya,' said Catherine and Fiona together.

Raheem took out his laptop and switched it on.

'Did you see your dissertation supervisor?' asked Catherine.

Aliyah started scribbling on her notepad. Why did she have to tell everyone what he was doing all the time? It was an old habit of hers. 'Yeah, I did. What about you?' said Raheem, nudging Aliyah with his arm. She seemed to be doing her best to not smile.

'I've got my meeting tomorrow,' Catherine replied briskly, turning her laptop screen around. She had certainly made an effort with her plan. If he hadn't known, he would have thought it was her actual dissertation.

'How was your summer? Did you go to the Caribbean?' he asked. Catherine was so lucky that her grandparents lived in Jamaica. Every summer she visited them and uploaded the most amazing photos on Facebook. It was definitely one of his wishes to go there. Maybe he could go with Sarah next year. Speaking of Facebook, he logged onto it on his phone and deactivated his account. Veronica had added him on Facebook the other day. He had changed the settings to hide his friend list, but Sarah would notice when she made her customary check on his profile.

'How's Sarah?' asked Fiona unexpectedly when Catherine had finished telling them about the islands.

Raheem wondered why, if Fiona was so concerned about Sarah, she couldn't just ask her herself. They'd never stopped nattering all through first year. 'She's good thanks. So ... any good movies on at the cinema?'

'Where else are they supposed to release? At the book store?' Aliyah asked sharply.

'Ha-ha,' said Raheem sarcastically as the girls giggled.

Hannah was sitting with some friends at the computers, chatting animatedly. Cheryl was with her group of friends at the tables near the windows. Veronica had told him that she would be going home after her lecture finished.

'I love that coat, Aliyah. Where did you get it from?' said Catherine, and the two girls started talking about shopping. The subject switched to make up, which ensured that Fiona got involved. They continued to chat for another half an hour before Catherine and Fiona decided to leave. The good thing for Raheem was that he managed to get on with looking at journals he could use for his dissertation.

'Catch you later,' said Catherine as she and Fiona headed for the second floor's back entrance.

Raheem waited until they were out of sight before rounding on Aliyah. 'Why did you have to say that I was in my dissertation meeting?'

Aliyah raised her eyebrows. 'Oh my God, Raheem – and you say women are sensitive.' She started typing. 'You need to stop being such a baby sometimes.'

'Don't get funny with me.'

Aliyah looked up from her laptop. 'Or what?' Raheem grabbed her in a headlock. 'Ouch, that hurts!' she said shrilly.

Some of the students stared at them and he let go. He had forgotten that they were on the second floor and they had to speak as quietly as possible. Aliyah swept her hair from her face and saved her work. 'Come on, let's go to Parkview café and I'll buy you a coffee. I think that will calm you down.' She began packing her things away.

'You've become very smart,' Raheem told her as he saved his work and logged off.

'I've always been smart,' she said brightly.

They left the library and went down the stairs. As they reached the ground floor, Raheem glanced at the sofa where Daniel had been sitting earlier. He was probably fast asleep by now.

'Do you think I've gained a bit of weight? Be honest,' said Aliyah as they walked down the corridor.

She looked exactly the same to him. 'I wouldn't say you'd gained weight, you're just a bit easier to see than usual,' said Raheem slyly.

'You cheeky little monkey!' Aliyah hit him with her bag. That was one of the great things about her. She was always up for a laugh and joke.

Raheem went past her and turned around so he was walking backwards.

'What are you doing?' she asked.

'Let me tell you a joke,' he said. 'So what do you call – ooohhh, shit!' He fell on his backside. He had just tripped over Rachel, who was bending down next to the vending machine.

'Sorry. You okay?' she asked as he got up quickly.

Aliyah was doubled up with silent laughter.

'I'm fine.' Raheem gritted his teeth and glanced around. Miraculously, no one except Aliyah had seen him drop to the floor.

'Hi, Rachel,' said Aliyah when she finally stopped laughing.

'Hey Aliyah, you good?'

'I am indeed, how are you?'

'I was good, until my crisp packet got stuck.' Rachel pointed ruefully at the vending machine. The crisp packet was halfway out of its slot and, unlike him, hadn't fallen down. It was the ready-salted Walker's one, the most boring crisp flavour of all time.

'I'll go ask security, they have the keys for the vending machines,' said Aliyah.

'Forget your security,' said Raheem and he banged on the vending machine with his fist. The packet dropped out of the slot.

'Thanks. Can't believe I didn't think of that!' Rachel took her crisps. 'How's your uni work going?'

Raheem and Aliyah chatted with her for a few minutes before making their way to the café. 'I've left my phone charger upstairs,' said Raheem, clapping a hand to his forehead.

Aliyah heaved a dramatic sigh and they returned to the second floor to get it. They passed the vending machine again on their way back, which now had an out of order sign on it. Bill, one of the security guards, was trying to open it with his key. 'Another one broken. They seem to think it's a punchbag,' he said to Raheem.

'Silly people' said Raheem, nodding in agreement.

'You should charge for damages,' commented Aliyah innocently.

Raheem grabbed her arm and led her down the flight of steps and out of the back entrance to the university. They crossed the road and entered Parkview. Adam and Zack were queuing outside the lecture theatre, both looking a bit drowsy after their meal. Raheem and Aliyah went into the café on the lower ground floor, got their drinks and sat at a table near the windows. It was really comfortable sitting in the café when it was raining outside. Aliyah began telling Raheem about her trip to York with her family the previous week. For Raheem, moments like these with Aliyah were the best part of university.

Chapter 6

Monday: the worst day of the week made worse by the fact that the university library was open to the public until 9pm.

The raindrops thundered against the roof of the library where Raheem was sitting with Samir, Sarah and Rachel. He had asked Samir to go with Rachel to the West Park campus, but Samir said that they were going out together later and it would be more convenient to set off from the city campus. He'd asked Sarah to go with him to the West Park campus, but she had said she was going out later and it would be more convenient to set off from the city campus. As usual, they had both caused him inconvenience.

Aliyah was in a meeting with her dissertation supervisor, and thankfully Veronica was not at university today. Raheem had called her that morning from the men's toilets, which was one of the few places Sarah couldn't follow him, and she'd told him she would probably go home after her work shift finished.

'Great idea, you need to have a bit of a break after work I guess,' Raheem had said. The further away Veronica was away from the university today the better.

As was usual when Sarah and Rachel were together, there was a slightly tense atmosphere.

'How did you find the lecture, Sarah?' asked Samir.

Why couldn't he just keep his mouth closed? He was always taking digs at Sarah for attending Raheem's lectures. He told Raheem that it was too controlling.

'It was fine thanks, Samir.' Sarah's tone made it perfectly clear that she had no interest in continuing the subject. They had been sat here for the past hour and apart from giving each other cold smiles, Sarah and Rachel had not spoken to each other.

Raheem kept his eyes on his criminology book. Even though it was raining outside, a cigarette might calm his nerves. 'Just going for a cigarette.' He got to his feet. Sarah tutted.

'In this weather?' Samir asked.

'No, in *that* weather.'

'I thought you said you'd quit?' asked Rachel, her head on Samir's shoulder.

Raheem shouldn't have mentioned he was going for one. 'I did. I quit smoking Marlboro Red cigarettes and changed to the Marlboro Gold brand now.'

Samir laughed but stopped abruptly as Sarah shot him an angry look. She had always blamed him for Raheem's smoking habit, even though he'd had nothing to do with it.

Raheem strolled through the library and went down the stairs. It had been an irritating day, and the miserable weather wasn't improving his mood. It was so annoying for both Raheem and Samir when their girlfriends refused to get on. He'd reached the ground floor when, to his horror, Veronica entered the library. What was she doing here? She had told him this morning she would go home after work. He tried to hide behind the bookshelf, but she'd already seen him.

'Hey,' she called as she approached him.

Raheem pretended to tie his shoelace to explain why he was kneeling behind the bookshelf. 'What are you doing here?' he asked, standing up and giving her a quick hug.

'I do study here, you know. I just finished work earlier and thought I would come here instead.'

There was a short pause before Raheem said, 'I know. I was joking. I'm so glad that out of all the places in the world you could have gone to, you chose here. Anyway, I got a lot of work to do. See you around.'

He turned around and walked up the stairs, but Veronica followed him. What else did he expect? 'What the hell? That's a bit rude!' she said indignantly, grabbing his arm. He nearly tripped on the stairs and grabbed her by the shoulder to steady himself. 'What's wrong with you Raheem?'

He tried to think what to say, but all he managed was to wave his hand around as though trying to catch a fly. The situation was perilous. 'I'll meet you on the third floor in a bit,' he said tentatively. He already knew what the answer would be.

'No, I'm going to the first floor. We're sitting together today, I'm sick of you always finding excuses to not sit with me' Veronica snapped. Women could be stubborn sometimes.

'No! I mean,' Raheem lowered his voice as people stared, 'I'm sitting on the third floor. It's really noisy on the first floor.'

Veronica looked at him sceptically. 'How do you know it's noisy on the first floor if you're not sitting there?'

This wasn't going the way he'd hoped. 'Erm, yeah, you're right. What I meant was, I'm sitting on first floor, but it's noisy so I'm just going to the third. How about you go to the third floor and I'll meet you there?'

Thankfully, Veronica nodded. 'Ten minutes – and if you're not there, I'm coming to the first floor,' she said as she started climbing the stairs.

'Twenty minutes?' called Raheem.

'Ten honey.'

He was stuck. It was too risky. He would have to leave the university with Sarah. She would give him an earful, but if she met Veronica she could give him a fistful.

Raheem was just about to go to the first floor when he remembered he couldn't leave with Sarah as Veronica was expecting him in ten minutes. He paced frantically up and down the staircase on the ground floor, thinking frantically. He would see Veronica on the third floor and then, when Sarah called him to see where he was, he'd pretend to Veronica that one of his friends was calling him. He'd just have to keep making excuses to switch between the floors until one of the women decided to go home. What a disgusting situation he had landed himself in.

He was about to go to the third floor when Jermaine walked down the stairs carrying his university bag. 'You alright, Raheem?' he asked.

'Not too good, not too bad. Are you going home?'

'Yep. I was supposed to go to the cinema later with Fiona but my car broke down and she doesn't drive.'

'Count yourself lucky if that's the only problem you've got,' said Raheem darkly.

'Are you okay, mate? You look worried.'

'I'm fine, thanks.'

Jermaine nodded before making his way towards the exit.

Hold on. Maybe there was a way out of this situation. 'I can drop you home if you want,' called Raheem. Dropping off one of his friends would be the perfect excuse to leave the university. Veronica would think he was being kind, and Sarah wouldn't have a problem because she knew Jermaine. He looked at Jermaine expectantly.

'Cheers, but I've got my mate picking me up,' Jermaine replied. 'He's parked outside. I appreciate the offer. I'm going to tell Sarah her man is a top guy.'

That was the end of that idea then. 'Thanks, but there really is no need to mention it. I don't like it when people say good things about me,' Raheem said tonelessly.

'Fair enough,' Jermaine chuckled.

'I'll let you go then. Take care.' Raheem forced a grin. They shook hands and Jermaine departed, pulling his hood up as he went.

Raheem hurried towards the third floor but his phone rang as he reached the second. Sarah was calling him. 'Hello?' he said nervously as he answered.

'Can you come back? I need to—' said Sarah, then the line went dead. The signal was always hard to maintain on the second floor.

The door to the third floor was just above him. Nearly five of his ten minutes had passed, but if he went to see Veronica now, Sarah would think he'd disconnected the call on purpose. But he could only go see Sarah for a few minutes otherwise Veronica would head down to the first floor. He turned round and sprinted down the steps to the first floor, past some startled students. He'd just reached the entrance when the door swung open and Sarah walked out.

'Phone disconnected, I swear, Sarah. Signal's shit on the second floor!' Raheem said hurriedly.

Sarah looked at him in surprise. 'What's up with you? I accidentally disconnected the call.'

'Oh ... right. Why did you ring?'

She tossed back her hair and took her umbrella out of her bag. 'I have to... Hold on, what were you doing on the second floor? I thought you went outside for a smoke?'

Why did they always do this to him? ' I accidentally pressed the wrong button on the lift and ended up on the second floor, was going down to ground floor for a cigarette but met a friend, spoke to him, came down the stairs, you called, signal went off, came here, met you, don't feel like going for a cigarette anymore.' Raheem took a deep breath.

'Okay, I was just asking' said Sarah.

'No problem. So why did you call?'

'I need to go, honey. I'm picking Natasha up from the train station. She's come to stay with me tonight because we're going to Jason's birthday party later. I thought she was arriving at seven, but it's actually six.'

'Oh, thank— I mean, *that's* why you rang? And I thought … erm… You leaving me, then?'

Sarah smiled and kissed him on the cheek. 'I'm sorry. Jason did ask me to bring you but I thought you might not want to go as you're not his biggest fan.'

Raheem was so relieved he didn't bother responding to her little dig. 'Say happy birthday to him for me,' he said. 'I didn't know his birthday was going to be on the second of November this year, but hey, next year let me know the date when it happens and I'll make sure I come.'

Sarah grinned. 'That joke nearly had me laughing. Come to mine for tea tomorrow. And say sorry to Aliyah for me. I was meant to spend this evening with her.'

'Aliyah was telling me she wanted to see you,' said Raheem sadly.

Sarah glanced at her watch. 'Aw, I know. I feel so bad. I'm going to Birmingham over the weekend and I'm busy this week so I probably won't be able to see her until after I come back.'

Raheem waited. He shouldn't have overdone it.

'I guess I could get someone else to pick Natasha up,' she said thoughtfully. 'That way I can see Aliyah for a bit.'

He wanted to bang his head against the wall. 'No, I think you should go. It's a bit short notice to get someone,' he said quickly. 'You can see Aliyah some other time, I will let her know.' Sarah loved complicating things.

'You're right. I did tell Natasha I'd pick her up. Make sure you say sorry, though.'

'I haven't done anything wrong, why do I have to say sorry?'

'I meant, say sorry for me to Aliyah. I'll text her anyway.'

The door to their left opened and out walked Adam, accompanied by Cheryl. 'Hey, Raheem, it's been ages!' said Cheryl as she hugged him. Sarah tactfully pretended to be on her phone. Adam shook Raheem's hand and greeted Sarah.

'Sarah, this is—' Raheem began.

'Adam. We met last year.' Sarah gave no sign she'd seen Cheryl, who was ignoring her.

Raheem grinned awkwardly before remembering that Veronica was waiting for him. 'I'll see you around, guys. I just need to ... erm...'

'Join us in the student union later. I want to see if you can beat Adam at pool,' said Cheryl brightly. 'Ask Samir as well, and Rachel if she wants to come.'

He didn't really expect her to ask Sarah to come along, but it would have been nice if she had. 'If I'm free, I'll come down,' he said.

'See you.' Cheryl grabbed Adam's hand and headed down the stairs. Adam looked a bit confused as the door closed.

'She's such a pain, eh?' Raheem said cheerily to Sarah, who was smirking.

'Silly cow, thinking I give a shit if she ignores me. Like I wanted to speak to her anyway! Are they together then?' Raheem shrugged. 'Anyway baby, I need to pick up Natasha. I'll see you tomorrow.'

Not at all reluctant for Sarah to leave, Raheem kissed her before she went down the stairs. He leaned against the lift. That had been close. Maybe he could buy Jason a present for having his birthday today. Actually, there was no point; it wasn't like Jason had any choice over what day he was born.

The lift doors suddenly opened behind him and he fell backwards. 'Oh shit, are you okay?' Veronica shouted as he lay on his back, dazed.

'I'm good, thanks,' he mumbled, taking her hand and pulling himself up. Next time he would lean against the wall rather than the lift.

'Your ten minutes are up,' she said brightly.

'I figured that much out.' Raheem winced as he walked through the first-floor entrance. If Veronica had come thirty seconds earlier, he would have been in big trouble.

'Are Samir and Aliyah here?' she asked.

'They are, but I think Aliyah is in a meeting with her dissertation supervisor. Samir is sitting there with Rachel, his girlfriend. Don't mention anything about us to people, okay? We are just friends at the moment ... according to everyone.'

'Don't worry, I won't say anything.' Veronica slapped his backside. Hopefully no one saw this. 'Hiya!' she said as they reached the table.

Samir, who'd been talking to Rachel, jumped slightly at the sound of her voice. 'Hi, Veronica. What are you...? Good to see you.' He looked at Raheem in bewilderment.

Raheem sat down and picked up his criminology book. He would leave it for Samir to decide how to deal with this situation.

'So, Veronica, this is Rach- Sorry should I have said your name first?' Samir asked Rachel.

'It doesn't matter' said Veronica, laughing. 'Hi Rachel, I am Veronica.'

Raheem peeped over the top of his book. Rachel smiled at Veronica, although it looked a bit forced.

'I don't see you much on the first floor nowadays, Veronica,' Samir continued.

Veronica explained that she'd been sitting on the third floor recently to complete her work as the first floor was too noisy. She kept nudging her leg against Raheem's.

'So how did you guys meet, Raheem?' Rachel asked, interrupting Samir and Veronica's conversation. The atmosphere around the table changed slightly. Rachel was looking at Samir, despite addressing her question to Raheem.

'We met through a mutual friend,' said Raheem innocently.

Samir nodded and smiled at Rachel, who narrowed her eyes.

'So what about Samir and Veronica? How did *they* meet?' she asked, for some reason addressing the question to Raheem again.

Why did everyone expect him to do the talking? 'Erm... ask our mutual friend over here. Only he can tell you.' Raheem nodded at Samir, whose eyes widened. Feeling guilty, he took out his notepad and pretended to write.

'We met here at university earlier this year,' said Samir sheepishly.

'Same course?' asked Rachel.

'No, she does business management.'

Raheem needed to help Samir out because the situation was becoming dangerous. 'I'm just going to the campus shop – I need a drink. Anyone want anything?' he asked as he stood up.

'I'll come with you,' said Samir immediately, getting to his feet.

There was no way Raheem was going to leave Veronica and Rachel alone together. 'You sit down and do your work,' he said sharply. 'You know, Rachel, he gets distracted easily. Do you want to take him to third floor?'

'You both seem to get distracted easily, so I will go with Veronica while you get some work done,' said Rachel firmly. Raheem and Samir both looked uneasily at Veronica, who had no choice but to obey.

Veronica had just stood up when Aliyah appeared, carrying a plastic bag. 'Hiya, anyone want any snacks? Just got this from the campus shop.' She sat down next to Raheem and opened her bag. It was full of chocolates, crisps and drinks.

'You're a lifesaver Aliyah... I mean, no one needs to go to the shop now.' Raheem put his hand in the bag and withdrew a Coke can.

Rachel sat back down.

'Hi, Aliyah,' said Veronica smiling at her.

'Hey, Veronica, how are you? You look stunning,' replied Aliyah kindly.

Raheem smiled and turned his head to find Rachel looking straight at him. The smile disappeared from his face. Samir was staring at the ceiling. He had the look of a man who knew he was going to be questioned later by his girlfriend.

'Do I look stunning as well?' said Raheem to Aliyah.

'Hard question, to be honest,' said Aliyah.

'I think Raheem looks—' began Veronica.

'Stunning weather, eh? It's a solar eclipse!' Raheem quickly pointed at the window. As he had hoped, everyone except

Samir fell for it, which gave him enough time to mouth wordlessly and make gestures. Samir nodded to show he understood.

'So Aliyah, what did your dissertation supervisor say?' Samir asked when they'd all finished looking out of the window and Aliyah and Veronica had punched Raheem's shoulder for lying.

They whiled away another couple of hours in the library without anything drastic happening. Rachel and Veronica spoke to each other, but the conversation did not last very long. Aliyah was the chattiest, speaking to Veronica before striking up a conversation with Rachel. This allowed Raheem to quietly get some work done.

At half seven, Veronica decided to leave. She was going home with her moody cousin Jasmine, who was waiting for her outside. The window behind their table had a clear view of the university front entrance and ground floor. Jasmine had parked her Audi on double-yellow lines.

Samir and Rachel left not long after, Samir looking nervous. Hopefully he would get back home in one piece. Raheem and Aliyah stayed together in the library until nine o'clock. It had been a tense day but the last hour spent with Aliyah relieved some of the tension.

Ryan had texted Raheem to ask if he wanted to go to the gym in half an hour. A workout would do him good, so he replied to say he would meet him there.

'See you, Raheem. I'm just going to pick up my phone charger that Cath borrowed,' said Aliyah, putting her bus pass in her pocket.

It was still raining outside. There was no way he was going to let Aliyah get the bus alone at this time and in this weather.

'I'll drop you home,' he said.

'No, it's okay. You're going be late for the gym and Ryan's waiting for you,' she replied kindly.

'Doesn't matter, he won't mind.'

'Are you sure?'

Raheem nodded confidently. '*That* Ryan would have minded, but not *this* Ryan.'

If shopping with Sarah was a pain, with Samir it was ten times worse. They could never agree on anything.

Samir walked over and dumped the bread he was carrying into the trolley. Automatically, Raheem took it out and placed it back on the shelf. 'Get the brown bread,' he said to Samir, who promptly took the white bread from the shelf and threw it back into the trolley.

'We got brown bread last time and this isn't your shitty Tesco. It's Asda, where I work. I decide what we get when we come here.' He grabbed the trolley and started walking down the aisle, grinning stupidly at his colleagues as they acknowledged him.

They usually took it in turns to do the weekly shopping, but they'd had an argument about whose turn it was this time. Apparently Samir had gone into the shops the other day and bought a packet of sugar, which he counted as his turn to do the shopping. They had tossed a coin but it had landed in the gutter. As they didn't have any coins left and couldn't decide, the only fair thing was for both of them to go. Samir didn't want to do rock paper scissors as apparently Raheem had a trick in which he would always win. Raheem still didn't have a clue what trick that was.

'You got a crap store,' Raheem said as he caught up with Samir. He took the bread out of the trolley and placed it on the shelf next to a can of beans.

Samir put the bread back in and added the can of beans for good measure. 'You're so dumb that you're going to pay for the shopping with your card and still ask for your change.'

Grabbing an egg from the shelf opposite and cracking it on Samir's head was tempting but Raheem resisted. They paid for the shopping – with cash – and headed to the car park.

'Put the trolley back at least,' said Samir as he closed the boot.

'You go, man. I'm tired.' Raheem tried to open the car door but Samir had locked it with his keys.

'I'll take it back for you.' Liam was pushing an empty trolley.

'Fuck you,' said Samir as though it was most natural greeting someone could give.

'That temper of yours is going to get you done over one day,' said Liam, taking a step back. He pushed his trolley towards them, so that Raheem had to stop it with his hand before it hit Samir's car.

'Bastard,' called Samir as Liam walked away. Samir tried to follow him, but Raheem held an arm out. A police car was parked outside the entrance to Asda with two officers sitting inside.

'Let's go,' Raheem said to Samir.

'We still need to put the trolley back.' Samir looked expectantly at Raheem. It wouldn't be the wisest of ideas to give Samir a trolley to run over Liam in the presence of police officers, so Raheem grabbed it and took it back. As he was returning after putting the trolley back, he saw an elderly man heaving a bag into a boot. The man's trolley was slowly moving away from him due to the wind, and there were still two bags of shopping inside it. Raheem grabbed the trolley and picked up the remaining bags.

'Excuse me sir, that's my shopping you're taking' said the man as he turned around and saw Raheem holding his bags.

'I was just taking your bags out for you' said Raheem as he heaved them into the boot. They were quite heavy as they contained milk gallons.

'Sorry son, I should have guessed' said the man apologetically.

'It's okay. I'm not as devious as I look.' He put the man's trolley back for him and returned to the car.

'Katie's coming with us to Sensations tonight,' Samir said, as Raheem got into the passenger seat.

'Why?'

'Because she is. And she is—'

'Staying over, I know,' interrupted Raheem dully. Samir really had it sorted: weekdays with a blonde, weekends with a brunette; both girlfriends in different cities, chances of being caught hardly any.

'What you thinking about?' Samir asked.

66

Raheem hesitated. Something had been bothering him recently. 'I just get this … weird feeling about Veronica sometimes,' he said eventually. The words had escaped his mouth before he had known what he was going to say.

Samir frowned. 'What do you mean "weird feeling"?'

Raheem shrugged. For some reason, he kept getting a horrible feeling that Sarah and Veronica had some sort of connection. Veronica had told him she'd always lived in Leicester, and as far as he was aware, Sarah had only been to Leicester once, and that was with him when they had gone to visit his brother at his law firm. 'It's hard to explain,' he said.

They sat in silence for a few moments. Samir turned to Raheem with a serious expression on his face. 'You know, I honestly think you need to leave Sarah *and* Veronica. You're looking for love and you aren't going to get that with them.'

'Just drive,' snapped Raheem.

'I'm serious.'

'Anything else, or can you drive?' He was getting sick of both Samir and Sarah telling him to leave the other.

'There's one small thing, now you mention it.'

'Go on,' said Raheem dully, knowing that whatever it was wouldn't be good.

'Since that day at uni when Veronica was with us, Rachel has been asking me about her. I told her that she is just a friend, which is true. But then she asked if you were going out with her.'

Why did that not surprise him? 'And what did you say?' asked Raheem.

'I said you're mates, but she didn't seem convinced.'

'About me and Veronica, or you and Veronica?'

Samir shrugged. 'I don't know. I wasn't exactly keen on continuing the subject. But either way, you got to be careful. People will notice that you and Veronica spend a lot of time together. Just stick to being her mate, and not mating *with* her.'

'I am serious about Sarah. I don't know why you think I'm not.'

'So why are you chasing after Veronica?'

Raheem's phone buzzed with a message from Sarah, which saved him from thinking of a response. *Hey just got into Birmingham. Will call you later tonight xxx*

'You still coming out tonight?' asked Samir as he finally started to drive.

Raheem shook his head. Sarah was in Birmingham for two more days, but he didn't want to risk it. 'Nah. I've had enough of these late nights. Going to give it a miss.'

Samir glanced at him sceptically. 'I know you, bro. You will definitely come.'

'No, I won't.'

***

He shouldn't have come, but it was too late now. He stumbled as he made his way out of Sensations and grabbed Veronica's hand.

'You're so clumsy Raheem!' she shouted.

They reached the exit, where Samir was standing with Katie. He looked as though he was going to ask Raheem to reconsider, but before he could say anything Veronica shouted, 'Bye, guys!'

Katie waved at them both, clearly oblivious to Raheem's dilemma.

Veronica kissed his cheek as they crossed the road. 'Not here,' he muttered, looking around. As usual on a Saturday night, town was packed with people, the majority of them students.

They had come in Samir's car so they had to get a taxi back. Raheem felt as if he had barely got into the taxi when the driver pulled up outside his flat. He gave the driver a £10 note and told him to keep the change.

As he got out of the taxi, the driver said, 'It's £10.50, buddy.'

Grimacing, Raheem fumbled in his pocket for some change and found a pound coin. 'Just keep it,' he said as the driver took out his change pouch.

'Thank you!' called Veronica cheerily as the taxi drove off.

Raheem unlocked the door and turned on the lights in the hallway.

'Nice flat,' said Veronica as he closed the door behind them. She had drunk quite a bit in Sensations, and he didn't want to take her to his room until he was sure she was sober. They went into the living room and sat down on the sofa. He turned on the TV but Veronica grabbed the remote and switched it off. He needed to think.

'I just need to go to the bathroom,' he said as Veronica began stroking his hair. She giggled, which Raheem took to mean he could go. He hurried upstairs and locked the door behind him, staring into the mirror. He could drop Veronica home and forget this night had happened. He listened carefully to make sure she was not coming up the stairs, before taking his phone out and ringing Samir.

'Have you done anything?' was Samir's greeting.

'No, not yet, we just got back. Listen, I feel bad about this. What shall I do?' Raheem said quietly.

'I told you – leave it. I'm not serious with Rachel and Katie, but you are with Sarah. That's the difference.'

'But Rachel thinks it's serious,' Raheem accused.

There was a slight pause. 'Why are we talking about me?' Samir asked. 'I'm telling you that you'll regret it later. For once, just listen.'

'I got this close, and now you're telling me to leave it?'

'No winning with you, is there? If I said go for it, you'd start going on about Sarah. If I say leave it, you're going to cry about missing out on Veronica!'

'Raheem come down!' Veronica crooned from downstairs.

'Fuck's sake,' Raheem muttered.

'Sounds like she's as desperate as you are.'

'Okay, listen. I'm going to drop her back home.' Raheem made up his mind. He couldn't do it.

'Good idea. Let me know how it goes.'

'Will do.' Raheem disconnected the call. Taking a deep breath, he walked out of the bathroom and headed down the stairs.

'Look Veronica, I think—' he said as he entered the living room. Before he knew what was happening, Veronica had pulled his face towards hers and they were kissing. How long he stood there for he didn't know, but the next minute she was in his arms and he was carrying her upstairs to his bedroom. He laid her on the bed before locking the door. His brain didn't seem to be working properly.

Chapter 7

Why had he done it?

He had dropped Veronica at her flat within an hour of waking up. Not that it had been easy – he had to practically carry her to the bathroom to get ready as she had wanted to sleep for a bit longer. They hadn't spoken much in the car.

Raheem parked in the driveway, nearly bumping into Samir's car. He opened the front door to find Samir standing at the top of the stairs. He knew from the look Samir gave him that there was no need to explain what had happened the previous night.

'Katie is still asleep. I'll talk to you later,' he said as he went back into his bedroom.

Raheem stood rooted to the spot. What was he going to do now?

He did his best over the next few days to forget what had happened, but it was very difficult. Samir had thrown half the items in the living room at him after Katie had left, but other than that hadn't said much. Sarah, on the other hand, was annoyed at him for turning up late to pick her from the train station. 'I clearly told you to pick me at six, not five past six!'

Raheem wanted to get some advice from Aliyah but decided against it. He didn't want to lose her as a friend after she found out how much of an arse he was. He decided he'd stay with Veronica until he could figure out what to do. It would look suspicious if he ended it with her now.

It hadn't been worth it. The shame and guilt were worse than anything he had ever experienced. He would need to move on from this somehow, but it wasn't going to be easy.

***

If there was one aspect of university that Raheem did not like, it was group work. Most tutors would not allow them to pick their own groups, so they usually ended up with people they hardly knew. In addition, the mark was for the group so if one person performed poorly, it affected the rest. He really needed to get a first in his police powers module as it would allow him to take some pressure off when it came to his dissertation, which was worth forty percent of his grade for third year.

Raheem was texting Veronica when he was distracted by Jordan, one of the members of his group. 'So, Raheem, are you okay to meet up next Thursday at four in the group study room?'

Raheem had a lecture on Thursday that finished at three and he was going back to Manchester straight afterwards. 'Can we not do a bit earlier, like twelve?' he asked.

'We've already booked the room at four,' said Charlotte, a short girl with glasses and curly hair. She was the type who would sit in the first row in the lectures and always ask questions, both during and at the end of the class when everyone else was waiting to leave.

'Why you asking me then, if you've already booked it?' said Raheem irritably.

Samir, who had been sitting on the table in front with his group, heard him. He turned around and grinned at Raheem, but then saw Charlotte looking at him and turned back. He had once had an argument with her in first year because he'd been talking to Ryan during the lecture. Charlotte had turned around and asked him to shut up. Raheem could still remember the look on Samir's face when she'd said that.

'You nodded when we told you that we were booking it at four,' said Jordan just as Raheem received a text from Sarah asking him why he had missed her call earlier. She seemed to think he could answer calls halfway through a class.

'Exactly, so why are you asking me if you already booked it? Not like I got a choice,' he said, now starting to get really irritated. He would have to let his younger sister know that he would need to take her out on another day. She wouldn't be happy about that.

Sarah had just called him again and he had accidentally disconnected the call.

'Are you alright?' asked Michael, the final member of the group. Raheem saw him more often on nights out than in university.

'I'm okay, just annoyed about something.' Raheem made it clear from his tone that Michael was not supposed to ask what he was annoyed about. The good thing with having Charlotte in the group would be that her high mark would soften the blow of Michael, who had somehow managed to scrape through the first two years at university.

'So, Thursday it is, then?' asked Jordan.

Raheem raised his hand to his forehead in a salute. Jordan started making plans with Charlotte and Michael about their presentation, leaving Raheem free to make an excuse to leave and pretend he was going to the toilet. Aliyah smiled at him as he walked past.

Once outside in the corridor, he called Sarah, hoping she wouldn't answer. Predictably, she answered after the first ring. 'Why did you disconnect my call?' were her first words.

'I was in a lecture. I can't answer calls then.' Raheem tried to keep his voice calm. His patience was being put to the test by everyone today.

'You don't have a lecture this time on a Tuesday,' she said accusingly. So she had memorised his timetable.

'Sorry, I meant seminar,' he said through gritted teeth.

'I can't hear anyone around you.'

His patience finally snapped. 'That's because I've just gone outside the room. It's not my dad's university where I can answer calls from you halfway through a class,' said Raheem angrily. He disconnected before Sarah could respond, walked back to the classroom and tried to pull open the door. It remained shut. He tried again before realising he had to push it.

***

'You okay, Raheem? You look really angry,' said Fiona an hour later as she walked past him in the corridor with Catherine.

'I'm fine, thanks. Sarah is good as well,' Raheem said automatically, walking quickly in the opposite direction. He really needed some fresh air.

Samir and Aliyah caught up with him as soon as he was outside. 'I told Fiona you're stressed because your presentation group is bullying you,' said Samir. 'I told her you might be crying outside so I needed to go check.'

'Stop it, Samir,' Aliyah said firmly before Raheem could respond with a volley of swear words.

They walked into town, where Aliyah went into the post office to send a parcel. 'Been such a shit week,' said Raheem angrily, kicking an empty Coke can. It skidded across the ground and nearly hit a pigeon, which flew straight at him and narrowly missed his head.

'You deserve it. I saw you being a prick to Aliyah earlier,' said Samir sternly. 'I swear I felt like punching you. Make sure you say sorry to her.'

'I only said I'd never been better when she asked me how I was,' said Raheem grumpily. Everyone seemed to be against him today.

'It wasn't *what* you said, it's the *way* you said it.'

'I've heard that before.' Raheem took out a cigarette.

'I might as well have one too,' said Samir thoughtfully.

They stood talking about Veronica for a couple of minutes, until a man with long hair and ripped jeans walked up to them. 'You got a cigarette?' he asked croakily. The stench of weed coming from him mixed with body odour was unbearable.

'Don't have one, sorry,' Raheem said shortly. He had once given a sandwich to a homeless man near the university, but the man had thrown it away and asked him for money instead. That was really annoying as Raheem had been hungry himself at the time.

The man turned to Samir. 'Have you got one?'

Samir shook his head and withdrew his empty cigarette packet. 'Sorry, I only got this one,' he said, indicating the one he was smoking.

'Can I have the rest of yours, then?' asked the man.

'Erm ... okay then,' said Samir awkwardly.

73

'Cheers,' said the man. He took the cigarette from Samir's hand and walked off.

'The guy's fucked in the head,' said Samir as they watched him approach a group of lads who were standing outside Sports Direct.

Raheem finished his cigarette and threw it in the bin. He was desperate for the day to end but he still had another seminar, as well as a shift at Tesco's later on.

'I don't know how you and Sarah have lasted this long. I say you end it with her and also with Veronica,' said Samir suddenly.

'I can't just end it with Sarah. How many times have I told you?' It was alright Samir thinking it was that easy, but it wasn't. How could he end it with Veronica without giving her a reason? And he did like Sarah. He had just made a big mistake.

'Chat about it later,' muttered Samir as Aliyah returned.

'Sent it,' she said brightly.

'He got scared by a guy just before you came. That guy was going to knock him out until I intervened,' Raheem said.

'I've got you there for me if I ever get into a fight.' Samir clapped him on the shoulder as they walked towards Subway.

'Aww, that's nice,' said Aliyah.

'You wish,' said Raheem.

'And that's *not* very nice,' said Aliyah sternly.

Samir grinned and put his arm around Raheem's shoulder. 'He loves me really.'

Raheem smiled grudgingly. 'Where are you going? It's right from here, not left.'

'I'm sure it's left, I haven't been Subway in ages' said Aliyah, looking around.

'I'll ask someone' said Raheem and he walked over to a lady who was leaning against a wall, looking at her phone. 'Hi, can you tell me where'-

'I've got a boyfriend' she said abruptly without looking up from her phone.

Bloody hell. She was paranoid. Raheem made a face at her and walked back to the others.

'What did she say?' asked Aliyah.

'She said she has got a… sandwich from Subway earlier. You were right Aliyah, it was left. Let's go.'

'You should listen to Aliyah more often, trust me it will help you' Samir told him as they began walking.

'You should get a brain, trust me it will help you.'

'I've already got one, thanks for checking though.'

'Really? Bring it along with you sometime.'

'It's worth more than yours.'

'Yeah it would be, seeing as it's never been used before.'

'Both of you stop it' said Aliyah as they entered Subway. Unsurprisingly, there was a queue.

'What can I get you, love?' asked the lady behind the counter.

The menu was behind the counter. Raheem had not been to Subway in a while. 'Could I get a twelve-foot – I mean twelve-inch tuna sandwich?' he said, correcting himself a little too late.

'He said twelve foot!' muttered Aliyah. The next thirty seconds were painful as Raheem endured Aliyah and Samir's sniggering.

'Any salad?' asked the lady.

It didn't look very appealing. 'Could I get everything apart from cucumber, tomatoes, peppers, olives, jalapenos, onion, carrots and sweetcorn.'

Samir and Aliyah burst out laughing.

'Sorry, I meant could I get lettuce and nothing else. Got it the wrong way round,' said Raheem apologetically.

'Bless you. Looks like you're having a bad day.' She smiled and Raheem forced a grin.

Once they had their sandwiches, they sat on the only remaining table next to the window. 'Are you sure you're okay, Raheem?' asked Aliyah.

'I'm fine thanks. Sorry about earlier Aliyah, I didn't mean it,' he said.

'It's okay,' she said kindly.

They ate their sandwiches before going back to the university for their seminar. Samir and Aliyah chatted, leaving him to ponder in silence about the mess he was in. He couldn't just leave Veronica. It wasn't her fault.

'Where are you going? Seminar is this way,' Aliyah said. Raheem had been about to enter the library.

'Oh right, I forgot.' He walked back to them.

They went down the corridor, past the smaller university cafe and turned left after going down the stairs. Daniel was sitting on his own in the café, staring at his phone.

'Really need to go to the toilet. That sandwich was heavy,' Samir said as they waited for the lift. He did look a bit queasy.

'Nearest toilets are on the first floor, next to the bio-medicine labs. It's a bit of a walk to be honest.'

'If only they were twelve feet away, or even better twelve inches,' sighed Aliyah as the lift opened.

Raheem had no response.

***

To take his mind off his problems, Raheem accepted Adam and Zack's offer to play on their team for a football match in Roland's Fields. Zack had been badgering him about it for the past few weeks. So far, things had not gone to plan. There were ten minutes to go, and their team was losing 2–1.

'Pass the fucking ball, man!' Raheem shouted in exasperation as Adam blasted his fourth shot of the match wide. If he'd only rolled it across the box then Raheem would have had an easy tap in.

'Bro, you were offside!' Adam shouted as he jogged back to the centre circle.

Raheem threw his arms in the air as the goalkeeper took his goal kick. He miskicked, and the ball went straight to their teammate, Luke. 'Luke, look!' yelled Raheem, pointing to where he wanted the ball. Luke chipped the ball forward. Raheem tugged on the shirt of his opponent, who stumbled, and he was suddenly one on one with the goalkeeper. He made to place the ball in the left corner but was fouled by the defender.

'Penalty!' yelled his team in unison. The referee blew his whistle and pointed to the penalty spot. Raheem had already picked up the ball and was hurrying to place it on the spot.

'Let Jimmy take it, he's never missed a penalty,' said Adam.

Raheem wagged his finger at him and said, 'I've got this, don't worry.'

Their opponents were still protesting at the referee. The guy whose shirt Raheem had tugged had just got a yellow card for his constant nagging.

Finally, everyone was behind the ball, waiting for the penalty kick. Raheem stepped forward, but his left leg slipped as he took the penalty. The ball went flying over the bar as Raheem fell on his backside.

'I told you to let Jimmy take it!' snapped Adam as their opponents let out howls of laughter.

Muttering furiously, Raheem got up, but the defender whose shirt he had pulled began fist pumping in front of him and swearing. Raheem pushed him in the face, and his opponent fell on the ground, rolling around and clutching his face as if he'd been shot.

'What the fuck you doing?' shouted one of his teammates, squaring up at Raheem.

'What you going to do about it?' snarled Raheem.

There was a mêlée, involving both sets of players. Zack grabbed Raheem and tried to drag him away, but the referee blew his whistle, walked up to Raheem and showed him a red card. The player he had pushed was still on the ground, though he had finally removed his hands from his face. Ten seconds later, he was back clutching his face as Raheem had thrown the football at him. He trudged off the pitch, scowling. Life was shit at the moment.

***

There was only one person whose company Raheem enjoyed no matter what mood he was in, or what mood she was in. After he had finished his shift at Tesco in the morning, he'd called Aliyah to ask her if she wanted to come for a walk with him on Saturday afternoon at Burydale Park. As always, Aliyah didn't let him down.

They were halfway around the lake when she said, 'You look a bit stressed lately.'

He hadn't told her about what had happened with him and Veronica, but Aliyah knew him so well that she would definitely have picked up on him not being his usual self.

'I'm fine, just been a bit tied down with uni work,' he replied, moving further away from the edge of the path in case he fell in the lake. That would be a sure way to get his stress levels up again.

'Is everything okay between you and Sarah?'

Raheem stopped in his tracks and looked at her. 'Yeah, everything is fine. Have you heard anything different?'

'No, I'm just asking. I thought it might be something like that,' said Aliyah.

It was something like that, but the less Aliyah knew the better. 'I'm afraid to say that for once you're wrong.' He smiled at her as they resumed their walking.

'I'll probably be wrong in my revision notes as well, so you might not want to risk borrowing them,' she said, grinning.

'When it comes to uni work, you can never be wrong.'

'Stop the flattery, mister. I always knew third year would be hard, but this is ridiculous. We have another presentation to do and I've heard that they are stricter with the marking for essays and exams in third year, is that true?'

'What you hear is not the truth, and what the truth is, you don't want to hear.'

'Oh wow, such an amazing dialogue!'

'Ha-ha, I'm just amazing Aliyah. I would have thought that by now you would have worked that out.' They continued talking for another fifteen minutes as they finished their walk.

The past couple of weeks had given Raheem time to reflect on his situation. He had spoken with Samir and reiterated that he needed to be with both Sarah and Veronica until he could work out what to do. As daft as it sounded, the only way to ensure he didn't hurt either of their feelings was to date both of them without them finding out. He couldn't just leave Veronica like this. Samir had not thought much of this idea, but when Raheem had reminded him he was seeing both Rachel and Katie, he'd relented. But Raheem was not going to bring Veronica to his flat again, that much he was sure of.

'Can I drive your car? I need some practice because my driving lesson was cancelled this week,' Aliyah asked as the car park came into view.

'No! You nearly crashed it last time,' Raheem said sternly. Aliyah had almost smashed into a lamppost. Apparently, she had panicked when he had sneezed.

'That wasn't my fault! You distracted me!' she said predictably.

'I said no.'

'Please?'

'Maybe if you say pretty please.'

'Pretty, pretty please?'

'No, you said it twice. I only asked you to say it once.'

Aliyah stopped in front of him, hands on hips. 'If I beat you in a race to the car, will you let me drive?'

There was no chance of that happening. 'Okay, then, that's a deal.'

She grinned and turned her back to him. 'I get a two-inch head start.'

'Fair enough.'

Raheem's car was fifty meters away. He checked his shoelaces to make sure they were tied and said, 'On the count of three. Ready?'

'Ready,' said Aliyah.

'Okay. One … two— Argh!'

Aliyah elbowed him in the stomach and ran towards the car. He chased her, still winded, but she was already halfway there. She reached the car two seconds before him and leaned against it, panting.

'That's cheating!' As Raheem grabbed her in a headlock, the back of his elbow smacked into his wing mirror. Aliyah was beside herself with laughter as he let go and straightened it. Thankfully, there was no damage. He turned back to Aliyah who had her hand held out.

'Keys, my dear,' she said sweetly.

He took his car key out his pocket. Aliyah grabbed it enthusiastically and got into the driver's seat. Feeling more cheerful than he had done in a while, Raheem also got in.

Chapter 8

As they neared the end of November, the exams and deadlines loomed nearer and the late nights in the library started for Raheem and Samir. They had both made steady progress with their dissertations. Raheem had met Steven for their second appointment, and it had gone pretty well.

The exams were usually after the Christmas break, but this year the university had decided to have them before Christmas. Doing late nights in the library was all part of the experience. It was usually the regular clubbers who were to be found at one in the morning in the library, bleary eyed, trying to get through their work.

Energy drinks, coffee cups and snacks littered the desks as Raheem clicked the submit button on his screen. He would hand in the hard copy of his essay on Monday because the university offices were closed at weekends.

The library was quiet, despite being half full. Whether it was the first or third year, Raheem usually ended up submitting his essays within a few hours of the deadline. Tonight, he had managed to submit three days before, so he was quite pleased with himself.

Veronica was working on her report but she still had almost a week before her deadline. Yawning, she put her arms around his neck and pecked his cheek.

'What you doing?' he asked as he moved his face away.

'Can't even get a kiss?' she asked grumpily.

'You need to finish your work,' said Raheem gently. She rested her head against his shoulder.

Jason entered the first floor and sat at a computer in the far corner. Raheem moved his chair slightly to the left so that Jason could not see him. Sarah was aware he was in the library tonight, but he didn't want to take any chances. She wasn't aware who he was with, and he would rather keep it that way.

He stood up and told Veronica he'd be back in ten minutes, then walked around the back of the library and left through the side entrance so that he wouldn't have to pass Jason. In the corridor he bumped into Hannah, who was sitting against the wall texting on her phone. 'Hello,' he said as he sat down next to her.

Hannah looked up and beamed when she saw it was him. 'Hey, good to see you,' she said.

'What are you doing here so late?'

'Just working on my disso,' she said. 'I wasn't feeling well the last couple of days so not got through much work. What about you?'

'I just submitted my youth crime justice essay, such a relief. Are you feeling better now?'

'It was just a cold. Get them at this time of the year. Feeling better now thanks.'

'Good. Where are you sitting?'

Hannah pointed at one of the computer lab rooms opposite them on the right. 'Got this weird guy trying to chat to me, there are only us two in there' she said.

'I *must* have a look.' Raheem peered through the glass pane. Liam was sitting at one of the computers with his back to the door, staring at his screen. It looked as though he were watching a movie. Raheem grinned and turned to Hannah. 'I think he's your type.'

'No way! He just kept asking me random questions! I'm sure he was the one who was looking at me that day when I was with you.'

'I think it was, you know. He must have feelings for you.'

'He can keep his feelings to himself.' Hannah pretended to shudder. 'Guess what type of guy I want?' That was pretty obvious.

'Someone tall?' asked Raheem. 'Do you know the advantage of having a partner who is taller? When it rains, they always know before you and can get the umbrella out so you don't have to.'

'Ha-ha, I want a *mixed-race,* tall guy. I find them so fit.' She was certainly very picky.

'I'm a big believer in interracial couples,' said Raheem innocently.

Hannah didn't seem to hear him; she appeared lost in thought. 'Most people tend to be with partners from the same ethnicity.'

'That's not always the case; I'm Asian, but I... I mean Samir's Asian, but he's with... It's not always the case,' Raheem said eventually. The less he spoke about Sarah or Rachel, the better it would be for him and Samir. 'I'll catch you later, Hannah. If that guy says anything to you, ring me, but I honestly think you should give it a go. You just never know, he might be the one you have been searching for all this time.'

'Shut it!' said Hannah, hitting him with her bag.

'I'm joking,' he said hastily. He said goodbye to her and made his way down the lift to the ground floor, checking his messages on his phone.

There was one from Samir: *Meet me outside the uni entrance will b there five mins. Need to go Tesco. Bring the facemask I left in your bag.*

Facemask: Samir always wore them in winter, the ones that surgeons wore in hospitals. The fact that he looked so ridiculous didn't seem to bother him.

Raheem headed back to his table. He told Veronica he was going Tesco with Samir and took a facemask from his bag. He asked if she wanted him to bring anything back for her but she still had some of her pasta left from earlier.

The cold air hit him the moment he walked outside. He put up his hood and wrapped a scarf around the bottom half of his face. He had only waited a minute when Samir arrived, shivering because the white cardigan he was wearing was not very thick.

'How was Sensations?' Raheem asked as he handed him the mask. They started walking towards the Tesco at the end of the road.

'It was okay. I went with Rachel – she'd booked the weekend off work so didn't go back home.'

'What about Katie?'

'I told her I was busy. She bought me this cardigan last week. It's good, eh?'

'It hurts my eyes, bro, it's so bright.'

'Better than that jumper Sarah bought for you!' Samir had a point. Raheem had only worn it whenever he was seeing Sarah alone, either at her apartment or at his place. It was too risky to wear in public.

The Tesco Express was open twenty-four hours, which was convenient for students. Raheem had been tempted to get a transfer to this one, but had decided against it. It was too close to his university, and there would be too many familiar faces. Samir and a couple of their friends had come into his Tesco store last year when he had been working. Thankfully, his manager had been lenient to him after he had heard Raheem tell Samir and his friends to fuck off. Some managers wouldn't be as relaxed about it. Samir had gone inside to get himself a packet of cigarettes when Raheem's phone buzzed with a message from Sarah asking how his revision was going. He was about to respond when raised voices from the wall behind the entrance to Tesco made him rush towards the sound. Even though he was more than a hundred feet away, there was no mistaking Samir's voice.

He turned the corner. A tall man, whose back was turned to Raheem, was advancing towards Samir. 'Whoa, chill out!' called Raheem.

The man looked at him. He was at least six feet three and had lean muscular arms. He had a gold chain around his neck and a silver watch on his left wrist. 'You fucking starting as well?' he snarled, taking a few steps towards Raheem, who did not step back.

Samir walked around the edge of the path and stood next to Raheem. Even beneath the mask, Raheem could tell Samir was having second thoughts about this. 'Is this the only guy you could find to start with?' Raheem muttered, lowering his scarf slightly so that Samir could hear him.

'Don't worry about it. There are two of us and he's drunk,' Samir whispered back.

Raheem decided to take the defensive route. Drunk or not, a couple of punches from this guy would knock them both out. 'Look, we can sort this out calmly, can't we?' He took a step forward and raised his hands.

The man said something that Raheem could not understand. He was definitely drunk, and stoned, judging by the smell of weed that was coming from him. He was slowly edging towards them.

'That's fine by me. You go your way, we go ours. See you later,' Raheem continued, stepping back.

The man said something else but his speech was slurred. He was now directly in front of them. Samir's patience snapped. 'What the fuck you on about? We can't understand what you're saying and there are no subtitles either!'

Before Raheem could move, the man punched Samir. It was lucky he was drunk because the punch missed his face, which was his target, and hit him on the shoulder. Nevertheless, Samir dropped.

Instinctively, Raheem threw a punch of his own, landing it on the side of the man's face. The man staggered backwards but was still standing. He ran towards Raheem, who stuck his leg out and tripped him . 'Come on, let's go!' shouted Raheem to Samir.

'Get this twat off me then!' The man had fallen on top of Samir, who was still down after the punch.

Raheem made to pull him off, but the man suddenly got up. Out of nowhere, he elbowed Raheem on the side of the face with such force that he staggered back and fell over. Slightly dazed, he got up and aimed another punch, which caught the man on his jaw. The man stumbled backwards and Samir, finally back on his feet, fly-kicked him in the back and sent him face first into the large bin near the wall. He hit his head on the bin and lay face down on the ground, motionless.

For a second that lasted an eternity, Raheem and Samir looked at each before simultaneously sprinting away from Tesco. They ran for a full minute before they reached the entrance to the university – or at least Raheem did. Samir hurtled through the front door and into the ground floor of the library.

Still panting, Raheem went to join him. He failed to get through the security barriers the first time because he forgot to scan his university card, and he banged his leg against the barrier. Cursing, he took his card out of his pocket and scanned it.

'Nice one,' said Samir, raising his hand for a high five.

Raheem was about to return the gesture, but halfway through raising his hand he changed his mind and slapped Samir across the face instead.

'What the fuck?' demanded Samir angrily, rubbing the side of his face.

'Why the hell did you start with him for?' asked Raheem. Now the adrenalin was leaving him, he realised they could be in serious trouble.

'He started with *me*. I was just about to go into Tesco and he was looking at me funny. When I asked him what he was looking at, he just started swearing! What do you think I am, a bitch who's going to not say anything back?'

Raheem shook his head in exasperation. 'He was drunk, you should have ignored it!' When Samir didn't respond, he added, 'If he reports this to the police we're fucked. You do know that, don't you?'

'What do you mean police? It's not like we killed him or something. He was still breathing when we ran away. I think.'

If only life were that simple. 'Bro, this isn't school where you punch someone and you get a detention. This could be classed as assault!'

'He is the one who started it so that won't be classed as assault. Plus, one of my mates works at that Tesco and she told me that the camera at the back never worked, so that guy can't prove anything.'

Raheem was about to swear again but the sound of the lift coming down next to him made him stop. This time he wasn't leaning against it. He gestured at Samir to be quiet as it opened and a group of girls came out of it.

'Hi,' said Samir, even though he didn't even know them. The girls giggled and walked on, looking back at them both. 'That middle one was alright,' he said, staring at them as they walked away.

Distracted, Raheem took another look. She *was* alright. She had a figure to match Veronica's. Then he remembered what had just happened. 'Did you know that guy? I could hardly see his face, it was so dark.'

'Nah. But our faces were covered so he didn't see us.'

'We could still get done for—'

The door next to Samir opened and out came the last person Raheem wanted to see: Liam. 'You were sitting upstairs, weren't you?' asked Raheem.

'I can sit where I want. You don't own this place, do you?' Liam said as he walked past.

'Bitch, I'll bang you out!' Samir stepped towards him, but Raheem held him back. The last thing they needed was another fight in full view of the security guards.

Liam raised his middle finger at them and walked away. The bastard would always make sure there was some sort of security around when he provoked them.

'Guy's gone cheeky nowadays, hasn't he?' said Samir. 'I've noticed that. Last year he never said anything to us. What's changed?'

'Why are you always starting with people?'

'You're the one who spoke to him first! So what if he was sitting upstairs? What's that got to do with anything?'

'Why can't you stand still?'

'There's something stuck under my cardigan!'

Samir put his hand underneath his cardigan and withdrew a silver watch. It was the same watch the man they'd fought had been wearing.

'You nicked his watch?' asked Raheem incredulously.

Samir looked bewildered. 'I swear I don't know where it came from.'

Raheem was really starting to lose it now. It was bad enough them attacking someone, but this made it even worse. The chances of them being reported to the police were increasing. 'What do you mean you don't know where it came from? Did your dad's dad give it to you? Or did it magically drop from the sky into your pocket?'

'My dad's dad is also your dad's dad and it must have got stuck when you tripped him onto me!'

'You stupid, *stupid* idiot!'

The lift opened again; they'd been arguing so loudly they'd not heard it coming down. It was Veronica. Samir quickly put the watch in his pocket. 'There you are. What's up?' she asked, looking from one to the other.

Raheem and Samir exchanged glances. 'Nothing. We – er – nothing,' mumbled Raheem, not meeting her eyes.

Veronica frowned. 'You didn't go to Tesco, did you?' she said coolly, reminding him of Sarah.

Samir looked at Raheem, who shook his head very slightly. Samir got the message to keep quiet and not interrupt.

'Well?' she demanded.

Raheem cleared his throat. 'We did go to Tesco.'

'What took you so long? Tesco is around the corner!' Veronica raised her voice.

It was time for the old trick. 'Yeah, but we didn't go *this* Tesco, we went to *that* Tesco...'

Behind Veronica, Samir was pretending to bang his head against the wall. Veronica looked at Raheem, her face expressionless. 'You could have just said that first,' she said.

Relieved, Raheem forced a smile.

'So, which of you is going to drop me home?' she asked, although she was looking at Raheem expectantly.

'I'll do it. I'm dropping Samir home first. He's got to clean up some of the mess he has made at Tes— in the flat.'

'What have you done?' asked Veronica they moved towards the entrance.

'Had a party last night, didn't clean up afterwards,' replied Samir.

'Thanks for the invite,' she said crossly.

'It was lads only. Sorry. That's why Raheem wasn't invited either.'

They both glanced in the direction of Tesco before heading in the opposite direction to the university car park.

A car drove past them. 'You're sexy!' shouted a man from the passenger seat at Veronica.

'Just like your mum!' Raheem shouted back. He didn't know what made him say it.

'Leave it, Raheem, he's just an idiot,' said Veronica affectionately as the car turned the corner and blasted the horn.

'Yeah, no point in getting into another– I mean, a fight,' said Samir.

'Raheem's not a troublemaker, are you, babe?' Veronica said adoringly.

'Nope, I'm a good boy, never in trouble,' he replied as they reached the Parkview car park.

Raheem started the engine and turned the heater on to maximum.

'Where's your bag, baby? Have you left it in the library?' asked Veronica.

'Dumb fucker,' muttered Samir.

'I'll come with you. Let's go get it.' Veronica got out of the car.

Raheem threw the keys at Samir and got out. Veronica grabbed his arm as they walked back towards the university. 'I hate it when you're away from me,' she said, kissing his cheek.

Raheem could only muster a painful smile. The further away he was from Veronica, the better it would be for both of them. But when, and how, was that going to happen?

***

To Raheem and Samir's relief, they heard nothing from the police – or anyone else for that matter – about the incident outside Tesco. Two weeks had passed, during which they handed in one of their essays and sat an exam. Raheem found the exam reasonable enough. Once he'd spent a few weeks back home in Manchester during the Christmas holidays, he'd be ready to come back and continue his dissertation before the start of the second semester near the end of January. He had written nearly four thousand words – but there were still two more exams and a presentation to complete before then.

***

Raheem bade goodbye to Rebecca in the staff room and went upstairs to the shop floor. It was just as busy as it had been when he'd finished his shift ten minutes earlier. Tracy and Jamie had come to the store a while back, and Raheem had been delighted to hear that Tracy had got a new job and her life back on track.

He wanted to buy a drink but the queue on the till and self-scans meant that he'd be waiting a while. He managed to squeeze out of the store, before being welcomed by a strong gush of wind outside. He was just about to light a cigarette when a voice spoke behind him. 'I need to talk to you, Raheem.'

He turned. Rachel was leaning against the wall of Tesco. 'Hi, Rachel. What you doing here?'

'I've been waiting to speak to you alone. After you finished work was my only chance,' she said.

So Sarah knew his timetable at university and now Rachel knew his work shifts. Being stalked by women wasn't as exciting as he'd imagined it would be back in his college days. 'The thing is … I need to go, I'm in a rush,' he said tentatively.

'I won't take long,' said Rachel firmly.

He had an idea what this was about; Samir had warned him it might be coming. 'Okay, then. Let's go around here. I'm just going to have a cigarette.' Rachel followed him around the corner, where the side street was empty. 'So what is it, everything okay?' Raheem put the cigarette in his mouth.

Rachel took a deep breath. 'Is Samir cheating on me?'

He took his time lighting his cigarette. 'No, she's just a friend,' he said calmly.

Rachel's blue eyes rounded in surprise. 'How do you know she's just a friend when I haven't mentioned a name yet?' She had a point.

'I meant that normally when a woman thinks a guy is cheating on her, the woman who she thinks her boyfriend is cheating with is usually just a friend of her boyfriend. You get me?' He seemed to be spending half his time trying to wriggle out of dangerous situations. He waited as Rachel mulled over his words.

'Is Samir going out with Veronica?'

'No, they're just friends,' said Raheem firmly.

Rachel's expression was difficult to read. 'Swear down.'

He put his hand to his heart. 'I swear down Samir is not going out with Veronica.' It wasn't a lie, although he wouldn't be able to swear anything if she asked him about Katie.

Rachel looked a lot more relaxed. 'Well, I best be off then. Sorry for asking, it's just – you know, one of those things,' she said awkwardly.

Raheem nodded. 'I understand. Don't worry.'

'Thanks. How's Sarah?'

'She's great.'

They looked at each other for a few seconds before Rachel said, 'Catch you later. I'm meeting a couple of friends at Starbucks. Come and join us. I think you've met Kevin and Leah before.'

For a second, he was tempted by the offer. It would be a welcome change to relax and have a normal conversation. But he had promised to take Sarah to the cinema later tonight and he needed to go home and get ready. 'Thanks, but I'm a bit busy this evening, got a few things to do. But you have a good time, and thanks for offering.'

Rachel smiled and walked away. Raheem turned his back and looked at his phone, which had a text from Veronica: *When we going cinema, haven't been in a while? X*

'Yeah, come with me and Sarah tonight. I can't wait to introduce you to each other,' he muttered, putting his phone back in his pocket. Just then, someone tapped him on the shoulder. He jumped in surprise and turned around, but it was only Rachel again.

'Sorry did I scare you?' she said.

She had scared the living daylights out of him. 'It's fine,' he said airily.

Rachel seemed a bit hesitant. 'In regards to our conversation, there is no need to mention it to Samir, if that's okay?' she said finally. 'I don't want him to think that I suspected him.'

He couldn't help feeling sorry for her, but the truth would be worse for her to hear. Rachel was not time passing as Samir had told him. Normally he would have told Samir to get his act together and leave Katie, but in the position he was in himself he would just look like a hypocrite. Two wrongs didn't make a right though. He would still mention it, but the chances of his cousin listening weren't very high. 'Don't worry. I won't mention it to Samir. Anything I hear, I don't even tell myself, let alone others.'

'Thanks.' She turned and walked towards the main street. This time Raheem made sure she was out of sight before heading for the train station car park.

'Can you watch where— Yes, Dan, good to see you!' He bumped into Daniel, who was going in the opposite direction.

Daniel peered at him for a few seconds. 'Hi … you okay?' he said, once he finally recognised it was Raheem. He'd lost even more weight since Raheem had last seen him. His hair was unkempt and he had dark shadows under his eyes.

'I'm good.' Are *you* alright?' Raheem asked.

Daniel nodded.

'Are you sure? We can talk if you want?' said Raheem. Daniel had been like this ever since ever since he had come back to university in September.

'Do you know where the nearest toilets are?' Daniel asked.

Raheem caught a whiff of what smelt like vodka. 'There's some in Sainsbury's round the corner,' he said, pointing to it.

Daniel squinted. 'Cheers... Well, I'll see you around Raheem.' He hurried off without another word.

Something was up with Daniel, but it looked like he didn't want to share it. It could have been something to do with failing the previous year.

Raheem glanced back at his Tesco store. Ashleigh and Rebecca were scanning items frantically on the tills. Joe was surrounded by customers. Even Andrew was on the shop floor, restocking the shelves as quickly as he could. He hurried away in case he was asked to do some overtime.

Chapter 9

Board games were near the top of Raheem's dislike list – they were just so boring – but that wouldn't be a good enough excuse for Sarah.

He opened the living-room door to find her lying on the sofa watching TV. Not that he was surprised to see her. Samir had texted him to let him know she was there. 'What a surprise! Where's Samir?' he asked.

'He's gone to pick up Aliyah and get some food. We're all having a game of Ludo,' she said brightly.

'Good. At least we can have some fun while no one else is here.' Raheem took off his top and she lay on top of him. Sarah did her mischievous grin and bit his neck. He never liked it when she did that, but he didn't want to give her another reason to start an argument. They had patched up when they'd gone to the cinema a couple of days ago.

It was really comfortable lying with Sarah on the sofa in front of the fireplace. He always preferred the fire to the radiators; it gave the room that romantic feel. As Sarah was telling him about one of the new managers at her workplace, Raheem's thoughts drifted to Veronica. Something needed to happen soon. He couldn't keep going on like this…

'What you thinking about?' asked Sarah.

Raheem ran his hands through her hair. 'I was thinking, how come you look so sexy all the time?'

Sarah giggled and raised her head from his chest. 'I'm not going to let you win in Ludo. You can try all the compliments you want.'

'I can assure you, I didn't say it so that you can let me win.'

Just then Samir's car pulled up in the driveway. Raheem hastily put his top back on and sat down on the sofa as the front door opened.

'Shall I leave these in the kitchen?' Aliyah asked.

'Yep, just put them on the table please,' said Samir.

Raheem stood up and went into the hallway. Aliyah was carrying two bags. 'Why is Aliyah carrying the bags?' he asked. 'Hi, Aliyah,' he added hastily.

'Hiya. I told him I would carry them.' Aliyah smiled back at him. She was wearing the purple cardigan that Raheem had bought for her last year.

Samir raised his middle finger at Raheem.

'Who are you swearing at, Samir?' asked Sarah as she came into the hallway.

'No one,' he said casually, apparently not realising his finger was still up.

Sarah raised her eyebrows and hugged Aliyah.

'I think we should eat first, before we play Ludo,' said Raheem.

'No, let's play Ludo, wait for the food to get cold and then eat,' said Samir sarcastically.

Aliyah sniggered and even Sarah managed a grudging smile. That was probably the first time she'd ever smiled at something Samir had said. They sat at the kitchen table and settled down to their food.

'How much did they charge you for it, Aliyah?' asked Samir.

'You made her pay for it, you little—!' interjected Raheem loudly, choking on his food.

'He nearly had a heart attack!' exclaimed Samir as Raheem, coughing and spluttering, went to the sink to get a glass of water.

'He was just looking out for me. That's what besties do,' said Aliyah kindly.

'We once ordered a pizza' said Raheem. 'The guy asked us if we wanted it in four slices or eight. Samir told him that he was really hungry so cut it in eight, as if that made a difference!'

'Eh, when did this happen?' shouted Samir as they all burst out laughing.

An hour and a half later, however, the atmosphere was tense. Aliyah and Sarah both needed to get a number one on the dice to win the game. Raheem still had two more tokens to take around the table. Samir had all four of his in his zone, having not managed to get one safely around the board.

'Listen, we give up. It's just you two.' Raheem moved his and Samir's tokens off the board.

'No! I don't give up. Anything can happen.' Samir put them back on the board. They all looked at him. 'But maybe it's asking too much,' he said sheepishly, moving them off again.

Sarah rolled the dice. It landed on number three. Only number one would do.

'Who you supporting, Raheem?' asked Samir slyly.

Aliyah and Sarah both looked at him: Aliyah was smiling but Sarah looked serious. The best way around Samir's stupid question was to be diplomatic. 'I want them both to lose,' he replied, smiling. Sarah glared at him and Raheem's smile faltered.

Aliyah rolled the dice and it landed on number five.

'I thought that was a one!' said Raheem in a falsely cheery voice.

Sarah threw again and got a two.

'Here, let me take a go for you, Aliyah.' Raheem picked up the dice.

'That's not fair! You can't do that, you already let Aliyah off by not killing her when you landed on her!' said Sarah indignantly. She could be really competitive sometimes.

'I would have been in danger myself if I'd killed her. I decided to play safe!' When Sarah still didn't look happy, Raheem added, 'I'll take one go for you as well.'

'Fine,' she said.

Raheem rolled the dice for Aliyah's go and it landed on number one. Aliyah was the winner.

'Oh my days!' shouted Samir.

Sarah was staring at the dice as Aliyah raised her arms in celebration. 'Well played, Aliyah. I think Raheem was lucky for you,' said Sarah brightly.

'Thanks. To be honest, the whole game is luck,' said Aliyah modestly.

Raheem made sure he did not look at Sarah as he started packing up the board. Despite the fact that it was only a game,

Sarah would be angry with him for playing for Aliyah and winning the game for her.

'Samir came last,' said Raheem loudly, trying to change the subject. Samir threw a cushion, which hit him on the face.

'Right, I think it's time to play a game of Monopoly that requires brains, not luck,' said Sarah briskly.

'He's got no chance of winning if you need a brain,' said Raheem and Samir together, pointing at each other. They both rolled around laughing and it took a full minute before they stopped.

'The person who comes last in Monopoly washes the plates!' said Samir as he went to his room to get the board. Sarah and Aliyah began chatting, which allowed Raheem to reply to Veronica's text messages. It was wrong for him to be doing this, but he had no choice.

They were halfway through the game when Raheem said, 'Can I show you all a magic trick?'

The other three looked at him. 'Go on then,' said Aliyah.

Raheem raised his hands. 'I need you all to raise your hands.'

Aliyah was the first, followed by Sarah and eventually Samir. Raheem put his hands into Samir's jeans' pocket and pulled out a wad of Monopoly money notes.

'Samir, you little cheat!' said Aliyah as Samir tried to snatch them back.

'How did you know?' he asked moodily as he sat back down.

'Because I would have done the same thing if I'd gone to get the Monopoly board from my room,' Raheem sniggered.

Aliyah was beside herself laughing.

'So, you would have cheated. Is that what you're saying?' Sarah demanded. Talk about killing the mood.

'No, I was joking. I'm not a cheater like him.' Raheem avoided making eye contact with Samir. He knew they were both thinking the exact same thing. Thankfully, Sarah did not elaborate.

They played until Raheem won the game. Sarah was going to drop Aliyah home on the way back.

'I'm going to go gym for a bit' said Samir as the girls left.

'Shut the fuck up and get inside' said Raheem. Samir slouched into the kitchen to wash the plates. He had come last again.

***

As ever when it was exam and deadline time, the university was packed. Getting a space in the library was a luxury.

Raheem spent most of his time with Aliyah on the third floor. They made notes together and tested each other on practice exam questions. Samir occasionally joined them, but more often than not he was with Rachel on the first floor. Veronica flitted between floors, sometimes bringing her friends with her to sit at the table with them.

Raheem had reminded her on more than one occasion not to mention to anyone that they were together. He also told her that whenever he was with Aliyah, Veronica needed to sit with them on the pretext that she was seeing Aliyah and not him. When Veronica asked him why he was so scared of other people knowing they were dating, he changed the subject.

He had been studying in the Parkview building on Mondays whenever Sarah was with him. Thankfully Veronica would be at work on Monday mornings and usually went home after her shift finished. That didn't stop her from always texting him whilst she was at work. He supposed he should be thankful that Veronica was a good distance away whenever Sarah was at the university. He had tried to swap his Wednesday evening shift permanently for Monday mornings, but was not successful. Most of his colleagues were students and had different timetables at University.

Raheem had sent an email to Ben, one of the student representatives, asking if he could raise the issue of allowing members of the public to enter the university on Mondays. Ben emailed back saying that the university had no plans to reconsider. When Raheem asked why, Ben sent him another email with pound and dollar signs. It looked like he would just have to hope that Sarah and Veronica didn't meet before he finished his third year.

***

Raheem was walking around the lake in Burydale Park with Sarah a week before he left for Manchester for the Christmas holidays. Sarah had rung him last night to say that she had something important to tell him.

Jason, the most irritating human being on earth, probably on any planet, happened to have chosen to come to the park the same day.

Raheem slouched moodily behind Sarah and Jason as they began another round of the lake. Once those two got started, they would never shut up.

'How was the financial reporting exam? It was so hard last year,' said Sarah.

'It was okay. I'm pretty sure I passed it. How's your work going?' Jason replied.

Raheem resisted the temptation to throw Jason into the lake. Sarah wouldn't take too kindly to it, particularly if Jason drowned.

After three-quarters of an hour, they completed their walk. Thankfully, Jason had a dentist's appointment in twenty minutes. He shook Raheem's hand and hugged Sarah before walking away a lot more quickly than he had done around the lake.

'He's so lovely.' Sarah locked arms with Raheem as they headed for their favourite bench.

Raheem bit back a retort. What did Jason have that he didn't? Maybe he was the type who listened to Sarah's every demand. That would be it – why else would she call him lovely?

They reached their bench, which had a perfect view of the lake. This was where they had shared their first kiss; whenever they walked in the park, they made sure that they sat on it.

Sarah sat down and Raheem lay with his head on her lap. 'What was it you wanted to talk to me about?' he asked as she stroked his hair.

She did not respond straightaway but looked across the lake, deep in thought. 'Aaron has moved to Stalford for six months. We have started speaking again recently,' she said quietly.

Raheem sat up. Sarah rarely spoke about her family; it was a subject she did not like discussing with anyone, including him. Her mother had passed away when she had been four years old and her father had re-married. He knew that she had a half-brother called Aaron, but they hadn't spoken for many years. Sarah had told him when they first started dating that it was just her and her dad at home. So that was why she'd been going back to Birmingham more often than usual during the last few months. 'Is everything okay?' he asked.

Sarah tied her hair back in a ponytail before responding. 'We've sorted things out. I'm talking to his mum…my step-mum as well. Dad really wanted us to get on. After all, he is my half- brother. The issue was never really with him, more with his mum. But that's in the past now. We all want to move on from it and start fresh.'

Raheem nodded. 'When did Aaron move up?' he asked.

'He got his flat a few weeks ago. He came to open his company's new office here and will go back to Birmingham in May.'

Why hadn't she told him this earlier? As though she had read his mind, she continued, 'I wanted to wait and see if things were okay between me and Aaron before I told you. Hope you don't mind.'

He couldn't blame her for that. 'You did the right thing. I'm glad things worked out well,' he said. They embraced. If only he could wind the clock back and not have cheated on her. Now, more than ever he regretted it.

'I've told him about you. He wants to meet you, if that's okay?' said Sarah as they broke apart.

'Erm, what exactly does he want to meet me about?' Raheem asked slowly.

Sarah raised her eyebrows. 'He's my brother, and naturally he is looking out for me.' She sounded much more like her old self. 'He wants to make sure that I'm with someone who can take care of me and isn't messing me around. Any brother would do the same.'

Raheem was not particularly thrilled about that, but he didn't want to let her down. 'Let me know when he wants to meet,' he said brightly.

Sarah beamed. 'Great! We'll sort out a date when you come back from Manchester after Christmas. He was going to meet you yesterday, but he had a call from his office in Birmingham and he needed to go back there.'

'What does he do?'

'He's an IT consultant. His company opened an office in Stalford last month.'

'Was this the only city they could find to open their office?' muttered Raheem.

'What?'

'I said it was a good job they opened their office here.'

Sarah held his face in her hands. 'I'm already looking forward to you meeting him!'

He smiled, but his nerves were jangling. Sarah still looked as though she wanted to tell him something. 'What is it?' he asked.

She opened her mouth but closed it again and shook her head. 'Nothing,' she said pleasantly.

Past experience had taught him that no matter how much he asked, she would not change her mind. He lay down and put his head on her lap again. They stayed there for another hour before deciding to go home.

Raheem drove back to Sarah's apartment and they kissed goodbye. As he was about to drive off, Sarah was still standing outside the gate to her apartment, watching him. 'What's up?' he asked, reversing his car back and lowering the passenger seat window.

Sarah looked as if she were in two minds. 'I'm just going to say that Aaron is nice, but he doesn't like anyone messing him around, so please make sure you behave. His sense of humour is very different to yours.'

'I will behave. Don't worry.'

She blew a kiss at him before opening the electric gate with her fob. Raheem sat back in his seat. This was the last thing he needed.

Chapter 10

The clock at the front of the exam hall showed it was 2.30pm. Raheem still had half an hour to answer his final question: *Discuss how social changes can affect policy development.*

Aliyah was scribbling away to his right. As though she could sense him watching her, she looked up and he grinned at her. He couldn't help it; she always gave him a reason to smile. Aliyah smiled back. For a few seconds they looked at each other before the examiner walked past, coughing slightly. Raheem pulled a face and returned to his paper.

Two hours later he was with Aliyah, Samir and Rachel in Broadway Shopping Centre. It was rammed. Everywhere they looked, they could see Christmas lights and decorations. 'It's so busy,' moaned Raheem as they stood just inside the north car park entrance, holding the coffees they'd bought from Café Nero.

'I know, Raheem. Who would have thought it would be busy so close to Christmas?' Aliyah rolled her eyes.

'Don't try be funny with me,' said Raheem, pretending to throw his coffee at her.

Aliyah must have thought he was actually going to do it because she jumped backwards and nearly bumped into the security guard. 'Sorry,' she said breathlessly as the guard gave her an angry look. He looked absolutely shattered and Raheem couldn't blame him. The build up to Christmas was hectic in any shopping centre, let alone the busiest one in Stalford.

'Can you two keep your violence at home and not in public?' Samir finished his cup and threw it in the bin. He wasn't the biggest fan of shopping either, but Rachel had made him come.

'So, what's the plan?' asked Aliyah.

Rachel, who'd been busy looking at the shopping centre map, said, 'I need to buy some new gloves and scarves. It's going to snow in Newcastle next week apparently.'

'You guys always get the snow up north. We haven't had any for the last two years,' said Aliyah. 'It used to snow a lot more before.'

'Good. I hate snow,' said Raheem. It was one of those things he'd enjoyed as a kid but now it was just an inconvenience.

'I'm sure it's got nothing to do with the fact that you got whitewashed last year in Manchester,' retorted Aliyah. 'I wish I'd been there to see it.'

Everyone except Raheem laughed. Some teenagers had thrown snowballs at him last year while he was trying to clear his car. He had tried to run after them but tripped and fallen face first into the snow. Most unfortunately, Samir and Rachel had witnessed it.

'Come on, let's go to Next. I can get my stuff there,' Rachel said.

'I'll come with you to Next. Aliyah, you go with Raheem to Boots – you said you wanted to get a few things,' Samir instructed.

'Let's stick together,' said Raheem.

Samir shook his head. 'No, I can't stand shopping with you. You're the worst person to shop with.'

'Look who's talking' said Raheem.

'So, you're just going to dump him on me?' asked Aliyah.

'Sorry about that, but you're the only one who can keep him under control. We'll meet you in the food court in forty-five minutes.' Samir grabbed Rachel's hand and set off, leaving Raheem and Aliyah together.

'Come on, then,' said Aliyah. Raheem finished his coffee and lobbed it into the bin before following her. 'I hope I passed the exam today,' she continued as they went up the escalator. Aliyah always liked going through the exam afterwards, but sitting it once was more than enough for him.

'Don't worry, you'll pass. What do you need to get?'

'A facial scrub, eyeliner and shampoo,' she replied as they entered Boots. Half an hour later they were still there. Aliyah had not managed to pick a facial scrub, eyeliner or shampoo.

'This shampoo looks good, I think' said Raheem, but before he could pick it up his phone rang. Veronica was calling him. 'I'll be back two minutes,' he said.

Aliyah nodded, her eyes still scanning the shampoo shelf. Raheem hurried out of the store and answered the phone.

'Where are you?' Veronica demanded before he could say hello.

'Just in…'

'Boots?'

Raheem nearly dropped his phone in panic. 'No,' he said stupidly. There was a pause. 'Hello?' he asked, gritting his teeth. Veronica had gone back to Leicester the previous day, so how did she know?

'Don't lie. I know you're in Boots with a girl. I've just been told,' she said accusingly.

'Who told you?'

'One of my mates has seen you. With another girl. Who are you with, Raheem?'

There was no privacy in this world. 'I'm with Aliyah. Samir and Rachel are here as well!' Raheem grimaced, waiting for Veronica's response.

'Oh.' She paused. 'Sorry. I think my friend made too much out of it.' Apparently Veronica had made nothing of it.

'Which friend is this?' he asked, doubting he would get an answer.

'Just a friend from uni. But why did you say you weren't in Boots when I asked?'

They never gave up. They always found something to cling onto. 'I answered the call *outside* Boots, so technically I wasn't *in* Boots when you asked me.'

'Ha-ha. I guess you're right. Anyway, I'll ring you later tonight. Love you.'

'Love you too. Bye.' Raheem was not at all reluctant to end the conversation. He put his phone back in his pocket. He'd taken one step back into Boots when it rang again. For goodness' sake!

'We just said bye,' said Raheem wearily as he answered.

'What are you on about, Raheem?' came Sarah's voice.

For the second time in a few minutes, he nearly dropped his phone. 'Nothing, nothing! I thought it was Samir!' he said hastily.

102

'Must be easy getting our names confused as they both begin with the same letter,' said Sarah coolly.

There was no point responding. The situation was too dangerous.

'Where are you?' she asked predictably.

'Just in Broadway.' Raheem decided on the spot it was best not to lie.

'With?'

'Aliyah, Samir and Rachel. It wasn't my idea. I hate shopping with everyone. Except you.'

'I can tell how much you like shopping with me. Shall I come down to Manchester during the holidays? I've got the full two weeks off.'

'I think it might snow, you know,' Raheem said casually. For the first time in years, he hoped it would, so badly that no one could possibly drive. Or get the train.

Sarah tutted. He spent the next two minutes telling her how much he would miss her during the holidays before they ended the call. As Raheem went back inside Boots, his phone rang again. 'Fucking hell!' he muttered angrily. He checked who it was before answering. It was Samir.

'Where are you? Come to the food court,' said Samir.

Three times in ten minutes Raheem had been asked where he was. Why did everyone want to know? 'Coming man. Give me one minute,' he said grumpily before disconnecting. He took deep breaths to calm himself. The next person who asked him where he was would be getting a right earful.

He jumped when he received a tap on the shoulder, but thankfully it was Aliyah. She was carrying a bag with her items in it. 'Where were you? I finished five minutes ago,' she said.

Raheem smiled meekly. The person *after* Aliyah who asked him where he was would get an earful, and judging by the fact his phone was ringing yet again, that person would be Samir.

***

It was nearly two in the morning, but Raheem was finding it difficult to sleep. He was going through his text messages with Sarah from earlier that day.

Are you even missing me? she'd asked.

Yeah course I am xx

You're not acting like it

Really I am! xxxxxxxxxxxxxxx

How's your family? X

They good thanks how's Aaron x

He's good, can't wait till you meet him when you come back! xxx

Looking forward to it already! x

Raheem began scrolling through his messages with Veronica.

Miss you xxx, Veronica had texted.

I miss u too. x

Aww, don't worry, we will meet up soon xxx

Yeah sure x

Do you wanna have a chat on the phone? xxx

No I wanna have a chat on the tv instead ☺

My baby is so funny xxx

Ha-ha I'm just with my family at the moment but will call you tomorrow x

Great speak to you then! xxx

He put his phone on his bedside table and stared into the darkness. It was only a matter of time before Sarah or Veronica found out. Would Sarah forgive him if she discovered that he'd cheated on her? He wouldn't deserve to be forgiven, that was for sure, and the hurt he would see in Sarah's eyes would be the worst punishment of all. If only he'd listened to Samir. If only he had not begun talking to Veronica. He had been about to drop her off home that night but she had kissed him first. Not that it made him feel any less guilty.

He needed something to distract him. He grabbed his phone and called Aliyah. She answered straightaway. 'Hi, Raheem.'

'Hey, how you doing? Sorry for the late call, I couldn't get to sleep.'

'Me neither. I was thinking about the exams we had.'

'Don't worry, you'll be fine. What you been up to?'

'I watched *The Lion King* with my niece. She's staying over with us for a week during the holidays.'

'I bet you liked it more than she did! It's all about the life of- I mean circle of life.'

'Yeah, you're right! What have you been up to during the holidays?'

They spoke for almost two hours. Something about talking to Aliyah put him at ease, no matter how bad he felt. At 4am, his eyelids started to droop. Aliyah's voice was getting softer and softer. He wished she could keep talking until he fell asleep but he needed to let her sleep too. She wouldn't tell if him she was tired.

'Aliyah, thanks for answering but I think you need to sleep.'

She stifled a yawn. 'I guess you're right. You take care now.'

'Will do, bye.'

'Bye.'

He switched off his phone and put in on his bedside table before closing his eyes. He couldn't wait to see Aliyah again.

***

It was Saturday afternoon at the Broadway Shopping Centre. Raheem's Christmas break had given him to time to reflect on his situation and he still had no idea what to do about Veronica.

He'd been tempted to call her on a couple of occasions and try end it with her but had backed out each time. How could he end a relationship without a valid reason? It wasn't as if they argued all the time or hardly spoke. He would just have to make do for now.

The one promise he'd stuck to was not to stay over in her flat or let her stay at his. But he needed to think of something quickly because she would surely pick up on that sooner rather than later. She had already hinted to him that they should spend the nights together at her place whenever her cousin Jasmine went back to Leicester for the weekend.

Sarah had called him at nine o'clock while he was still in bed to remind him that he was supposed to be taking her shopping. Raheem had promised her they'd go once he returned from Manchester, but he had forgotten to book a day off work. He called in sick, coughing as hard as he could down the phone; it was either that or Sarah giving him a load of grief for the next month for committing the unforgivable crime of missing shopping.

She came out of the fitting rooms for the fourth time. This time she was wearing a lilac-coloured dress and heels. Most unfortunately, the world had not ended on 21st December.

'What do you think?' she asked, giving him a twirl and nearly twisting her ankle.

'Great. I think it really suits you. Come on, let's pay,' he said, also for the fourth time.

Sarah put her hands on her hips. 'You've said that every time. I don't think you're even interested.'

A staff member who was folding jeans heard her and grinned at Raheem.

'What can I say? Your beauty is to lie... I mean die for' he said innocently. The staff member was shaking with silent laughter. Raheem didn't like that dress but he just wanted to get out of here.

'Don't try being cute with me. Then again, I do like this dress.' Sarah checked her reflection in the mirror.

'Brilliant. I'll wait for you at the till.'

Sarah went back into the fitting room again. The staff member who'd been laughing popped his head around a clothing rail. 'To lie for, eh?' he said.

Raheem raised a finger to his lips and pointed towards the fitting room. The man nodded, still grinning, as Raheem turned away and headed for the till. Sarah eventually joined him and he paid for her outfit. Sarah always paid for his clothes when they went shopping and he paid for hers.

'Come on, then. What are we waiting for?' Raheem turned and saw her fiddling with her bag.

'I need to return this cardigan I bought last week from Debenhams. I didn't get the chance to try it on in the store and it doesn't suit me,' she said. 'I should have listened to Natasha. Also, it has a little hole near the sleeve.'

Raheem bit his tongue to stop himself saying something. That was typical Sarah. When she was shopping with her friends, she didn't bother trying on anything, whereas when she was with him she wanted to try on everything in the store. 'I need to make a call. I'll wait for you in the car, if that's okay?' he said, instantly regretting that he'd said he had to make a call.

'Who do you need to call?'

'Just Samir. Something about his dissertation. He needs a bit of help and I promised him I'd ring him today while I was with you.' Why hadn't he just said he needed to go to the toilet or something?

'Okay, I'll go on my own then,' said Sarah coldly. Without waiting for a reply, she moved past him out of the store. Cursing to himself, Raheem walked out of the front entrance into the car park. He had no choice but to call Samir now, in case Sarah checked.

After what seemed like an age, Samir answered. 'Hello,' he said groggily. He sounded as though he were still in bed.

'It's me speaking. Don't ask me why, just keep the call on, and after a few minutes I'll disconnect it,' said Raheem tonelessly.

'It's also me speaking, and okay,' replied Samir, yawning. That was the thing with guys. No questions.

'Are you still in bed?'

'Yeah. Need to go library in a bit and get some work done. Katie has just left. I dropped her off at the train station earlier.'

'You're wasting your time with Katie. How many times have I told you? Stick with Rachel.'

'You can't take it that both my girlfriends are fitter than yours.'

'In your dreams bro. Ver-Sarah is better than both of yours combined. Anyway, go back to sleep. I'll disconnect in a bit.'

'Okay.'

Raheem put his phone down on the passenger seat. A car was reversing into the bay next to him, getting very close. 'Fucking hell,' he muttered. People seemed to be obsessed with parking close to him. There were kids in the back of this one, and he knew they would hit his car when they opened the door.

He was just about to indicate to the driver to park properly when Sarah called him. He disconnected the call to Samir and answered. 'Sorry, I was on the phone to—'

'Can you come into Debenhams? Like now?' she interrupted.

'Uh, why? What's up?' he asked nervously. Veronica was still in Leicester. Surely she hadn't come back early, and to Broadway of all places?

'They are not letting me get a refund, they're only offering me an exchange and I don't want that. I want a refund!' she said shrilly.

Raheem started laughing. 'Give me two minutes and I'll be there,' he said, relieved.

'What's funny about that?'

'Nothing! Just seen this guy dancing in the car park, that's what I was laughing about.'

'Right.'

'I'm coming now.' He got out of his car, hitting his door on the car next to his. 'Shit!' he said angrily, running his hands through his hair as the driver got out.

After apologising profusely to the driver, he went to Debenhams. Raheem had offered the driver some money for the scratch, but he'd accepted that he'd parked too closely and told him not to worry about it. Thankfully for Raheem, the car he'd hit was an old Nissan Micra as opposed to a Mercedes.

A few minutes later he was in Debenhams with Sarah, who was arguing with a supervisor. She had lost the receipt and the policy was no refund without receipt – not that the policy mattered to her.

The supervisor was a blonde woman Raheem had seen a few times on his nights out during his first year at university. From the way she was looking at him, it seemed that she also recognised him. 'Hi,' said Raheem, smiling at her.

Her blue eyes took him in before she greeted him. He suddenly remembered he was with Sarah and hastily asked why they could not get a refund. Sarah had been insisting the hole near the sleeve had been there when she'd tried it on at home.

After five minutes of negotiating, with many smiles from Raheem, the supervisor agreed to a refund. To his surprise, Sarah did not look pleased. She went to the till to collect her refund and then walked out of the store, leaving Raheem to hurry after her. 'Did you like my negotiation skills Sarah?' he asked as he put his arm around her.

'Really good Raheem. I hope they are as good next time, when it's not a pretty blonde,' she replied coldly.

'What's that supposed to mean?' No matter what he did, it seemed that Sarah would never be pleased with him.

'You know what I mean.' She still wouldn't look at him.

Raheem couldn't understand what the issue was. He'd got her what she wanted and still she was not happy. 'Come on, babe. I had to be polite, didn't I? Otherwise, she wouldn't have given you the refund.' He kissed her on the cheek but Sarah did not respond.

'I think the issue is that you got a bit jealous seeing me chatting to her,' he said quietly, watching her closely for her reaction.

Sarah grinned, which Raheem took as a good sign. 'Maybe,' she said, finally looking at him.

'Well, all I can say is that she might be good looking but with you around she has no chance with me.' He should have thought of that when he was with Veronica. If Sarah was upset about the way he and the supervisor had smiled when speaking to each other, he couldn't even begin to imagine how she would react if she found out about Veronica.

They embraced once they were outside Broadway. 'Oh look, he's here! Let go, Raheem.' Sarah broke apart from him suddenly and looked over his shoulder. Raheem had just moved in for a kiss, but she shook her head and gestured with her eyes. 'I told you this morning on the phone that Aaron was meeting us today. Have you forgotten?' she hissed. 'Look behind you. He's walking towards us.'

Eh? He didn't remember that part. 'Oh, right. Sorry,' Raheem said hastily. He turned around, hitching a smile on his face.

A tall, well-built man was walking towards them. Raheem couldn't see his face clearly but something about him looked familiar. Only when he was fifty feet away did Raheem realise, with a shock that wiped the smile off his face, that the man walking purposefully towards them was the one he and Samir had fought with outside Tesco that night.

Chapter 11

Avoiding looking at Aaron, Raheem sipped his coffee. Sarah was sitting between them, clearly wanting one of them to speak. After nearly two minutes of silence, it must have dawned on her that she would have to break the ice. 'So, as you know, Aaron, this is Raheem.'

They both nodded but did not speak. Raheem had been sitting with one side of his face on his palm, trying to hide as much of it as possible. He wanted more than anything to leave.

'I think it's better if I leave for a while. It might be easier for you to talk,' said Sarah.

Raheem wanted to leave; he didn't want Sarah to leave. 'No, it's okay Sarah. You stay. I think—' he began

'Give us half an hour,' interrupted Aaron.

Sarah got to her feet. 'See you later.' She smiled at them both and fleetingly placed her hand on Raheem's shoulder as she left.

He looked at Aaron. 'Where do you work again?' It was all he could think of saying. He kept reminding himself that he'd had a scarf wrapped around his face the night of the fight and Samir had a facemask on, but he was worried his eyes would give him away.

'I'll tell you about me later. I want to get to know a bit about you first,' Aaron replied.

'No problem, ask away.' Raheem finally removed his hand from his face and sat up straight.

Aaron took a sip of his latte. 'Sarah has told me a lot about you. She has nothing but nice things to say.'

Raheem nodded. Part of him was relieved, but the rest was drenched in guilt.

Aaron continued. 'We come from a diverse family, as you're probably aware. I'm assuming your family doesn't have an issue with you being with a woman who's from a different ethnicity?'

They didn't have an issue because they didn't know, but he didn't want to tell Aaron that. 'We are very, um, libertarian when it comes to stuff like that,' said Raheem defensively.

Aaron looked at him as though he were trying to be funny. 'You mean liberal?'

'That's what I meant.' Raheem waved his hand dismissively.

Aaron looked as if he were having second thoughts about the 'nice things' Sarah had said.

'Due to family problems, me and Sarah haven't seen each other that much over the last few years but at the end of the day she is my sister. It's my job to look out for her.'

'I understand.'

Aaron had said he wanted to learn about Raheem, but he was talking about himself. 'I just want to make one thing clear to you.' They both leaned slightly towards each other as he continued, 'I don't want you messing my sister around.'

There was a short pause. 'Why would you think I'd do that?' asked Raheem calmly, although his insides were squirming.

Aaron took his time responding. 'You're a good-looking guy, Raheem, and you go to uni. I've been at uni myself, I know what it's like. I don't want you to do anything to break Sarah's heart. That's all I'm saying. I'm sure you understand what I mean.' It was quite clear what he was implying.

'What makes you think I would cheat on her?'

'I'm not saying you would.'

There was nothing to be gained from prolonging this dangerous topic. 'I get you,' said Raheem eventually. They sat in silence for a few moments.

'So, you're originally from Manchester, aren't you?' Aaron said.

Glad of the change of subject, Raheem told Aaron more about himself, after which Aaron told him about his work. He seemed to be one of those people who would take ages explaining a simple thing.

Raheem's phone buzzed with a message. She-Who-Must-Not-Be-Named had texted him to say she would be returning to Stalford tomorrow. He hastily put his phone back into his

111

pocket. 'Yeah, Stalford is a great place to live,' he said when Aaron finally shut up.

Aaron looked at him, his eyes narrowing. 'You know, I keep getting this feeling I've seen you before. You look familiar.'

Raheem's heart sank. 'You also look familiar, but I can honestly say that we have never met.'

Aaron looked at him thoughtfully. 'You know what? I think I have *heard* you before. Your voice sounds familiar.'

'I once sang a song on the radio. That's definitely where you would have heard me.'

For the first time during their conversation, Aaron smiled. It was a relief to know that he could do something as friendly as smile. 'Really?'

Raheem nodded. 'So where do you go on nights out?' he asked before Aaron could ask him what song it was. He'd never seen him at Sensations or any other club on a night out.

It was Aaron's turn to look uncomfortable. 'I've kind of stopped going out recently.'

'What do you mean?' It was a nice change to be the one interrogating as opposed to being interrogated.

'Do you work at Tesco, Raheem? Sarah mentioned it.'

She might as well have told Aaron his whole history. Why mention Tesco? Aaron was wearing a different watch to the one he had been wearing that night. His old watch was in Samir's drawer, but most unfortunately, Raheem would be unable to tell him that. 'Erm … yeah, I work at Tesco part-time. Not the one near uni though, one in the city centre.'

Raheem waited with bated breath. Aaron was going to tell him about the fight. He knew it. A few seconds went by and Aaron had still not said anything. 'So how come you have stopped going on nights out recently?' asked Raheem again.

Aaron sighed. 'Look, I'm going to be honest with you. I'd rather just get it out.'

Raheem sat up in his chair. 'Go on, then.'

Before Aaron could say anything, Raheem felt a hand on his shoulder. Sarah had returned. 'Hope you both actually said something while I was gone,' she said, smiling at them.

'I don't know if we said the word "Something" but we definitely spoke' replied Raheem.

112

'Ha-ha, good one. Aaron, you need to be aware that Raheem has got the worst jokes ever.' She sat between them. Raheem wanted to know what Aaron had wanted to tell him, but now Sarah was here Aaron didn't seem to want to discuss it.

They spent another hour in the cafe before deciding to leave. It was a good job that Aaron didn't seem to be the sharpest of people. Sarah had been right; he had a totally different sense of humour to Raheem.

They both insisted on dropping Sarah home. In the end, she tossed a coin and Raheem called correctly. They said goodbye to Aaron and went to sit in Raheem's car. 'How was it?' she asked eagerly the moment they got in.

'It was good,' replied Raheem, leaning across and kissing her. He had rarely seen her look so happy. How long that happiness would last if she ever found out about Veronica, or the fact that he and Samir had a fight with Aaron, was something he did not want to think about.

***

'Please tell me you're fucking joking?'

'I'm not joking, Samir.'

'What are the chances of that happening?'

'About as likely as you saying something helpful. In other words, none.'

Samir sat back on the sofa, still looking as though he did not believe what Raheem had just told him. Raheem received another text on his phone from Veronica, asking him why he hadn't responded to her first one.

'What you going do about Veronica?' asked Samir.

Raheem puffed out his cheeks. 'I don't know, but the more time I spend with Sarah, the more I feel like being with Veronica. The more I am with Veronica, the more I feel like being with Sarah.'

'Why's that?'

Raheem scratched his head. 'Not sure. It's hard to explain.'

Samir looked at him thoughtfully. 'To be honest, I think you have an ego thing.'

'Ego thing?'

113

'Basically, with Veronica it's your ego. You just want to be with her because it gets you thinking you've achieved something. You know all the guys at uni like her, you've seen it yourself when we've gone on nights out with her. She's always getting the attention. Samir took out his phone and sent a text message.

'Who do you keep messaging?' asked Raheem. 'I've noticed you're on your phone a lot more. Have you got another girlfriend?'

'I'm messaging Rachel. Don't change the subject. Just tell me, am I right, or am I right?'

Raheem considered it for a moment, before saying, 'So what should I do? Aaron basically told me that if he catches me cheating on Sarah he's going to knock the shit out of me.'

'I have an idea how to avoid that ever happening.'

'How?' said Raheem, sitting up straighter. It seemed that the day when his cousin would give helpful advice had finally arrived.

'You forget about Sarah and Veronica,' Samir said abruptly as he stood up.

'What?'

'I said you forget about Sarah and Veronica. It's best you end it with both of them.'

Raheem threw the remote at him. It narrowly missed Samir's head and went straight out of the open window.

***

Nothing dramatic happened over the next couple of weeks. Aaron was busy with his job, so Raheem never got the chance to ask him what he had wanted to tell him. Raheem and Sarah were being more polite with each other than usual, but nothing out of the ordinary.

As Raheem had anticipated, Veronica kept asking him why they always had to meet outside and never in his flat. He made excuses that Rachel and Katie kept asking to stay over. Veronica had unloaded on Samir about cheating on Rachel; She had always thought Katie had been Samir's friend. That had been the most uncomfortable ten minutes Raheem had ever

114

experienced as he agreed with Veronica whilst Samir looked at him in disbelief.

It was a cold Monday afternoon in the last week of January. Raheem was sitting in his first seminar of his second and final semester. 'Everything okay there, boys?' called Michelle. The class turned around as Raheem and Ryan looked up from the back row.

'All good, thanks,' said Raheem.

Michelle gave them a reproachful look before addressing the class.

'I need five tickets for the United match this time. My brother wants to go as well,' muttered Raheem.

'It will be £160 if you need five,' whispered Ryan.

'Shut the fuck up! That's a rip off!' Raheem protested indignantly.

'Are you *sure* everything is okay?' Michelle was staring at them. She was not as successful at keeping the anger out of her voice this time. 'If anyone wants to leave, be my guest,' she continued when neither of them responded.

Raheem suddenly stood up and walked slowly towards the door. The entire class was silent. He took an empty chewing-gum packet from his pocket and put it in the bin before walking back to his seat.

***

'I'm going to miss you when we leave uni, Raheem!' said Hannah half an hour later as they were walking down the corridor.

Ryan had gone to his appointment with his dissertation supervisor on the eighth floor, a task made a lot harder because the lifts were broken. The whole class had started laughing when Raheem had returned to his seat because they'd thought he was about to leave. He had even made Michelle crack a smile, which was one of the greatest accomplishments of his life.

'At least *someone*'s going to miss me.' Raheem raised his voice as he passed Aliyah and some of her friends who were standing in line outside the student union coffee bar. Aliyah gave him a smile, which he returned.

Hannah continued to follow him, even though he had no clue where he was going. They carried on through the corridor until they reached the entrance to the library. 'Where's Samir? I haven't seen him for a while,' she asked. Right on cue, Samir walked through the university entrance with Rachel.

'Lucky you. I have to see him every day,' said Raheem, as Samir spotted him and came over.

'Hi, we were just talking about you!' said Hannah.

Rachel said hello to Raheem, who returned the greeting. They had been nicer to each other since they had spoken outside Tesco before Christmas.

'Hope it was something good,' said Samir.

'Is that even possible?' Raheem said.

Samir aimed a kick at him. 'What you up to, anyway?' he asked as they went into the library.

'I need to make more notes on the seminar we just had,' Raheem said. He had made some notes but getting a good mark in Michelle's module on criminology theory would go a long way towards securing a first-class degree. He would have settled for a two-one degree, but getting a first would be a huge bonus. It wouldn't have been possible without Aliyah.

'How are you getting on with your dissertation?' Rachel asked him as they climbed the stairs.

'Not bad. I need to add my survey and interview results. Thanks for filling out my questionnaire,' he replied. He might as well get started on that, and he could do the notes for Michelle's module with Aliyah.

He had conducted interviews with students just before the Christmas holidays. Some had been really interested in his dissertation topic, others irritated. Maybe sitting at their table uninvited and shoving his questionnaire under their noses had something to do with that irritation.

Hannah said she was going to the third-floor silent-study room to do some reading. They said goodbye to her and entered the first floor.

'Watch it, man,' muttered Raheem as a guy who was staring at his phone barged into him as he opened the door.

'Silly twat,' said Samir. They headed to a table in the centre of the library.

'Didn't even say sorry,' said Raheem angrily as they sat down on their table.

'I know. You need to learn to say sorry, Raheem. It will go a long way.'

So Samir had called *him* the twat? 'You're always cheating-I mean chatting shit. I don't know how Rachel copes.'

Rachel stroked Samir's hair. 'I think he's hilarious.'

Raheem took out his laptop. He needed to get a good couple of hours work done today, and the less hilarious Samir was the better.

After ten minutes, it became clear that Samir was not in the mood to work. He kept putting his hand on Rachel's lap, at which she giggled, irritating Raheem. 'Why don't you two go back to the flat?' he suggested politely the fourth time it happened.

'Not like you to make a good suggestion, is it?' replied Samir, grabbing Rachel's hand and standing up.

Raheem smiled sarcastically and waved them off. Perhaps now he would finally be able to concentrate.

Aliyah had texted him to say she would join him in the library soon. Raheem started creating graphs to show his questionnaire results but he was distracted by someone taking a seat opposite him. He looked up, grinning, expecting to see Aliyah. Instead, Aaron was taking off his blazer.

Raheem's grin disappeared. 'What you doing here?' he asked, taken aback.

'I've come to see someone. University is open to the public on Mondays,' Aaron replied defensively. He held out his hand and Raheem quickly shook it, his mind working frantically. Sarah had told him she was going out with Natasha and their girl gang during the day so couldn't come to the university, and Veronica was at work this time on a Monday.

'What you thinking about?' asked Aaron.

'Nothing,' said Raheem automatically. The last thing he needed was Aaron to be here in a library full of students who had seen him numerous times on nights out. 'So, what was that thing you wanted to tell me about the other day?' he asked

117

before Aaron could dictate how the conversation went. He must have had a haircut over the weekend, as the left-hand side had a horrible line design. It would be better not to comment about it.

'I had a drink problem over the last year.' For someone who liked to drag out a conversation, that was pretty upfront.

'You had. So, you don't currently have one?' Raheem asked.

'I'm working on it. I just went through a bad phase. Got into a bit of trouble here and there. But I want to get my life back on track.'

'That's good. Does Sarah know about this?'

'Yeah, she does. I also used to get high quite a bit, but I haven't told her that. One of the reasons I wanted to work in the new office in Stalford was because I wanted a bit of a change. Sarah felt that maybe meeting some new people, like you, might help.'

'Change can be good,' Raheem said reassuringly as he checked his phone. He had three missed calls from Veronica but as it had been on silent he hadn't realised. Why was she calling him when she was at work?

As he stood up to go to the toilet, Hannah walked past their table and acknowledged him. Aaron's eyes followed her to where she sat down with her friends. 'Who is that?' he asked.

'Just a friend,' said Raheem. Aaron had still not mentioned anything about the fight. Maybe he'd been so stoned that night that he'd forgotten about it, or he didn't want to tell him about it. Raheem wasn't going to encourage him to do so, that was for sure.

He needed to return Veronica's calls – they must have been important if she'd called him three times from work. He got another text, telling him to call her urgently. She had probably finished early today and needed a lift or something. He made to leave but remembered something and turned back to Aaron. 'You told me you had a drinking problem. What caused it?'

Aaron was about to respond when he looked over Raheem's shoulder and raised his hand. Raheem turned around to look and his jaw dropped. Walking towards them, wearing more makeup than a model on a catwalk, her handbag swinging from her hips, was Veronica.

Chapter 12

If his legs could have moved, Raheem would have run out of the door but he seemed to have lost all feeling in them. He stayed rooted to the spot as Veronica reached their table. She was busy messaging on her phone and didn't seem to realise he was there.

'Hey,' said Aaron as Veronica sat next to him. She smiled then spotted Raheem. For a fleeting moment her eyes widened in shock, but Aaron was having a coughing fit so didn't notice.

'Veronica, this is Raheem. Raheem, this is Veronica,' choked Aaron.

Being introduced to someone he had slept with was really strange. Raheem tried to speak, but the lump in his throat prevented him from doing so.

'Hi, Raheem, nice to meet you,' said Veronica.

Raheem stared at her before nodding his head. His throat was still dry. Veronica extended her hand and he shook it. For the briefest of moments her hand tightened on his.

'Have you guys not met each other before?' Aaron asked, looking from one to the other.

They had. Too many times.

'No, we have never met. I don't think we have – I mean, I haven't seen you before.' Raheem found his way to his seat and sat down.

'I've seen you around uni,' Veronica said sweetly.

What the hell was going on? How did Veronica know Aaron? Raheem ducked under the table to tie his shoelaces, or rather untie them first so that he could tie them again.

'Sarah is out at the moment. I'll introduce you to her in a couple of weeks,' Aaron said.

'That's fine. How do *you* guys know each other?' Veronica replied.

Raheem lifted his head and banged it on the table.

'Raheem is the lucky man who Sarah is with,' Aaron said.

Shit. Shit, shit, shit.

Veronica gave Raheem a filthy look as he re-emerged, having tied his shoelaces three times. 'Oh, I never knew,' she said tonelessly.

'You wouldn't have known, would you? I just told you for the first time now,' said Aaron.

It was time for Raheem to leave. He couldn't take the tension anymore. His brain was scrambled. 'Anyway guys, good chatting to you but I really need to go. I'll catch you next time.' He got to his feet.

'No worries.' Aaron nodded at him.

Veronica was still giving him daggers. 'I'll see you around,' she said.

'Yeah, sure. What s-subject do you study?' Raheem wiped his forehead with his sleeve.

'I do business management. What about yourself?' said Veronica. She really was a natural when it came to acting.

'I do criminology with psychology.'

'I wish I did psychology. It really would help me understand people,' she said coolly.

Wow. The audacity. 'Ah, right, cool. To be honest, I haven't found it very helpful in understanding wom-people. Well, see you around.' Raheem turned and walked towards the entrance before hurrying back to pick up his bag, still unable to comprehend what had just happened.

***

Samir had driven back to university thinking that Raheem was going to announce he'd won the lottery. Instead, they were now heading out for their third cigarette in an hour. 'I told you not to get with Veronica,' he said angrily. 'But you don't listen! Are you happy now?'

It was a bit rich of Samir to lecture him about cheating, but Raheem had no one to blame but himself. Aaron and Veronica had gone into town an hour ago. Samir had met Aaron briefly, although Aaron had guessed who he was because Sarah had told him about Samir. There were so many women that Aaron could have been in a relationship with. Why Veronica of all

120

women? There were so many people they could have had a fight with. Why Sarah's brother? He had always got that feeling that Sarah and Veronica had some sort of connection. Now he knew that Aaron was that connection. He couldn't imagine a worse situation to land himself in. Life was not fair.

'Isn't that Jasmine?' asked Raheem as a group of women walked up the path outside their university.

'Why? Do you want to go out with her as well?' muttered Samir, fumbling in his pockets for a lighter.

Jasmine saw them looking and came over. 'Hi,' she said. Without waiting for a response, she took Samir's cigarette from his hand and lit it. 'Bye.' She casually walked away to re-join her friends.

'At least she had a lighter this time,' said Raheem.

Samir was looking aggrieved. 'What the fuck? Who does she think she is? She always nicks something off me.'

'Shut up. Don't start with her now.'

'Why you acting like it's my fault?'

'Listen, I'm not in the mood for your—'

'Look who it is, Dumb and Dumber.' Liam walked past them and entered the university.

Simultaneously, Raheem and Samir threw their cigarettes to the ground. 'I've been looking for an excuse to beat the shit out of him,' snarled Raheem as they walked back inside.

Liam was next to the security desk. 'Alright, fellas, how's things?' said Bill as they approached.

'Good, Bill. How's the missus? Still angry about the cancelled holiday to Spain last summer?' asked Raheem, glaring at Liam.

Before Bill could reply, he was distracted by his colleague who, by the sounds of it, had lost one of the keys to the back entrance.

'Dumb and Dumber, eh?' said Raheem quietly as he took a step towards Liam. They couldn't do much in front of the security guards, but after what had just happened he needed to take out his frustration.

'It's time to show him what happens when you get cheeky,' muttered Samir.

Liam had a strange smile on his face. 'I need to show *you* something, though,' he said mysteriously.

'Feel free, but don't be long. I'm in a rush to batter you before I go,' said Raheem.

Liam delved into his bag and took out a camera. It was one of those silver Toshiba ones that you could pick up from Argos. He held it up to their faces. 'Take a look at this.'

Raheem glanced at the screen and what he saw made his heart stand still. It was a picture of him holding hands with Veronica in Sensations. The photo changed; the next one showed Samir with his arms around Katie, with Raheem and Veronica in the background. Raheem had his hand on Veronica's waist.

The picture changed again. This one showed Veronica kissing Raheem on the cheek next to Samir, who was dancing with Katie. The next two were of Raheem sitting with Veronica in the library and Samir holding hands with Katie in town.

'Good quality, aren't they?' said Liam.

Good? Raheem had never seen anything so bad.

'I've never seen you two so quiet. What's the matter?' Liam leered at them.

Samir opened his mouth to speak but no words came out. Liam put his camera in his bag and put his arms around their shoulders. 'I think it's time we had a little chat,' he said.

'Here?' asked Samir, his voice a bit higher than usual.

He shook his head. Still with arms around them, he started to walk towards the library. 'No, I don't think so. I'd prefer somewhere a bit quieter.'

They had no choice but to go with him. Liam eventually let them go as they entered the ground floor of the library. 'Over here.' He pointed to the sofa in the corner where Raheem had seen Daniel looking depressed a few months ago.

Raheem and Samir sat side by side. Liam sat on the single seater opposite them.

'Look, don't show—' Samir began but Liam raised a finger to his lips.

'I think the time has come for me to do the talking,' he said. He glanced around. 'You two think you're some big guys around here, don't you?'

'No,' said Raheem.

Samir kept looking at the security desk, as though hoping the guards would go on their break simultaneously. Raheem didn't have the heart to tell him he was wasting his time.

Liam saw Samir looking and clicked his fingers. 'Look at me when I'm speaking to you,' he said. Samir's eyes snapped back to Liam. 'I'm going to get straight to the point. My course finishes on Friday, 13th May. I'm going to leave for the States two days later.'

Why was he telling them this?

Liam glanced around again before leaning forward. 'Five thousand pounds. I want that money, in cash, on Saturday 14th May.'

Five thousand pounds! Raheem and Samir looked at each other in disbelief.

Liam clicked his fingers again. 'You're lucky it's not more. But £2500 each sounds reasonable to me. If you don't give me the money, I'll show these photos to your girlfriends. I've done my research; I know where they live. I could have shown you these photos earlier but I just wanted to make sure I had all the information.'

'Where do they live then?' asked Raheem.

'Apartment 612, Sixth floor, Holt Gardens, and 24 Station Terrace,' he rattled off. So he had done his research.

'But he doesn't know which one lives where,' said Samir hopefully, as though that made a difference.

'Shut up, man,' muttered Raheem.

Liam was looking delighted. 'Breaking your ego is so satisfying. Also, I know you attacked someone. Remember that night when I saw you near the lift? I know it was outside Tesco.'

Why had they spoken so loudly that night in the library?

'Don't know what you are talking about,' Raheem said.

'You're lucky I have no proof,' he said quietly. 'But if I ever hear that police are looking into an incident that happened that night, I *might* give them a tip off.'

Raheem and Samir said nothing.

'There's only one way I'll give you the camera without the money,' continued Liam.

123

'How?' asked Raheem a little too eagerly. It was not as if his bank account were loaded. Dealing with two girlfriends was expensive.

Liam looked around yet again to make sure no one was passing. 'If you can set me up with that tall girl you're always with – Hannah. I'll hold a house party. Bring her there, she can have a few drinks and you two leave us together.'

He was having a laugh. 'Are you stupid?' said Raheem angrily.

Liam shrugged. 'I've been checking her out for the last year or so, but she knows you morons so I can't approach her. I've always had a thing for tall women, if you know what I mean.'

What the hell was he on about? 'She's got a nice body, goes to the gym and is tall. That's always been my type,' continued Liam, his expression misty eyed. 'It's one of my wishes to be with a British woman. That accent is so strong compared to the American one.'

'We can't do that for you,' said Samir in disgust.

Liam stood up and swung his bag over his shoulder. 'Your choice. I'm happy with the money instead. I'll tell you where you need to give it to me at a later date. Cash only. But Saturday 14th May is the *only* day you're going to give it. Not sooner, not later. So you better be free that day. Is that understood?'

Raheem had a sudden idea. 'Give us your number. At least we can discuss it?'

Liam looked at him thoughtfully. 'I reckon you're not as thick as this dog over here.' He nodded at Samir. 'But you're still dumb. No messages, no calls. Only face to face. I will let you know the location. I don't want to be done for blackmail now, do I?'

That was the end of that idea, then.

'You give me the money, I'll give you the camera and you can keep it.' Liam sniggered. 'It's a decent camera.'

Reluctantly, they nodded. Liam took one final look at them. 'Anyway, best be off. What's your address again? Just so I know where to go if you don't turn up with the money. Thirty-two, Ridge Way Grove?'

If he'd managed to get their girlfriends' addresses then how could they expect him not to know theirs? Still sniggering, he glanced back at them as he walked out of the library.

Samir put his head in his hands. Raheem put his hands on his head. They were screwed now.

***

Raheem called Sarah the moment he got back home. 'Are you okay? You sound worried,' she said.

'Everything is fine. Just thought I'd check how you are,' he replied.

Samir called Rachel once Raheem had finished with Sarah, but she didn't answer. He spent the next few minutes fretting until he received a text from her to say that she was with some friends and would call him later.

'She's put a kiss at the end of the text so everything is fine,' said Raheem reassuringly, as he handed Samir his phone back.

***

Raheem paced the living room as Samir punched the cushion into a more comfortable position. They had messed up alright. It wasn't just the fact that Liam had those pictures; he was demanding £5,000. It wasn't an impossible amount, but it was still a lot of money. Raheem's dad was expecting him to have some savings towards a deposit for a house, and Samir's dad expected the same of Samir. They had fleetingly thought of selling their cars, but they knew their parents would be suspicious. Plus, they still had their rent to pay until the end of May for their current flat.

They both dismissed the idea of trying to set up Hannah with Liam. Hannah was their mate and they'd never do that to her. They would rather give him the money. That much they agreed on.

Raheem stopped pacing and sat down on the floor. Earlier that day they'd received their results for the previous semester. They'd both done pretty well, but they weren't in the mood to celebrate. He didn't know what to do. All he knew was that if

Sarah found out, Aaron would find out. Samir would also be in trouble because those photos confirmed he'd known about Raheem and Veronica. That was assuming he survived Rachel's reaction. She would be after Raheem as he'd lied to her about Samir. And he hadn't even started thinking about the hurt they would cause their girlfriends.

Why had he cheated on Sarah? For him to do it with Aaron's girlfriend made matters a hundred times worse. But Liam didn't know that – or did he?

'Do you reckon he will show Sarah and Rachel the pictures?' asked Samir.

'Yeah, he will,' said Raheem. 'Remember when you asked me why he was being mouthy with us this year? Now you know why. He's planned this all along. We need to do something.'

'Like what?'

Raheem knew what the first thing they needed to do was, but after that he had no idea. 'First thing we need to do is talk to Veronica,' he said eventually.

'I told you not to be with her!'

'Keep your voice down!'

'Fuck you, arsehole. This has happened because of you. You never listen! You're so dumb, you see.'

'Swear down, Samir, you say one more thing and the only thing *you're* going to see is my fist in your face! Just shut the fuck up. I'm stressed as it is.' But all that happened when Samir shut up was that Raheem's mind went blank. They needed to find a way out of the situation. But what that way was, he had no clue.

Chapter 13

The moment the class was dismissed, Raheem said a hurried goodbye to Aliyah and headed for the library. Aliyah had not spoken to him during the lecture, communicating only through moody nods of the head. He couldn't complain because he'd been irritable with her all day, but that was because he'd not been sleeping well recently.

He hurried through the corridors, acknowledging Jermaine and Fiona as he walked past them. Aaron and Sarah were at work, so the library was the safest place to meet. Samir had texted him that he was on his way.

Inside the library, Hannah was with some friends on the way out of the ground floor. Her friend Lauren smiled flirtatiously at him. The last thing Raheem needed right now was another girlfriend.

'Hi, Raheem. You okay?' said Hannah brightly.

'I'm okay, thanks, just need to go do some work.' He gave her a quick high five, then entered the lift and pressed the button for the first floor. He still hadn't worked out how Liam thought he had a chance with Hannah. As if staring at her all the time was really going to make her fall in love with him.

'Room 104,' he muttered, checking the door numbers. Students had to book these rooms, because they were for group study. He reached it and peered through the glass pane. Veronica was sitting on the table. Raheem knocked, entered and glanced under the table. He needed to be sure they were alone.

'What you looking under the table for?' Veronica asked as he down put his bag.

'Just wanted to have a look at your legs,' he said casually.

Her eyes widened. 'Shut up! Someone could hear us!' she hissed.

'Well, they all know, don't they?' Raheem's voice was becoming louder with each word. He was in no mood to mess around. 'Let me tell you the full story, and then I have some questions for you madam.'

'I'm all ears,' she replied.

Just then, Samir barged into the room.

'Can you knock next time, please? You nearly gave me a heart attack,' said Raheem irritably

Samir walked out of the room and closed the door before knocking and re-entering. He sat on the computer desk, looking at them as though he were watching a film.

Raheem turned to Veronica. There was no point beating around the bush. 'Actually, before I *tell* you I want to *ask* you a question,' he said.

Veronica nodded. 'Normally when people ask something it's a question.'

He really wasn't in the mood for sarcastic comments, least of all from Veronica. 'Why didn't you tell me you had a boyfriend?'

'Why didn't you tell me you had a girlfriend?'

No matter how long he had thought about how he would justify the answer to that question, no justification was acceptable. 'Erm, okay, listen. Let's get straight to it. Yeah, I lied. I had – I mean, I *have* a girlfriend. Sarah.' The mention of her name sent a shiver down his spine.

'You know, I was thinking about this last night,' Veronica said thoughtfully. 'You've cheated on your girlfriend with the girlfriend of your girlfriend's brother.'

That sounded about right. He looked at Samir, who was texting on his phone. 'Can you get off your fucking phone? Who do you keep texting, your invisible friend?'

Samir looked up. 'I'm texting your dad.'

'Stop it, you two. I'm so confused!' said Veronica shrilly.

'Confused?' said Raheem angrily. 'I get I fucked up – at least I admit it – but what were you doing with me all this time? And why didn't you mention anything about Aaron?'

'There was no need to mention it! We weren't technically together; we were on a break! I wanted to see if I got on with you and then I could end it with Aaron. I should have guessed you had a girlfriend. No wonder you never invited me to your flat after that first night and kept making excuses.'

Raheem stared at her incredulously. 'So basically, you thought you'd get in a relationship with me and then decide who you preferred?'

'I feel so bad,' Veronica whispered.

And he felt great, didn't he?

'At least there's no proof we were together, Raheem. I've deleted our calls and messages from my phone,' she continued reassuringly. 'Make sure you do the same.'

That really was a big help. 'Wow, that is so clever of you, problem solved, I can't believe I never thought of that, how silly of me!'

'What do you mean?'

'You tell her, Samir. I don't have the energy,' said Raheem wearily.

'Tell me what?' said Veronica suspiciously.

Samir explained about the fight they'd had with Aaron, and about Liam. He didn't mention anything about Liam's request regarding Hannah. Veronica listened without moving an inch.

'The fight happened that night when you saw us on the ground floor in the library and Raheem was saying he'd gone to Tesco,' Samir finished.

'See, I told you I'd gone to Tesco. I wasn't lying,' Raheem said. Veronica smacked him across the head with her handbag.

'You're a fucking dog, Raheem!' she screeched. She swung her handbag again, narrowly missing him. Samir got up, eased her into a chair and took her handbag for good measure.

Raheem's blood was beginning to boil. 'Why you blaming me for everything? You were cheating as well!' he snarled. That still didn't justify what he'd done, but he needed to get his anger out somehow.

'Oh my God, Aaron is so possessive. Anyone would have done the same! Then he started getting drunk every night when we were out and I couldn't cope! I *wasn't* with him when I went out with you!' She looked as if she were about to cry.

Samir motioned at Raheem to calm down, but it was too late. Veronica was sobbing with her head in her hands. Samir got up from the table and put his arm around her. 'Don't worry, everything will be okay,' he said consolingly.

'It's not that,' spluttered Veronica, wiping her tears on Samir's jacket. He did not look best pleased but, given the situation, allowed her to do it.

'What is it then?' asked Raheem.

Veronica found a tissue and wiped her eyes. 'It's just... I don't know.'

Raheem's anger slowly ebbed. They'd both done wrong and nothing would be achieved by blaming each other. He put a hand on her shoulder 'We'll sort something out, don't worry.'

Veronica nodded, drying her eyes. 'I'm just so confused,' she spluttered.

'About why you and me got together?' asked Raheem.

'No, I don't mean that. It's just I can't decide between you and Aaron now!'

Eh?

'Whoa, what do you mean you can't decide?' Raheem's temper was rising again and his sympathy disappeared as quickly as it had come. Veronica looked at him, her face expressionless. 'You're with Aaron, I'm with Sarah. Forget about me and what happened between us,' he said angrily.

'How can I just forget it like that?'

'The same way you forgot you were with him when you went out with me!'

'I wasn't with him, we were ... on a break! Unlike you and Sarah!'

'Stop always comparing this to me and Sarah,' said Raheem exasperatedly.

'Why? It's the same thing. But at least I've got an excuse. Aaron cheated on me. Long story, and I'm not going into it, but I officially wasn't with him when I met you! Get that into your thick head.'

It was no use arguing with her. They had to be on the same page if they were to get out of the mess they were in. 'Look, Veronica, we both did wrong,' said Raheem in a voice of forced calm. 'We both felt that our girlfriends – I mean boyfriends ... no that's not right... What the fuck is the right word, Samir?'

'Partners, I think.'

'Isn't that when you're married?'

'Doesn't have to be, but feel free to think of your own word if you don't like it.'

Now was not the right time to have a debate. 'As I was saying,' said Raheem gritting his teeth, 'we both felt our *partners* were possessive, we... I cheated on mine and you "were on a break". We realise our mistake and we need to move on. Is that okay with everyone?'

Thankfully, Veronica nodded. Samir raised his hand.

'What?' asked Raheem.

'What shall I do about Rachel and Katie?'

Brilliant. Just what they needed.

'Bloody hell, I forgot about that,' moaned Raheem. 'Look, the main thing is that we need to get that camera. Also, Aaron will know that *you* knew that me and Veronica were going out together. We can deal with Sarah and Rachel later. We need to get rid of the evidence on that fucking camera. It's Aaron you need to worry about. From what I'm aware, he's got a lot of lads in Birmingham and they're crazy down there. I will need to call back-up from Manchester to deal with that.'

'He doesn't need any "lads". He can knock the shit out of both of you if he wants to,' said Veronica bitterly.

'Excuse me, I banged him out outside Tesco,' said Raheem, prickly.

'I helped as well' said Samir.

'You helped start it you daft twat.'

'Shut up, both of you!' said Veronica angrily. 'We need to work together.' There was a minute's silence, before she stood up. 'I've got a seminar now. We can arrange a place to meet to discuss this properly and decide the next steps.'

'That's fine by me,' said Samir. They both looked at Raheem.

'That's fine. Just one thing Veronica.' This was the hard part, but he needed to say it. 'We are only friends. There can be nothing further between us. We can't change what *has* happened, but we can change what *will* happen.'

Veronica looked as though she were going to cry again.

'Oh, shut up, man! You talk so much crap,' said Samir, smiling. 'Come on, Veronica, I'll walk with you to your class.'

'Thanks,' she said quietly.

'I'll meet you back here. We need to start our reports for Michelle. Don't forget we've still got a degree to complete,' Samir added to Raheem.

Raheem sat down. He could not let this overwhelm him. He still needed to live life as normally as possible. With a pang, he remembered that Michelle had asked for three thousand words for her report. Swearing under his breath, he took out his laptop and started to work.

***

Raheem spent the next few days trying to think of solutions to his problems, but his brain didn't seem to have any. Neither did Samir's, for that matter, which came as no surprise.

Sarah wasn't telling him off as much as usual, but she wasn't acting so differently that he thought something was wrong. Liam kept grinning at Raheem and Samir whenever he saw them in university and making gestures that looked as though he were taking a picture of them. He seemed to be coming to the city campus more often, despite the West Park campus being where most of his classes were. He would usually book the student meeting rooms and sit in there most of the day. They were not particularly thrilled about that.

Aliyah, on the other hand, was still annoyed with Raheem. She strode across the corridor towards the university exit. He ran past her to open the door before she could get to it. 'After you, madam,' he said, opening it for her and bowing.

She ignored him and headed through the automatic doors instead. Raheem hurried after her. She seemed to be heading for the Northern Tower, which was located opposite the university. They'd had some of their seminars there last year, and he'd studied there with Sarah sometimes in his first year when she was irritated by the noise on the first floor of the library.

'Are you not going to speak to me?' he asked, pretending to look upset as he caught up with Aliyah. She glanced at him as he walked alongside her but didn't respond, though the corners of her mouth were twitching as she tried not to smile.

They crossed the road and walked up the path towards the Northern Tower. They walked around the side of the building to enter from the courtyard entrance.

'Let me tell you a joke' said Raheem. 'What do you call a person with no body and no nose? If you don't know the answer it's okay, because nobody knows!'

Aliyah sniggered but did not speak. He would have to try something else. He grabbed Aliyah's arm and said, 'I like your watch. What time is it?'

'Raheem!' she screeched, trying to wrench her arm from his grip. He let go and her hand swiped through the air, hitting him on the nose.

'Argh!' he shouted, falling on the ground dramatically.

'Sorry Raheem it was an accident, are you okay!' Aliyah wailed, dropping to her knees beside him.

He closed his eyes and held his nose. It didn't hurt at all, but he was trying to cover his face so she couldn't see him grinning. 'I think my nose is broken. Call an ambulance quickly,' he muttered through his hands.

'I'm so sorry!' said Aliyah shrilly, panicking and taking out her phone.

Raheem removed his hands from his face and sat up. 'It's okay, I think it's fixed now.'

Aliyah turned to look at him, her phone still in her hand. 'I hate you! You scared me!' She squeezed his nose hard.

'That hurts!' he yelled, and she let go. His nose really was throbbing now.

'Serves you right.' Aliyah nudged him on the back with her foot. They both laughed and she held out her hand to help him up.

'I can't believe I have to fake pain for you to speak to me,' Raheem said indignantly as they crossed the courtyard and entered into the tower. There were a few students sitting outside waiting for their seminars. Northern Tower also had a café, although not as big as the Parkview one.

'Oh yeah, I forgot I was angry with you.' Aliyah ran into the lift which had just opened. He tried to follow but the doors closed, Aliyah waving at him as they slid shut.

She usually sat on one of the tables on the second floor when she came here. He had just turned around to take the stairs when the door to his right opened and Liam walked out of the toilets, followed by a member of staff who was on his phone. He saw Raheem looking at him, smirked and did his picture-taking gesture. It took all Raheem's self-control not to walk up and clobber him in the face.

Unclenching his fists, he headed upstairs. He found Aliyah at the corner table taking out her books and notepad. 'Wasn't difficult up the steps, was it? You took a while,' she asked as he sat down.

'Nope, it was really easy. Got a bit of exercise and burned some calories.' He sat next to her.

Aliyah started reading her notes from the lecture they'd just attended. 'Why have you been so moody recently?' she asked sternly.

The administration team's office door opened and a staff member walked out, turning off the lights behind him. The building was open until 9pm for students but the offices closed at five.

'Actually Aliyah, I need to talk to you about something.'

Aliyah had been concentrating on her notes but at Raheem's words she looked at him with concern. 'Is everything okay?'

Raheem took a deep breath. He'd decided the previous night to tell Aliyah the truth about his situation, firstly because he trusted her, and secondly because she always gave him good advice. However, he didn't know how to start to explain the problem he was in.

When he didn't speak, Aliyah said, 'Are you going to tell me, then? I've got something I need to tell you as well.'

'Go on, you tell me first,' he said. He should have planned his explanation better, but at least now he had a bit more time to decide what to say.

Aliyah put down her pen. 'I'm getting engaged in August.' A stunned silence greeted her words. She started tying back her hair, avoiding Raheem's gaze.

'You're what? he asked slowly.

Aliyah finished fixing her hair. 'I'm getting engaged.'

Raheem stared at her. He had not been expecting this. 'Why?'

Aliyah glared at him. 'What do you mean, "why"?'

'Whoa, sorry,' he said, taken aback.

Aliyah expression softened almost to one of pity. 'Sorry, Raheem, I didn't mean to get angry. I'm just a bit nervous about it. I don't really know him that well, but my family want me to get engaged so I've rushed into it. His dad's an old friend of my dad. The wedding will be end of this year, after which I'm moving to Glasgow.'

'G-Glasgow?'

'Yeah. That's where he lives.'

It was though a shard of ice had pierced his heart. Never had he been more lost for words than he was now. He had expected Aliyah to be with him always, but soon she would be gone.

'Why the sad face? Aren't you happy for me?' she asked.

Raheem blinked and looked at her. 'Course I am.'

'You don't look happy.'

He turned away and looked out of the window. Some students on the ground floor were sitting at tables opposite the café and chatting. He and Aliyah had sat there plenty of times last year having their heart-to-heart talks after their investigative psychology seminar on Friday afternoons.

'I am happy, just sad that you're going to be far away in Glasgow,' he said quietly. She looked at him sympathetically. 'Have you told anyone else?' he asked.

Aliyah shook her head. 'No, you're the first one. I was only planning on telling you and Samir for now. Please don't tell anyone. I'll announce it to others once I'm officially engaged. It's just going to be a small engagement ceremony and then the wedding at the end of the year.'

'What did Samir say when you told him?' Raheem was still trying to digest the news.

Aliyah looked confused. 'I haven't told him yet. I was planning to tell him after I told you.'

'Oh yeah, sorry, I just got a bit … mixed up…' What sort of friend was he? He hadn't even asked for Aliyah's soon-to-be fiancé's name. 'What's his name?'

'Imran.'

135

Raheem took out his phone and pretended to read a text message.

'So, not even a congratulations?' asked Aliyah.

What was wrong with him? His best friend had announced she was getting engaged and he hadn't congratulated her. 'Sorry, I forgot. Congrats.' Raheem smiled and hugged her.

'You're coming to my wedding,' said Aliyah as they parted.

'Is that a request or an order?'

Aliyah smiled. He would have to cherish each smile now. He had never before appreciated how her smile brightened his day; now each one would be precious before she went away. 'It's an order,' she said.

Raheem nodded. 'I will do. Definitely.'

They sat in silence. This had been the last thing he'd expected Aliyah to say but, more than that, he couldn't understand why he felt so empty inside. When he couldn't sit in silence any longer he asked, 'What does Imran do in Glasgow?'

'He is an accountant.' Aliyah took out her phone. 'That's him, the one in the middle. The other two are his brothers.'

Imran looked exactly how Raheem would have imagined Aliyah's husband to look. Articulate, mature face with square-rimmed glasses. 'You two will look great together,' he said as he handed back her phone.

'Aw, thanks. So have I got your approval?' Raheem nodded, his throat still a bit tight. Aliyah put her phone back in her pocket and was about to pick up her pen when she looked at him again. 'You wanted to tell me something as well, didn't you?' she said.

'Yeah, I did.'

She looked expectantly at him. He grabbed her hand and held it with both of his own. 'I just wanted to tell you Aliyah, that the best thing that ever happened to me was having you as a friend.'

Chapter 14

It was a rainy afternoon in the second week of February and Raheem was sitting on his own at the Parkview Café. Aliyah, who'd been asking him why he was so quiet, had left earlier as she had a work shift that evening. The automatic doors to the café's back entrance opened and Samir entered with Rachel.

Samir spotted him and muttered something to her before making his way over. 'What you doing here on your own?' he asked, sitting opposite him.

'Nothing,' said Raheem.

Samir turned towards the counter. 'Excuse me. Two iced coffees, please,' he called, raising his hand.

The assistant behind the counter looked up. 'You have to order at the till, mate. It's not a restaurant,' he called back.

Samir pulled a face when the staff member turned the other way, then slouched over to the counter. He came back and handed one of the iced coffees to Raheem.

'Thanks,' said Raheem as he took it.

'What do you mean "thanks"? Since when do we need to say thanks to each other?' asked Samir irritably.

Raheem sipped his coffee. It tasted horrible.

'Is it Sarah?' Samir asked when Raheem did not respond.

'Why does everyone always ask me about Sarah?' Raheem banged his fist on the table.

'Fucking hell, bro. Calm down.'

'Sorry, I'm just—' began Raheem, not knowing what he was going to say. Samir was looking at him with a confused expression. 'Aliyah told me about her engagement,' Raheem said eventually.

'You should be happy.'

He knew he should be happy. He didn't know why he wasn't.

The doors opened again and Daniel walked in wearing a woolly hat and a thick black jacket, accompanied by some friends. Raheem and Samir raised their hands to get his attention. He saw them and came over.

'Dan the man! How you doing?' asked Samir as Daniel sat down.

'I'm good, mate. How are you guys?'

'Not too good, not too bad,' said Raheem, which was the most diplomatic way he could put it.

'Want a drink?' asked Samir, standing up.

'I'm okay. I can't stay too long, I've got a lecture to go to in half an hour,' said Daniel. 'Do you guys have salt in your coffee?'

'No, why?' said Raheem.

'Why are there salt packets on the table then?'

Samir, who had just taken a sip from his coffee, spat it out on the floor. 'Shit, have I put in salt instead of sugar?'

No wonder the coffee had tasted bad.

'Looks like it' said Daniel.

'We still got plenty of time to talk, sit down Dan,' said Samir, even though Daniel was sitting and he was the one standing. He sat down when Daniel pointed this out to him. 'How you getting on with your work? Were the notes helpful for your exams?' Samir continued as he cleaned the salty coffee on the floor with a tissue.

'They were really helpful, thanks, both of you. Appreciate it.'

Raheem lost track of the conversation. Aliyah had told him here in this very café that she planned to get married once she graduated. It had totally slipped his mind. It was because she was going to be far away. That's what bothered him…

It was a few seconds before he realised that Liam was sitting with a couple of friends at the far end of the café. He had just got up and was heading towards the toilets. This could be their chance. 'Samir, listen, Liam is leaving – let's grab him.'

Samir and Daniel both turned to look. 'We can't do anything to him here,' Samir muttered, but Daniel still heard him.

'What's up?' he asked.

'Nothing. That guy was supposed to get us tickets for a concert,' said Samir. 'We already paid him but he hasn't given us them yet. We're going give him two more days.'

Raheem clenched his fist in frustration. The fact that Liam was so close yet they could not do anything was unbearable.

'I wouldn't trust him, to be honest,' said Daniel quietly.

Raheem and Samir looked at each other. 'Do you know him, Dan?' asked Raheem. Daniel nodded. 'Why did you say you wouldn't trust him?'

Daniel shifted in his chair slightly. 'Nothing... He's just... I don't know,' he mumbled.

'Just tell us,' said Samir.

Daniel was looking as though he regretted entering the conversation. He stood up. 'My lecture starts soon. I need to go.'

'Sit back down. You aren't going anywhere. Tell me what lecture it is and I'll give you the notes for it,' said Raheem sharply.

Daniel sat back down. Something had been up with him this year and today Raheem was going to find out what it was. 'You've changed this year, Dan,' he said. 'We're your friends. If you don't tell us, who're you going to tell?'

Liam came back from the toilet, picked up his bag and left the café through the doors that led to the main university building. He hadn't noticed them, otherwise he would have done his stupid camera pose.

Daniel took a deep breath. 'So basically ... it happened last year.'

As he explained, Raheem could hardly believe what he was hearing. Samir's mouth remained opened the entire time. Once Daniel had finished, there was a stunned silence.

'So let me get this straight,' said Raheem eventually. There was a lot to go through. 'You liked this girl called Amy, who was also friends with Liam. You bought her a new watch—'

'What watch was it?' interjected Samir. 'Sorry,' he added after a look from Raheem.

Raheem repeated, 'So anyway, you bought Anna a watch—'

'Amy,' interrupted Daniel.

'Fucking hell man, let me finish,' snapped Raheem. Samir patted Daniel on the arm sympathetically as Raheem continued. 'So you bought *Amy* a new watch for her birthday and you went to her birthday party. You also planned to tell her you liked her.

Liam had bought her a box of chocolates. He asked for some of your wrapping paper and later that evening he swapped the two gifts around. You took his present, thinking it was the watch?'

'That's right,' said Daniel quietly.

'Could you not tell when you picked up the present that it wasn't a bloody watch but chocolates?' Samir demanded.

Daniel shook his head. 'I never got the chance! We went in one of Liam's mate's cars and the presents were in the boot. Liam handed me my gift bag when we got out. The size of that chocolate box was the same as the watch box and I didn't think to check. He must have swapped the presents and card envelopes when he opened the boot. The worst part is, I know Amy hates chocolates and it was such a cheap gift to give her on her birthday.'

Seriously? How could he have been so stupid? 'So, what was that part again where he told Amy to open the presents after you all left?' asked Raheem.

'Liam told Amy to open the presents after we left. There were quite a few people at the party and he said something might get nicked. She put them in her bedroom and locked the door. She text me the next day to say thanks for the chocolates. I got confused so I asked what other presents she got. Then she mentioned that Liam had bought her a new watch.'

Samir let out a whistle.

Raheem scratched his head. 'And you never bothered telling her that you'd bought it?'

Daniel shook his head, looking miserable. 'I didn't want to start a fight with Liam. One of his mates is a drug dealer and I felt nervous about confronting him. That was also the week my watch went missing.'

'*Your* watch went missing?' said Raheem and Samir at the same time, so loudly that people turned to stare.

Daniel shifted in his chair again. 'Yeah... I was stoned in my flat. I'd started getting high around that period... Liam and that drug dealer and another guy called Alex were also there.'

He paused, as though Raheem and Samir would reprimand him for allowing them into his flat. When they didn't speak, he continued. 'I remember taking off my watch and putting it on the dining table so it didn't get wet when I went to the bathroom. I forgot to pick it up. When I went back into the sitting room, Liam and his mates took me outside and said we were going to go into town for a night out. When I returned to my flat, my watch wasn't on the table anymore.'

Samir was shaking his head in disbelief. Raheem didn't have it in him to have a go at Daniel for his stupidity. 'Did you ask them about it?' he asked.

'I asked Liam the next day if he'd seen it, but he said no.'

What had Daniel expected him to say? Raheem sympathised with Daniel and, from the look on his face, he could tell Samir also felt sorry for him.

'My mum bought it for me. I had to tell her I'd lost it,' mumbled Dan.

What was it with these people that they loved losing their watches? First Aaron, now Daniel.

'What about Amy? Please don't tell me she started going out with Liam after he'd given her the watch you bought for her,' Samir said.

Surprisingly, Daniel smiled. 'No way. She said he'd asked her out on a date but when she said she only saw him as a friend, he got all offended and asked for the watch back. She told me she returned it. But I reckon he has sold my watch and the one I bought for Amy.'

'You can still ask Amy out,' said Raheem encouragingly.

Daniel shook his head. 'No, I can't. I've liked her since I met her and I think she knows, but up until last year I didn't have the guts to ask her out on a date. Even if Liam had my watch, I know I couldn't confront him about it. I'm just a coward.'

'That's not true,' said Raheem sharply.

Daniel didn't look convinced. 'It's too late. Me and Amy hardly talk now. She probably thinks I'm too clingy.'

Samir frowned. 'Clingy? Like your proper sticky or something?' It was hard to tell who was the stupidest at the table, but Samir had the edge with that comment.

'Clingy, as in I always message her first and I always make an excuse to talk to her,' explained Daniel. 'She's still friendly, but I know she deserves someone better than me. I'm someone who's always drunk and who failed last year.'

141

'You're not the only one who likes getting drunk' muttered Raheem.

'What?' said Daniel.

'Nothing.' Now was not the time to talk about Aaron.

'Trust me, there's nothing wrong with you, Dan. You're just making your life worse by having this mentality,' Samir said firmly. 'Look at the state of you. You look so depressed.'

Words were not enough for Raheem. 'You'll be alright, Dan. But you know who won't be? That fucking rat Liam, because I'm going to find him and I'm going to shove his head down the toilet!'

He stood up, but Samir grabbed his arm. 'If you shove his head down the toilet, we won't have heads on our shoulders, so sit down!'

'What will happen to your heads?' Daniel looked puzzled.

'Nothing, Dan. It was just a figure of speech.' Raheem was breathing heavily as he sat down again.

No one spoke for a moment, then Daniel said, 'I should have seen the warnings signs. Phil told me his camera went missing last year when he was sharing a house with Liam.'

Raheem and Samir glanced at each other. 'What camera was it?' asked Raheem.

'A silver Toshiba one,' said Daniel.

Of course it was a silver Toshiba camera; Raheem had seen his and Samir's photos on it. This was getting too much.

Daniel stood up. 'I need to go, I have a lecture in a bit. I'll see you guys later. Thanks for … listening to me. I feel a bit better now that I've spoken to you.'

'I know Liam looks like a rat, but he's turned out to be a fucking snake,' Samir said as Daniel walked away.

'He's not just a snake, he's the fucking basterlicks in the Harry Potter movie. You know, that massive snake he fights at the end,' snarled Raheem.

'You mean basilisk, not "basterlicks",' corrected Samir.

'Same thing, man.' He couldn't believe Liam would stoop that low.

'I was thinking of getting a new watch,even though I still check the time on my phone' said Samir thoughtfully.

142

'Why do you need a watch? Your time is going shit' said Raheem.

'Your time is going good, isn't it?'

'Don't talk about watches. Aaron's probably wondering what happened to his.'

'You prick. I *told* you not to be with Veronica.'

'At least I don't put salt in coffee…'

Still bickering, they headed out of the café.

Samir took out his cigarette packet and gave one to Raheem. They definitely needed a cigarette after the chat with Daniel. 'We need to set Dan up with Amy. What do you reckon?' Samir said.

'Yeah, we do. But then again, I reckon any woman who hates chocolate isn't worth it,' sighed Raheem.

***

Two weeks had passed since they had spoken to Daniel. Valentine's Day came and went. Raheem took Sarah to a restaurant and then headed for a night out in town with her. Samir spent the first half of the day with Katie, then spent the evening with Rachel. He still hadn't learnt his lesson. But then again, as Raheem knew himself, ending a relationship with someone for no reason was very hard.

They made sure they would be in different night clubs later that night but argued over who was going to go to Sensations. They tossed and Raheem won, so Samir had to spend a full ten minutes on the phone trying to explain to Rachel why they were going to Control, the second-best club in Stalford, while Raheem sniggered in the background.

'Here, you might as well wear this,' snarled Samir, throwing Aaron's watch at him.

'No, thanks.'

Aaron had finally introduced Sarah and Veronica to each other. From what Veronica had told him, Sarah hadn't seen her before. That was one thing that had gone right. Veronica said she'd gone on a date with Aaron on Valentine's Day. He had tried to kiss her but she'd told him that she needed more time to think.

Raheem hadn't asked Aaron anything about Veronica. Aaron would probably end up telling him that he had cheated on her, but there was no benefit in talking about it to him. It wasn't like he would be understanding if he found out Raheem had cheated on Sarah.

***

Raheem hummed to himself as he stood outside the Odeon cinema. It was one of the rare sunny days they'd had this month. He was waiting for the rest of the group to arrive. Samir was supposed to come, but Katie had turned up out of the blue and wanted to go shopping with him.

Sarah pulled up in the car park and she got out, along with Aliyah. Grill and Pepperz was opposite the cinema. All those times he'd gone there with Aliyah…

Aliyah waved at him as they came towards him. He waved back, before noticing that a car was driving up. Aliyah and Sarah were in conversation and hadn't seen it. They stepped onto the road when the car was less than twenty feet away.

'Aliyah, stop!' shouted Raheem.

The driver slammed on the brakes just in time, ten feet away from them. Aliyah raised her hand apologetically and let the car pass, before making her way over with Sarah to Raheem.

'Are you okay?' asked Raheem.

'I'm okay, thanks,' said Aliyah.

He hugged Sarah, before saying, 'Samir couldn't come.'

'Why not?' said Sarah, examining her reflection on her phone.

'He … was busy.'

It would be better if he didn't show Sarah the text he had just received from Samir.

Fucking hell, Rachel is also at Broadway with her cousins, I forgot she had booked the weekend off work!

'Aaron's on his way,' Sarah informed him.

They stood outside waiting for Aaron, which gave Raheem enough time to text Samir back.

Get the hell out of there, make any excuse to Katie. Why did you have to go Broadway today of all places??

144

After a couple of minutes, Aaron's Mercedes arrived with Veronica in the passenger seat.

'Hiya,' said Sarah as the couple joined them. Sarah and Veronica hugged, bumping their jaws against each other's cheeks. You could tell there was a bit of tension between them; they were just two people who would probably never get on. Veronica hugged Aliyah before smiling at Raheem.

'Right, does everyone know who's who?' said Aaron.

Raheem was getting sick and tired of Aaron's introductions. 'Yeah, we all know each other. Come on, let's go in,' he said cheerfully, turning towards the entrance.

'One second, Raheem.' Sarah pulled him by the arm. Veronica looked away pointedly.

'I know you're Aliyah, but I don't think we've ever met.' Aaron held out his hand.

'I know you're Aaron, and this is the first time we've met,' said Aliyah, smiling and shaking it.

Raheem stared determinedly at the ground, avoiding eye contact with everyone.

'Well, nice to meet you. I'm Veronica's boyfriend – in every way,' said Aaron. Everyone laughed except Raheem, who could only manage a painful smile. Were Aaron and Veronica in a relationship? Were they friends? Were they still on their break? It was fucking ridiculous.

'You're turn, Raheem,' said Aaron, winking at him.

He didn't see the point in this, as they all knew who he was. 'I'm Raheem, Sarah's boyfriend, in nearly every way.'

Sarah slapped his arm him as they all laughed. He tried to laugh along with them, although he wasn't finding anything funny.

'Shall we go in, then?' said Veronica brightly.

Aaron held the door open. They were just about to join the queue to buy tickets when Aaron said, 'Guys, this is on me today.' He took out his wallet.

'Chill, I've got it,' said Raheem pulling out his own wallet.

'Nope, I'm paying today and that's final.'

'You can pay next time, Raheem,' said Veronica kindly. They looked at each other and Raheem knew they were both thinking of the time they'd gone to the restaurant with Samir.

'Okay, looks like I'll have to listen,' he said resignedly.

Aaron and Veronica joined the queue to buy the tickets.

'You never *have* to listen to me,' muttered Sarah. Thankfully, Aliyah was making a phone call so didn't hear that comment.

'You're my boss. I always listen to you,' said Raheem, shaking his head to the music.

'People are looking. Stop shaking your head!'

Raheem stopped. 'See, you're the boss' he said as Aliyah rejoined them. They waited another few minutes until Aaron and Veronica returned with the tickets and snacks. They had bought drinks, Doritos and jalapenos, together with a couple of packets of chocolates.

'Let's go then,' said Raheem.

'Look, Raheem, that bear is so cute!' said Sarah longingly, pointing at a stall which had large teddy bears.

'This one's on you.' Aaron nudged him.

Veronica turned to Aaron. 'Excuse me, you need to get me one too.'

They went to the stall, Raheem walking behind the others.

'Afternoon ladies and gents, my name is Tom. Who is going to go first to win a bear for their ladies?' said the man at the stall.

'It's them who want to win it for us,' said Raheem.

Sarah stepped on his foot. 'We have to win it?'

'Yep, rules are on the board,' said Aliyah, pointing.

They read the rules. From what Raheem could make out, you had to throw the ball through one of the small gaps in the wall. You either had three goes at winning one bear, or you could take one go at winning two bears. You were only allowed to play once, as apparently these were some rare and special stuffed bears.

'Aaron, you better get me this. Take three goes,' said Veronica, who finished reading first.

'Three goes it is, then.' Aaron handed a pound to Tom.

'She seems very demanding,' said Tom as he put the coin in the jar.

'She is, yeah,' muttered Raheem to Sarah.

Sarah raised her eyebrows. 'How do you know that?'

It hadn't been the best thing to say, but then again he'd been saying stupid things at stupid times a lot recently. 'I mean all women are high maintenance,' he explained as Veronica pointed out which bear she wanted.

'Even me?' said Sarah sternly.

'No, you're not.'

'So you're saying that I'm not a woman?'

'No I didn't say that.'

'You're saying I'm cheap, eh?'

'You're priceless, so that doesn't count has high maintenance.'

Sarah blew him a kiss just as Aaron got ready to take his go. He threw the ball and missed the hole by a yard. It was a shit shot. 'Aaron, concentrate!' cried Veronica.

Raheem caught Aliyah's eye and they grinned.

'Sorry,' said Aaron, looking flustered. He threw again and this time managed to get it in. The girls started clapping. By the time Raheem joined in, they had stopped.

'Well done! That's the bear, as promised,' Tom said, handing Aaron the bear.

'He's so cute!' said Veronica affectionately.

'And now your turn, sir. You want the three goes for one bear, or the one go for two?' said Tom.

'Take the three goes, Raheem. You don't want to risk it,' said Aliyah.

'No pressure, babe, but you know I love my teddy bears.' Sarah squeezed his hand as Raheem picked up the ball.

'Good luck!' said Aliyah.

Raheem put down the ball. 'I'll take the one go for two bears.'

'If you miss, we won't have another chance. You can only play once!' said Sarah indignantly, but Raheem's mind was made up.

'He seems very confident,' said Tom.

'I am confident.' Raheem took a deep breath and picked up the ball. The holes looked a lot smaller when you were aiming at them. He raised his arm and chose the hole slightly to the right of centre. He checked his aim one final time before throwing the ball. To his delight, it went straight through the gap. Everyone cheered and clapped, none more so than Raheem.

'Well done!' Aliyah gave him a glowing look.

Raheem took the bears and handed one of them to Sarah. 'See, I told you I'd get it.'

'I always had faith,' she replied, taking it.

'I never knew you were into teddy bears,' said Aaron, taking a picture of his phone with Raheem holding it. He would probably put it on his Snapchat story. More publicity, just what he didn't need at the moment.

'I'm not.' Raheem grinned. 'There you go.' He handed the other bear to Aliyah. She hesitated. 'Take it or I'm going to rip its head off,' he said firmly.

'Thanks.' They looked at each other before Raheem turned to the others. 'Come on, let's go, the film's about to start. I don't want to miss the adverts.' He walked off towards the cinema screens.

'It's screen seven,' said Veronica, looking at her ticket.

'What did I say? It was screen three hundred?' said Raheem as Sarah caught up with them. Aliyah and Aaron were twenty feet behind them, carrying the snacks.

'Alright then, smart arse' said Veronica, sniggering.

Sarah didn't look best pleased with that comment from Veronica, who was walking between him and Sarah. She held out her hand for Raheem to grab right in front of Veronica, who had to stop as Raheem grasped it.

'Sorry,' Sarah said to her as she stepped in between them.

Raheem gave Veronica an apologetic look. She raised her eyebrows at Sarah, who thankfully was not looking. He hoped they wouldn't start fighting; he would be the one who would be in the most trouble if that happened.

The cinema was already half full, despite the fact there were still fifteen minutes to go before the film started. They walked towards the back where they found five free seats at the end of a row. Veronica sat at the end with Aaron next to her. Sarah looked as if she wanted Raheem to go next but he nodded at her to go ahead. Aliyah was behind him.

The lights dimmed.

'If we don't like the film, shall us two just go to Grill and Pepperz and leave the others here?' he whispered to Sarah.

'No, we're staying until the end. Stop messing around,' she whispered back as she rested her head on his shoulder.

Raheem turned to Aliyah. 'If we don't like the film, shall us two just go to Grill and Pepperz and leave the others here?'

Aliyah grinned. 'That is a great idea. And if we don't like sitting our exams, we'll do the same then as well.'

'Is that a deal?'

'Deal. Whenever we don't like something, we'll always do that.'

He was going to miss their banter when she left. He would never have another friend quite like Aliyah. He sat back in his seat. All three of the bears were face down at their owners feet. After all that trouble to win them in the first place.

Chapter 15

Winning teddy bears was all well and good, but it wouldn't solve his problems. Raheem turned off the heating and returned to the living room. 'Okay, one final time so there's no confusion,' he said, sitting on the sofa.

'How many times do you have to hear the same thing before it gets into your head?' demanded Samir. He'd been very lucky last week at Broadway; he'd had to pretend to have a migraine for Katie to finally abandon their shopping trip. The quicker they were out of this mess, the better.

'So, Veronica. Just to be clear, you definitely don't want to be with Aaron?' asked Raheem.

'For the twenty-fourth time Raheem, no,' she replied irritably. 'It's not the same with him anymore. He's fucked up too many times and I want to end it. We can be friends but nothing more than that. I shouldn't have even come to the cinema that day. I don't want to be in a relationship at the moment. Guys are just too much hassle – no offence.'

Guys were too much hassle? She was perfect, wasn't she? At least things were finally clear as to where Veronica was in regards to Aaron. What wasn't clear was why Veronica was acting innocent in all of this. He didn't know, but there was nothing to be gained from arguing.

'Right, that's sorted then,' said Raheem. 'So how are you going to tell Aaron?'

Veronica shuffled her feet. 'I don't really know. I guess I'll try hint that I want to end it. I'm just worried about those pictures. Can't you beg that Liam guy to get rid of them? I don't want the word spreading of what I – you did.'

'I'm not begging him,' said Raheem dismissively.

'Can't you put your ego to one side?'

'I've got no ego! But I'm not going to beg him. And even if I did, he'd show them anyway.'

'Why did you have to pour your drink over him in the corridor last year?'

'That wasn't me, it was him.' Raheem pointed at Samir.

'Served him right, he's a bastard' said Samir stubbornly.

They were going around in circles. Raheem was worried that Aaron would go back to drinking if Veronica broke up with him. From what Aaron had told him, the split with Veronica had contributed significantly to his alcohol problems. Sarah was not aware of this. She had asked him on more than one occasion to keep an eye on Aaron and support him as best as he could. But there was no point in trying to get Veronica to be with someone she didn't want to be with.

'Okay, Veronica, you do your best to end it with Aaron. Do it gradually though, make all the hints that you can that you don't want to be with him. We will try think of something regarding that camera.'

Veronica stood up and stretched. 'I'll try. But believe me when I say, he doesn't give up easily.'

Samir grabbed his car keys from the table. He was dropping Veronica home before going to the library to do some work. Raheem said goodbye to them, then went upstairs to his bedroom. He collapsed onto his bed, staring at the ceiling.

As if his university work wasn't challenging enough, he now had to rack his brains to think of how to get his hands on that camera. The problem was that Liam wouldn't carry it around with him; the only way to get the camera was to corner Liam and threaten him, but that was too risky. They only saw him at university and if they attacked him there was a big chance they could get kicked out. Being so close to finishing their degree, they didn't want to take that chance.

Raheem remembered the conversation he and Samir had with Daniel. He felt sorry for Daniel but given the circumstances they were in, they couldn't really do anything for him. If only Daniel had told them last year when it happened, they would have beaten up Liam so badly he wouldn't have been in any fit state to return to university for his third year. They had seen him quite a few times in the city centre on nights out last year, but since he had shown them the pictures they had only seen him at the university.

The room was slowly getting darker but Raheem couldn't be bothered to turn on the light. He tried to think of something else, but all that came to mind was Aliyah going to Glasgow after she got married, which made him even more depressed. Everywhere he looked, it seemed as if he were stuck. Each time Sarah or Aaron called him he got anxious, thinking Liam had shown them the photos. Samir was having the same problem whenever Rachel or Katie called him. Simply paying Liam to get the camera was not enough. They needed to punish him, not just because of the pictures but also because of what he had done to Daniel.

Raheem took out his phone and started browsing the internet. He checked the sports headlines before reading a couple of articles. One was about how to change your luck, but it wasn't very useful. All it said was that helping others was a way to bring you luck. If that was the case, surely everyone in the world would be helping each other.

Samir's car pulled up in the driveway an hour later. Raheem turned on the lamp and pretended to be texting on his phone as his cousin came into his room carrying an envelope. 'Here, read this. I printed it off earlier,' he said, lobbing it at Raheem.

Perplexed, Raheem opened the envelope to find a piece of paper folded inside.

Aaron wants us to help him be with Veronica.

Veronica wants us to help her split up with Aaron.

Aaron is Sarah's brother, who we both attacked and took his watch. (By mistake.)

You have cheated on Sarah with Veronica.

I've cheated on Rachel with Katie.

Liam has got evidence of this and wants five grand.

And we need to make sure we pass our third year.

But apart from that, we got nothing to worry about.

'It's good isn't it? It gives a summary of the problems,' said Samir.

Raheem glanced down at the paper again. The biggest problem he had was not even on there. 'Yeah, it's brilliant,' he said dully.

'Thank you.'

'But imagine how much better it would have been if you'd written the fucking solutions,' snapped Raheem, throwing the paper at him.

Samir sat down on the bed with an uncharacteristically serious look on his face. 'That's what we need to work out,' he said. 'But in the meantime, I think we need to help Dan. I get a feeling that might help us with our solutions.'

Talk about coincidence. Raheem had been reading that article a few minutes ago, and now Samir was suggesting the same thing. But there was one problem. 'How can we help Dan?' he asked.

***

The idea sounded good, but it seemed that Daniel didn't have confidence in it. 'That will make her think I don't like her,' he blurted.

'Don't be silly, Dan. That's what women like,' said Veronica brightly. 'Someone who has a bit of mystery.'

She was resting her head on Raheem's shoulder and he wished she wouldn't. The student union bar downstairs was busy. They had booked the room upstairs for an hour, but you never knew who might randomly walk in.

Daniel still didn't look convinced. Raheem leaned forward slightly so that Veronica's head slipped from his shoulders. 'Look, you got nothing – ouch, don't pinch me! – you got nothing to lose. From what you told me, Amy seems to think you need her. Once she sees you and Veronica are flirting, she'll get jealous.'

Veronica had rested her head on Samir's shoulder instead. When Daniel didn't respond, Raheem added, 'In regards to what happened in the past, just forget about it and move on. Our job is to get you back with Amy. When's the last time she texted you first?'

'On Christmas Day,' said Daniel moodily.

'What did she text?'

'Merry Christmas.'

'Thanks, but Christmas was nearly three months ago. So what did she text you?'

'I told you, Merry Christmas.'

'Is that it?'

Daniel nodded glumly. 'Only time in the last six months she has texted me first.'

'Who are *you* texting?' asked Raheem sharply, swivelling his head around.

Samir looked up from his phone. 'Your dad.'

Raheem turned back to Daniel. 'I guarantee that Amy will text you first after she sees you with Veronica. If she doesn't, you can slap me.'

'That's not fair! You never gave me that option,' said Veronica. She was still acting innocent in all this.

Daniel smiled. 'Fair enough.'

Samir put his phone back in his pocket. 'So, repeat the plan for me, Dan, just so we know that you know what's going to happen.'

'Amy always sits on the second floor on her own on Wednesday and Thursday between three and five,' Daniel said. 'That's when she does most of her work. You two are going to sit at her table and you're going to ring me and ask to borrow one of my books.'

'Perfect,' said Samir.

'So, I'm going to bring the book upstairs. When Amy notices me, I'll say hi and sit down as well. After a bit, you two will go away and Veronica will arrive.' Daniel went a little pink and glanced at Veronica, who winked at him.

'Go on, lad, keep going,' said Raheem, clapping his hands.

'And then Veronica is going to start talking to me. I'm going to give her attention, compliment her. We are going to talk for a bit—'

'You need to introduce Amy to her. Still talk a little to Amy' said Raheem.

'Oh yeah. So, Veronica is going to ask if I want to go Sensations with her later this week. I'm going to say I'm a bit busy but will let her know. Then we'll go for a coffee together. I'm going to ask Amy if she wants to come—'

'No, you're not. Calm down,' Raheem interjected.

Daniel looked puzzled. 'But it would be rude not to ask her to come with us.'

'Exactly! So, what you're *going* to do is ask her if she'd like you to bring a coffee back for her.'

'Because that way, it's not rude that you ignored her, but you're making it known that you want to be alone with Veronica,' said Samir impressively.

'Good one. You two should have gone to Oxford Uni,' said Veronica.

'I almost got offered a place at Cambridge University,' said Samir.

'Really?'

'Yeah, I—'

'You actually believe that this donkey nearly got a place at Cambridge?' asked Raheem incredulously. Samir started laughing.

'He said it so convincingly,' said Veronica defensively.

Raheem turned back to Daniel as Veronica began slapping Samir. 'So, you got it?' he asked.

'Yep,' said Daniel.

'If she doesn't text you within three days, you can slap me as well.' Samir jumped up from the sofa to avoid Veronica.

'I'm not going to slap you guys. I really appreciate your help,' said Daniel seriously. It was nice hearing something positive for a change. Daniel stood up and swung his bag over his shoulder. 'I need to go, meeting one of my mates in town. I'll see you later.' He went down the stairs and out of the side exit of the union bar.

'That went well enough' said Raheem, turning to the others.

'You both seem to be experts on every woman except your own girlfriends' sighed Veronica. 'That's the thing with guys. They think they are too clever sometimes.'

'I am clever though.'

'But your problem is you think the rest of the world is stupid.'

'Let's just help Dan, we can decide who the stupidest is after' said Samir, yawning.

Helping others was all well and good, but it was hard to see how that would help them get out of the mess they were in.

***

155

It was an irritable Monday afternoon. Raheem had just finished his lecture. Aliyah had gone to the third floor to study with some course mates on a group presentation. Sarah had texted him to ask (or rather tell him) she was coming over to his tonight to make up for the fact that she hadn't been able to come to university today. Raheem and Samir had already had two arguments about this, as Rachel also wanted to come to the flat tonight.

'Move your shit, man, I need to sit down,' said Raheem as Samir plonked his bag and jacket on two separate chairs.

'Alright chill out' Samir said as he picked up his bag and put it on the floor. They were sitting at one of the corner tables on the first floor of the library. Ryan, Hannah, Jermaine and Fiona were sitting at the opposite side, but Raheem wasn't in the mood for talking. He hadn't slept well the previous night. His morning shift at Tesco hadn't helped, either; he'd been told off by one of the supervisors for taking too long on his break. He'd only gone fifteen minutes over; it wasn't like the store had collapsed without him being there.

'Did you ask Aliyah to send you the notes from the lecture?' he asked as he put his head on his arms and closed his eyes. He really wanted to sleep, but he needed to continue his psychology essay.

Critically discuss the major ethical problems involved in researching human behaviour with reference to psychological research.

'I'll ask her now,' said Samir sheepishly, taking out his phone.

Raheem kept his eyes closed. He had recently been having dreams of dropping Aliyah off to the airport so she could catch a flight to Glasgow. During his waking moments he would remember the great times they had together. Aliyah had told him that once University had finished she would start the wedding shopping, and Raheem would have to come with her. At least that way he would get to spend more time with her before she left.

'Shit,' said Samir suddenly.

156

Raheem looked up. Aaron had just entered the first floor. Despite the fact that they were sitting at the table furthest from the entrance, he spotted them immediately and came over.

'Just what we need,' said Raheem exasperatedly. 'Why do they allow the whole world to enter this fucking uni on Mondays?'

'You said you'd send them an email telling them not to.'

'I did, but they're like you, they don't listen!'

'Yes, lads, just on my break so thought I would come see you,' said Aaron, sitting down.

'What's new?' asked Samir.

Judging by the way Aaron was dressed, it seemed as if he had just come from work. Unfortunately, his office was only a ten-minute walk from the university. Aaron leaned forward slightly with a purposeful look on his face. 'I have thought about Veronica and come to a decision.'

Raheem sat up straighter. Looked as if there would finally be some good news. Aaron looked over his shoulder before saying, 'I've decided that I want to be with Veronica again. I'm going to tell her this when I meet her in a few days. Time to move out of the friend zone.'

Raheem slouched back on his chair. Great. That was the exact opposite of what they wanted to hear.

Samir was more successful in pretending to look pleased. 'Are you *sure* about that?' he asked pointedly.

'Positive. In fact, it's down to both of you. You made me realise I'm not as bad as I thought I was.'

Aaron was right. He wasn't as bad as he thought. He was even worse. What were they going to do now? Veronica had made it clear she didn't want to be with Aaron. Raheem ducked under the table, pretending to tie his shoelace so that Aaron couldn't see him swearing.

Aaron sat with them for the next half an hour before deciding to go back to his office. No matter how many hints Raheem and Samir gave him to move on from Veronica, he didn't seem to understand.

'What we going to do now?' asked Samir.

'I don't know. It's the worst—'

157

'Can I borrow your notepad, please?' Liam had just sat down in the seat Aaron had vacated. Why did the wrong people always turn up at the wrong place at the wrong time? 'Can I borrow your notepad, please?' he repeated.

Samir, looking bemused, handed Liam his notepad. He flipped through to the back and began ripping out pages. 'What the fuck you doing?' asked Samir indignantly, but Liam raised a finger to his lips.

When he had ripped out at least ten pages, he threw the notepad back. 'Time for some fun' he said, scrunching up each page. The first one he threw at Raheem, which hit him on the forehead; the next one hit Samir directly on his nose. The third was also aimed at Samir and the fourth at Raheem. He threw five and six simultaneously at them.

A few college girls who were regular visitors to the library on Mondays were laughing and pointing from the table nearest to theirs.

'Look, security!' Raheem called, looking over Liam's shoulder. He got another paper thrown at his face for his lie.

'See you around,' said Liam lightly as he threw the last page at Raheem. He picked up his bag and hurried out of the library.

Samir turned to Raheem, rubbing his nose. 'This is all your fault. I *told* you not to be with Veronica!'

Raheem picked up the notepad from the table and threw it at Samir's face.

***

Aliyah had passed her driving test. She had told him that he had driven past her during her test but he hadn't noticed her. Nevertheless, anything positive was a welcome change. Raheem was getting increasingly nervous and, from the looks of it, so was Samir. He didn't seem to be speaking to Katie as much and was spending increasing amounts of time with Rachel. It looked as if he had finally started to appreciate Rachel.

Veronica had been right about one thing: Aaron couldn't seem to take no for an answer. Raheem was just reading a text message from him, his frustration growing with each sentence he read.

You orite Raheem? To be honest with you, Veronica seems different now. I really want this to work but she seems to see me more as a mate than a boyfriend. I don't know what's changed in her but for some reason I'm thinking she is with someone else ... I need you to find out what she really thinks of me. Cud u do that? Just find out if she still plans on being with me? At least that way I know. You reckon you cud do that? And don't tell her that I told you to ask.

He handed his phone to Samir. 'He's crazy,' said Samir, handing the phone back once he had read the text.

'I got my exams and dissertation due, and he wants me to spend my time trying to convince Veronica to be with him.'

Raheem and Samir were at their usual table on the first floor in the library. Ryan and Hannah were next to each other on the computers, both typing away. In the centre, Jason and his group of friends were crammed together at a table, books stacked in front of them. Jason saw Raheem looking before getting up and coming over to them.

'Do I have a sign on my forehead that says come talk to me?' muttered Raheem angrily.

Jason was wearing his orange baseball cap, which clashed horribly with his dark-blue shirt. He looked like a Jaffa Cake packet. 'You okay, lads?' he asked, but had enough sense not to take a seat.

'Not bad, Jason,' said Raheem tonelessly. Samir had taken the perfect opportunity to make a phone call.

'How's the dissertation going?' asked Jason.

'Good.'

'How's Sarah?'

'Very good.'

'She showed me a picture of the jacket she got you the other day. What did you think?'

'Very, very good.'

Jason seemed to realise he wasn't going to get any follow-up questions from Raheem. 'Got to get back to my revision, lot of work to do,' he said. Raheem nodded dully as Jason returned to his table.

Ryan picked up his bag and walked out of the library, leaving Hannah alone at her desk. Samir, who had coincidentally finished his phone call the moment Jason left, saw him looking. 'Can you do some work?' he asked. 'One minute you're talking about Aaron, then you're looking at Hannah. I reckon they would make a good couple, both so tall!'

Raheem returned to his laptop. They were both very tall... that was so hilarious, wasn't it...? Hold on. 'Say that again,' he said slowly.

'I said, Aaron and Hannah would make a good couple.'

How had he not thought of it before? 'You're a genius,' said Raheem happily.

Samir put his hand on his heart, closed his eyes and nodded before abruptly typing on his laptop. He stopped after a few seconds. He had no clue about the idea he had just given Raheem. 'I'm depressed. We might as well go chat to her,' he said. He had still not cottoned on.

'Best idea you ever had.' Raheem stood up.

'What you on about?' Samir said but Raheem was already moving to Hannah. 'Hello,' he said, sitting on the desk next to her computer. Samir joined them and sat on her other side.

'Hi. What brings you two here?' Hannah grinned at them.

'Just came to see what you're up to,' said Raheem innocently.

'It was my idea,' said Samir loudly, swinging his legs under the desk with no regard for the person trying to work next to him.

Some of the students were giving them disapproving looks. Liam was sitting a few rows ahead of Hannah at the computers.

'Can you two Humpty Dumpty's find somewhere else to sit instead of on a desk? It's just that you're distracting people from working,' called a guy with glasses, who was sitting on the same row as Liam. Some of the students laughed, though none as hard as Liam. He started doing his camera pose.

'Humpty Dumpty sat on a wall, not a desk, you stupid idiot,' called Raheem. The guy who had called out put in his earphones.

'Yeah, you fat, skinny little—' Samir began.

'Leave it. He's got his earphones in, he can't hear you,' interjected Raheem.

Hannah had clapped her hand over her mouth. A couple of girls were laughing at what Samir had said and he looked pleased with himself, even though he'd made no sense.

'Come to our table, Hannah. That way Einstein over there can concentrate.' Raheem stood up.

Samir looked as though he wanted to go talk to the girls who were still giggling at him, but grudgingly followed them back to their table. But it was his mention of Aaron and Hannah that had given Raheem an idea. There was one way for Aaron to get over the disappointment of not being with Veronica. Hopefully, Hannah was still single.

***

'Are you out of your mind?' asked Samir, half an hour later.

Raheem smiled mysteriously. Samir had clearly had not grasped the brilliance of his idea.

Hannah was back at her desk. Einstein had taken out his earphones.

'Look, Veronica doesn't want to be with Aaron, agreed?' asked Raheem.

'Yeah but—'

'Hannah likes tall, mixed-race guys, that's what she told me,' interjected Raheem.

'Yeah but—'

'Aaron is tall and mixed race.'

'Yeah but—'

'That day when I met Aaron here, I could tell from the way he looked at Hannah that he was interested.'

'I don't know. I wasn't there.'

'Doesn't matter, you still have to agree.'

'Why? What I don't see, I don't believe.'

'Have you seen Switzerland?'

'No.'

'Does that mean Switzerland doesn't exist?'

'I … heard about it, innit? There's a difference.'

161

'Just listen.' Raheem looked around to make sure nobody was in earshot. Past experience had taught him to be more careful. 'If we introduced Hannah to Aaron, it would make it a lot easier for him to forget about Veronica,' he said. 'That's two problems solved, Veronica's and Aaron's.'

Samir considered for a moment. 'That sounds okay, actually.'

'There you go then.' Raheem swung back on his chair, before gripping the table to stop himself from falling. They had the information they needed from Hannah to get this started, but pulling it off was a different matter entirely.

Chapter 16

Raheem now had ten weeks left at university and eight weeks until the day of reckoning on May 14th . Liam had still not told them where he wanted to meet for them to give him the money.

Raheem had decided to take Aliyah to Grill and Pepperz after their seminar finished. He had rung Samir, asking him if he wanted to join them, but Samir had said that he was going to spend the evening working on his dissertation. That was the first time ever Samir had chosen to study on a Friday evening.

'I hate traffic,' Raheem groaned as he put on the handbrake yet again.

Aliyah, who was busy uploading pictures on Instagram, looked up from her phone. 'You *are* traffic.'

'When you getting a car, then?'

'Hopefully in the summer, so will have a few months to drive you around before I leave for Glasgow.'

There were at least thirty cars ahead of him, all stationary. They wouldn't get there for another fifteen minutes at least. He turned the music louder, but Aliyah turned it back down again. 'Let's talk instead,' she said brightly.

When Sarah turned the music down in the car, they always argued about it. In a sense that was good because by the time they had finished arguing they'd be at their destination.

'Tell me a joke.' Raheem released the handbrake and moved his car forward two inches.

'No, you tell me,' said Aliyah stubbornly.

'How can you double your money instantly?'

'How?'

'Put it in front of a mirror!'

'Wow, that is so clever.' Aliyah clapped sarcastically. It was not even funny, but they both couldn't stop laughing. 'Okay, calm down,' said Raheem as they reached the traffic lights. The traffic ahead had eased, meaning that they would get there in the next five minutes.

'I was laughing because that was one of the jokes you said to me when we met for the first time.' Aliyah beamed at him. 'Remember, outside the Parkview Café at uni?'

'Oh yeah, it was. I still remember that day.' Raheem had been thinking about that day more often recently, going through every detail he could recall.

'When I met you, I never thought I'd like you. Honestly, I thought you were a right idiot.'

'What changed?'

Aliyah thought for a moment before saying, 'I don't even know, to be honest.'

'At least you changed your mind. I still don't like you.' He moved his head back as Aliyah aimed a slap at him.

'You think you're so funny, don't you?' said Aliyah, messing up his hair. ' You had *better* change your mind.'

'I'll try change it, but I can't promise that the new mind I get will be better than the one I will be changing.'

She twisted his ear.

'You are really hyper today.' It didn't matter whether she was moody or hyper, either way he loved her company.

'I had your Red Bull can this morning. I think it's got to me.'

'*That's* where it went, you little thief. I spent five minutes shouting at Samir.' Raheem turned into the car park.

'Hurry up, otherwise we won't get seats. It's always busy on Friday,' said Aliyah as he carefully reversed into a bay.

'Alright, chill out madam!'

Aliyah got out before he'd even stopped and hurried towards Grill and Pepperz. Raheem sat and smiled to himself, before following her. As he'd expected, the restaurant was full but the good news was that they were second in the queue.

'Are you okay to sit on the sofa? I'll give you a shout when your table is ready. Be about five minutes,' said the waitress.

'Which sofa, there are a few?' asked Raheem. The waitress frowned at him. Aliyah turned away to hide her laughter. 'Listen, I need a cigarette to calm down,' he continued as the waitress walked away.

'When are you going to stop smoking?' asked Aliyah exasperatedly.

'When I find a reason to quit,' he replied.

'You're reducing your life span by ten years. Isn't that enough of a reason?'

'I'd rather live till seventy-five than eighty-five.' This time, he had to dodge her leg as she aimed a kick at him. He went outside, but she followed him. 'Go back inside. What if it's our table next?' he said.

Aliyah leaned against the wall. 'She said our table will be ready in five minutes. She probably put us down the queue because she thought we were laughing at her.'

'Really? More like you couldn't be without me.'

'Well, we've only got a couple of months until left at uni, so make the most of every moment.'

His good spirits dipped at her words.

'I bet you forget about me once uni finishes,' Aliyah continued.

'You're right. I won't remember you.' Raheem put his cigarette packet back in his pocket. He didn't feel like having one now.

'So rude.' Aliyah pretended to look offended.

Raheem turned to face her and looked her directly in the eye. 'Because I only remember those people who I forget, so there's no chance of that happening with you.' He raised his arms wide, hoping for a hug, but Aliyah turned and walked inside saying, 'I need to go to the bathroom.'

Raheem walked back into the restaurant with his arms still raised. 'Your table is ready,' said the waitress bluntly when she spotted him. 'I know there are lots of tables to choose from but your table is number thirteen.' He slouched off, sat at the table and picked up the menu. He had still not decided what to order when Aliyah returned. 'You left me hanging,' he said.

'Sorry,' she replied, grabbing the menu out of his hands.

Their food took fifteen minutes to arrive, by which time Raheem had entertained Aliyah with his jokes.

There was no time for jokes when they started to eat. Raheem dropped his knife and fork on the table, having given up trying to cut his chicken.

'Let me show you how to do it.' Aliyah stood up and moved next to him.

'I can manage,' he replied grumpily.

Aliyah ignored him and took his knife and fork. 'So, you cut it like this,' she said. A boy on the table next to theirs was laughing at him.

'And now it's cut, you eat it with your fork.' Aliyah picked up a piece with his fork and put it into his mouth before sitting back on her chair. The chicken was really chewy as usual. It was only because of Aliyah that he would ever come here.

'I hope your husband hates Grill and Pepperz,' Raheem said.

'If he hates it, I'll divorce him.'

Raheem laughed, but the thought of Aliyah coming here with someone else made him feel lonely. It was their special thing and shouldn't be shared by anyone else. 'Do you know what the biggest reason for divorce is?' he asked as he finally managed to cut a piece of chicken by himself.

'What?'

'It's marriage.'

'You really are so hilarious.'

'It's a statement of fact!'

Aliyah shook her head. 'So, how are things with you and Sarah?'

Raheem took his time swallowing his chips before responding. He'd not had much contact with Sarah over the last few weeks. They had met a couple of times for food. He had assumed that she understood it was due to his deadlines and dissertation, but then again Sarah had rung him last year when he was sitting in his exam room. He doubted something as trivial as revision or his dissertation would stop her.

'It's fine, haven't really seen her much recently as I have been busy,' he said.

'What about Veronica and Aaron?'

'They're fine as well. Why? Have you heard something else?' he asked quickly.

Aliyah raised her eyebrows. 'No, I was just asking. I've noticed you get very defensive with questions, recently.'

Raheem looked down at his plate.

'I think Veronica is one of the prettiest girls at uni,' Aliyah continued. 'We went to town the other day after Uni. She has a great sense of fashion.'

His body temperature had increased and it had nothing to do with the extra hot sauce on his chips.

'If you weren't with Sarah, would you ask her out?' Aliyah asked.

Why was she asking him that? He decided to play safe. 'I don't know. That's a hypocritical question.'

'You mean hypothetical?'

'Yeah, *hypothetical.*'

Aliyah played with her food for a few seconds, seemingly lost in thought. 'I've been looking online for jobs in Glasgow. There's a lot of demand for social work up there and that's what I want to get into.'

'That's good. You'll get a job there straightaway after you graduate.'

'Fingers crossed.' Aliyah poured herself some water from the jug.

They stayed for another quarter of an hour. The drive back to Aliyah's house was quick as there wasn't as much traffic. It was the first time he'd been disappointed by a lack of traffic.

They said goodbye and Aliyah got out. She'd asked him if he wanted to come inside, but he declined because he needed to clean up his flat, as Samir had politely reminded him earlier. She headed up the footpath. He wanted to call after her to come back, but Aliyah continued until she was at the front door. She opened it and gave him a wave. Raheem's hand was still raised after the door had closed.

***

It was time to help Dan the man. As planned, Raheem and Samir had gone to the second floor at half three on Thursday afternoon. Raheem peered through a gap behind a large bookcase.

'What if we ask if we can sit down and she says no?' Samir whispered.

'I'll ask, that way she won't say no,' Raheem whispered back. Amy was reading through some notes she had been writing for the last ten minutes. It was now or never. 'Come on, we need to go, we been behind this bookshelf for ages.'

167

Together they walked out from behind the bookshelf to the far corner of the second floor where Amy was sitting. It was a good job there weren't any spare tables, otherwise it would have looked weird to sit with her. Raheem had seen her around uni over the last couple of years but had never spoken to her. She still hadn't noticed them, despite the fact that they were mere feet from her.

Raheem cleared his throat and she looked up. She had jet-black hair and large hazel eyes, which had a permanently surprised look. 'Hi, is it okay if we sit here? There are no more free tables and first floor is too noisy,' he said.

Amy smiled and moved some of her books to the side. 'Sure. That's why I never sit on the first floor – can't concentrate.'

'Thanks.' Raheem took the seat opposite her and Samir sat next to him. They took out their books and notepads.

Five minutes later, she had not said another word to them. It looked like they would have to start the conversation. Just as Raheem was thinking what to say, Samir spoke. 'Nice weather eh?' If there was a list of how not to start a conversation, talking about the weather would probably be near the top.

'Hmm, it is a nice day. I really don't want to be stuck inside but I've got a lot of revision to do,' said Amy without looking up.

Samir picked up one of his books and raised it to his face. It looked like Raheem would have to take over. 'Have you got that book, the big blue criminology one, Samir? I checked earlier and there aren't any left in the library,' he said.

'No, I don't. Dan's got it. You can ask him,' said Samir loudly.

Amy looked up from her notepad.

'Do you reckon he'll lend me it?' Raheem took out his phone.

'Course he will, Dan always helps others. I've never met anyone as helpful as him.' Samir was really overdoing it.

Raheem texted Daniel to come to the second floor. Five minutes later, Daniel joined them.

'I thought it might be you when they said Dan. How've you been?' asked Amy as Daniel sat down.

'Yeah, Daniel is not really a common name!' said Raheem. No one laughed.

'I've been alright, just busy,' said Daniel. So far it had all gone to plan.

They sat around for another five minutes before Samir made an excuse to go to the toilet so that he could ring Veronica. Daniel and Amy continued chatting; Daniel seemed to have got back some of his confidence.

'Veronica's coming in two minutes. We'd better go,' muttered Samir as he sat back down.

'Okay.' Raheem trusted Veronica to play her part convincingly. If she could act as if she didn't know him in front of Aaron, this would be easy.

'Thanks for the book, Dan. I'll give it back to you tomorrow. We're just going to go to silent study room on third floor,' said Raheem as he and Samir stood up.

'No worries. I'll see you later.'

'Bye,' said Amy.

Raheem winked at Daniel as he headed out of the door. 'It went alright, eh?' he said as they waited in the corridor for Veronica.

'I fucked up though, when I asked about the weather,' said Samir.

'When have you never fucked up on something...?'

They waited a minute before Veronica turned up.

'You know what do to,' said Raheem.

Veronica grinned and gave them twirl. 'How do I look?'

'So good that I'm starting to feel a bit jealous of Dan,' replied Raheem.

Samir put his arm around Raheem. 'They're sitting on the back table,' he said to Veronica. 'You do what you need to do. I will keep hold of Raheem, in case he gets a bit too jealous.'

Veronica grinned, before heading into the second floor. Raheem and Samir turned to go down the stairs, but before they reached the door it opened and Rachel appeared with her mate, Emma.

'What's going on here?' said Rachel as she saw Samir holding Raheem.

'Nothing. He just got a bit emotional. The stress of uni is getting to him,' said Raheem as Samir let go and hugged her.

'You poor thing, you should have called me,' said Rachel sympathetically, patting Samir's head.

'Emma, isn't it?' Raheem asked as he stepped ever so slightly in front of the entrance to the second floor.

169

'Sure is,' replied Emma.

'What are you guys doing?' Samir was still holding onto Rachel.

'We were just going do some revision together. I could barely understand the lecture we just had, it was so hard,' said Rachel. 'Why don't you two join us?'

The girls really had to choose the second floor, didn't they?

'You know what really helps before revising? A nice coffee. Come on, let's go to the café,' said Samir. Raheem was not in the mood for a coffee with salt in it like last time.

'He is thoughtful, but if he was *very* thoughtful he'd have suggested that you ladies need a cold drink,' said Raheem. 'So, we should go student union instead.'

'Come on, then, student union it is,' said Samir.

Raheem pressed for the lift and they entered it.

'I'm sure I saw Veronica coming this way. Ask her if she wants to come with us,' said Rachel.

'She has a deadline today so she won't be able to make it,' said Raheem as the lift doors opened.

'She does business management, doesn't she?' Rachel asked as they crossed the ground floor. There were a lot of angry students gathered around the IT helpdesk.

'Erm… yep... I haven't really seen her in a while,' said Raheem. 'Ladies, are we okay to meet you at the student union in a bit? Just need to go for a cigarette.'

'What do you want? We can order while we wait,' Rachel offered.

'No, don't worry; I am getting it today. We'll see you soon.'

'Don't be too long,' said Rachel as she and Emma headed towards the union bar.

'I really needed a cigarette but I left my pack at home.' Samir was fumbling in his pockets.

Raheem searched his pockets but couldn't find his own pack. 'I think I lost my deck.' He checked his bag.

'You need to quit smoking, lads. It kills.' Liam was sitting on the sofa near the stairs.

'We said we will give you the money on the 14th,' said Samir irritably.

Liam stood up. He looked back and picked up his keys, which had dropped out where he'd been sitting. 'That's why you should never carry keys in your pocket. So easy to lose,' he said as he put them in his bag.

'I think you need a girlfriend. You seem lonely,' said Raheem. It wasn't the best thing to say.

Liam walked up to them. 'If I don't get my money, you two won't have any girlfriends either.' They had no reply to that. 'Also, if you try act smart one more time, I will increase the price.' He walked back to the library, shoulder barging Samir on the way.

'Come on, let's go,' said Raheem. They would have to go to the campus shop to buy cigarettes. He was about to leave the ground floor when two identical yellow lighters on the floor next to Samir made him stop. 'Are they yours?' he asked, pointing at them.

Samir looked down and picked them up. 'Yeah, must have dropped them. They always fall out my pocket' he said. 'Come on, I've got two cigarettes left. I was only messing when I said I'd left my deck at home.'

Two yellow lighters...?

'Do you want to smoke inside instead?' Samir called. Raheem followed him outside. 'What happened over there?' Samir asked, lighting his cigarette.

Raheem shrugged. He didn't know what it was, but something had popped into his mind and disappeared straight away. He didn't know why two identical lighters would have that effect. Perhaps he was overthinking.

'I wish he had that camera on him,' said Samir bitterly. 'I would have taken it off him within two seconds, not like he can do anything about it.'

'It will be at his residence but fuck knows where he lives,' replied Raheem. 'He won't carry it around with him. That's why that day he showed us the pictures, he was stood next to security, in case we tried to take the camera off him.'

'Really? I thought he was stood there because he was learning how to be a security officer.'

'Can you tell me where you learnt to be a comedian?'

'Can I borrow your lighter, please?' It was Jasmine. She was dressed in office wear and looked exhausted. 'I have a cigarette this time,' she added when she saw the looks they were giving her.

Samir slowly passed her one of his lighters.

'Are you just a social smoker then?' asked Raheem.

Jasmine nodded. 'Only when I'm stressed.'

She always seemed stressed when she saw them. Veronica had told Raheem that she'd told Jasmine that they'd split up but were still on speaking terms and not to mention it to him.

'Had a long day at work?' asked Samir.

'It was terrible, hence the stress,' sighed Jasmine. 'I should never have got a job here; it's too hectic for anyone working in Law. I should have stayed in Leicester. I would do anything to go back. I'll see you later guys. Our Madam Veronica forgot to hoover this morning and I've got friends coming over, so I've got some cleaning to do.'

'She didn't give me my lighter back!' said Samir indignantly as she walked away.

'You've got a spare one!'

Samir huffed and took out his flat keys and a couple of old iPhones. 'I need to sell these phones. I keep forgetting.' He held out the keys to Raheem. 'Where can I get copies of these cut? Need a spare, just in case.'

'What is it with you and two versions of everything?' Raheem asked. 'Two lighters, two girlfriends, two phones, two keys...' Hold on... The thought that had fleetingly entered his mind when he saw the lighters on the floor returned but this time it remained.

'You got that look on your face that you get when you're going to say something stupid,' said Samir apprehensively.

Raheem didn't answer. It was a reckless idea. A dangerous idea.

'What is wrong with you today?' said Samir loudly.

'I think ... we need to talk to Jasmine. And keep them two phones. Don't sell them.'

'Why?'

Jasmine was still visible in the distance. It looked like there might be a way to get that camera after all.

Chapter 17

'Fucking hell Raheem, do you think I'm some sort of actress?' demanded Jasmine angrily as they walked around the lake. Samir, who had been feeding the ducks opposite the sign which stated clearly not to feed the ducks, caught up with them.

'Please, Jasmine, it's the only way,' Raheem pleaded, hiding behind her as a dog ran past.

'I said no. I don't have time for your little games. I'm busy as it is.'

And he had thought it would be easy. 'Think about it at least,' he said. This was their only hope.

'No means no,' said Jasmine irritably.

Raheem picked up a stone and threw it as hard as he could into the lake, nearly slipping off the path and falling in the lake himself.

'I'm going for a jog' Jasmine continued. 'Meet you at the back entrance – you need to drop me back home. Veronica has texted to say she needs my car a bit longer.' She put in her earphones before setting off at a quick jog.

Raheem and Samir went towards the bench near the back entrance of Burydale Park and sat down. 'Bad luck,' said Samir, taking out a water bottle

'Was such a good idea as well,' said Raheem bitterly, grabbing the bottle from Samir and downing half of it in one go. He'd thought about it last night and decided it was the only way. Liam wouldn't carry the camera with him, it would be at his residence, but they would need a set of keys to get in whilst he was not there. They would need to get to Liam's bag to steal his keys, get them cut and return them without him realising. But for all of that, they needed Jasmine.

'You need to offer her an incentive,' said Samir wisely.

'Like what? Offering to sleep with her for a night?' Raheem leaned back on the bench and closed his eyes.

'I said incentive!'

173

Raheem kept his eyes closed. What could he offer Jasmine as an incentive? Veronica couldn't do it because Liam knew her, and there was no one else they could ask.

Samir's phone began ringing. 'Hello, Danny boy. How can I help?' Raheem could guess why Daniel had called. 'It's been one day, Dan, calm down. Amy will contact you soon, okay? I need to go now. I'll ring you later.' Samir disconnected the call and shook his head. 'I said three days to him, not one day.'

Raheem could easily have fallen asleep on the bench. He thought back to when he'd gone to Parkview café with Aliyah, the day she'd told him her plan was to get married after graduating. So much had happened since then. He was looking forward to starting work after studying but getting that first job would be difficult. Like Aliyah had said, it wasn't what you knew, it was who you knew.

'Jasmine seems so stressed about her job. She told me earlier she wants to go back to Leicester but apparently it's hard to get into a law firm there,' said Samir.

'What?' Raheem opened his eyes.

'I said Jasmine wants to get a job with a law firm in Leicester. What you smiling for?'

'You're the biggest accidental genius I've ever met,' said Raheem happily, taking out his phone.

Aliyah had been right: it was *who* you knew, and it looked as though Raheem could offer Jasmine an incentive. He just hoped his brother wouldn't let him down.

***

Recently, things seemed to be falling into place by accident – not that Raheem was complaining. He had asked Jasmine to email him her CV and a covering letter, which he promptly sent to his brother. Raheem got a call a few days later to say that as long as Jasmine didn't have a fake law degree, the job would be hers at the end of May as one of his brother's staff members was leaving then. Raheem had not told Jasmine yet. He felt it would be better to hang fire for a couple of days and reconfirm with his brother in case he changed his mind.

Starbucks in the city centre wasn't the most exciting place to be on a sunny Saturday afternoon. It was quarter to two; they had told Aaron to meet them here at half one.

'Where the hell is he?' Samir was looking out of the window at the high street.

'Probably finding somewhere to park. You know what it's like finding parking in town.' Raheem glanced out of the window towards the big Morrison's store. Hannah would be finishing her shift at two o'clock and they had the perfect view of the entrance.

'There's no back exit, is there?' Samir asked.

'There is, but all staff enter and leave by the main entrance,' said Raheem.

'You want me to go for a cigarette just after two o'clock?'

'Yeah, stop asking questions! Just make sure when you see Hannah it doesn't look like you were waiting for her!'

'Alright, calm down you little bitch.'

They had waited another minute when Aaron finally came in. 'Remember, no overacting,' muttered Raheem.

'Says you.'

Aaron was looking smart in a shirt and dark-blue jeans. His sunglasses were on top of his head. 'Alright, lads?' He shook hands with them both as he sat down.

'Good, bro. Listen, let's order first then we can chat,' said Raheem.

'Sounds a good plan.'

'It's a great plan. Trust me,' said Raheem.

Samir went to place their order and came back carrying two cups.

'Where's my espresso?' asked Raheem indignantly as Samir handed Aaron his latte.

Samir opened the lid of the cup he was holding. 'This one is espresso – I forgot to order my hot chocolate. Shit.'

'At least give me mine,' Raheem said as Samir walked back to the till. He handed Raheem his drink before hurrying back to order his hot chocolate.

He returned after a minute and sat next to Raheem, who turned to Aaron. There was no time for small talk. 'I got your text about Veronica. Are things not working out?' Raheem asked.

Aaron placed his cup on the table. 'No, I don't think they are. It's almost as if she doesn't want to get back together again. We haven't kissed in a whole year!'

'Even you've had one in that time,' Samir muttered to Raheem.

'What's that?' Aaron asked as Raheem kicked Samir under the table.

'He said that *is* a long time,' said Raheem.

'Yeah, it is.'

'So just to be clear, did you cheat on her? Is that how all this started?' Raheem asked.

'Well, kind of.' Aaron shifted uncomfortably in his chair.

Why didn't he ever give a straight answer? 'Look you might as well be honest, that way we can help you be with Han— Veronica.' Raheem corrected himself just in time. He really needed to control his mouth. It would have been a bit of a giveaway if he'd mentioned Hannah.

'It wasn't exactly cheating,' said Aaron defensively. 'I was in the club and a bit drunk and kissed another woman who happened to be a friend of Veronica's.'

Raheem had heard it all now. Kissing your girlfriend's friend was apparently not exactly cheating.

'Interesting,' said Samir thoughtfully.

'I know, but it was a mistake. It's not as if I slept with her. I'm not that much of a bastard.'

Raheem coughed as he sipped his espresso.

'Everything okay?' asked Aaron.

Raheem nodded and wiped his mouth with a tissue before saying, 'Look Aaron, personally, I think if there's no trust then there is no point in continuing.'

Aaron looked taken aback. 'It's not just that. I mean ... I did sometimes get really angry at her and shouted... I get angry easily – but that was when I was drinking heavily.'

'You don't look the type to start on people,' said Samir.

'I'm not. I sometimes think that I should just move on from the past.'

For once, he had spoken sense; now was the moment to press the advantage. 'You're right, Aaron. You shouldn't worry about the past. I gave Samir the same advice,' said Raheem seriously. Samir frowned. Raheem continued, 'Samir also cheated on his girlfriend. He made a mistake, she dumped him, he got depressed. I was the one who helped him get his confidence back. Then he went on a couple of dates and managed to move on and get his life back together. Look at him now. He is with Rachel for the past two years and they have never even argued once.'

Samir was shaking his head in disbelief; Aaron, on the other hand, was hanging on his every word.

'So basically, what I'm saying is never mention to a woman that you cheated in a relationship,' said Raheem. 'They are funny creatures, women. Once they know you've cheated, they will always suspect you. Let's hope you stay with Veronica, but if not and you find someone else, don't mention your past to them. Samir might be better to talk to about that, though. I've never cheated, so I wouldn't know.'

Raheem's speech was met with silence. Aaron looked like he was pondering his words.

'I don't suppose you can find out what Veronica really thinks without her knowing that I've asked you to find out?' he said tentatively.

He just wouldn't let go of Veronica, would he?

'That won't be a problem,' said Raheem.

'Thanks, appreciate it.'

Raheem nudged Samir. It had just turned two. 'I'm just going for a cigarette,' said Samir, standing up.

The moment he left, Raheem turned to Aaron. 'I know you like Veronica. But I honestly think you need to move on.'

Aaron looked at him in surprise. 'But I thought you were going to find out what she really thinks about me?' he said accusingly.

'I will do,' said Raheem. 'But I don't want you going back to your old ways if she doesn't want to be with you. That's what I'm more concerned about. I honestly reckon you should go on dates pretty quickly when she— I mean *if* she says no.'

Aaron avoided answering and took out his phone. It seemed like he didn't want to think what would happen if Veronica said no. They sat in silence for a couple of minutes until the door to Starbucks opened and Samir walked in, accompanied by Hannah who was carrying three large Morrison's bags.

'Hi, Hannah, what a surprise. Come and join us,' said Raheem.

Samir hurried into the chair next to Raheem.

'Hey, guys,' she said. 'I'd just finished work and saw Samir outside. I'm not disturbing you, am I?'

'Not at all,' said Raheem, waving his hand. Hannah sat down on the seat next to Aaron.

'This is Aaron,' Samir told Hannah.

She smiled at Aaron, who smiled back.

'I don't think you've met Hannah yet, have you?' asked Raheem. 'Aaron, stand up a second, that chair leg looks loose.'

Aaron stood up, which allowed them to see how tall he was.

'It looks okay, sit back down' said Raheem.

'I think I saw you in university that day when I was with Raheem,' Aaron said to Hannah as he sat back down.

'I remember wondering who you were. I'd never seen you in uni before,' said Hannah.

'I was visiting Raheem. I finished uni a couple of years ago. I'm working in Stalford until May because we've opened an office here.'

'What did you study?'

'Computer forensics. What do you study?'

'Wow, that's sounds interesting. I do criminology and psychology, same as Raheem and Samir.'

'Trust me, your course definitely sounds more interesting than mine. Are you doing a dissertation this year?'

They seemed to have forgotten that Raheem and Samir were there, which suited them perfectly. Aaron's latte sat forgotten on the table. It was now time for the final part of the plan. Raheem nudged Samir again, who took out his phone under the table and rang Raheem.

'I'll just get this call. Back in a bit,' Raheem said as he walked away. He headed towards the toilets around the corner so they couldn't see him. Once outside, he stood and waited for a couple of minutes.

'Excuse me, are you wanting to go in?' said a staff member who was walking past.

'Oh no, er … I changed my mind,' said Raheem.

The man looked nonplussed as Raheem pocketed his phone and returned to the table, trying his best to look worried. 'Samir, we need to go. Michael's been taken to hospital; he's had another panic attack.'

Aaron and Hannah stopped talking and turned to look as Samir leapt up dramatically from his chair.

'Is everything okay?' asked Hannah.

'Just one of our mates, he's had a few panic attacks recently,' said Raheem. 'Stress of uni, I guess. We need to go and see him.'

Samir put on his jacket. 'Hannah, are you okay getting home? Those bags look heavy. We can take them and drop them off at yours after we come back from hospital.'

'Thanks, love, but I should be fine,' said Hannah kindly.

No one spoke for a few seconds. What the hell was Aaron waiting for?

'It's going to be a bit of a walk to your flat from here. It's better to go in a car,' said Raheem pointedly.

'It's okay, I usually get a taxi,' said Hannah.

Aaron was still silent.

'That's a waste of money, Hannah,' said Samir impatiently.

'I can drop you off. I'm parked close by,' Aaron said eventually. It had taken him long enough.

'Great! You drop off Hannah when you guys are finished. Take your time, though,' said Raheem happily.

'Do you know where she lives?' asked Samir.

'That's for Hannah to tell him. Let's go!' said Raheem in exasperation. Samir really was going to find a way to fuck this up.

'Oh… Yeah, you're right.'

They said goodbye and hurried out of Starbucks. 'What a plan, eh?' said Raheem once they had walked a short distance away.

'They hit it off quite well, better than I thought they would,' replied Samir.

'Hope it stays that way.'

'Well, we'll find out from Hannah next week. Don't text her and ask, though. That way it looks obvious.'

'No? You don't say?'

'I nearly messed up when I said that thing about you getting a kiss before him!' said Samir ecstatically.

'Oh yeah, tell me about it,' said Raheem darkly. They could laugh about it now, but if Aaron had heard they certainly wouldn't have been laughing.

'I couldn't help it. Sometimes shit just comes out and I can't control it. I think me and you have the same problem.'

'Yeah, we do. The only difference is my shit comes out of my backside and yours comes out of your mouth.'

'Wow, you're funny! Teach me how to be like you.'

'Thick twat. How the hell was Aaron meant to know where Hannah lives?'

Samir laughed. 'Fuck knows why I said that.'

They continued chatting as they walked to the car park. On a couple of occasions, Raheem thought he saw Aliyah, but when he looked closer it was someone else.

'Just out of interest, why did you say the name Michael?' asked Samir as he turned the car on.

Raheem grinned as the memory of being with Aliyah on the first day back at university last year returned to him. 'It's a common name. If anyone asks, we can say it wasn't *this* Michael, it was *that* Michael.'

***

Their plan seemed to have worked. Hannah told them that she and Aaron would be meeting up for coffee again later in the week. 'He's really nice,' she said.

Hopefully Aaron had taken their advice about moving on and would not mention his drink problem. That was a sure way to put off any woman. In the meantime, Raheem and Samir had been working on their dissertations. Aliyah had kindly offered to proofread some of their work, for which they were both extremely grateful.

It was on a wet Monday afternoon that Raheem was sitting with Sarah on the third floor of the library. The atmosphere was a bit tense.

'Aaron mentioned that he went for coffee with you two,' said Sarah casually as she texted on her phone.

Raheem had just finished the first paragraph of his essay, but at Sarah's words he looked up from his laptop. 'Which two?'

'You and Samir, obviously. Not like you two ever do anything without each other.'

Raheem returned back to his laptop. 'Yeah, we did. Why?'

He shouldn't have said the last part. Sure enough, Sarah put her phone down on the table a little harder than necessary and said, 'I was just asking. Can't I ask anything?'

Raheem didn't have the energy to start bickering with her. 'I'm just going to the toilet. Be back in a bit.'

Sarah didn't respond. As Raheem left through the back entrance, he passed Aliyah in the corridor who was heading into the computer labs with a couple of friends. She asked if he wanted to join them, but Raheem told her that he was with Sarah. Aliyah said she'd meet up with them later before she went home.

Raheem pushed open the door to the toilet. As luck would have it, Liam was drying his hands next to the sink. Automatically Raheem turned and tried to go out, but Liam had seen him in the mirror. 'Oi!' he called as Raheem stepped back into the corridor. Raheem screwed up his face in frustration and went back in.

'You having a nice little chat with your girlfriend?' asked Liam.

Why was his timing always so bad? 'I wouldn't say it's a nice chat,' Raheem said grimly.

Liam smirked. 'It definitely won't be nice if you don't have the money on 14th May.' He threw the paper towel at him, narrowly missing his face.

'Where do you want to meet for the money?' Raheem asked as though nothing had happened. Last year, the prick would not have dared look him in the eye, let alone throw things at him. How times had changed. For the worse.

Liam was about to respond when the door opened and a couple of guys walked in. He tapped his nose and left. Raheem washed his hands before heading back to his table. 'Fucking bastard' he said angrily as he pushed open the door to the third floor.

Sarah was not alone at the table; Jason was also there and, to raise Raheem's blood pressure further, he was sitting in his chair. They were so busy yapping that they didn't notice Raheem watching them. 'Ahem,' he said, clearing his throat.

Jason looked at him and immediately jumped up. 'Sorry, didn't realise I had taken your chair. Sit down.'

He was being asked to sit down on his own chair! Raheem slowly sat as Jason said, 'How you getting on with—?'

'Get a chair, Jason,' interjected Sarah.

'I'll get one for you!' said Raheem enthusiastically. He grabbed an empty chair from the next table and placed it between him and Sarah. Jason looked pleasantly surprised, but from the way Sarah was looking at him it was clear she wasn't buying it.

'You were asking something, Jason?' Raheem said politely.

'I was asking how you're getting on with—?'

'Have you been to the new dessert place on Manor Road? We were *supposed* to go the other day,' interrupted Sarah. That was what she was annoyed about? It had totally slipped Raheem's mind.

Jason turned to her. 'Sarah, it's got the best desserts in the city. You two need to go.'

'Really? What did you get?' Sarah asked.

Raheem sighed and looked around the library. Liam was grinning at him and making the camera pose. If only he wasn't in this situation, he would walk up to him and punch his teeth out. Sarah and Jason were now talking about organising a trip to Alton Towers in the summer with their friend group in Birmingham. That was also depressing, made even worse by the fact that Sarah told Raheem that he would also be coming.

When he went back to his laptop to continue his essay, he was met with a blank screen because the battery had died. Scowling, he opened his bag to take out his laptop charger but it wasn't there – he had left it back at the flat. He had also forgotten to save the paragraph he had written before he went to the toilet.

Sarah was laughing at something Jason had said. Liam raised his middle finger at Raheem. Making his mind up on the spot, Raheem decided he was going to ring Jasmine this week and tell her that they were ready for their plan. They needed to find out where Liam lived and who he lived with. Ideally he had wanted to get that information before he and Samir asked Jasmine to help them but he needed to do something. The problem they had was that Liam would definitely notice if they followed him home. Raheem knew a couple of people Liam hung around with, but there was a chance they would tell Liam if either he or Samir asked for his address. They couldn't take that risk; one mistake and their whole plan would go down the drain. What they really needed was someone who knew Liam, but knew them as well. Someone they could trust.

Raheem received a text on his phone. It was from Daniel.

Going for dinner with Amy later tonight!

Sometimes the obvious things were the hardest to notice.

Chapter 18

Raheem had talked it through with Samir and they were both in agreement: Daniel was the best man for the job. Samir had gone back home to Manchester for the weekend , so Raheem went on his own to visit Daniel in his apartment.

He told Daniel that Liam had pictures of them on his camera with other women on nights out and was threatening to show their girlfriends. He didn't mention who the 'other women' were.

'So, it's definitely Wednesday, 11th May?' Daniel made a note on his phone.

'Correct,' said Raheem. 'So, you need to have a house party that night and call James and Callum.'

Daniel made another note. James and Callum were uni mates of his and they were Liam's flatmates. They had to be out on the night Raheem and Samir broke in.

'And you are going to get the keys cut?' asked Daniel.

'Yep.'

'How are you going to get his keys without him realising? And how will you make sure he's also out on the night you break in? I don't think he will come if I invited him to my house party to be honest.'

Raheem began pacing around the apartment. 'I've got another plan for that,' he said. There was only one way to guarantee Liam would be out and he'd be discussing that with Jasmine, once she'd confirmed that she would be able to do it.

Raheem leant against the window ledge. The plan was risky and a lot could go wrong. The only suitable time to carry it out would be a few days before 14th May, which was the day they were due to give the money. Whatever happened, he couldn't live with himself if Sarah found out he'd cheated on her. Aaron would be fully justified in beating the shit out of him. He didn't want to put Sarah in a position where she would see her boyfriend fighting with her brother. Rachel would also be devastated if she found out about Samir. He could not let that happen.

***

Two days after speaking to Daniel, Raheem was sitting on a bench in the city centre having just finished work. He had been on the till most of his shift because a couple of colleagues had called in sick, and his legs were aching. He was just about to get up when Aaron walked out of Hugo Boss opposite, accompanied by a group of friends. Aaron spotted him (as he always did) and, after a quick chat with his friends, made his way over purposefully.

Raheem stood up just in case Liam had shown Aaron the pictures and he was about to punch him. He would probably still get knocked out, but he had a better chance of defending himself if he was standing.

'Raheem, what are you doing here?' Aaron asked happily, shaking his hand enthusiastically.

Maybe Raheem wouldn't have to defend himself after all. 'Just finished work,' he said.

'Good, good,' Aaron muttered, more to himself than Raheem.

Aaron looked as though he wanted to tell him something. He finally stopped glancing around and said, 'Me and Hannah are serious about each other.'

Now that was the kind of news Raheem wanted to hear. 'That's great,' he said, grinning.

'Cheers. We've not known each other long but it was obvious from the start, to be honest,' said Aaron modestly. Good job he didn't know that Raheem was probably even more pleased about this than he was.

'We knew you two would be perfect,' said Raheem happily.

Aaron's smile slowly disappeared. '*We* knew? Who else knew?'

Shit. He had fucked up. Again. 'I mean... When I say we ... me and Samir.'

'You mean that you and Samir thought that me and Hannah would be perfect.'

185

'That's right,' said Raheem, relieved.

Aaron looked thoughtful. 'But I haven't told Samir yet.'

Oh yeah. Raheem hadn't thought of that. 'I mean, I *know* you will be perfect because... I *know* what I think because I am ... me,' he said. 'I know Samir knows you will be perfect ... because I *know* him and I *know* how he thinks ... if that makes sense.' It didn't make sense even to him, truth be told.

'You have a complicated way of explaining simple things.' Aaron grinned. 'I best be off. Got a few things to get. I'll let Sarah know once things progress. I haven't told her about Veronica yet. I'll pop down to yours sometime this week.'

'Anytime, bro,' said Raheem as Aaron headed back towards his friends. That was one problem solved. It now seemed as if Veronica wouldn't have to worry about Aaron anymore now that he was serious about Hannah. But it didn't change anything regarding the pictures.

He took out his phone and checked his messages. There was one from Jasmine.

Hey, I had an interview at your brother's law firm and he offered me the job, starting in June! I'm happy to help you once he sends me the contract and I have it in writing. Deal? and thank you so much x

***

'The last time I saw you this happy was that night when you were in bed with me,' said Veronica as they headed towards the train station.

After the most awkward pause in history, Raheem grinned shiftily. He had just finished telling her about Jasmine's offer to help them. He'd also told her about how he and Samir had convinced Aaron he needed to move on. He didn't mention anything about Hannah. Veronica had said that Aaron had hardly been in contact with her over the past few weeks.

They were heading for the train station together. Veronica was going back to Leicester for the weekend to see her family. As she went inside to get her train, Raheem stood and remembered the night he'd been with her in his flat.

His misty-eyed expression must have lingered because a woman walked towards him and said, 'Have you never seen a lady before?'

'I have, but not one as stupid as you,' was his response. He looked at her, before taking a step back and clapping a hand over his mouth. It was Sarah.

'What the hell did you just say to me, Raheem?'

Raheem took another step back. His heart was hammering against his chest, both about what he had just said and whether Sarah had seen him with Veronica. 'I didn't know it was you,' he said quickly, glancing towards the train station. Veronica wasn't there.

'Don't lie! You were staring right at me when I walked up to you!' said Sarah furiously. Some passers-by looked at them.

The last thing he needed was for her to cause a scene in the city centre. 'I didn't know it was you,' he pleaded, putting his arm around her.

'Don't touch me.' She moved his hand away.

'Babe, what the hell? Would I ever call you stupid? I swear I didn't know it was you!'

'So who were you looking at? What are you doing here?' she snapped back.

He smiled, relieved that she hadn't seen him with Veronica.

'What's funny!?'

'Nothing... I was just – seeing my friend off at the train station. *He* is going back home for a few days.' It was true that he was seeing off a friend at the station, though he'd rather keep the name of the friend private.

Sarah had that familiar suspicious look on her face. 'I don't believe you,' she said quietly.

He was in trouble now alright. There was an alleyway to his left. If Sarah started shouting at him, he'd rather it happened somewhere quieter.

'Look, let's go over here.' He nodded to the alleyway. She didn't say anything but walked past him and turned into it as he followed. They walked halfway down before going behind a wall. There were some old flats behind them, but nobody was outside.

Raheem turned to face Sarah. 'Look, I swear down I didn't know it was you. I would never say something like that to you and you know that, so let's get that out of the way.'

Sarah didn't reply. Raheem hated it when she did that; it was an annoying habit of hers. Usually, it meant she'd accepted what he said but couldn't bring herself to admit it. But he needed to be sure. 'So that's clear then?' he asked.

Sarah folded her arms and nodded. 'Why have you not contacted me recently?'

First it was what he'd said, then it was who he'd dropped at the train station, and now it was that he'd not been in contact as much as usual. 'I've just been busy. You know what final year of uni is like, plus I've taken a bit of overtime at work recently.'

Sarah looked over his shoulder at the flats as though trying to think of another accusation to level against him.

'How's Jason?' he asked casually. Whenever his name was mentioned she was usually happy.

Sarah's eyes swivelled back at him. 'I don't know what you've got against Jason. I've been feeling down recently and he's been there for me.'

'Was I supposed to have a dream that you were feeling down? You never told me,' said Raheem angrily. She'd been distant with him for a while now, and if it wasn't about the fact that she knew about him and Veronica he didn't know what else it could be.

'There is no need to mention it, you should be able to tell' said Sarah coldly.

Laughter behind him made him turn around. A group of students were heading out of the flats, one of them wearing a Winnie-the-Pooh costume. It was then it clicked. 'Hold on, are you angry because of that teddy bear thing at the cinema?'

Those bears were more hassle than they were worth. Sarah looked away, which was enough to tell him that his guess was probably right. Now he thought about it, she'd been like this with him since then.

'Look, I got one for Aliyah because it wouldn't have looked nice if both you and … Veronica – that's her name, isn't it? Anyway, if you two had got them and Aliyah didn't, it would have looked bad. I would have done that whoever it was.'

188

Sarah stared at him. It was impossible to tell what she was thinking. 'Can you cook for me tonight at your place?'

Raheem scratched his head. Women were really weird sometimes. 'Yeah, sure. I've been looking for an excuse to make stir-fry for a while.'

'At least you remembered I like that,' said Sarah.

'Obviously, I wouldn't forget.' Raheem smiled. He was still a bit taken aback at her sudden mood change, but he had gotten away big time today. He'd been so daft to walk with Veronica in the city centre on a Friday evening when neither Sarah nor Aaron were working. He couldn't make the same mistake again. He really needed to think before doing stupid things.

Sarah grabbed his arm and rested her head on his shoulder as they began walking. 'Aaron seems in a good mood recently,' she said. 'Ever since he met you, he's changed. I'm so glad you two get on. I was initially worried that you wouldn't.'

'Hmm, yeah,' said Raheem.

'Have you got your car? I got a taxi into town to return something. Fiona dropped me off as I couldn't be bothered to try find parking,' she said softly.

'I have my car, but I've parked near the market so it's a bit of a walk,' he replied.

'The longer the better. I like our walks together.'

They continued talking on their way to the car park. All was okay. For now.

***

Raheem was waiting impatiently in his car in the university car park. Samir had said he would be five minutes but it had been fifteen. Just as he was about to ring him, the passenger door opened and Samir got in.

'Why have you bought envelopes? You've never sent a letter in your life,' said Raheem.

'It's all classed as stationary,' said Samir as he start putting them in the glove compartment. 'You never know when you'll need some—' He broke off.

189

Liam was standing in front of Raheem's car. He walked around and sat in the back seat. 'What you doing?' asked Raheem angrily.

'Just need a lift to my lecture in Parkview,' said Liam innocently.

They were parked one hundred feet from the entrance, but there was no point arguing. Raheem turned on the engine and drove forward.

'Can you park a bit closer, please?' said Liam smugly.

Raheem positioned his car as close to the entrance as possible without going onto the path.

'I'll take a few of them, if you don't mind.' Liam nodded at the remaining envelopes in Samir's hand. 'I think they might come in handy.'

Samir held them out without looking at him. Liam took a handful of envelopes before getting out of the car. 'Cheers for the lift, fellas' he said brightly before disappearing into the Parkview entrance.

Samir turned to Raheem. 'Was being with Veronica really worth it?'

'Fuck off!'

Raheem started to drive, but a noise behind him made him look back. Liam had left his car door open, and it had hit a bin.

***

It was a sign of how bad things were that Raheem and Samir had decided to go to West Park campus on Tuesday afternoon to work. It was Samir's idea. He said it would be good to get a change of environment and, seeing as Liam had been coming to the city campus recently, at least they wouldn't have to see his disgusting face. Raheem didn't like the idea of going to a different campus just to avoid Liam, but reluctantly agreed.

The West Park campus was not nearly as good as the city one; for a start, the city campus women were definitely better looking. The West Park campus was very old and its stone walls made it a depressing environment. The good thing, however, was that Aliyah had decided to join them.

'You two seem a lot calmer. We should come here more often,' Aliyah said as she handed Raheem his laptop having rewritten the conclusion for his essay.

'That's because there are no distractions,' yawned Samir. He was right about that. They had both silently got on with their work today.

'Pass me that Coke can,' said Raheem. Samir lobbed it at him and he opened it, which was a mistake. Five minutes later, he returned to the table having dried himself in the bathroom.

'You're so dopey sometimes. Didn't you think it would do that after Samir threw it?' Aliyah asked as he sat back down.

'He doesn't think about anything Aliyah, that's his problem' said Samir.

Raheem smiled sarcastically.

They were sitting on the ground floor, which had the largest study space. The security team had their desk right next to the entrance. It was much harder to sneak in hot food here compared to the city campus. He had been here a few times before in his first and second year with Sarah. She preferred it and had told him it was a lot more peaceful.

They worked for another hour before Aliyah said she was going to see one of her friends on the second floor. On the pretext of going to the toilet, Raheem went out of the library. He was going for a cigarette, but Samir was getting quite a bit of work done today and he didn't want to distract him.

'Hannah was here,' said Samir when Raheem returned back to the table.

'Oh, yeah, she goes to the gym here.' The sports facilities and scenery were definitely better than the city campus. At the back of the field they had the tennis courts, football and rugby pitches, as well as the gym.

'She was in a rush,' Samir continued, 'but said to tell you that the same guy was checking her out again earlier outside the gym. She says you'll know who she is on about.'

Raheem did not immediately register what Samir had said. 'Who was checking her out?' he asked.

'She said the same guy was checking her out. She told me to tell you.'

'So what shall I do? Do you want me to … oh, fucking hell.'

'What's up?'

Raheem closed his eyes. Every single one of Samir's ideas was useless. He knew who'd been checking out Hannah. He was here today, too, and they'd come to West Park to avoid him.

'What's up?' he heard Samir ask again.

He opened his eyes. 'Did you have to pick today to come here, you clown?'

'What you on about?'

Before Raheem could say another word, a scrunched-up ball of paper hit his head.

'Hi,' said Liam as he sat down on Aliyah's empty seat. Raheem glared at Samir, who shrugged apologetically.

'Isn't that your girlfriend?' Liam nodded towards the entrance. Like the pair of idiots that they were, they fell for it and looked. Liam howled with laughter and stood up. 'Fucking morons,' he said. Why did he always seem to find them?

'This chocolate looks nice. I didn't manage to have any lunch earlier.' Liam put his hand in Aliyah's bag and took out a chocolate. In an instant, both Raheem and Samir stood up. Liam hurried away with the chocolate in his hands.

'Leave him, people are looking,' hissed Samir as he held Raheem back, but Raheem couldn't care less. Liam was now near the exit of the library. Raheem managed to get free from Samir's grip but his elbow caught him in the face. The only thing that stopped him from running after Liam was Samir's high-pitched scream of pain.

'Oi!' shouted one of the security guards as Raheem pulled him to his feet.

'It's fine, it's fine, it was an accident,' said Samir, wincing. Everyone in the library was staring at them. The security guard shook his head and went back to his desk. Liam had disappeared.

After two more cigarettes, and plenty of swearing and arguing, Raheem and Samir were back at their table. Raheem had only calmed down in the last five minutes. 'He really is pissing me off,' he muttered angrily.

Samir, whose cheek was still a bit red, said, 'You need to think of the bigger picture. We can't do anything to him.'

192

That was true, but anger that he had never felt before had flared inside of Raheem the moment Liam had delved into Aliyah's bag.

'Anyway, who was the one that was checking out Hannah?' asked Samir after a few moments.

'Your dad,' snapped Raheem just as Aliyah arrived. Samir stopped rubbing his cheek.

'What's up with you?' she asked Raheem.

'He got upset when you went and he couldn't cope without you,' said Samir quickly before Raheem could say anything.

'Don't worry, I'm back now.' Aliyah patted Raheem's arm. She opened her bag. Raheem and Samir glanced at each other. 'I forgot my chocolate today,' she said grumpily as she rummaged through her bag. Raheem didn't have the heart to tell her what had happened. The fact he couldn't do anything made him even more frustrated. He put his arm around her shoulder and said, 'If you had to pick one thing to eat, what would it be?'

Aliyah stopped rummaging in her bag. 'I was going to say Grill and Pepperz, but I'm more in the mood for a curry so I'd say the lamb curry from Akbar's.'

'Come on, then. Let's go. Treat is on me today.'

'Aw, that's so nice of you but I'll just buy something from the canteen,' said Aliyah kindly.

'Nope, we are going Akbar's. No arguments.'

'Okay. Let me just do a bit more on my essay and we'll go in a bit. Why's your cheek red, Samir?'

Samir said he'd banged it on the table when he had ducked down to pick up his pen.

Raheem had to get Liam back for this, but how? Liam had proved he was devious, and Raheem was convinced he would try to trick them somehow even if they gave him the money. There was a reason why he had told them that he only wanted the money on the last day before he departed for America; it couldn't have been a coincidence. Raheem had tried to point this out to Samir, but he had said there was nothing in it.

And Liam had seriously thought they would bring Hannah to his flat and leave her there after she had a few drinks?

'Smile, Raheem.' Aliyah pointed her phone camera at him and he obliged as she took a picture. Aliyah had done so much to help him, and he couldn't even do anything to Liam after he'd gone into her bag.

Aliyah saved her work and logged off her laptop after ten minutes but before Raheem could get up she said, 'Hold on, we need a group selfie.' She took out her phone again and took a selfie with Raheem and Samir on either side of her. 'That's such a lovely picture,' she said, showing them. 'Are you okay to drop me home first? I need to get changed.'

'That's fine,' said Raheem. His mind was made up. Getting the camera wasn't enough. They needed to do more. It was time for Liam to have a taste of his own medicine. Only problem was, what could he do to get back at him?

Chapter 19

Raheem needed to get the blue ball in otherwise it would be virtually impossible to win the frame. Samir stood in front of the pocket, watching gleefully.

'Move out of the way, you're distracting me. That's why I missed those other shots,' snapped Raheem.

Samir smirked and moved away. 'Yeah right. More like you're just shit at snooker.'

Raheem scowled, bent down and hit the cue ball. It hit the blue but he'd hit it harder than he meant to, so it cannoned off the jaws of the pocket and headed up towards the other side of the table. To cap it off, the white ball rebounded off the side cushion and went straight into the middle pocket. It was a foul that had lost him the game.

Samir was beside himself laughing. 'You shit bag!'

'I know you been practising.'

'Rachel's got into snooker so I've been coming with her recently. Let's go for a cigarette before Aaron turns up. He's called us here and then he's late himself.'

They left their cues on the table and went down the steps of the snooker centre. They passed Ryan and a few of his mates who were going up to the pool tables on the first floor. 'I think I know who lost,' said Ryan when he saw them.

'I kicked your arse last time,' replied Raheem, which shut Ryan up. They said goodbye to him and his friends and went outside in the warm spring air.

'What do you reckon it's about?' Raheem asked Samir as they lit their cigarettes.

'Don't know. We just have to wait and see, don't we' said Samir as a black Mercedes entered the car park.

***

Why was life such a bitch? In any other circumstances, they would have loved what Aaron had shown them. It would have been hilarious.

'I've told you that the only time I had any sort of interaction with him was when we had a fight in Sensations in first year,' said Raheem, handing Aaron his phone back.

'But you told me you had a fight with him because he tried to grope one of your friends, that Cheryl,' said Aaron. 'What if he does the same to Hannah?'

Raheem pretended to tie his shoelace, which seemed to be a regular occurrence whenever he was with Aaron.

'This sort of shit happens. Lots of women get these types of messages,' said Samir reassuringly.

Aaron had told them that Hannah had left her Facebook open on her laptop and he'd seen messages from Liam on there along the lines of, *Hey, let's meet for a coffee* and *Why aren't you replying to me?*

'Personally, I think you're making a mole hill out of a mountain,' Raheem said as he eventually finished tying his laces.

'It's mountain out of a mole hill, isn't it?' asked Samir.

Aaron shrugged. 'I just don't feel right doing nothing. End of the day, just because this sort of stuff happens often doesn't make it right.'

They spent another ten minutes trying to convince Aaron not to come to the university to confront Liam; that was not an option at the moment, not for Raheem and Samir. Eventually, Aaron relented.

'Look, we see Hannah at uni all the time,' said Raheem. 'We'll keep a look out for her, but I think it's best you don't mention—'

'Mention this to Hannah or Sarah. I won't,' interjected Aaron. 'I blocked him from her Facebook before she came back, but I thought I'd discuss it with you first seeing as he goes to your uni and you might know him. She hasn't seen the messages. I'm keeping the screenshots on my phone though, just in case. But I need to tell you both one thing.'

'Go on,' said Raheem tentatively.

'I'm not going to tell Sarah or Hannah, but if something else happens then I'm coming to your uni to find him.'

Shit. It would take Liam two minutes to find out that Aaron was related to Sarah, then Raheem and Samir would be the ones who were fucked. But if they argued anymore about this, Aaron might become suspicious as to why they were so keen for him to not confront Liam.

'That's fine. We'll keep an eye out anyway,' said Raheem. It looked like Liam really was fascinated by Hannah. It would have been so funny seeing Aaron look for him. That would have allowed them a perfect opportunity to get their own back. But in the situation they were in... Raheem picked up his cue and took a shot, but his cue had not been chalked properly. The white ball bounced off the wall.

'When's the last time you played snooker, bro? You're actually rubbish,' said Aaron.

Raheem gave Aaron his cue and sat down. Unknown to Samir, who was laughing his head off, an idea about how to get revenge on Liam, had sprung into his head. They already had the plan for getting the camera. By sending those messages to Hannah, Liam had done them a huge favour.

Raheem didn't know what was worse: the fact that Liam seriously thought he had a chance with Hannah, or that he thought sending weird messages would actually work. He had also sent them a message a few days later, which was pretty self-explanatory. Raheem and Samir had returned to their table on the first floor of the library to find a note on it: *Burydale park café. Saturday 14th May 11am.*

***

Jasmine had received her contract and signed it. That was one big headache out of the way because they couldn't carry out the plan without her. Aliyah was still helping Raheem with his work, despite having her own to do. He did mention this to her on a couple of occasions, but she insisted on doing it. He knew her proofreading and small additions were worth extra marks, and words could not express how grateful he was.

Veronica was hinting she wanted to get back together with him, which he found extremely irritating. Why couldn't she understand it wasn't possible?

197

Aaron was being even more irritating than Veronica. He kept calling Raheem and Samir and asking them if they'd seen Liam near Hannah. He seemed to think they were his private investigators.

Then there was Sarah. She was complaining that Raheem was not spending enough time with her. Raheem turned up outside her apartment one afternoon after a long, gruelling shift at work. He knocked on her door just as the door near the end of the corridor opened. 'I hate you!' shouted a female voice.

Raheem continued knocking, but his attention was on the door from which the raised voices were coming. A woman walked out, saw Raheem watching her and stalked off down the stairs, swearing at the top of her voice.

'Ouch!' Sarah was clutching her forehead. He had continued knocking after she had opened the door.

'Sorry,' said Raheem hastily as he stepped inside. Her apartment was spotless as usual; nothing was out of place. All the dishes were clean and the worktop surfaces were gleaming.

'You're so clumsy,' she moaned, rubbing her forehead.

'I said sorry.'

Sarah sat down on the sofa in a huff. She folded her arms as he sat next to her and put her legs on the table, staring at the blank television screen. 'You seem so off nowadays. It's like your mind is somewhere else on the rare occasions you're with me,' she said stiffly.

Rare occasions? 'I've just been busy with uni work. You know what final year is like, it's hectic.'

'I know that, but it's not just you. Aaron is acting really strange.'

Oh no. That was not what Raheem wanted to hear. 'In what way?' he asked, gritting his teeth.

'I don't know. Whenever I mention anything about Veronica he just … changes the subject, like *you* always do when you got something to hide. Are they still together?'

Raheem stood up. The last two people he wanted to talk about with Sarah were Aaron and Veronica. He went to the fridge and opened it. 'Are you cooking anything for me today? I had a nasty shift at work and I'm starving.' He frantically searched for something he could take out to explain why he'd gone to the fridge. He found a can of Coke and took it out.

'See, you just did it again!' said Sarah shrilly.

'Did what again?' Raheem wearily raised his arms as though surrendering.

'Just changed the subject,' she said angrily.

'What you on about?' said Raheem, exasperated, opening the can. He had just shaken it when he had raised his arm and grimaced as the cold cola dripped down his arm. The second time that had happened to him.

'I've just cleaned up, Raheem!' Sarah stood up and grabbed a wad of tissue from the roll on the table.

'It's not my fault,' he retorted, holding out his arm for Sarah to wipe it. Instead, she bent down and cleaned the floor where the Coke had spilt. Muttering furiously, Raheem grabbed some tissue and wiped his arm before heading to the bathroom to wash his hands.

When he came out, Sarah was lying down on the sofa reading a book. He tried to kiss her but she put the book in the way.

'Why do you have to be like this, Sarah?' he groaned, sitting on the floor and leaning against the sofa. He had wanted to come and relax to get away from his problems, but Sarah was making them worse. He'd have been better off doing some overtime at work. At least there he got paid for tolerating people.

He took out his phone and went through his messages. Veronica had sent him a smiley face. Why did women send random messages at random times? He replied with a thumbs-up emoji. Daniel was asking if he had any notes from last year about the exam on young offenders. He texted back that he'd email them later. There was a message from his sister asking him why he hadn't come home last weekend. He texted to say that he'd drive back tonight and stay over.

It had started to rain. He turned the television on and flicked through the channels. A reality show was on and he read the subject: *I think my boyfriend is cheating on me.* He quickly changed the channel and settled on watching *The Simpsons*.

199

'Can you turn the volume down a little bit?' Sarah's voice came from behind him.

Raheem switched the TV off.

'I said turn it *down*, not turn it *off*.'

He turned it back on but put the volume all the way down to mute.

'What's your problem, Raheem?'

'I've put the TV on!'

'You put it to mute!'

'Because you said it was distracting you.'

'I never said that.'

'You implied it.'

'Whatever. You never admit you're wrong.'

Raheem got up suddenly. 'I admit I was wrong to come here,' he said as he went to the door. To his annoyance, Sarah didn't respond. It was only when Raheem walked back towards her that she looked at him.

'You changed your mind quickly' she said.

'I dropped my car keys, actually.' Picking them up from the floor, he left her apartment. Staying over at his house in Manchester would be a good idea. He needed a break because when he came back it would be time for action.

***

As with all plans, back-ups were needed in case things messed up.

'Do you not think he'll get bored?' muttered Samir as they went back up the stairs.

Raheem glanced back at the sofa on the ground floor where Daniel was sitting, looking perplexed. At least perplexed was better than depressed. 'We only need an hour max. You definitely know the way to the key shop?'

'How many times are you going to ask that?'

'Never know with you.'

They reached the third floor and turned left towards the student meeting rooms. 'Imagine if today was the only day he put his keys in his pocket,' Raheem said as they strolled down the corridor towards the room at the very end.

'Don't say that, you're jinxing it,' said Samir moodily as they opened the door.

'What if he is a total psycho?' asked Jasmine the moment they walked in. For someone who always looked cool and moody, she was looking nervous.

Raheem sat next to her and turned his chair to face her. 'Look, he is weird, I will admit that. Anything happens, you just give me a call and I'll be there as quick as I can. Also, it's a public place so you'll be fine. And remember, you're going to tell him your name is Anita.'

'What exactly do I say again?' she asked.

'Where do you think you're going? Sit back down,' said Raheem sharply as Samir opened the door to leave.

'I need to check if that prick is actually in the room. Its ten past two – he might have cancelled his two o'clock booking.'

'Oh. Right.'

Raheem turned back to Jasmine. 'All you need to do is start a conversation with him. Just say something like "have you booked this room"? He'll say he has, and then you just talk. Say you need somewhere to sit down and concentrate as the library is too noisy. He will let you sit down. You talk to him for a bit and then say that you need to go into town and get a few things, but you won't be able to carry the bags back to uni. He'll offer to come with you, but if he picks up his bag you tell him to leave it because he won't be able to help you carry your things. That is so important. Once you two have left, I'll take his keys from his bag. Samir will get them cut while I wait here. You need to keep him away for a minimum of forty-five minutes. Asda is a ten-minute walk from uni, so that shouldn't be a problem. Samir will be back by then, and we'll put the original keys back in his bag before you guys return and keep the copy. Simple.'

A stony silence greeted his words.

'Can't we just go to the uni café or something? Why town?' asked Jasmine finally.

'Because you need to carry some bags. What's the point of telling him to go to the café? He will take his bag with him,' Raheem explained patiently. 'And make sure you don't give him your number. Give him the number of Samir's old phone that I gave you.'

'What if he takes his keys out of his bag and brings them with him?' she asked.

'Then you're just going to have to find a way of taking them out his pocket,' said Raheem, although how Jasmine was supposed to do that he had no idea. Maybe she could try sneaking them out if she gave Liam a hug or something. He really hoped they wouldn't have to resort to that.

'And when I get back to uni, shall I call the taxi then?' Jasmine asked.

'Yeah. Tell him you'll link up soon.'

Jasmine looked at him with an almost pitying expression on her face. 'I would have done anything to get a job back in Leicester. You've helped me with that, so I'll help you with this.' *Help* her get the job? He had practically *got* her the job.

Samir walked back in. 'He's there. The room is booked until five o'clock. We won't get a better chance than this.' They both looked at Jasmine expectantly.

'I'm ready,' she said, just as Raheem got a call from Daniel. 'You can go to the toilet, Dan... yeah, that's fine. Cheers,' he said.

'I feel so bad that he has to ask for permission to go to the toilet,' Samir said as Raheem disconnected the call.

Raheem nodded, but he could not take any chances. It would be typical of Sarah to turn up unannounced. She had a dentist appointment in the afternoon, but if it was cancelled she'd probably come to see Raheem. Monday was the only day they could carry out the plan because Jasmine was allowed to enter the university as a visitor.

'Are you sure Rachel is at West Park?' asked Raheem, before remembering he'd already asked the same question twice today. Samir nodded irritably, and they both wished good luck to Jasmine as she left the room.

'She'll be fine,' said Samir.

'Are you trying to convince me or yourself?'

'Both.'

Raheem stretched his legs onto the table. All they could do now was wait and hope.

They had not heard from Jasmine since she'd left almost an hour earlier. Raheem was just thinking that it might be a good idea to sneak down to the second floor and check on her when he saw a message on his phone. He heard Samir's phone buzz, too.

It was from Jasmine. *We are in town on way to Asda. He left his bag in room, didn't even bother bringing it with him! Not sure if the keys are with him or in the bag. Let me know once I am able to come back. Been easier than I thought tbh.*

Elated, Raheem looked up to find Samir grinning at him. 'Yes!' he said punching the air.

'How did you know? Did she text you as well?' asked Samir happily.

'Yeah, she did. Come on, let's go.' Raheem hurried to the door. Samir remained where he was. 'What?' Raheem asked.

'Where do we need to go? Aren't we waiting for Jasmine to text us?'

What was he on about? 'We need to get the keys, you stupid idiot!' said Raheem.

Samir's phone buzzed with a message. He read it and looked up at Raheem. 'Jasmine just messaged to say they are in town and he's left his bag. Let's go get the keys,' he said.

'So what were you happy about before?'

'Rachel texted that she has a surprise for me when I go to hers. I'm going there tonight.'

Raheem shook his head and signalled for Samir to follow him. Samir's surprise could wait; the last few times they'd been surprised had not exactly been great. It would be better to create a WhatsApp group going forward so that they received the messages at the same time.

They hurried down to the second floor to the student meeting room and peered inside. As expected, it was empty except for Liam's university bag and the computer on which he had locked the screen. The student meeting rooms on either side of them were occupied, but hopefully no one would notice.

'You stay out here. If someone comes, block the entrance to the door so they can't see inside,' said Samir.

'Alright,' muttered Raheem as Samir pushed open the door.

Samir started unzipping the bag as Raheem kept watch. He pulled out a packet of biscuits and put them on the floor next to him. If the keys weren't in the bag, this would be the biggest waste of time in history. Raheem glanced down the empty corridor. A seminar was going on in the IT lab a few doors down.

'All sorted.' Samir opened the door carrying a bunch of keys.

'Keep your voice down!' hissed Raheem. Thankfully, no one had been walking past. But there was still a problem: Liam's bag was unzipped and the packet of biscuits was still on the floor next to it. Mouthing obscenities, Raheem entered the room and put the biscuits back inside before zipping up the bag.

'Oh shit, I forgot about that,' said Samir as Raheem returned.

They hurried back up the stairs, before Raheem remembered that they still needed to get the key cut. 'Do you definitely know where the—?'

'Yeah, man! Stop asking me that!' said Samir irritably as he headed back down the stairs.

Raheem hoped he would see Samir before he saw Jasmine or Liam. Otherwise there could be trouble.

***

He needn't have worried. Samir managed to get the keys cut and returned ten minutes before Jasmine texted them to say they were coming back. They put the original keys back in Liam's bag and hurried up to the third floor. The only problem was Raheem had forgotten to tell Daniel he could leave. Daniel had been keeping watch at the library entrance for two hours before he remembered.

'I'm glad that's over. He got weirder and weirder the longer we talked,' said Jasmine as poured herself a drink from the fridge. 'He's already messaged me three times! I'm glad I didn't have to give him my real number.'

'We told you he had that side to him,' said Samir darkly. 'Remember; just respond to his messages normally. Be a bit flirty with him if you want.'

'That is going to be so awkward.'

'I understand, but we don't have too long left to do this.'

'A promise is a promise.'

Raheem gazed out of the window. They still needed to break into Liam's flat, which wasn't going to be easy. Jasmine's part wasn't done yet.

His phone buzzed with a message from Sarah, the first one she'd sent since the argument in her apartment.

We meeting Aaron for DINNER (1pm) on Sunday at Nando's, he wants to introduce us to someone. Any problem sort it out with Aaron. It is his invite.

He had an idea who Aaron was going to introduce to him and Sarah. Once again, he would be introduced to somebody he already knew.

Chapter 20

Raheem kissed his dissertation before placing it in the drop-in box. 'Don't let me down,' he muttered to the box. Unsurprisingly, it did not respond.

There was no going back now. He had double- and triple-checked his dissertation during the past week and had given it his best shot. He went out to the corridor to Samir and Aliyah. 'All done' he said.

'Great. Are you going to be nice to us now?' asked Aliyah as they went down in the lift. She had submitted hers a couple of days earlier and Samir had submitted his that morning. Raheem had been a bit tetchy with them while he had fretted about his own.

'I'm always nice!'

They got out of the lift and left for the Parkview car park through the back exit.

'I just need to make a call. I'll meet you outside,' said Samir.

'You can make the call in front of us. Why are you being so secretive?' asked Raheem.

Samir smiled as he went inside and left Raheem and Aliyah waiting.

It was the best day of the year so far. There was not a single cloud in the sky, and there was a gentle breeze. Raheem and Aliyah had been waiting a couple of minutes before Samir returned. 'You guys go. I can't come,' he said.

'Why not? Is everything okay?' asked Aliyah.

'No, you're coming,' said Raheem.

Samir shook his head. 'Try to understand.'

Understand what? They argued for another minute before Raheem gave up. 'You're just selling us out for Rachel, aren't you?' he demanded.

'She needs me to come see her so I have to go.'

'Traitor,' said Aliyah.

'Go do your stuff, then,' said Raheem.

Samir clapped Raheem on the shoulder and said bye to Aliyah before heading back into the university.

'Looks like it's just me and you,' said Aliyah as they walked to the car park.

'I know. I'm gutted,' said Raheem.

They were going to Burydale Park for a walk. It had been Samir's idea; they'd all been stuck in the library during the warm weather, finishing their dissertations, so a long walk and fresh air would be good.

The park was busy for a weekday. Aliyah sat on the bench in front of the lake as Raheem queued for the ice-cream van. It took him nearly ten minutes to get to the front of the queue. He carried the two ice creams carefully to where Aliyah was sitting waiting. 'It's so busy. I don't know why— Whoa!'

He'd been about to hand Aliyah her ice cream when a dog ran past him. Not being a fan of dogs, he jumped and dropped the ice cream before she could take it. 'I hate dogs!' he said angrily as it spread on the ground . He'd have to get her another one, but the queue was even longer. 'You can have this one,' he said, holding his own ice cream out to Aliyah.

'Thanks, but it's okay,' she said kindly.

'Just take it,' said Raheem firmly.

'It's fine, Raheem.'

'Are you sure?'

'Yeah.'

'Okay then.' Raheem threw his ice cream on the ground next to Aliyah.

'You're mad!'

Raheem grinned and sat next to her. 'We got just over one month left, eh?'

'I know, I can't believe it. Final day May 27th,' said Aliyah. They sat in silence for a moment, looking across the lake.

'How's your soon-to-be fiance?' asked Raheem. The same sinking sensation tingled inside of him as it always did when this subject came up, but it would be rude not to mention it.

Aliyah started explaining the plans for the engagement and then the wedding. She had no idea how much he'd been

207

thinking about her recently. Any moment he wasn't with her felt wasted. He would always be there for her...

'What is it, why are you looking at me like that?'

Raheem blinked. 'Nothing.'

Aliyah looked at him sceptically. 'You didn't listen to a word I said, did you?'

Raheem grinned. 'No, I didn't. I was too busy thinking of the times we spent together.'

Aliyah smiled; her smile was the most comforting he had ever seen. They were sitting very close to each other on the bench and their knees kept touching.

Raheem took out a cigarette and was about to light it when Aliyah snatched it out of his hand and threw it in the lake. 'Smoking doesn't suit you,' she said sternly. He put his cigarette packet in his pocket.

'It's okay, you can have one. I don't want you going into moody mode again,' she said.

'No, you're right. It doesn't suit me. I'm trying to give it up.'

Aliyah looked delighted. 'Starting from today?'

If only it were that easy. 'Erm ... no, not yet. When I finish uni.'

Aliyah ruffled his hair. 'Right, listen, let's do this. You have to say one thing about me that you don't like, and I will say something about you that I don't like.'

'No, you're very sensitive. I'm saying nothing.'

'No, you have to.'

What was it about Aliyah that he did not like? Even when she was moody with him he found it endearing as opposed to irritating. 'There's nothing I don't like about you,' he said. 'Give me one sec, let me think,' he added hastily as Aliyah raised her hand for a slap. He thought for another ten seconds before saying, 'You always roll your eyes. I don't like that.'

He actually found it funny when Aliyah rolled her eyes but he couldn't think what else to say. As he'd expected, Aliyah rolled her eyes at his words. 'Your turn now, and you can't say smoking. I know that if it wasn't for smoking I would be perfect,' he said.

Aliyah thought for a moment. 'We would be here all day. Not enough time.'

'You're hilarious. You should be a comedian.'

'I know,' she said brightly as she stood up.

'Where you going?' asked Raheem.

'Come on, let's walk around the lake.'

Raheem gave fake yawn. 'Let's just sit here instead.'

'I said come!'

'Bloody hell, someone's got a temper.'

'I know, I can be quite demanding, but I don't think you've seen that side of me yet.'

Unfortunately, there wasn't much time left for him to see that side of Aliyah. They went down the path together and started to walk around the lake. It usually took Raheem thirty minutes to walk that route with Sarah, but with Aliyah it generally took twenty-five minutes. Today it took them forty five minutes. He was walking slower than usual.

He had been coming to Burydale Park on his own in the evenings recently, sitting on the bank of grass and staring into the sunset. He wanted to tell Aliyah this but decided against it.

'I'm shattered. I want to eat something,' said Aliyah as they completed their walk. She sat on the bench they'd been on earlier.

'Let's go to the café. They don't do bench service, even for you.' Raheem held out his hand.

Aliyah chuckled and grabbed it to raise herself up. 'Stop using my lines on me, think of your own.' They walked to the café and placed their order.

They reminisced about their time at university together. When they finished their food, they went to the bank of grass where Raheem had often sat. Aliyah was talking about the places in Scotland she wanted to visit once she got married. Raheem leaned on his elbow and watched her. He would much rather talk about the past than the future. If only he could live it again.

***

Raheem slowed down his speed on the treadmill before coming to a halt. He wiped his face with his towel then made his way to the changing rooms. An hour later, after a cold shower in his flat, he got dressed and drove to pick up Sarah. She had called him yesterday to remind him he was due at Nando's and to remember to collect her at 12.45.

The drive to Sarah's took the usual fifteen minutes. She was already waiting for him outside the gate to her apartment. It was 12.46. Maybe one day he would get somewhere on time.

'Hi,' he said as she got in.

She gave him a quick peck on the cheek. 'How's your revision going?'

'It's going okay. Got my dissertation out of the way.'

'I'm glad I never had to do one for accounting, it would have been so stressful. Main thing is that you have done it.'

She had her sunglasses on and was wearing her favourite light-blue dress. They didn't talk much on the way. Raheem turned the music on, but for once Sarah did not ask him to turn it down. She had also not reprimanded him for turning up a minute late. He didn't know whether that was a good thing or bad thing.

Aaron and Hannah were already there when they entered Nando's. Sarah held his hand as they walked towards them.

'Raheem!' shrieked Hannah, so loudly that people stared. She cupped her hand over her mouth, pink in the face.

'I told you that you'd be surprised,' said Aaron, smiling.

'Sarah, this is Hannah. Hannah, this is Sarah. Ladies this is Aaron. Everyone, this is me' said Raheem, before Aaron could start his long introductions. Sarah and Hannah embraced.

'I thought I'd seen you somewhere. It must have been with Raheem.' Hannah smiled at Sarah as they sat down.

'Yep, you do look familiar.' Sarah returned the smile.

Hannah turned to Raheem. 'I can't believe you never told me.'

'He told me not to!' Raheem nodded at Aaron.

'It was our little secret,' said Aaron.

'One of many cigarettes- I mean secrets.' Raheem grinned at Sarah, who did not crack a smile. He turned to Aaron. 'How's work?'

For the first few minutes Raheem and Aaron did the talking, but the longer they sat there Sarah and Hannah spoke with each other. Sarah definitely got on more with Hannah than with Veronica. By the time their food arrived, they were in full flow about shopping and clothes and had arranged to go to Broadway Shopping Centre together the following week.

Raheem took out his phone under the table and messaged Samir as planned. His phone buzzed with a text message. It was from Jasmine, and it was in their WhatsApp group.

Wednesday 11th May, we are going to a restaurant. I'm going to meet him there.

Raheem texted Daniel to confirm his house party for that night. A date was the only way to ensure Liam would be out and distracted the night they broke into his flat.

'We're going to see Adele on the 11th of May in Newcastle. You both have to come with us, we have two extra tickets,' said Hannah.

Raheem quickly put his phone in his pocket.

'Wow, I'm definitely coming.' Sarah gleefully clapped her hands.

Everyone looked at Raheem. 'I can come as long as it's not on the 11th,' he said.

'It *is* on the 11th though!' said Hannah.

Oh dear. How unfortunate.

'I really would like to go but I – erm – I'm covering one of my colleagues at work that night.'

'Aw, no!' said Hannah.

Aaron was also looking disappointed. 'You had to pick that night to cover someone?' he demanded.

'My colleague covered my shift when I needed it so I just returned the favour,' said Raheem.

Aaron and Hannah tried convince him to cancel, but eventually relented. 'What are we going do with the spare ticket, seeing as Raheem doesn't want to come with us?' Hannah asked.

'It's okay, I'll ask Jason,' said Sarah. Everyone on the table looked at her.

'Jason?' asked Raheem.

'Yes,' she replied icily.

Why Jason out of everyone? She was just doing this to piss him off.

'Are you *sure* you can't come, Raheem?' asked Hannah.

For a split second, he almost said he could but then he remembered Jasmine's text. There was no way he could go. 'Nah, I can't cancel on my mate at work. You know Ashleigh, don't you, Sarah? The one that was either male or female? Anyway, I would have come but as I can't then you can take Jason. On this occasion.'

After a rather awkward pause, Aaron's phone vibrated with a text. He frowned when he read it but thankfully Sarah was too busy shooting annoyed looks at Raheem to notice.

'I need some fresh hair, feeling stuffed. Raheem, you coming?' Aaron stood up. Eager to get away from Sarah, Raheem got up too. 'We'll be back in a bit,' Aaron told the girls.

They went outside the entrance and behind the wall. 'I just got this message.' Aaron passed over his phone. 'I don't recognise the number.'

Raheem faked a look of surprise as he read the message: *Stay away from Hannah if you know what's good for you.* 'What the hell?' he said.

Aaron took his phone back and tried to call the number. Samir had better not answer his old phone by mistake. One phone was with him, the other was with Jasmine who was using it for messaging Liam. Raheem had told Samir that morning under no circumstances was he to answer any calls on that phone.

'Gone to voicemail,' said Aaron.

'How would that Liam get your number, though? You haven't got it on your Facebook, have you?'

Aaron nodded. 'You can't stop me now, Raheem. I'm going to get him.'

'What? No!' Raheem grabbed Aaron as he turned to go back inside. 'I mean, we need to find out if it really is Liam.'

'Who else would it be?'

Sarah and Hannah were chatting merrily together inside. Raheem had to say it now. 'Look, let me and Samir find out if it really is him. We need to be certain. Because if either of us – or you – beat the shit out of him and it isn't, me and Samir are kicked out of uni with no degree, and you could lose your job – that's assuming we avoid going to court.' He hated doing this, but it was the only way.

'But you said that last time,' said Aaron in frustration. 'How do you think I'm feeling that someone is sending me this shit and I'm not doing anything? I've dealt with bigger stuff than this before, bro.'

'I know that, but please, one final time, I'm asking you to follow what I say,' said Raheem calmly. 'Me and Samir will try to find out more about Liam. If it is him, you can do whatever you want to him.'

He could totally understand where Aaron was coming from, but they needed to look at the bigger picture. This was essential for their plan to get back at Liam.

'That's a deal,' Aaron said reluctantly.

'Let's go in.' Raheem opened the door.

'But I'm still going to have a word with Hannah about this,' Aaron said.

'No!' said Raheem. He grabbed Aaron again and pulled him back outside. There was always someone that would mess up, wasn't there?

'I need to ask Hannah if she knows him!' said Aaron, exasperated.

'You guys have just started off together. You don't want to ruin it,' said Raheem quickly. 'She's going to get freaked out by this and you could end up losing her!'

'Alright, I won't! But you and Samir need to find out for me.'

'We will do, promise,' said Raheem firmly. 'What did Sarah say when you told her you weren't with Veronica?'

Aaron looked a bit taken aback by the sudden change of subject. 'She was a bit upset I hadn't told her sooner, but other than that she was fine. I don't think she liked Veronica, to be honest.'

'And you definitely haven't told Hannah about Veronica?' asked Raheem nervously.

'No, as you said, there's no point bringing up the past,' Aaron replied as the door to Nando's opened and Sarah and Hannah appeared.

'You two have been ages,' said Sarah.

'We were just coming back in,' said Raheem. 'What we doing now?'

'We're going bowling.' Hannah held out her hand for Aaron and they made their way to the bowling centre opposite.

Raheem held out his hand and Sarah grasped it before following. Hopefully there wouldn't be a teddy bear stall there.

***

Raheem didn't seem to be the only one who couldn't make up his mind about things. He had been working on his essay (*Develop and justify a proposal for a crime prevention project*) in one of the student meeting rooms with Aliyah, who had left half an hour ago to set off for work He had offered to drop her to work but she had said her sister was picking her up. He was about to go to the campus shop to get a drink when Samir walked in, followed by Veronica. Both of them looked agitated. 'What's wrong?' he asked.

'Ask her.' Samir pulled Raheem off his seat and sat down on it.

Veronica took a deep breath. This wasn't going to be good. 'I want to be back with Aaron,' she said.

After two full minutes of silence, Raheem raised his face from his hands. 'What do you mean, you want to get back with Aaron?' he asked. He couldn't believe what he was hearing. After all that effort, and now Veronica had decided she wanted to be with Aaron?

'What's wrong with that? We were dating for a year and we still have feelings for each other!' Veronica protested.

Raheem rested his head against his arms again. He was losing the will to live. It was only when Samir threw a pen at his head that he sat up straight. 'Look, Veronica, you need to move on,' he said.

Veronica glared at him. 'Why is it such a big deal if I want to be with Aaron? Nothing happened between me and you. I thought we agreed on that, remember?'

Raheem winced at her words.

'I'm waiting.' Veronica folded her arms.

Raheem ran his hands through his hair. 'Samir, are you single?'

'If Liam shows those pictures to Rachel, then I will be.'

'Veronica, are you single?' Raheem continued.

'Yeah, I am, duh. Thanks to you.'

'You two might as well get together.'

'Shut up, Raheem! I'm serious!' said Veronica furiously.

Raheem connected his laptop charger and logged back on. Just when things looked like they would improve, something always happened to fuck them up.

'Have you told Aaron about getting back together?' asked Raheem.

'No, I haven't – though now you mention it, I might as well tell him now.' Veronica took out her phone. Instinctively Raheem leapt from his chair and snatched it off her.

'What are you doing? Give it back!' she shouted, making a grab for it.

Raheem pointed behind Veronica's back and she fell for it. As she turned to look behind her, he lobbed the phone to Samir who quickly put it in his back pocket.

'Don't mess me around, give it back now,' demanded Veronica as she turned around. Her eyes fell on his jeans' pocket.

'You can't be back with Aaron,' said Raheem.

Veronica put her hands on her hips. 'Why's that, may I ask?'

It would be better to take the offensive route. 'I thought you said you can't deal with him. He's got a temper.'

'People can change.'

'He might not have changed.'

'Give me my phone. Now.'

'No, you can't be with him. Sorry.'

'Why not?'

They had no choice now. They would have to tell her. 'Because he is with someone else,' said Raheem quickly, as though it might be less of a shock for Veronica if he spoke fast.

Veronica froze, gaping open mouthed at Raheem, one of her hands in his jeans' pocket. He held it. 'I'm sorry, Veronica. Aaron felt there was no future with you. He did initially want to get back with you, but then ... then he met Hannah and it helped him get over you.'

'Hannah – the one on your course?'

Raheem nodded. He could guess what was coming next.

'How did they meet?' asked Veronica.

Raheem pointed at Samir. 'He will tell you. I just need to go – I'll be back in a bit.' He made to get past Veronica, but she grabbed his arm and pulled him back.

'Stay here!' she ordered. 'Tell me, Samir, how did they meet?'

Samir went into an explanation about the day at Starbucks when they were with Aaron and Hannah had met them. He told the story as though they'd just happened to meet Hannah as opposed to it being planned. Raheem kept his eyes on the floor, his shame rising with each word.

'So let me get this straight,' said Veronica when Samir had finished. 'You two were with Aaron in Starbucks, and you saw Hannah outside at precisely that time.'

Raheem and Samir nodded nervously. She didn't believe them. She looked at them both, and suddenly smiled.

'Are you okay?' asked Raheem uncertainly.

'Course I am,' she said brightly. 'If it was meant to be, then it was meant to be.'

'What was meant to be?' asked Raheem.

'If Aaron and Hannah were meant to be together, they would have met. I believe in destiny. Whoever I'm supposed to be with, I will meet them one day,' Veronica said confidently. 'We were not meant to be together, so don't think about the past otherwise you will always be regretful. Come on, Samir, you need to print off some work for me. I've left my student card at home so can't log on to the printers. I'll see you later, Raheem.' She walked out of the door that Samir held open for her.

'Make sure she's okay,' said Raheem.

'I will do.' Samir looked at him. 'Is there anything you want to tell me?' he asked.

There was. Something Raheem should have told him sooner. But he couldn't do it.

Raheem shook his head and Samir left the room. He would have to keep his feelings to himself.

Chapter 21

The big night arrived. Sarah had texted Raheem to say that she'd call him once she had returned from the concert. Raheem had texted back to say that she should go to sleep and he'd ring her tomorrow. He didn't want her calling him tonight.

It was quarter to nine. Once he got the text message from Jasmine that she was in the restaurant with Liam, he would set off for Liam's flat with Samir.

***

'Who you texting?' asked Raheem as he started the engine.

Looking annoyed, Samir held out his phone. 'Rachel. She wants me to come to her flat.'

'Did you not tell her you weren't feeling well earlier this morning? I told you to tell her.'

Samir shook his head. 'I forgot. That's what I'm telling her now, that I feel sick.'

Raheem clapped sarcastically, just as he received a text from Jasmine on the WhatsApp group.

He has arrived. Please hurry up as he has already drunk a lot. This is gonna be so awkward!

Raheem let her know they were setting off. 'It's show time,' he said.

They didn't talk much on the way. Daniel had also messaged to say that both James and Callum were at his house party.

The satnav showed that he was one minute from his destination. Raheem turned into Woodland Avenue narrowly avoiding the kerb.

'Twenty-four … twenty-six…' Samir muttered, looking out of the window. Raheem pulled over to the left and parked his car. 'Go further, its forty-two,' Samir said.

Raheem shook his head. 'It's better we park here and walk in case someone notices the car.'

The street was dark; a couple of the streetlights didn't seem to be working. Cars were parked all along the road, but nobody was out. Now was the hard part. If those keys didn't work…

***

'Close the door, quickly,' whispered Raheem as he stepped into the hallway. The kitchen and living room lights were on. He was just about to take the key for the bedroom out of his pocket when the front door slammed behind him. He jumped and landed on Samir's foot.

'Argh, watch it!' hissed Samir angrily, hopping on the spot. The door behind him was closed.

'Why did you close it so hard?'

'*You* said close it quickly!'

This guy – honestly. Raheem motioned to Samir to follow him upstairs. There were four doors in the landing. The door to the bathroom was ajar and the light had been left on. Raheem wasn't worried about that. He and Samir also left their lights on in their flat when they were out at night.

He turned to Samir, who was tying his shoelaces. 'Have you left the bag at your dad's house?' he asked sarcastically.

Samir glanced back down the stairs to where his university bag was right next to the front door. 'Sorry,' he said, and hurried down the stairs to get it.

'You ready?' Raheem asked as he returned. Daniel had said that Liam's bedroom was the one on the left.

'No, after all this effort, I'm shitting it. Let's go back.'

Raheem took out the key, put it in the keyhole and turned it. The lock opened with a satisfying click.

Liam's room was quite big. The walls were littered with posters of American baseball players. An Xbox console was on the floor next to the bedside table. It wouldn't surprise Raheem if that was also stolen.

'Do you think he'd notice if I used his toilet?' asked Samir.

'Yeah, he would. Your shit stinks like … like shit, so hold it in,' Raheem replied. They needed to be as quick as they could.

Jasmine had told them to message her the moment she was free to make an excuse to leave. She had hinted to Liam as they had suggested to her that they would head out for a night in town after the restaurant. Not that there was any chance of that happening.

Raheem strode across the room and opened the drawer next to the bed. 'Bet it's in here.'

He was wrong; the only thing in the drawer was a laptop.

Samir bumped him out of the way. 'My turn. Let me show you how to do it.' He opened the second and third drawers at the same time so hard that they nearly fell out. The second drawer had university books in; the third held a mixture of underwear and socks.

'You check inside the wardrobe, I'm going to check under the bed.' A familiar feeling of panic was fluttering in Raheem's chest. He'd been so sure that the camera would be in one of the drawers.

Samir strode to the wardrobe and began looking inside, whilst Raheem checked under the bed. There were two large suitcases, but there was nothing in them except a few clothes. Liam had already started some of his packing.

'I found it!' Samir said excitedly. The top of Raheem's head smacked against the wooden underside of the bed as he had raised his head in excitement. 'Fuck, it's just an alarm clock.'

Raheem clenched his fist in annoyance and stood up. He checked under the duvet and pillow with no luck as Samir went through Liam's university bag.

'Let's check downstairs in the living room.' Raheem tried to keep his voice calm.

Fifteen minutes later, they were back in Liam's bedroom having checked everywhere in the house except James's and Callum's rooms, which were locked.

'What a wasted effort. I bet he's taken the camera with him,' said Samir angrily.

Raheem sat on the floor. Jasmine had messaged, asking if they'd found the camera yet. Liam must have taken the camera with him, and if he had, they would just have to revert to plan B and grab him before he reached home. That's not what they had wanted to do, but it looked as if they had no choice. Samir was daydreaming out of the window. 'Think of something then,' Raheem snarled.

Samir opened the wardrobe to check it again. Raheem ran to the bathroom and took a quick glance inside. Nothing.

'Yeah, it's really going to be in the bathroom, isn't it?' said Samir sarcastically as he sat on the bed. 'Where would you hide something in a bedroom?'

Raheem let out a sigh. He had never had to hide anything in his room – well, except his cigarette packets. He used to put them on top of his wardrobe, the one place no one would see when they were in his bedroom...

Hold on. They hadn't checked on top of the wardrobe. Raheem flung Samir off the bed and stood on it...

***

'I still don't get why there are two copies,' whispered Samir.

The ecstasy they had felt when they had found the camera had disappeared. Raheem was sitting on the floor, Samir next to him. They had deleted the pictures off the camera, but they had also found two brown envelopes on top of the wardrobe. The envelopes looked exactly like the ones Samir had bought, the ones Liam had taken off him in the car. Inside the envelopes were the same photos that Liam had taken of them. One envelope had Raheem's pictures with Veronica; the other had Samir's pictures with Katie.

Raheem looked closely at the envelopes. There was a miniscule letter S on one of them, and a small R on the other one. 'Look at this,' he said, pointing them out.

Samir look bemused. 'What does that stand for?'

Raheem shrugged.

'What's Hannah's surname? Is it Richardson?' asked Samir.

'Yeah, it is,' said Raheem slowly.

'That's it, then!' said Samir excitedly before hushing his voice as Raheem glared at him.

'What you on about?' said Raheem.

'S and R, it stands for Hannah Richardson!'

He wanted to throw Samir out of the window. 'You clown! Hannah begins with H!'

220

Samir looked as if Christmas had been cancelled. 'Oh yeah.'

Raheem turned his attention back to the envelopes and photos. Liam had told them that if they didn't give the money, he would show the photos to Sarah and Rachel. He had told them he knew where they lived...

Raheem suddenly stood up. Sarah and Rachel ... S and R!

'What?' said Samir

Raheem picked up Samir's bag, took out his notepad and carefully tore out ten pages. Now he knew what Liam had been planning to do all along. All of a sudden his mind was clear and he knew what he had to do.

'What are you doing? Tell me!' demanded Samir.

Raheem dropped the bag and turned to him. 'Those two envelopes with the photos are for Sarah and Rachel. Liam was going to give us the camera, but he'd printed off the photos. Once we gave him the money, he was going to drop these off at Sarah's and Rachel's!'

Samir gaped. 'That little bastard! *That's* why he only wanted the money on his last day here, so we couldn't do anything to him before he left.'

'Exactly. My instincts were right. And I can guarantee you, once he gave us the camera and took the money, he wouldn't be coming back here on Saturday. He would either go back to America the same evening, or he would be staying somewhere else that night and go the next day. That way we would never have found him either.'

Raheem's phone buzzed with a message, as did Samir's. Jasmine had texted to say that she could only keep Liam there for another fifteen minutes maximum. They needed to go, but there was one final thing they needed to do.

'Have you got a black pen?' asked Raheem.

'Yeah, I have.' Samir rummaged in his bag and handed him the pen.

'Good. Take my car keys. Your envelopes that you bought that day will still be in the glove compartment. Bring them here. I'll message Jasmine back.'

'Why do you need the envelopes?'

'Please, just do what I say.'

As Samir hurried out of the room, Raheem put the pieces of paper he had ripped out on the bed. He could take the photos and leave the camera now that they had deleted their pictures, but Liam's sneering face kept looming out of the darkness at him.

Liam wasn't likely to check his camera and the envelopes. The hard part would be copying the letters S and R as Liam had written them. But it was only two letters. Shouldn't be too difficult…

***

Samir kept watch as Raheem locked the front door. They strolled casually back to Raheem's car, hardly believing what they'd done. They had taken care to make sure Liam's bedroom looked exactly how it was before they entered. The original envelopes with the photos were in Samir's bag. They'd left the camera on top of the wardrobe, along with the envelopes which now had paper folded in them. If Daniel hadn't realised that a watch had been swapped with a box of chocolates, Liam would hopefully not realise that the envelopes with the photos had been swapped with paper. Raheem had weighed the envelopes on the weighing scale in the bathroom, one with the photos and the other with the paper, and their weight was exactly the same.

The moment they got in the car, Raheem started to drive. Samir texted Jasmine to tell her that they'd meet her in the car park outside the restaurant. She would tell Liam her friend had come to pick her up as she wasn't feeling well.

Sarah had texted him to say she, along with Aaron, Hannah and Jason, would be setting off for Stalford soon. It would take them at least an hour and a half to make it back from Newcastle. Barring a disaster, Raheem would be back in his flat well before she arrived.

***

Raheem was reading through his text message exchange with Aaron.

222

Raheem had written: *You were right. I think it is him. I spoke with a couple of people who know him and apparently he likes to harass women. I've been told every Saturday morning he goes for a walk in Burydale Park. We will get him then.*

Aaron replied: *All the evidence pointed that way, but good job you made sure. I'll come to yours Saturday morning, we will go together.*

No worries, see you then, don't mention anything to anyone else for now.

I won't dw

Dw?

Don't worry

OK

Raheem put his phone on the table. Jasmine had told Liam to meet her in Burydale Park at ten o'clock on Saturday morning. He knew Liam, being the desperate guy that he was, would meet her there and change the time of his meeting with Raheem and Samir. He would go for a nice walk together with Jasmine before things got a bit kinky. Once that was done, he would meet them and leave with the money. Or rather, that's what Liam thought would happen.

'Who are you texting?' asked Aliyah sharply.

'No one,' said Raheem innocently as he put his phone in his pocket. Aliyah continued her conversation with Rachel. Raheem took out his phone again and read the message from Jasmine.

I have told him to meet at the park at 10 on Saturday. How many times are you going to ask?!

Samir had spent the day touring the university looking for Liam. They needed to make sure that he saw them so that he would confirm the change of time. But they still had the rest of today and tomorrow; Liam would find them one way or the other.

'I remember Samir used to always bring me to this café in first year,' said Rachel dreamily.

'Raheem hates it here, don't you?' said Aliyah.

'No way. Parkview Café is the best café in the world,' replied Raheem. Okay, maybe not the best café in the world but it was definitely a place that held special memories for him, the most special being with Aliyah.

'Samir has just messaged to say he's busy with his work,' said Rachel. 'He says to order without him.'

Yeah. He was busy with work, the type of work that would keep Raheem with Sarah and Samir with Rachel.

'Let's order then. It's on me today, Raheem,' said Aliyah as she saw Raheem taking out his wallet.

'It's okay,' said Raheem but Aliyah grabbed his wallet from his hand and put it in her bag.

'You still going to have that boring pasta that you've been having for the last two years?' she asked as she got up.

'It's actually really nice —' Raheem began but then broke off. Liam had just entered the café. He saw Raheem and gestured with his head to meet him outside the café entrance.

'What's up?' Aliyah said.

Raheem stood up. 'Yeah, just the pasta please. I'm going for a cigarette while you order.'

Aliyah thrust his wallet at him. 'You need to quit.'

'I will soon. Back in a bit.' He went outside into the bright sunshine.

Liam was standing next to the entrance to the underground car park. 'Change of plan,' he said. He waited, as though expecting Raheem to say something, but Raheem had decided to keep his mouth shut as much as possible. It would be typical of him to somehow to give Liam the impression that something was wrong.

'Meet me at the café in Burydale Park at *one o'clock* on Saturday instead. 'Bring the money in a bag. When you give me the money, I am going to call a taxi. Once the taxi arrives, I will hand over the camera.'

Although Raheem had resolved to speak as little as possible, Liam would find it odd if he agreed without asking anything. 'Why at one o'clock?' he blurted out. 'I thought you had said eleven.'

'Shut up and just be there with the money at exactly one o'clock, okay?' snapped Liam. 'Tell you're fucking cousin as well. Don't forget, you are going to give me the money *first*, before I give you the camera. And remember, if you don't turn up, you know what's going to happen.' He made a throat-slitting gesture and walked away towards town.

Raheem received a text from Samir: *I can't find him, he must be at west park but you're going there not me. I've been running around a like a dog all day when I was supposed to be revising!*

Raheem texted back to tell him what Liam had said, before going back inside the café. They would definitely have to do some running on Saturday. Hopefully they'd be running after Liam as per their plan, and not away from Aaron.

Chapter 22

Daniel had sent a message. *Hi, guys. So Liam set off for Burydale Park fifteen minutes ago. He got the bus. I searched in his bedroom and none of his stuff is there. You were right Raheem, he probably checked into a hotel last night and left his things there before he goes back to America. The camera and envelopes were gone from the top of the wardrobe. He has his backpack with him. Callum and James were sleeping so don't think they heard anything. I'll message you once I'm at the park and I see him on the bench next to the lake. I'll return the keys to you next time I see you. Good luck.*

Raheem replied, *Dan, u r a fucking legend!*

Then Samir chipped in. *Dan, u r a fucking legend!*

Stop copying my messages, Raheem texted.

Stfu

Haha you two are legends! Daniel chipped in.

I know I am, Samir said.

And, of course, Raheem had the last word. *I am I know*

Raheem rang Jasmine; she needed to tell Liam she'd been delayed setting off. Liam not taking their mobile numbers had been the biggest blessing in disguise. If he'd taken their numbers and messaged them, they'd have had no chance of pulling this off.

Raheem's phone rang, showing a private number. As he answered the call, a wasp landed on his hand. 'You little bastard!' he said angrily as he dropped the phone on the sofa. The wasp flew out of the open window; thankfully it had not stung him.

He was slamming the window shut just as the doorbell rang. Aaron was outside. 'You ready?' Raheem asked as he opened the door.

'Sure am,' said Aaron.

He sat down on the single seater, but Raheem remained standing. 'I reckon he's at the park,' he said.

'So I'm going to wait at the entrance to the woods at Burydale Park in my car?'

'Correct. You wait there out of sight. Me or Samir will ring you if we think we see him.'

'Let's go, then. Where is Samir?'

'He's upstairs, I'll go call him. You wait for us in your car.'

Aaron stood up. 'Is that your phone?' He pointed at the sofa.

'Oh yeah, it is.' Raheem picked it up. It would have been a disaster if he'd left without it.

As Aaron got into his Mercedes, Raheem jogged up to Samir's bedroom to tell him it was time to go, before going into his own bedroom. He opened his bedside drawer and took out Aaron's watch and Samir's old phone on which they'd been using to send the messages, put them in his jacket and zipped the pocket. Then he texted Jasmine and Daniel to let them know that he and Samir would be at the park in half an hour.

***

Despite everything he'd told himself, Raheem was nervous as they entered Burydale Park. There was so much on the line, but he'd gone through every detail with Samir the previous night, and they were sure there were no loopholes. They just had to be convincing and they would pull this off.

Daniel had rung Samir and told him he could see Liam on the bench at the halfway point on the path around the lake, where Jasmine was supposed to meet him. The halfway point was where the entrance to the woods was.

'I'm going to ring Jasmine. She needs to tell Liam she'll be there in fifteen minutes, that way he'll stick around,' said Raheem.

'Go for it.'

Hopefully this would be the last time Jasmine would have to speak to Liam.

'I've said I will be there in fifteen minutes,' she said, the moment she answered.

'Nice one. We're going to get him now.'

'Good luck! And don't mess anything up!'

'We won't, don't worry. Thanks for your help Jasmine.' He ended the call and looked at Samir. 'Let's go.'

They set off around the lake. Daniel was on the café balcony, which had a perfect view of the lake; he was speaking to Samir to let him know Liam was still there. Aaron was in his car at the entrance to the woods.

As they reached the grapevine yard, Samir ended the call to Daniel. They peered through the bushes. Liam was sitting on the bench with his rucksack, looking at his phone. There was no one around him. Raheem put his hand in his pocket to make sure Aaron's watch and Samir's old phone were still inside. This was it.

'Ready?' breathed Raheem.

'Ready.'

'Go!'

Together, they ran at Liam – or at least Raheem did. Samir swore in pain as he lay on the ground, having slipped on the grass. Liam heard him and, by the time Raheem looked back to the bench, he was running full pelt down the path into the woods.

'Don't ring Aaron yet!' Raheem shouted at Samir, who had got to his feet and taken out his phone. He ran as fast as he could after Liam; it was essential he caught up with him before he got to Aaron. Liam, despite carrying the rucksack, was more than matching him for speed. Samir was running behind them. They needed to catch up with him in the next minute otherwise he would make it out of the back entrance of the woods.

'I'll give you the money! Stop!' Raheem shouted.

Liam looked back, stumbled over a branch and fell headfirst onto the ground.

'Aha!' shouted Raheem happily, but he shouldn't have got so excited. Next moment, he found himself on the floor after tripping over the same branch. 'Grab him, grab him!' he shouted, scrambling to his feet.

He needn't have worried; Samir had already jumped on top of Liam and pinned him down. Raheem hurried over. 'Keep him down like that,' he said as he unzipped Liam's rucksack. The camera was inside, as well as the envelopes with the paper in which Liam would have dropped off at Sarah's and Rachel's once he had given them the camera. He quickly slipped the phone into the rucksack and Aaron's watch into Liam's back pocket. Liam, lying on his stomach with his face pinned to the ground, didn't seem to notice. Raheem then took Liam's real phone from his pocket and held it out to him. 'What's your phone code? Tell me otherwise you're going to regret it.'

'One, three, five, seven' panted Liam.

Raheem put the code in and went onto Liam's camera album. He scrolled through the photos in the past year. Thankfully, Liam had not taken any pictures of the printed photos on his phone. He deleted the messages and number of the phone that Jasmine had been using.

'Your phone is shit, I don't want it' said Raheem as he put it back into Liam's pocket.

'Time to call Aaron, I think,' said Samir.

Raheem took out his phone and rang Aaron, who answered straightaway. 'We got him. Come through the woods and follow the path – you'll see us.' Aaron didn't even respond as he disconnected the call.

'Ease off him a bit in case he dies,' said Raheem. 'Ease off – but don't let go!'

Samir loosened his grip slightly.

'I'll give you the camera! Let me go!' Liam panted.

'Let me think about it... nah,' said Raheem. 'If you don't be quiet, I'm going to break your face.'

They had waited a minute before a noise made them look around. Next moment, Aaron appeared.

'We got him,' said Samir as Aaron walked up to them. He let go of Liam as Aaron turned him onto his back. He offered no resistance, which was a smart move seeing he was outnumbered three to one and all of them were bigger than him.

'Take him behind the trees and bushes,' said Raheem. They could not take any chances that someone would come along this path. People, particularly cyclists, used it as an entrance to the park. Aaron grabbed Liam's left arm as Samir grabbed his right.

'Raheem!' A voice that Raheem had no trouble recognising called his name. Heart banging against his chest, he turned around. Sarah was hurrying towards them.

Chapter 23

'Oh shit,' muttered Samir. Shit? They were in deep shit.

'Listen to me, both of you,' said Raheem hurriedly as Sarah drew nearer. 'Don't say anything, let me talk.' Why the hell was Sarah here at the worst possible time? Raheem hitched a smile on his face as she reached them.

'What is going on?' she demanded, staring at him in shock.

'Nothing,' said Raheem brightly. 'How was your concert?' Everyone stared at him. It had been worth a try. What did they expect him to say?

Sarah turned to Aaron then nodded at Liam. 'Who is he?' Aaron looked at Raheem for help, but what help could Raheem provide now? 'Is anyone going to tell me?' she asked when no one responded.

It was clear that neither Samir nor Aaron were going to say anything. Then Raheem remembered he had told them not too. 'Why are you here?' he asked Sarah casually, knowing full well he would have to explain why *he* was here. He'd not planned for this and he couldn't believe his bad luck. He would rather have met a lion here than Sarah. If there ever was a time to keep calm under pressure, it was now.

Sarah's eyes flew back at him. 'I heard you on the phone this morning.'

'Phone?' asked Raheem, but then he remembered. He'd dropped his phone on the sofa when the wasp landed on his hand, and it must have been Sarah who had called him. He had not disconnected the call. Sarah would have heard every word he and Aaron had said. He wasn't going to let a wasp mess this up for him. 'But why did you ring on a private number?' he asked.

'Because I gave my phone to my work colleague to make a call yesterday and forgot to change the settings back on my phone! What is going on?'

'He is cheating on you!' shouted Liam suddenly.

There was a shocked silence. Raheem's heart started beating faster again, but as long as he remained calm and convincing then Liam couldn't prove anything. 'What the fuck you on about?' he said dismissively.

Liam had a horrible smirk on his face. 'Oh, so you don't know what I'm on about? Let me go, so I can show you.'

Sarah and Aaron were staring at Raheem. 'Go on, let him go,' he said calmly

Liam looked more shocked than anyone else as Samir and Aaron let him go. He quickly opened his bag and took out the camera, before turning it on. One minute later, he was still searching. 'Well?' asked Raheem. Liam's face went pink and he began opening the envelopes.

'What is he doing?' asked Samir.

Liam stared at the blank sheets of paper, his face expressionless. The urge to laugh was so strong, but Raheem had to keep a clear mind.

Thirty seconds went by and Liam was still staring at the papers in his hand. Then, without warning, he tried to run, but Samir had anticipated it and stuck out his leg. Liam fell back on the ground.

'Can someone please explain to me what's going on?' asked Sarah.

Raheem turned back to her as Samir held Liam down again. 'Can I speak first without interruption? I will explain everything,' he said. Sarah folded her arms.

'I think that means go ahead!' called Samir.

Raheem walked past Sarah and turned around to face the others. 'So basically, Aaron saw a message on Hannah's Facebook from Liam where he was saying weird things. Then Aaron got a message on his phone telling him to stop seeing Hannah. Aaron told me and Samir. We put two and two together and realised it must have come from Liam. We agreed to find out if it really was him.'

'I never sent a phone message!' Liam shouted but Raheem walked up to him and slapped him across the back of the head.

'Can I ask why I was not told any of this?' asked Sarah.

'Raheem told me not to tell—' began Aaron.

'Raheem told Aaron- I mean, I told Aaron to not tell you because I didn't want to worry you,' said Raheem. 'Aaron, show her the messages you got and the Facebook message Hannah got.'

Aaron walked over and held out his phone to Sarah.

'Keep going,' said Sarah, once she had finished looking.

'So anyway, Aaron came today because me and Samir had … erm… worked out that it was most likely Liam who'd sent the message on Aaron's phone. It was because he had sent the Facebook messages earlier so it made sense. I asked a few people at uni about him and they said he was the type who would do something like this. So Aaron met us at our place this morning – that's when you must have called and that fucking wasp… yeah, so when we came here, I told Aaron to wait in the car at the back entrance. Then he arrived.' Raheem nodded at Liam.

'But how did you know he'd be here?' asked Sarah sceptically.

'Because one of the girls we asked about him told us that he always comes to the park on Saturday mornings. She usually goes for a jog here with her friends and she told me he is always here on Saturday's,' said Raheem patiently. 'Probably to find women and harass them. Me and Samir used the code word, which was "Hannah". He looked at us suspiciously, so we knew it was him. We started chasing him through the woods, Samir rang Aaron ... and that's when you must have seen him run into the woods and came here.'

Raheem looked at them all impressively. Sarah was watching him with her mouth slightly open.

'He's lying!' shouted Liam.

This time, Samir slapped Liam around the head. 'Speak when you are spoken to!'

Liam fell silent.

'One moment, Samir,' said Sarah.

She was about to step forward but Raheem held out his arm. He wanted there to be no doubt in her and Aaron's minds. 'Wait, babe. Aaron, ring that number that you kept getting the messages from.'

As Aaron rang the number, everyone stared at Liam's phone in Samir's hand. It didn't ring. 'See it's not—' Liam began but Raheem cut him off.

'What's that noise?'

A buzzing sound was coming from Liam's bag. Samir, a little too enthusiastically, began shaking Liam's rucksack. Out dropped Samir's old phone. The one they had been using to send the messages to Aaron. The one Raheem had recently slipped into Liam's bag.

'Caught red handed!' Samir shouted, pointing at Liam.

Aaron lunged at Liam, but Raheem grabbed him. 'Not yet,' he muttered as he dragged him away.

'That's not my phone!' yelled Liam.

'What was it doing in your bag, you little liar?' shouted Sarah.

'Your boyfriend is cheating on you, and Samir is cheating on his girlfriend, Rachel!'

'He's lying, we just need to find out why he is lying' said Raheem calmly. Sarah was staring directly into his eyes, so he made sure he maintained eye contact. There was no way he could let Sarah find out, not for his own sake but for hers.

'So why is he saying it, then?' she asked. 'I get the Hannah part, – I get these random guys sending me messages on social media. But why would he say you were cheating on me? And Samir is cheating on Rachel? And what have that camera and those envelopes got to do with anything?'

'He's crazy, Sarah, he —' said Samir, but Sarah raised a hand and he fell silent.

'I want to talk to him,' she told Raheem. It was no good protesting. If he refused to let her talk to Liam, it would look suspicious.

'One moment!' Samir raised his hands as Sarah walked up to him and Liam.

'No, I just want to speak to him.'

'But before you do, let me make sure he isn't carrying anything dangerous on him. He could have a knife or something,' said Samir solemnly.

Sarah looked a bit taken aback by Samir's thoughtfulness. She glanced at Raheem, as though he should have thought of that.

Raheem held onto Liam as Samir searched his pockets. 'No knife, just his watch' said Samir, taking care to make sure Aaron could see it. 'People normally wear watches on their wrist, but like I said, this guy is fucked in his head and keeps it in his pocket.'

'Hold on.' Aaron frowned, a look of dawning comprehension on his face.

'What?' said Raheem eagerly.

'That's *my* watch,' said Aaron slowly.

Liam looked bewildered. 'I don't know where that's come from,' he said.

'*Your* watch?' asked Raheem.

'Yeah. I lost it that day I got attacked outside Tesco,' said Aaron. It wasn't an attack exactly, but on this occasion Raheem didn't mind.

'You what?' exclaimed Sarah. She seemed to have forgotten about her questioning. Aaron launched into the story of the "attack".

'And why did no one bother telling me this?' Sarah asked when he'd finished.

'I didn't know, either. Did you Raheem?' asked Samir.

'No, no. First time I've heard about it.'

'I felt there was no need to mention it' said Aaron awkwardly.

Sarah sat down on a log with her head in her hands.

'These two were the ones who attacked you that night,' said Liam quietly.

'Have you got no shame? How much do you lie?' demanded Raheem. ' You and one of your friends probably attacked him. We know you hang around with some people who like stealing.'

'There were two people I reckon' said Aaron, frowning as he tried to remember. 'I was so drunk so can't remember everything. He must have had a... hold on, how do you know it would have been his friend? I never told anyone there were two people?'

234

He had a point. Bloody hell. Aaron normally wasn't the sharpest of people. Why try be clever now, today of all days?

'Come on Aaron, you really think this guy could attack you on his own?' said Raheem cheerily. 'He must have had someone, or a few people with him, one on one he would have no chance against you!'

Before anyone could stop him, Aaron ran forward and started punching Liam on the face. Liam's screams were loud enough for the whole of Stalford to hear. Raheem and Samir grabbed Aaron and, with great difficulty, managed to pull him away.

'Aaron, stop!' shouted Sarah.

Aaron was swearing, Sarah and Liam were both screaming. They would get caught.

'Everyone shut up!' yelled Raheem as Aaron's elbow caught him in the face, just like it had six months earlier when they had fought outside Tesco. Liam was curled up on the ground, clutching his face and sobbing. It was time to take charge. 'Sarah, Samir, calm Aaron down. I need to keep hold of Liam.'

Aaron stayed where he was, breathing heavily. 'Go over there,' instructed Raheem, pointing at a log thirty feet away. He went to Liam and turned him on his back. He had a nasty bruise under his left eye.

Raheem sat him up and grabbed his shoulder so that he couldn't run away, not that he looked in any fit state to run.

'How did you get into my flat?' muttered Liam. Aaron was sitting on the log with Sarah whilst Samir kept guard.

Raheem turned back to Liam. There was only one way to end this once and for all. 'Samir, come here,' he called.

'Who? Me?' Samir asked.

'Is anyone else here called Samir?' said Raheem in exasperation. Samir hurried over. 'You need to call Hannah,' Raheem muttered. 'Pick her up from her flat and bring her here.' Without further ado, Samir headed up the path towards the car park.

'Where's Samir gone?' called Sarah.

'To get Hannah. We want to see if she knows him,' he said, nodding at Liam.

'Why would he say you and Samir were both cheating?' asked Sarah.

'He's fucked in the head that's why,' said Aaron. 'Don't listen to him, Sarah.'

That was one less person to convince, but Sarah still seemed a bit hesitant and Raheem had to make sure she believed him. 'Aaron, come here and hold him down, but don't do anything else,' he said.

Aaron strode forwards and held Liam down. Raheem went to Sarah and grabbed her hand. 'What's the matter?' he asked quietly.

She looked at Liam, then back at Raheem. 'I get why he would stalk Hannah, but why would he say you cheated on me?'

He hated himself so much, but he had to lie. For the greater good. 'Because he wants to get me and Samir back for beating him up in first year,' he said firmly.

'Why did you beat him up?'

Raheem explained how Liam had tried to grope Cheryl back in first year, and how he and Samir had hit him in front of everyone. 'I can call Cheryl, if you don't believe me.'

Sarah bit her lip. 'Have you still got her number? You told me you'd deleted it?'

Seriously? Is that what mattered to her most at this moment? 'I'll ask Samir when he comes back. I don't think I've actually got her number.' He did have her number but there was no harm in waiting a bit.

Raheem went back to Liam and knelt down next to him. 'You go back there now,' he said to Aaron, who trudged back to the log. Raheem waited until he was out of earshot before turning to Liam. 'Don't say another word,' he muttered. 'We will let you go. No one will hurt you if you keep your mouth shut.'

'Just tell me how you got into my flat.'

'I said shut up. One more word and I swear I'll knock the fuck out of you. You deserve it, you bastard. I knew you'd try doing us over. Just don't say anything. Do you understand?'

Liam nodded. Raheem lit a cigarette to calm him down, but made sure he stayed within ten feet of Liam in case he tried to escape. They had nearly done it. If it was only Aaron, they wouldn't have needed to call Hannah, but with Sarah he had to provide as much evidence as he could.

They waited fifteen minutes before Samir returned with Hannah, who was looking scared. Samir had texted Raheem to say that he'd explained everything to her in the car on the way here.

'Hannah, sorry about bringing you here, but can you confirm who this is?' said Raheem, turning Liam around.

Hannah took one look at him and said, 'He's the one who was trying to chat to me that night in the computer room, remember, Raheem? And he was acting weird outside the gym at West Park. I told Samir about it. He has been starting at me at uni all year.'

Perfect, Hannah. Sarah looked a little more reassured.

'Samir, do a video call with Cheryl and ask her if she remembers him,' said Raheem.

Samir obliged and within moments, Cheryl was on loudspeaker explaining how Liam had groped her in Sensations two years ago.

Raheem turned to face Sarah and raised his arms. 'What more proof do we need? The messages, the phone, Aaron's watch, Hannah, and now Cheryl.'

Sarah suddenly walked over to Raheem and Liam. 'Get him up, Raheem. Don't argue.'

Raheem exchanged a nervous glance with Samir as he hoisted Liam up. Sarah's expression was unfathomable. Raheem's nerves began jangling again. Suddenly, she raised her hand and slapped Liam across the face with all the strength she could muster. When he fell back on the ground, Hannah ran forward and kicked him on his back.

Raheem grabbed Sarah as Aaron lifted Hannah off her feet. Together they pulled them away from Liam.

'Leave him, babe, he's not worth it.' Raheem tried to avoid Sarah's flailing arms. She only stopped resisting when the back of her hand accidentally hit his face. Why did everyone always have to end up hitting him?

Raheem told Aaron to take both Sarah and Hannah to his car. They returned the watch to him, and Aaron and the girls left. They had wanted to tell the police but Raheem had shouted them down. They could do without that.

'Let me go, please,' Liam pleaded with Raheem and Samir. His cheek was still red from where Sarah had slapped him and the bruise underneath his eye was swelling up.

Raheem and Samir looked at each other. Raheem could tell that, like him, Samir wanted to punish Liam a bit more, but because Liam was practically begging meant that they had to let him go.

Samir pulled Liam to his feet. Raheem picked up the camera. 'This wasn't yours,' he said as Liam looked at it.

'And this wasn't yours, either,' said Samir as he pocketed his old phone which they had slipped into Liam's rucksack. 'Shall we tell him how we did him over?'

Raheem was tempted but decided to play safe. 'Nah, we got what we wanted.'

Without another word, they walked up the path that would lead them out of the woods. When they turned around, Liam was standing where they had left him, his backpack hanging limply from his hand.

Raheem and Samir both did the camera pose, which Liam had so irritated them with, before turning their back on him. Revenge was sweet.

Chapter 24

How they had managed to get away with it was unbelievable. Liam had gone back to America empty handed. But it was more relief than anything else that they felt. A big disaster had been avoided and Raheem had learnt his lesson. Never again was he going to cheat.

They spent the next few days revising for their exams. Friday 27th May would be their last official day as students and it was also the day of their final exam.

Daniel had finished his second year. Raheem and Samir went to see him in his flat as he was packing his bags.

'Dan, you really helped us this year. We just came to say thank you,' said Raheem.

'You guys helped me with my work. I'm certain I've passed.' Daniel grinned.

'And Amy?' asked Samir.

Daniel zipped his suitcase shut before turning to them. 'We kissed last night.' He ducked for cover as Raheem and Samir jumped on him.

***

'Aren't we supposed to be revising?' Raheem asked as they sat in McDonald's car park with their McFlurries.

'You got a point.' Samir moved his seat back to a more comfortable position.

That day with Sarah just before the start of his third year flashed through Raheem's mind. It was in this McDonald's car park, and he'd been parked in the same bay. It would be fair to say that a lot had happened since then.

'Me and Katie have split up,' said Samir abruptly.

'What?'

'Me and Katie have split up. Long story short, I was the one who ended it. And I am never cheating on Rachel ever again.'

Raheem stared at him.

'I've decided I need to change,' Samir continued. 'No more flings. I haven't told Rachel about Katie, and I don't intend to. I don't want to see the hurt in her eyes. I can't change the past but I can change the future. And I want my future to be with Rachel.'

Raheem was half-expecting him to laugh and say it was a joke but Samir turned to look at him. 'You don't cheat on someone you love, Raheem. Remember that. Initially, I was with Rachel just for time pass, but now she is everything for me.It just took me a long time to realise.'

'So what you saying, that I should leave Sarah?' Raheem frowned.

Samir nodded.

'You're out of your mind,' said Raheem. 'Fair enough, with Veronica I admit that was an ego thing. But I do want to be with Sarah. What happened with Veronica was a mistake.'

'Are you convincing me that you want to be with Sarah, or are you trying to convince yourself?'

Raheem hesitated. 'I do want to be with Sarah,' he said.

'Why couldn't you say that straightaway, then?'

Raheem was stunned by the impact of Samir's words. Why had he hesitated? Maybe it *was* time to be honest with himself.

Samir looked him straight in the eye. 'You need to make a decision,' he said quietly.

Raheem sat back and closed his eyes. Samir was right: he had to decide. If he was honest with himself, he'd known deep down for the past few weeks that it would come to this.

***

They were back in the flat. Raheem had called Sarah and asked if he could come to her place. Sarah had said she'd come to his instead. She had sounded a bit nervous on the phone.

No matter what he told himself, he was dreading breaking the news to her, but she deserved someone better than him. Most of the times he'd argued with her over the past six months were more to do with him being angry at himself and feeling guilty. But Samir was right: they both had to change. Too much had happened for them not to.

'You know, in the future we'll look back at this year as the best life lesson we ever had,' said Raheem. 'You were right about helping Dan. It did change our luck.'

Samir nodded. ' Problem with being right all the time is it is boring. Are you sure you want me to stay in the flat? It might be better if I go out.'

'No, I want you to stay in the kitchen. I'm not sure how Sarah will react, but in case she tries to attack me or something, I need you there to calm her down. She is going to be gutted, and so am I but I need to be honest with her.'

Sarah's car arrived. A lump rose in Raheem's throat. 'Get a glass of water, she might need it,' he said.

Samir dashed past Raheem into the kitchen as Sarah got out of her car.

Raheem steadied himself. 'Just relax,' he muttered as Samir came back in with a glass of water and put it on the dining table.

The doorbell rang. 'Go get it,' hissed Raheem.

'What, me?'

'Yeah, go!'

Raheem sat on the sofa as Samir left, but he was back on his feet again when Sarah came into the living room. Every item of clothing she was wearing, including her earrings, was something that Raheem had bought for her. That only made it even harder.

'Hi,' she said as Samir closed the living-room door. They stood for a split second before embracing. It was a longer embrace than usual and suddenly Raheem didn't want to let go.

'You look nice,' he said as Samir went back into the kitchen.

'Thanks,' she replied.

There was another pause before Raheem said, 'Can I get you something to drink?'

'I'm okay thanks,' she said softly.

He didn't want to break her heart, but he had no choice. 'Look Sarah ... there's something... I – I need to tell you,' he said.

241

Sarah's face stiffened. 'I need to say something to you as well.'

He needed a bit more time to gather himself. 'Sure. You first,' he said.

Sarah grabbed his hand in both of hers. She was going to apologise, and he was going hate himself even more when he told her that he was ending the relationship.

'I feel I like need to be honest with you,' she said. 'We haven't been the same for a while now ... and I just want to say something...'

Once she'd apologised, he would apologise as well and then break it to her.

Sarah took a deep breath. 'I'm so sorry, Raheem. I can't be with you anymore... I ... want to be with Jason.'

'What!'

Samir burst into the living room. 'What's happened?' he demanded, looking at them both.

Raheem let go of Sarah's hand and stepped back, horrified. He'd not been expecting that. 'She is dumping me! She wants to be with Jason! What the hell? No, you can't do this, Sarah!'

'Eh?' said Samir.

'Raheem, I'm sorry. What did you think I was going to say? I thought you were expecting this!' cried Sarah as he started pacing around the room.

Samir looked as if he had been struck by lightning.

'Expecting this?' Raheem's voice was higher than usual. 'I thought you came here to apologize to me!'

Sarah's expression of pity, which Raheem had hardly ever seen, turned to annoyance, which he had seen many times before. '*Me* apologize to you! You should be apologizing to *me*!'

'You've gone mad, totally mad!' Raheem was on his fourth lap of the living room, waving his hands in the air. He grabbed the glass of water from the dining table and downed it in one go. Sarah was going to leave him! For Jason! But hadn't he wanted to end the relationship with Sarah just a few minutes ago? Maybe he was the one who was losing it.

'Excuse me, you're the one who never made time for me, was always making excuses, used to hate going shopping with me!' she screeched.

'Who, me?' shouted Raheem, still doing his laps around the room. He wasn't watching where he was going and stumbled over his uni bag.

'And I've told you not to leave your bag lying around a million times, but you never listen!'

'You always find a reason to have a go at me!' said Raheem angrily, finally sitting down on the sofa. 'Those shopping trips did my head in! You could never make up your mind what you wanted. The shopping centre was always rammed, all chatty women not able to decide what they want, then when they finally decided on something, coming back the next week to return what they bought, it was torture!' All that could be heard in the room was their heavy breathing.

Sarah turned to Samir, who was standing in exactly the same place. 'Have you got nothing to say, Samir? You usually like to chip in your two dollars?'

'It's two cents, actually,' said Raheem, running his hands through his hair. He was starting to get a headache.

'Come into the garden,' said Samir to Raheem. 'Now,' he added when Raheem didn't respond.

Raheem followed him outside. Sarah had taken his place on the sofa and had her head in her hands.

'Get in,' said Samir, unlocking his car. Raheem flung himself in the passenger seat. 'What's your problem?' Samir asked as he got in.

'My problem?'

'Yeah, your problem. You were going end it with Sarah, so why are you angry now? Oh, let me guess. Is your ego hurt because she ended it?'

Raheem said nothing and folded his arms. What *was* his problem? The fact that Sarah ended it or that she was leaving him for Jason? Or was his problem his stubbornness, his ego?

Samir put his hand on Raheem's shoulder. 'Do you trust me?' he asked.

'More than I do myself,' replied Raheem.

'Then go inside, apologise to Sarah, and leave on good terms. You have been together for two years. I know it's not easy, but she and Jason have known each other for ten years. They suit each other. I just never wanted to say that to you. You're a good guy, and I know you will do the right thing.'

Raheem pondered Samir's words. He was a good guy? 'Do I have anything good about me?' he asked slowly. It was the first time he had ever doubted himself.

'Shut up,' said Samir firmly.

'No, tell me. Is there anything good about me? Look at the games I played with Aaron, Sarah, Veronica. I never once thought of the consequences.'

'First of all, *we* played the games. I'm not letting you take credit for everything. Secondly, the best times I've had in my life have been with you, and that includes all the fit women I've been with. Admit it, though, I've pulled more than you in life.'

'Alright, maybe one or two more. But mine have been sexier! Veronica, come on, she was just on a different level. You haven't dated anyone like her!'

'Thirdly, you helped Aaron when he was having problems. You introduced Hannah to him and look at him now. You always paid for us all when we went out. You helped Dan get with Amy, and you sent him your notes from last year. You got Jasmine a job she wanted. You backed me up in fights. Do I need to go on?'

Raheem was starting to feel better.

'Look at her,' said Samir, nodding his head to the sitting room where Sarah was sitting on the sofa, crying. Raheem's anger melted away as he watched her.

'You've cheated on her and she doesn't know even know about it,' said Samir. 'Let's be honest, you never gave her enough time. Did you see her face after she told you she wanted to end it? Look how much it hurt her to say it.'

Sarah was drying her eyes with the tissues he had left on the fireplace. All Raheem's anger had disappeared.

***

'I'm sorry, Sarah. You deserve someone better than me,' said Raheem five minutes later. Fresh tears poured out of Sarah's eyes as they stood opposite each other. A cup smashed in the kitchen.

'It slipped,' called Samir. 'I'll have your coffee in a sec, once I clean this up.' Talk about taking all the tension out of the moment.

Sarah grabbed his hand. 'I'm so sorry, Raheem. You're a great guy, honestly, and I've loved the time we spent together. I'll always remember it. But sometimes it's just not meant to be.'

'Don't be sorry, babe – I mean Sarah... Erm, it's going to take some time to get used to it,' said Raheem.

Sarah smiled sadly. Raheem was finding it difficult to continue speaking. No matter the complaints he had always made about Sarah, he was the one who had been in the wrong. Most of the time, not all the time though.

'You know, Raheem, I did tell Jason about my feelings,' she said quietly. 'He was always urging me to make it work with you. I sometimes got angry at him for saying good things about you. I know Jason has always liked me, but I swear he always encouraged me to be with you. Not many people can do that.'

'Jason is a good lad and he will definitely keep you happy,' said Raheem. He had never liked Jason, but if what Sarah was saying was true – and he had no reason to doubt her – then his respect for Jason increased.

There was a knock on the door and Samir entered. 'Where's the coffee?' said Raheem.

'Kettle is not working and the coffee is finished. I told you to get some the other day. He never listens, does he, Sarah?' said Samir.

Sarah smiled. 'You're right. You need to teach him to listen.'

The world really had gone mad if both Sarah and Samir were getting on.

Sarah looked back at Raheem. 'I've got a new job in Birmingham, starting in three weeks. I'm moving back.'

'Congratulations. Is it another accountancy firm?' Raheem asked.

'It's for Whitehall Property Developers, in their finance department.'

'Great, you can transfer some of their money to my bank account. Don't transfer all of it, though, they might realise.'

All three of them laughed. 'Your sense of humour will never change and it had better not.' Sarah beamed at him.

'Nope, it never will,' said Raheem. 'It's a big company and you deserve this opportunity.'

No one spoke for a minute until Samir broke the silence. 'I'm off to uni, got to revise for these exams. I'll leave you both to it.' He gave Raheem a thumbs up as he went.

'How about having tea at Burydale Park in the cafe, and then a final walk around the lake?' asked Sarah.

'I'm a coffee person, not a tea person, as I've told you enough times.'

'You know what I mean!'

'It's called dinner, not tea, and you cannot convince me otherwise.'

Sarah slapped his face gently and picked up her bag. 'I'm going with you on one condition.'

'Which is?'

'That I'm paying,' she said sternly.

Raheem nodded. 'But I'm driving, I guess?'

'You sure are, and you can't turn the music on.'

Laughing together, they headed outside.

***

Later that night, Raheem was lying in his bed going through pictures on his phone of him with Sarah. It had been the right decision to part ways, but it would take him a few days to accept it. He flicked through the pictures until he stopped at his favourite one of Sarah. It was the one he'd taken last year when they had gone to the Lake District, the one where she was doing her mischievous grin. She would always hold a special place in his heart.

Chapter 25

Raheem now had less than two weeks left of university and two final exams to sit, along with handing in his essay. As long as he got a minimum 70% score in his final exams and 60% for his dissertation, he was virtually guaranteed a first-class degree. Getting that 70% in his exams would not be easy though.

The lift door opened and he got out. He was going for a cigarette break after spending the last two hours on the first floor working on his essay with Aliyah. He had just taken out his cigarette packet when Jason entered the library.

Jason spotted him. Raheem stood where he was. For a full ten seconds they looked at each other, before Raheem walked up to him. 'You alright, Jason?'

Jason nodded, looking apprehensive. 'I'm good thanks... how are you?'

Raheem gestured towards the back of the library near the printers. Jason followed him, still with that apprehensive look on his face. At the last printer, Raheem turned to face him. 'I'm sorry, Jason.'

It was clear from the way Jason looked at him that he had not been expecting this. 'You're sorry?' he asked as if he were sure he had misheard.

Raheem nodded. He had never been good with Jason, and apologising was the first step to make up for his behaviour. 'I've always been an idiot towards you, even though you've never had a problem with me. I just wanted to say I'm sorry.'

Jason opened his mouth a couple of times but didn't speak. 'Say something then, or are you just going to stand there?' Raheem held out his hand.

Jason smiled and shook it. 'I never took anything you said to heart, so it's all good.'

They both laughed; it was the first time that had happened. Together at least.

'Look after Sarah, otherwise I'll switch back to my old ways,' said Raheem.

'I will do, Raheem. Thanks for being so, erm … don't know what the right word is so I'll just leave it as thanks.'

Raheem clapped him on the shoulder before walking towards the exit. That hadn't been too bad. Jason was actually alright. Really.

***

Sunlight was streaming through the open window. Raheem was about to have a cold shower to freshen up.

He'd just completed his final shift at Tesco. He had managed to get a transfer to a Tesco Express in Manchester, where he would work until he got his first full-time job. His colleagues had bought him a card and a Hugo Boss fragrance as a gift. Whenever he was in Stalford, he'd go back and visit them.

He had started climbing the stairs when the doorbell rang. He opened the door to find Aaron standing outside. 'Aaron, good to see you, come in.'

'Thanks.' He stepped into the hallway.

The kitchen door opened and Samir came out. 'Give me two minutes,' he said, acknowledging Aaron.

'How's things?' asked Raheem as they sat down in the living room.

Aaron was about to respond when Samir bounded into the room. 'I'll mop up after,' he said hastily as he sat down next to Aaron. They needed to make sure their flat was clean before they left, otherwise they wouldn't get their deposit back.

'You want a drink or anything?' asked Raheem.

Aaron shook his head and opened his mouth, before closing it again.

'What's up?' asked Raheem. He wouldn't be surprised if Aaron said he wanted to be back with Veronica. If the past year had taught him anything, it was to expect the unexpected.

'I feel really bad that Sarah left you,' Aaron said eventually. There was an awkward pause; he was looking a bit uncomfortable at how that had come out.

'We left each other,' said Raheem politely.

'That's what I meant. I feel gutted, to be honest. But, end of the day, if you both decided, then it's your choice.' Aaron looked genuinely disappointed, which Raheem appreciated. No one said anything for a few moments until Aaron continued, 'Thanks for your help. Both of you. With Hannah. I'm so glad I'm with her.'

'We didn't do anything. It wouldn't have been possible if you hadn't put the effort in yourself,' said Samir reassuringly.

They sat in silence again for a few moments, each of them absorbed in their own thoughts.

'So what you guys doing this evening?' asked Aaron.

'Not much. Why? You got something planned?' said Raheem.

'Final night out? Some of my friends are coming down from Birmingham tonight and we got a VIP room at Sensations if you want to join us?'

Aaron never managed to hear their response because both Raheem and Samir had run out of the living room and up the stairs towards the bathroom.

'Fuck off! I'm going first!' yelled Raheem as Samir grabbed him in a headlock.

'Piss off!'

'We don't have to go,' called Aaron as he came onto the landing. Raheem took advantage of the distraction to get out of the headlock and fling Samir to the ground, before running inside the bathroom and locking the door.

'We don't have to go, if you don't want to,' Aaron said again.

'We will go, Aaron. Now shut the hell up!' Samir yelled. Raheem had to hold onto the sink to keep himself steady as he laughed. It was going to be a wild night that was for sure.

***

Their night out wasn't the only final event of that week; they also had their last all-nighter in the library.

Samir held the door open for Raheem before quickly following him inside. They had not been caught bringing hot

249

food in the library during their entire period at university. They had taken it in turns to distract security whilst the other one went outside and collected the food. That was some achievement.

'Here you are, ladies.' Raheem placed the steak and chip boxes on the table.

'Thanks, guys,' said Aliyah and Veronica together.

Veronica took out the disposable plates from her bag. They were sitting in one of the student meeting rooms on the second floor. Raheem, Samir, and Aliyah, who was doing her first all-nighter in the library, were revising for their exam. Veronica, who had her final exam on Wednesday, seemed to have brought the entire business management library with her. There were at least ten books on the floor next to her chair.

They ate their way through the pizza and wings before Raheem put the rubbish into a black bin bag. He opened the door and glanced along the corridor, before putting it in the bin outside the IT labs.

'Right, come on, Raheem, back to revision,' said Aliyah briskly, taking her notes from her bag.

Raheem, who had just taken a cigarette out of his pocket, looked up. 'Can I go for a cigarette first?'

Aliyah shook her head. 'Nope, you can't go for a cigarette for the next forty-five minutes at least, starting from now.'

It was eleven o'clock. With a sulky look at Aliyah, he pulled his laptop and books towards him and started to revise. He had less than a week with her before he left for Manchester the following Friday. Each remaining moment he spent with her was precious.

'Veronica, you come to the first floor with me,' said Samir abruptly. 'Let these two revise. I'm just going to distract him otherwise.'

Raheem looked up from his laptop. 'Why? Stay here, it's our last all-nighter in the library.' He wanted to make the most of every second he had left, and Samir had been with him all the way.

'I think Samir is right,' said Veronica. 'You two will distract each other. You need me and Aliyah to keep an eye on you.' It took her a full two minutes to pack away her books. She handed the ones she couldn't fit in her bag to Samir.

'Let him go for cigarette breaks or he won't be able to concentrate,' said Samir to Aliyah.

'I'll monitor his behaviour. If it's good, I might consider it.' Aliyah smiled at Raheem.

'See you around. We'll be on the first floor should you decide to visit us,' said Veronica. She left the room with Samir, leaving Raheem and Aliyah together.

Raheem turned to Aliyah. 'That's not fair. If I behave then you *might consider* letting me go for a cigarette?'

'Yep,' said Aliyah simply. 'I think that is fair. You mess around once, and I am not going to let you go.'

They looked at each other for a moment before Raheem returned to his laptop. He was going to miss Aliyah more than he could ever tell her. But he wasn't going to tell her anything. He needed to stick to the promise he had made to himself.

They worked in silence for almost half an hour before Raheem texted Samir to meet him outside the university entrance in fifteen minutes. The forty-five minutes set by Aliyah would be up by then.

'You know what? You've behaved, so you can go for one a bit early,' said Aliyah as she put down her pen.

'You're so kind, but I'm going in fifteen minutes as we agreed. I just wanted to talk to you about something.' Raheem saved his notes on his laptop.

He had to tell her now. He had spoken with Samir and decided that he couldn't hide his split with Sarah from Aliyah – they were best friends, after all.

Aliyah stopped writing and turned to look at him. 'I'm listening,' she said.

It would be better to not beat around the bush. 'Me and Sarah have split up.' If ever there was a silence so still, he had never experienced it before.

'How come?' Aliyah whispered.

Raheem told her that he and Sarah had come to a mutual decision and didn't mention anything about Veronica or Jason. He expected Aliyah to ask more details but, to his surprise, she asked no further questions.

251

'I've moved on, and so has Sarah,' he finished. She was looking at him as though expecting him to continue, but he didn't know what else to say. Thankfully, Samir chose that moment to ring him. 'I'm coming outside now – two minutes,' said Raheem. Aliyah was still looking at him.

'Now, or in two minutes?' Samir said.

'Two minutes.'

Raheem put down the phone and stood up. 'Back in a bit.'

Aliyah nodded and returned to her notes. Raheem left the room and leant against the wall. The temptation to go back inside and tell Aliyah his feelings was overwhelming. Taking a deep breath, he turned right and took the stairs to the ground floor, passing Ryan who was going in the opposite direction and looking frantic. From what Raheem could make out, Ryan had only just realised that his criminology theory exam was tomorrow as opposed to the following Monday.

Adam and Zack were sitting on the tables next to the vending machines, eating as they revised. They had not been as successful as Raheem and Samir when it came to sneaking in hot food in the library – Zack had been caught at least five times during the past three years. Raheem spoke to them briefly before going outside.

Bill, who was on his phone as usual at the security desk, nodded at him as he walked past and joined Samir outside. It was a balmy May night and neither of them had brought their jackets.

'Yo,' said Raheem lighting his cigarette.

'You managed to get any revision done? Me and Veronica keep chatting and now one of her mates has joined us. She never shuts up. I might have to sit on my own tonight.' There was no chance Samir would get any revision done with two chatty women.

'Come back with me and Aliyah. I actually went a full half an hour working.'

Samir shook his head. 'I moved so you could get your revision done. I'll sit with Ryan on the first floor. Me and him work well together.'

'Yeah, you would, seeing as you both don't know what the fuck you're doing. Apparently, he only realised an hour ago that his exam is tomorrow.'

'I know.' Samir laughed. 'That's Ryan for you. Did you tell Aliyah about you and Sarah?'

Raheem nodded and closed his eyes as he blew out smoke from his cigarette. There had been more to tell Aliyah, but he had left it too late.

***

It was four in the morning and Aliyah's eyelids were drooping. Having done it many times before it was easy for him to stay awake through the night, but she was always asleep by midnight at the very latest.

'You look like you're going to pass out any second.' Raheem saved his work and shut down his laptop. He'd got through a solid night's revision and was more confident about his exam now.

Aliyah nodded, bleary eyed. 'It was worth it.'

'Come on, I'll drop you home.'

'Let me just take a power nap and then we can go,' she yawned, stretching.

Raheem took out his phone and texted Sarah. She had just messaged him to ask how his revision was going. It looked like she was also having a really late night. Or a very early morning.

He was just about to go upstairs to see Samir and Veronica when Aliyah's head drooped onto his shoulder. He looked down at her, his lips an inch away from her forehead. Time seemed to have stopped. Part of him wanted to wake her up, but the part closest to his heart wanted to stay exactly where he was.

The seconds ticked by and still Raheem sat where he was, unable to move.

***

Veronica and Jasmine had gone back to Leicester. They had both come to see Raheem and Samir before they left. Raheem was sad to see Veronica go, but she and Jasmine had made plans to meet him and Samir in London over the summer. Nevertheless, these goodbyes were getting too much for him. He'd need all his mental strength tomorrow, that was for sure.

Two things he wouldn't miss were exams and assignments. Raheem sat through two hours of writing, after which his hand was aching. The moment the exam finished, he rushed outside for a cigarette. He was joined by Samir, who told him that Aliyah would meet them in ten minutes. Their final exam had taken place in Northern Tower and they were standing around the back of the building in the courtyard.

'Throw your cigarette away,' muttered Samir, nodding at the gate opposite. Sarah and Aaron were walking towards them.

Raheem stubbed his cigarette out and dropped it into the bin next to him. It would be disrespectful to say goodbye to Sarah whilst doing the very thing she'd hated when they were together.

'Hi,' said Aaron.

'You alright?' said Raheem, shaking his hand. Sarah smiled at him. Samir and Aaron were both looking at him expectantly. What was he supposed to do?

'Can we talk?' asked Sarah.

Oh. He was supposed to say that part.

'Sure,' said Samir. He and Aaron walked around the wall and out of sight.

Raheem and Sarah looked at each other. This was it. A new beginning. 'Look Sarah—' he began awkwardly. He expected her to cut him off but she didn't. 'Erm, what was I saying? Oh yeah. Look, I'm sorry for the way everything turned out, but like I told you that … that day… you deserve someone … better than me.'

There was a pause. Sarah looked as though she were about to cry, but there was a firmness in her voice as she said, 'No, Raheem, you don't need to be sorry. I also made some mistakes. Like I said, it just wasn't meant to be. I will always remember our moments together.'

That had gone well enough but the sadness was building inside him.

'I'm definitely going to miss your rubbish jokes, though,' Sarah added.

Raheem dropped his bag on the ground and hugged her.

She wiped a tear from her eye as they broke apart. 'There is one more thing I need to say to you,' she said.

'Go on.' Raheem crossed his fingers behind his back. Surely she wasn't going to ask him about Veronica?

Sarah looked around to make sure they were alone. Samir and Aaron were nowhere to be seen and nobody was within a hundred yards of them. 'Aaron has really changed in the last few months. I know he's spent a lot of time with you and Samir, and he's changed for the better. I just want to say thank you. Both of you.'

Raheem breathed a sigh of relief. 'Thank God,' he muttered.

'What?'

'Nothing,' he said lightly.

Sarah was having none of it. 'You said "thank God".' She sounded much more like her old self.

'I didn't say that!' protested Raheem.

'You did, I heard you!'

'Okay I did say it. But I meant thank God as in that's who you should thank, not me!'

'Oh, is that what you meant?'

Raheem raised his hands, protesting his innocence.

'Are you two arguing again?' Samir and Aaron had returned not a second too soon.

'No, we weren't arguing,' said Sarah simply. No one spoke for a bit.

'Well, I guess it's time for me to say goodbye,' said Aaron, breaking the silence.

'I'll meet you in the car. I'm going to wait for Aliyah,' said Sarah.

Aaron nodded and turned to Raheem and Samir. He pulled them both into a hug. 'Shout me whenever you're in Birmingham,' he said as he let go.

'Will do, bro. You take care of yourself – and Sarah and Hannah,' said Raheem.

'Take care Aaron, we will meet again' said Samir.

Aaron grinned at them and set off back towards the gate where his car was parked.

Sarah turned to Samir. 'Bye, Samir. Look after Raheem.' She held out her hand.

'He will be looking after me.' Samir grinned as he shook it.

Sarah smiled at him then turned to Raheem, who held his arms wide. Samir tactfully pretended to be on his phone as they hugged again. 'Good luck with your results. I know you'll do really well,' she whispered in his ear.

'Good luck with your job. I know you'll do really well,' he whispered back.

They broke apart, just as the door behind them opened and Aliyah came out. She and Sarah embraced and exchanged farewells. The moment Sarah broke apart from Aliyah, she walked off. They watched her go to Aaron's car.

Raheem was happy and sad at the same time: happy that Sarah was beginning a new chapter in her life, desperately sad because he knew he would miss her.

Aaron opened the passenger door for Sarah, who was making rather a fuss about shutting her handbag. Eventually, with a final look in Raheem's direction, she got in. The car reversed out of the parking bay and drove onto the main road before disappearing around the corner. Sarah had gone, and all Raheem had left were her memories.

Chapter 26

Aliyah put her hand on his shoulder. 'Are you okay?'

Raheem smiled and nodded. He'd had some amazing times with Sarah, and he would always cherish those moments, but now he had to move on. Looking at the past would only increase his pain and regret. Samir was looking at him sympathetically. 'Come on, let's go,' said Raheem.

'I need to make a call, give me a minute.' Samir headed back into Northern Tower, leaving Raheem and Aliyah together.

Aliyah was looking in the direction that Sarah had just left. He could not be selfish anymore because, like Sarah, she was too good for him.

'We're still going to be besties, aren't we?' he asked, trying to keep his tone natural.

Aliyah nodded. She was now looking at the spot where she'd accidentally hit Raheem on the nose and thought she had broken it. 'Remember when you hit me over there?' he asked. If only he'd told her about his feelings earlier – but did he have them earlier? Or had he always felt this way about Aliyah and not realised?

Aliyah looked at him. 'Come on, let's recreate that. It was so funny.'

'Okay,' said Raheem, a little surprised. Normally he was the one to make that sort of suggestion. They walked to the spot and turned to face each other. 'I need to go behind you and then I'll put my hand on your arm and you need to hit me with your hand – not hard, obviously!'

'Don't worry,' said Aliyah, as he went up behind her.

Raheem raised his hand. 'Ready?'

'Ready,' Aliyah replied.

Raheem grabbed her arm. Aliyah turned around. 'Whoa, Aliyah, you look so—'

SMACK! She slapped him across the face. Shocked, Raheem staggered back and fell on the ground. 'Aliyah, what the— Are you okay?'

Tears were streaming down Aliyah's face as he lay on the ground, one hand still on his left cheek where she had just slapped him.

'What's wrong, Aliyah?'

With a scathing look at him, her face still tear-streaked, she hurried across the corner of Northern Tower and out of sight.

Two minutes later, Raheem was still lying on the ground unable to understand what had just happened. He took out his phone and tried to call Aliyah but she disconnected after the second ring. He tried again, but this time she disconnected after the first ring.

The door to his left opened and Samir walked out. He didn't look surprised to see Raheem on the ground and held out his hand. 'Get up,' he ordered.

Startled, Raheem grabbed Samir's hand and tried to stand up, but Samir let go and he fell back again. 'What is going on?' he shouted angrily, heaving himself up.

'You stupid, stupid, *stupid* idiot, Raheem.'

Raheem stared at him. 'Listen, can you just—'

'Shut up and let me speak.' Raheem fell silent. Samir took a deep breath. 'You deserved that slap. But you don't deserve Aliyah.'

Raheem stood stock still. How did Samir know? He opened his mouth, but Samir raised his hand and he fell silent. 'You still haven't worked it out, have you, Raheem?'

Worked what out? How could Samir know how Raheem felt about Aliyah? It was the only thing he had never told him. 'I don't know what you're talking about,' he said quickly. He was not going to admit anything to Samir. But he still didn't understand why Aliyah had slapped him.

Samir smirked. 'I kept telling Aliyah for the past two years that she should tell you, but she didn't want to do anything that would make you break up with Sarah.'

This was getting more and more confusing. 'She should have told me what?' asked Raheem.

'You really have the nerve to call *me* stupid?' Samir still had that forced smirk on his face.

'Explain then!' Raheem said angrily, although the only person he was angry with was himself.

Samir raised his eyebrows. 'Are you seriously telling me that you never knew about Aliyah's feelings for you? After all she's done for you and the way she's been with you, you still can't admit your feelings towards her?'

Raheem was as still as ice, trying to comprehend Samir's words. He never knew Aliyah's feelings? But that could only mean one thing... Aliyah had not only seen him as her best friend, there was more to it. All this time he'd been thinking that it was one sided, but it hadn't been. He just hadn't realised. Until now.

Samir shook his head. 'You know all that happened with Aaron, Sarah and Veronica? She is aware of it. I was telling her everything.'

It was as though someone had switched on a light in Raheem's head. Everything made sense. Now he knew who Samir kept calling and texting all the time. Why he had always tried to discourage him from being with Sarah. Why he had tried to chat up Veronica before she was with Raheem. Why he had always backed out and made an excuse whenever Raheem had asked him to join him and Aliyah when they went out. Why he had asked Veronica to sit in a different place that night in the library...

'Why didn't you tell me?' Raheem said eventually.

'Why didn't you tell me you liked Aliyah?'

Raheem shook his head. He couldn't do this now, he couldn't admit it. 'I liked her as a friend,' he blurted out. Never had any of his lies been as obvious as that one.

'I told you that day in the car, I know you better than you know yourself. Every time you're with Aliyah, I see the look in your eyes. It's been obvious. I've never seen that look with anyone else you've been with. It's time you admitted it.'

Raheem's throat was tight. He closed his eyes.

'Me and Aliyah have spoken a lot during the past two years,' Samir continued. 'She made me promise not to tell you, or to do anything that might make you break up with Sarah. I

259

broke my promise. I did try convincing you to end it with Sarah, not because I had anything against her, but because I knew the moment you two started going out with each other that it wasn't going to last long term. I honestly thought you'd tell Aliyah your feelings that night when I left you two in the library. But I was wrong. Do you realise how hurt Aliyah was? She thought you'd tell her but you didn't. The way you have been feeling about her since you finally realised you loved her, she has been feeling like that for two years. Only difference is, you were too thick to see it.'

Raheem opened his eyes. If only he had opened them earlier. He backed into the wall and sat down, his face in his hands. 'It's too late now. She's getting engaged soon,' he said, trying to keep his voice level.

To his surprise, Samir was smiling. 'Do I really even need to say this?' he asked, sitting down next to him.

'Say what?'

Samir put his arm around Raheem. 'There is no engagement. There is no wedding. That was my idea. It was one of my friend's pictures she showed you that day. I thought that was the one thing that might make you realise your feelings about Aliyah, and I think it did. But you still didn't admit it because, stupid as you are, you have a good heart. You didn't admit it to Aliyah because you didn't want to make her feel bad that she would reject you.'

Raheem stared at Samir. He was right. The moment he had realised he loved Aliyah was when she'd told him that she was getting engaged. He had taken her for granted, but when he imagined her with someone else, his love for her, which had always been hidden, had emerged.

Samir's phone began ringing. 'I'll come back in a bit,' he said, and he walked inside Northern Tower.

Raheem didn't know what to think. He was still trying to come to terms with what Samir had said. How had he been so stupid to not realise? He had always thought Aliyah was different to other women he knew, but he had never questioned himself as to why he thought that. He had always had this protective feeling towards her more than anyone else. He hated shopping more than he could ever tell anyone, but whenever he had gone with Aliyah, he had always enjoyed it. Aliyah had to pretend that she was getting engaged for him to finally wake up and realise. He had messed up. Big time.

After five minutes Samir returned. 'I just got a call from Aliyah.'

Raheem's heart rate increased again. 'What did she say?' he asked nervously.

Samir didn't respond and began walking back towards Northern Tower. 'Oi, what did Aliyah say?' called Raheem.

Samir turned around, his hand on the door handle. 'She says that you have got until twelve o'clock to find her. If you've any sense in you, then you'll know where she is. But if you don't find her before twelve, she says she never wants to see you again. I think that's fair.'

He went inside. Seeing Raheem still sitting on the ground, he poked his head back out. 'Your time starts now.'

What! How was that fair? 'Where is she? Tell me!' shouted Raheem, scrambling to his feet, but Samir just shrugged and closed the door.

Chapter 27

It was quarter to twelve. He had fifteen minutes. Where would Aliyah be? What did Samir mean when he said Raheem should know where she was?

'Burydale Park,' he muttered and began sprinting as fast as he could towards the university car park. That's where Aliyah would be, on the bench they always sat on.

He ran across the road, ignoring the cars blasting their horns at him. He couldn't care less. The only thing that mattered to him was that he found Aliyah. He flung himself in his car and started the engine when he stopped. Aliyah *couldn't* be at Burydale Park. That was at least a twenty-minute drive from the university, and she couldn't expect him to get there in fifteen minutes and find her in that time. She wouldn't be able to get there by then either.

The library: that was where they'd spent the most time together. Raheem turned his car off and ran back towards the university entrance. There were only a few people on the ground floor, and none of them was Aliyah. He ran inside, ignoring the stares he was getting from the staff and students.

There was no time to get the lift. He ran up the stairs and turned right onto the first floor. There were about fifteen people there – and Aliyah was not amongst them.

His watch showed the time as nearly five to twelve. He had just over five minutes left. He went out the first floor and ran up the stairs. He checked the second floor. She wasn't there. He ran to the third floor. Aliyah wasn't there. 'God help me, please,' he muttered, closing his eyes and putting his head against the wall.

His phone buzzed with a message. He took it out; it was from Sarah.

Going to watch the lion king when I get home tonight. Always the best movie to watch. One day you will also learn to like it haha x

Raheem put his phone back in his pocket. As much as he liked Sarah, now really wasn't the time to text her back. Heartbroken, he turned around to leave the third floor. He had no idea where to go next. Hold on…

His heart began thumping again and he quickly took out his phone. He opened his messages and read the one from Sarah again. *The Lion King… The Lion King…* The circle of life! That was it! Aliyah's favourite quote! She was waiting for him outside the Parkview Café, because that was where they'd met for the very first time!

Raheem ran down three flights of stairs and raced across the ground floor. One of the staff members, who was carrying some books, jumped out of his way and dropped the books on the floor, just as she had done on the first day back at university when Raheem had run after Aliyah after their seminar.

'Sorry!' shouted Raheem, without a backward glance. He turned left, ran down the corridor, through the double doors and down another flight of steps. He ran past the campus shop and turned right through the doors that would take him out the back exit. He was nearly there.

Chapter 28

For the second time in ten minutes, Raheem ran across the road despite it not being a red light. He raced through the entrance to Parkview and down the steps to the lower ground floor where the café was located. It was now 11:59. He jumped the last five steps, nearly stumbling but managing to keep upright. He ran through the entrance to the café. For the first time he could remember, it was empty. But Raheem wasn't interested in the café interior; what mattered to him was who was standing outside. He nearly laughed with relief.

Aliyah was standing with her back to him, leaning against the window next to the back entrance. Raheem's face split into the widest smile as he stared at the sunlight glinting on her hair. He had never truly appreciated just how beautiful she was. Yet she was still there, waiting for him.

Waiting for him? Today, more than ever, he needed to be on time. It was ten seconds to twelve. He sprinted across the café, just as Aliyah began to walk away. He reached the exit and shouted as loud as he ever had in his life. 'Aliyah!'

He was panting, a searing stich in his side, but he didn't care. As Aliyah turned around, a solitary tear slid down her cheeks. They stared at each other, Raheem breathing heavily, Aliyah as still as a statue. Thirty seconds passed and she still didn't say anything.

He knew what he had to say. 'I'm sorry.'

He couldn't take seeing her upset. He never could, and he never would. He took a tentative step towards her. She didn't move. He took another step. This time, her right hand moved ever so slightly. Aliyah was going to slap him again, and he couldn't complain if she did. She had every right to.

'I love you,' he said. Never had truer words come out of his mouth. He had loved her since he had met her. But he just never had it in him to admit it.

'You're lying, Raheem,' said Aliyah quietly.

Why did no one believe him when he spoke the truth? 'I'm not lying, Aliyah. I swear down I—'

'All you have done is never accept the truth,' Aliyah interrupted and Raheem fell silent. She was right, just as Samir had been right. He hadn't accepted the truth. He had taken Aliyah for granted.

'I did want to say it, Aliyah. Honestly I did. But I never thought you felt the same way about me,' he said desperately.

Aliyah shook her in disbelief. 'You never knew? Or you pretended you didn't know?'

'Look—' Raheem took another few steps towards her. They were only six feet apart now.

She raised her eyebrows. 'Another excuse? Were you so busy that you forgot?' she said coldly. 'Or did you think there was no need to mention it?'

'I—' Raheem began but he didn't know what to say. He needed Aliyah in his life. That was the only thing he knew.

'The truth is Raheem, you don't love me. I don't think you know what love is.'

Her words lit a flame inside Raheem. He would let his heart speak. 'Yeah, you're right, Aliyah, I don't know what love is!' He hadn't meant to say it so loudly, but the time had come to finally share his feelings. 'Thirteenth September 2010, I first met you. Right here. Something happened inside of me that day but I didn't know it was love. Every time we were together, I felt a connection with you that I'd never had with any woman before. Every time I came to uni, you were the person I wanted to see the most. Any day that I didn't see you was never a good day. I didn't know that was love. Every time we spoke, every time we went out together, every time we sat together, I remembered those times more than any others in my life. I didn't know that was love.'

It was a relief getting the words out after all this time keeping them to himself. More tears were coming out of Aliyah's eyes. The most beautiful eyes in the world.

'But that day you told me you were getting married, I felt as if I had left it too late,' he continued. 'That day I realised I had always loved you. But I thought I wasn't good enough for you.'

He was finding it difficult to continue but he had to. He got down on one knee. 'Don't leave me, Aliyah. Please. I can't live without you.' He extended his hand. The first day he'd met her flashed vividly through his mind.

Aliyah moved forward and took his hand, but then lowered it slowly and let go. 'I'm sorry, Raheem.'

Raheem had heard of a broken heart, but only now did he realise exactly how it felt. It was as though it would never be whole again. He closed his eyes. He deserved this pain. He had left it too late.

But then two hands held his face. He opened his eyes. Aliyah's face was a few inches from his, smiling at him as the tears continued to flow down her cheek. Raheem wiped them away with his hand.

Whether they were kneeling together for ten seconds or ten years, he couldn't tell. Slowly, their faces were getting closer and they were standing up. Raheem's hand found Aliyah's waist, hers were still on his face. She closed her eyes half a second before Raheem, and their lips touched.

Time really had stopped. It was as though someone had turned the volume down. All that mattered to Raheem was that Aliyah was with him and he was with her. After what felt like a lifetime, they broke apart.

'I'm so sorry,' said Raheem but Aliyah pressed a finger to his lips.

'You don't need to be sorry,' she whispered as he stroked her hair. They kissed again. He pinched his arm to make sure he was not dreaming. But this was real. His love for Aliyah was real.

He let go of her. 'You look gorgeous when you cry, but even more gorgeous when you smile,' he said gently. He got what he wanted as Aliyah smiled. He was going to make sure that smile always stayed on her face. 'I did promise I would attend your wedding,' he continued.

Aliyah nodded. '*Our* wedding.'

'Am I still allowed to tell you rubbish jokes?'

'Yes, you can. You look so cute when you say them,' she said, before giving him a bite on his neck.

266

'Don't tell me you also like biting!' said Raheem, jumping away from her and rubbing his neck. That had been the hardest bite he had ever received.

Aliyah's eyes widened. 'Also? Which other woman bites you?'

Unfortunately some of his habits, like speaking without thinking, didn't want to change. 'No one! I just meant... I like your top by the way. It really suits you. It looks as though it was made for you.'

Aliyah laughed. Raheem wished he could just stare at her all day as she laughed.

'I think *you two* were made for each other. I always knew it. I need to stop being right all the time!' said a voice that Raheem had no trouble recognising.

Samir was walking towards them, looking happier than Raheem had ever seen him. Raheem made to run towards him and hug him, but Aliyah got there first. Samir grinned at Raheem over her shoulder and patted Aliyah's head. He let go and Raheem strode over and embraced him.

'Thanks,' muttered Raheem as Aliyah beamed at them both over Samir's shoulder.

'No need to mention it,' Samir muttered back as they broke apart. 'I'm going back home tomorrow, so you might as well stay an extra day.'

'Why would I want to stay an extra day? Not like I have anything to do, or anyone to be with,' said Raheem.

'So mean!' Aliyah punched his arm.

Samir checked his phone, which gave Raheem time to give Aliyah a quick peck on the cheek.

'I need to go,' said Samir. 'Rachel is going back this evening and I promised her that I would spend the day with her after my exam. I'll catch up with you two later. Aliyah, if he messes you around, make sure you tell me.'

'Don't worry, I will. Although there won't be much left of him if he does mess me around,' said Aliyah affectionately.

Samir winked at them and headed back inside the café.

Aliyah turned to Raheem. 'Have you found your reason to quit smoking yet?'

'I certainly have,' said Raheem. He took out his cigarette packet, walked over to the bin and threw it inside, before returning to Aliyah.

'Tell me a joke, your most rubbish one ever,' she said brightly. His most rubbish joke ever? There could only be one.

'What do you call it when I say I'm going to give up smoking?' said Raheem.

Aliyah pondered for a few seconds before saying 'I don't know, tell me?'

'A joke!'

Aliyah grabbed Raheem and he lifted her off her feet. Never had he felt happier in his life.

'Long drive?' he asked as he let her go.

'That would be great,' Aliyah said. 'You will be taking me on these long drives for the rest of your life, so might as well get used to it. But I have one question for you, before we go.'

'Go ahead,' said Raheem.

'Why were you late? You had to be here by twelve!'

'I wasn't late! I came on time!'

'No, you were ten seconds late!'

'I love you, Aliyah.'

'I love you too, Raheem.'

He put his arm around Aliyah as they started to walk. To say it had been an eventful year would be an understatement.

Printed by BoD™in Norderstedt, Germany